THE BURNING BRIDE

Margaret Lawrence lives with her family in Middle West America in the house her grandfather built in the 1880s.

The Burning Bride is the third in her trilogy featuring Hannah Trevor. The first novel, *Hearts and Bones*, was published to much critical acclaim and was shortlisted for, among others, the Edgar Allan Poe Award for Best Crime Novel in 1996. The second novel, *Blood Red Roses*, was also greeted with much praise on publication.

Praise for Margaret Lawrence

'An absorbing blend of mystery, romance and history.'
Evening News

'A brilliant historical story of murder, love and passion . . .
Her attention to detail brings the era alive.'
Lincolnshire Echo

'An engrossing debut . . . a revealing and emotionally
honest novel.'
Manchester Evening News

By the same author

HEARTS AND BONES

BLOOD RED ROSES

THE BURNING BRIDE

Margaret Lawrence

PAN BOOKS

First published in Great Britain in 1999 by Macmillan

This edition published 2000 by Pan Books
an imprint of Macmillan Publishers Ltd
25 Eccleston Place, London SW1W 9NF
Basingstoke and Oxford
Associated companies throughout the world
www.macmillan.co.uk

ISBN 0 330 37265 3

A CIP catalogue record for this book is available from
the British Library.

Typeset by Intype London Ltd
Printed and bound in Great Britain by
Mackays of Chatham plc, Chatham, Kent

To Deborah Schneider.

This one's yours.

Set me as a seal upon thine heart, as a seal
upon thine arm; for love is strong as death:
jealousy is cruel as the grave: the coals thereof
are coals of fire, which hath a most vehement flame.

—Song of Solomon, 8:6

How He Killed the Ghost of Shame

Till the night when the habit of killing returned to him, he had almost forgotten the quickening joy of it, how it scourged the smear of shame from the heart and made it live.

It came sudden and wild, and when it was done, he felt no guilt and no fear of discovery. At Lamb's Inn and the Red Bush tavern, the Rufford farmers would drink their rum toddy and mutter of debts and grievances, and if they spoke of him at all, it would be only to say that the heart had gone out of him since the summer, that he was already dead in his soul.

They did not know how he lived behind glass, now, and saw the world huge, its parts bloated into monstrosity, nor how it reflected his ghost in its glare. His eyes stared out, amphibious and ancient, and he did not feel his wife's hands upon his body for the cage of faulted glass around his bones.

He had taken this stern, fragile country like an innocent bride to his bosom, bled for it, poured his sweat and his passion like seed deep inside it. Now he felt like a soldier who has slept unawares with the enemy and taken shame, like lovers' sweat, into his pores.

Only the killing redeemed him. He was a sword against the scorn of God.

He had been many months in prison – debtors, honest but floundering farmers like himself crowded casually in with thieves, counterfeiters, a murderer or two waiting to be hanged. Tax upon tax had been laid on them, debts from a war that set rich men free to get richer, but ground out all hope from the laboring poor.

In the winter it was very cold in the prison, the cells dug into the side of a hill and almost two feet below the level of the ground. During the worst of the cold, he had fought off sleep for five nights together, rubbing himself, chafing one hand with the other, marching in place because the cell was too crowded to pace back and forth. One man lost his foot to frostbite and gangrene.

After that he scarcely slept at all, only his feet marching up and down, up and down. His mind crashing against the blank glass cage of despair.

When the warm weather came, there was fever in the place. Of the twenty-six men in the cell with him, fourteen died. He himself caught it, lost his mind in it and began to rave.

There was a barred window, and the branch of a horse chestnut tree hung over it. A blue jay flew in and perched there, squawking its cry of 'Thief, thief, thief!' Two more dead were carried out, men he knew only as different-sized shapes in the reeking straw.

Somebody sang 'We All Believe in One True God'. Another jay answered the first.

After a while some other men came. 'Rebels!' cried the guards. 'Regulators!' He could hear shouting, thick boots kicking the door and wooden rams smashing against it, the same rhythm as the raucous bark of the birds in the tree.

Thief, thief, thief. Shame, Shame, shame. Down, down, down.

Then there was fire, burning shingles dripping like raindrops, black timbers falling, the smell of hot pitch in the wood. 'Freedom!' he heard a young man's voice shout. 'Justice for all the poor!' Somebody lifted him, some giant without a face, without eyes. Others took him up roughly, slung him into an oxcart. Wheels moved, rumbling over the ruts of a forest track.

On the homeward flight, fever dreams claimed him. He saw himself frozen, clear as an icicle, looking down at the bones of his feet through a skin that was ice. Then he was deep under the earth, the black dampness of prehistoric ferns in his mouth. Still alive with this weight of centuries upon him, he gazed up through amber and rubies to glimpse his wife's pale face.

Sheba, she had told him to call her. Sheba's face, high-boned and fragile, with skin soft as dogwood blossom. Sheba's breasts, with a fine blush of freckles just under each nipple, drifting down to her ribcage. Sheba's back, long and smooth, perfect as an unbroken snowfield.

Sheba, my queen, sweet and constant.

From under the sea, drowned and living, he saw her through fever and pearls.

When he came to himself, she was there by the fireside, she was real and alive. Sheba was weaving, the treadles of her great loom clacking and the beater-stick thumping as it smashed against the warp, a homely, comforting rhythm. Now and then she would leave her work to come and lay cool hands on his face or on his chest.

Home, he thought, and made his mouth form the sound of it.

But the word did not connect with any tangible memory of the room where he sat. The web of experience, the long knotwork of his own history – after the prison, he was no longer part of them. He did not belong to the waking world any longer, nor even to himself. He lived in Sheba as other men live in their bones.

As he healed and grew stronger, she brought him the last wild grapes of the Maine autumn, heavy with sweet purple juice, and ripe quinces and wasp-stung pears the Rufford biddies would not use. Sometimes she peeled the fruit with her teeth and passed it into his mouth from her own, her tongue reaching inside him, the taste of her mixed with the sweet–sour juice.

And yet his body did not desire her; he did not take her, scarcely even spoke to her. Instead, he worked long and hard, coming inside the cottage only to eat his food in silence and then go out to his fields again, reaping the late corn she had planted in his absence, trying to salvage what he could from the deepening cold. At night he fell down exhausted on the hearthrug by the fire, a foot from the bed where Sheba lay.

One night he came in to find her waiting, a pan of water warmed for his washing and clean linen laid out on the bed. She began to undress him and he did not resist her.

His chest was broad and strong, brushed with fine hairs, and a thin white scar from a British sabre ran nearly to his hip from the breastbone. Sheba took his blundering sex in her two hands and warmed it, her face laid close against him and her mouth on his small, foolish nipple.

'How dare you take your heart from me?' she whispered. 'God. I want you so. I shall die of it. God.'

She had had other men before he met her; her own body would not let her pretend otherwise. But there had always been a determined decency about her, an innocence she kept like a gift to give only at her own will, whatever else might be taken. He had never questioned her about the past. If she had been the most practiced whore, he would have forgiven her in those days, gentle as she was, and the war all around them.

God, his mind echoed as she slipped down his body, her thin arms around his wet thighs. *God forgive me my trespasses, as I forgive God who trespasseth against me.*

But this time he could not forgive.

As soon as he came to himself from the fever, he had seen at once that Sheba was pregnant again. For a long time he watched her, uncertain. He was no judge of mothering women, of how quickly their bodies grew great and unwieldy. Besides, he wanted the child badly, a child of his own, a fragment of their joining; he waited, worked, said nothing. Whenever he went to the town, he observed other men's wives. 'How long till her time?' he would murmur to their husbands, judging the heavy curve of the growing bellies under the loose short-gowns women wore, comparing them with his own wife's awkward, swollen shape.

Counting backwards, he knew the child was not his; he had been too long in the prison. For a while he tried to delude himself, to brazen it out in the town. But as she bent over him that night to coax him to her, he could no longer pretend.

'I love you so,' she said. 'You are the world to me.'

'Liar!' he groaned, and ran from her, naked and wet and howling, into the cold, tangled woods.

The midwife, Hannah Trevor, came next day on her old shambling pony; she, too, was with child, though it showed only slightly. The man climbed up to the loft above the kitchen and looked down through a knot-hole at the two of them, letting his eyes play along their bodies – how they swayed as they walked and seemed to balance the air against them like a burden-sack; how their voices were liquid and their eyes were bright and their skin smooth and translucent with gathering milk.

He stuffed a fist in his mouth to keep from retching, and tears of shame blinded him. In the town, the tavern sots would talk of Sheba now as they did of the midwife, calling her a slut and laying bets on which of them had had her.

But Sheba was proud, she would not have lain with such fools. No, it must have been some rich merchant, some fine man who did not stink of sweat, who came to her sweet and perfumed, and called her his mouse.

He despised them, all rich men and town-dwellers, all who lived in packs and sucked the nipple of progress. All his life they had stunted him, hedged him in, taken him for granted.

A townsman. A scornful, sneering thing in satin breeches and a velvet coat. Doctor, lawyer, merchant, chief. Squire, selectman, preacher, judge.

Ghostly faces swirled through his mind – men he knew, their laughing mouths mocking him. His rage caved in upon him and the frail bond was broken that had held him to living. Sheba was no longer his.

On the night after the midwife's visit, when the fire was banked and the skim of ice began to form across the water bucket, the man slipped out of the cottage, through the cluttered dooryard and into the night, bareheaded and coatless in the bittering cold.

Beyond the apple orchard where the woods grew thick, he could see the flickering of torches and hear the feet of men running, calling softly to each other now and then with the voices of owls. They were hunters come out from the village, frightening the deer with false fire and driving them into the guns.

Townsmen. Townsmen.

One of them had put seed into Sheba and it had taken sound root there as his own had never done. That was the real crime, the real shame. In the seven years of their bedding, there had been no living children carried to term. Now there was this unborn, this interloper. Already it had lived in her longer than any child of his.

Hate surged up in the man once more and he broke into a sweat. He sank down to his knees in the snow and growled, low, like an animal, his face scraping the trunk of an apple tree till there was blood on the bark. 'Christ,' he said. 'Christ.'

The torches still moved through the forest, the owl-men still called in the dark. He dug under the thin crust of snow for the fallen crab apples and stuffed them greedily into his mouth, handful after handful, till the front of his shirt was soaked with half-fermented juice and pulp as sweet as breast-milk.

Then he went back to the house where Sheba lay sleeping.

There was a single glass window of four panes, the thing he had gone into debt to provide her. In the winter months he was often out trapping or hunting, and with the wooden shutters nailed down night and day and only the hearthfire for light, she had begun to shrivel, mourning her life away. So he had borrowed ten pounds on the quiet from Siwall and sent to Boston for the glass.

That debt had begun his long ruin, but tonight he was glad of the glass, and of the moonlight that washed in through the small square panes as he stood looking down at her. Sheba lay on her back, naked in bed as always, her arms above her head so that her heavy breasts drooped slightly sidewise, a few hairs like down in the broad cleft of them. Her nipples were hard with the deep cold, the aureole around them blood-darkened and a network of pale blue lines under the thin skin, like the tangled blue threads on her loom.

She was very pale and young, only three-and-twenty, with the fine fair hair of a child. Very cold, too, as she lay there. The fire was banked for the night and her breath made a fog above her face and throat.

He pulled back the quilts to lay his palms where the alien child slept inside her, then slipped his hand between her legs and carried her juice to his lips. Standing alone in the middle of the dirt floor, he touched this spoor to his cheek, then to his forehead, then to his breast. On the whitewashed wall, he felt for the place they had once pushed against for balance, he lifting her body to meet him, her hips thrusting, driving him deeper and deeper inside her.

His rough hand found the spot, a small break in the chinking where the moonlight slipped through. He touched the place with his forefinger, as though truth might yet live there.

Then he picked up his long rifle and put the stock to his shoulder, sighting down the bore at her belly where she lay on the bed. With a sword he was hopeless, but he could put a lead ball into the soft bone behind a horseman's ear at three hundred yards.

Perhaps the child, breathing fear as it swam in her body, woke and warned her. For suddenly Sheba sat up with a soft cry, like wind rising in branches. From the clear night sky outside, impossible snowflakes had begun to fall.

'I will not tell you how this came into me,' she said quietly. 'But it is yours, if you will have it. I could have been rid of it, but I would not, for your sake. I give it to you. A gift.'

He could hear the scrabbling of mice in the loft above. The banked coals snapped and sizzled in the chimney draft. He lowered the gun from his shoulder and a cry came from him that was the grinding together of great, dry rocks.

'Whore!' he whispered, and struck her hard across the breasts. She did not cry out, only fell back onto the bed.

He snatched up the powder horn and the bag of shot from their nail, and was gone again, into the dark.

Where he went next, his mind remembered only as a great hollow chamber with many candles lighted. This room was the autumn woods where the men from the town were still hunting, their torches made of tallow-soaked cattails dancing and flaring, leaving trails of brownish smoke against the dark.

He made his way silently through the veil of dry snow-flakes, running and running, gasping for breath, his feet kicking the floor cloth of damp November leaves. Once he tripped over the root of a huge burr oak and fell face down in the wet mold. He lay still, the great hulk of Chine Ridge like an old bear dark above him.

Then all at once a hunter's torch flamed up on the narrow track beyond him, no more than ten yards off. A false owl cried, then another. A rifle shot, muffled and faraway. 'Buck shot!' came the cry.

False, he thought. *They are all false, the soft and the stupid, the powerful. They eat up the world like maggots. They have eaten my heart.*

The lone hunter, the townsman with the torch, was very close now, a man big-bellied from ale, stumbling and weaving with drink. He wore a dark-skirted coat and pale satin knee breeches, gleaming in the flickering light. There was a heavy stink of arrogance and stale rum and cheap wig-powder and greed, and a jingle of coins from a scrip that bounced at his side.

'Halloo, sir!' cried the townsman. 'Where are you? Come out, you black rogue, or I shall box your ears!' He turned round and round on the pathway. 'Why, the Devil take me! I am lost from all my friends!'

The absurd snow still drifted through the darkness, sizzling as it struck the flame of the torch. *Sheba,* thought the man in the darkness. *Sheba is bright, like a flame.*

His wife's name was a knife in his lungs and he dreamed that he stood by her bed-place, watching the pot-bellied townsman pull off his breeches and clamber on top of her. My *love*, she groaned in his mind's ear. My *darling dear*.

The townsman was very close now, almost upon the man where he lay hidden in the leaves. There was no need to aim, no time to regret or consider.

'Thief!' Sheba's husband cried aloud. 'Shame! Shame! Shame!'

He pointed the long barrel straight up at the pale, puffy face of the townsman, and fired.

The bullet plowed like a cannon ball through its target, entering the lip and travelling upward, shattering the top of the head. The townsman's body turned slightly, the splintered skull lolling on the shoulders, the shredded wig caught madly on a branch. One of the hands tried to grasp at it, as if to put it back on. The eyes stared and the mouth gaped with surprise. There was a sound like the bubbling of a kettle in the chest.

The marksman primed again, seated another ball in the barrel, then fired a second time, scarcely aiming. The pigeon-plump body lay still on the path, the torch smothering its light in the dirt. He put the gun down and drew a long breath, filling his lungs with clean air, feeling the long shame fall away from him.

'Come,' said a quiet voice behind him. 'It is done, and we may live.'

Sheba's pale shape floated in the dark like the torches, her loose hair smoking out behind her, her naked body white as the snow under his old army greatcoat. He stared down at the dead man, but he would not have known his own brother so. 'Who is he?' he said.

'A smut on the world,' she whispered.

'I am damned now,' he told her, his voice raw as gravel. 'From this night, I have no god but you.'

Sheba reached up her thin, cold hand and made the sign of a cross upon his forehead. 'Then I forgive you all your sins,' she said.

ONE

The Third Journal of Hannah Trevor, Midwife

I WRITE UPON MUSTERING DAY OF THE RUFFORD
MILITIA, THESE PAGES WHICH ARE MINE OWN

6 November, the year 1786

*Here begins the twelfth winter since I came to Maine, to Two
Mills Farm upon the River Manitac. A sour, cloudy morrow.
We have had in the night the winter's first dusting of snow.*

*I doubt not but it will come to civil war here as it has in
Massachusetts. Word is come from Boston of women's breasts
slashed by the governor's troops at Stockbridge, where the rebel
farmers are strongest, and of children's eyes put out with
bayonets.*

*Major Josselyn commands the militia that musters for
training this day at Great Meadow. If the Governor calls up
our Rufford troops to put down the rebels, Daniel must ride at
their head.*

*I have not seen him this fortnight, since the husking at
Towler's. The gossips say he is seen by the Night Watch wandering
the bank of the river, and when he is spoke-to, he answers them
nothing. He has gone twice to visit the grave of his wife at Gull's
Isle and he cannot forget her.*

I do fear it is foolish to wed.

I am near four months with Daniel Josselyn's child, and do not puke now at mornings. My breast aches me sorely, and grows great with milk. Made a poultice of sorrel well-roasted, which gave some relief.

I drink no more beer nor hard cider, as the Angel saith to the mother of Samson, *Drink no Wine nor Strong Drink and thou shalt bear a Son.*

Pray God the bargain be a sound one. The new cow gives milk of a foul weedy savor, the well water is brackish, and I long for a mug of good ale.

My Uncle banks corn stalks and pompion vines against the house and barn this day to stop up draughts. Young Ethan Berge assists him, for he has not his strength as before.

A wherry is come upriver to Burnt Hill Manor four days since with Master Royallton-Smith of Boston, who is father of Jem Siwall's bride. Have been summoned twice this three weeks to quiet her fusses, a pale lumpish creature with pink eyes like a rabbit. Gave maid's-hair tea, though nothing ails her but a husband who has wed against his will.

Charged five shillings for simple annoyance, and may go whistle until I am paid. The Rich will spend gladly for any Indulgence, but Necessity may wait for her hire till she turns to Green Cheese.

Have been two days from home with old Lady Jory, the mother of Mrs Hewins, who fell from her chair with a fit and broke the great bone of her arm. Gave comfrey in a poultice, and an ointment of boneset.

Doctor Clinch gives her overmuch laudanum. I took up a warming-pan and chased him out-of-doors.

Took my fee from Mrs Hewins in bayberry wax and a peck of Maiden Blush apples, for our old tree is fallen in the All Hallows' storm.

Tarried awhile with Mrs Flynn, whose husband was broke from Salcombe Jail with my Cousin. Gave sassafras for the jail-fever, as with Thomas Whittemore, and stitched some while upon her quilt of Burgoyne Surrounded. Leah Kersey at Sable Brook has bespoke me for her delivery.

Bargained with Mrs Kersey to set two fancy warps upon our great loom and our small. The patterns shall be Devil's Hoof and Wide World's Wonder, which last my daughter shall weave by herself to learn the skill. A deaf, silent woman must live like any other, and I fear no man will have Jennet to wife when she is grown, for all the sweetness of her heart.

Heard at dawn the passing bell rung beyond a count of sixty, which may token the death of old Lady Jory. I warrant she hath slept her life away with Clinch's drugs.

We dip the last of the winter candles this day from the tallow of gentle Bluebell, our old cow that is dead. If the rats do not get at them, forty dozen more will last to St Valentine's, with the fifty already laid down.

My Aunt Markham bakes Training Cake to take her mind from trouble and because it is Jonathan's favorite. We scarce hope to see my Cousin in this life again, for he is gone to hide in the Outward and there be as many deaths in such a place as in a sheriff's noose.

My Uncle says God feedeth the Prophet who hideth in the Wilderness. But in the Forests of Jerusalem, I think, it does not snow.

*My Aunt's Receipt for Training Cake: To a peck of fine
flour, add ten eggs beaten till their yolkes be the color
of lemon. Grate two good nutmegs, with a soupspoon
each of mace and cloves well pestled. Mash a cone of
sugar, and mix into the flour. Wash, dry and pick stems
from five or a half-dozen pound currants, and mince
your half-pound of candy-orange, lemon, and citron
very small. Next make you a possit of good cream, a
pint each of ale and sack-sherry, and then put into it
a pound and quarter of new sweet butter, and another
pound and quarter into a mug of good ale-yeast or
barm, and mix all very fine, with rosewater, juice of
orange, and sack-sherry as you desire. Bake very slow
in an oven not fit for bread, three hours or four, till it
have a fine crust on the top.*

*N.B. Having no lemon nor orange, use candied quince
and dried apricocks or red cherries. If you have not
sack-sherry, rum or brandy will serve.*

*Only be sure your nutmegs be not wood before you
grate them, as there be chapmen that carve out wooden
nutmegs and sell them to the scant-brained for unequal
reward!*

My aunt's quilt of China Dish is near finished and I piece upon
another, the last I shall make before I go to housekeeping at the
Grange at Christmas. It is a patch of my own contriving to
which I give the name of Bridges Burning, as I make it for my
marriage bed.

    I snap at my love for no cause, and we wrangle.
    I own, I am afraid to wed.

TWO

The Devil on Horseback

The morning proved dense and grey and windless, but for Maine in November it was clement enough. Unless flood, tempest, or hellfire prevented them, the women of Two Mills Farm had always made the last of their winter candles on November Muster Day.

By Christmas Hannah Trevor would be mistress of Mapleton Grange, Dan Josselyn's fine manor, and rich folk burned candles of wax bought ten pound at a time from the chandler. Unless she had a craving for it, Hannah need never dip a tallow candle in her life again.

It seemed too much like a fairy tale to be credited and, like a stone in her boot heel, the voice of reason grumbled: *Madam Midwife, you are eight-and-thirty, and froward. He finds you pleasant enough in the darkness, no doubt. But willful Hannah Trevor, learn once again to keep a husband's daylight rules?*

She stamped her foot on the sanded kitchen floor and set her Aunt Julia's pewter to rattle in the dresser. *Bother the rules! Bother wax candles! Bother pewter! I am as I am, and he may like me or lump me!*

Her sense of herself thus restored, Hannah tied on her old brown sailcloth wrapper and set to work. It was clock-winding day, and she went out to the chilly front hall to pull up the chain weights, then locked tight the door of the weight-box where the family's small savings were kept.

Finally she tied a woolen kerchief over her short, ash-brown curls, and glanced at herself in the hall mirror as she passed it. How Daniel would have laughed to see her, kerchiefed like a dairy maid!

I shall fail him, she thought suddenly, and it struck like a kick from the child in her belly. *I am not made for a gentleman's lady. I will wound him one day, deep, deep.*

Her first marriage had been like a shipwreck, and after James Trevor deserted her, Hannah swore never to marry again, not even for love. But that resolve had proved foolish delusion. Trevor was dead at last and in her heart she was married to Daniel already; if they might have gone to live on the moon, she would have felt nothing but joy.

But Rufford, Maine, was not the moon and even Daniel could not change the law. Once married, a woman was her husband's legal property until one of them died. Whenever Hannah Trevor let herself consider the risk of it, the blind folly of the laws and conventions that had bound her to a selfish, loveless rascal like Trevor and made her subject to every whim of his will, there was only one word for what she felt.

Surrender, she thought, and the clock ticked it back at her. Hannah sighed, picked up a bucket of tallow, and stepped out into the yard.

As soon as old Henry Markham finished his morning's milking, he and Ethan Berge, the new choreboy, had set up three fire-blackened oak poles in the dooryard. Where they met, they were tightly lashed with rope, and under this tripod the women built their dipping fire, the great black iron melting-kettle hung over it by a hook and trammel. It would hold just over forty pounds of melted beef tallow, with bayberry wax added for clean burning and fragrance, and it was wide enough to dip ten candles at once on wicks of homespun tow tied to willow sapling poles.

Aunt Julia's choice of a dipping day had earned her many a whisper of Toryism, for most women gladly forgot their household tasks on Muster Day and called it patriotic pride to cheer as the men marched and drilled. From the age of sixteen – though some boys added a year or two, unwilling to watch from the sidelines – to fifty or more, every able-bodied male was required to turn out for training just as they had done under the British governor, in readiness for their own defense. And every year their women trooped into town from the outlying farms and villages – matrons and grannies, old maids with ribbon cockades to their bonnets and some last faint hope of a husband, flirtatious young girls with a mind for mortal sin.

There were lesser company training days four or five times in the year, but this was the last and the greatest, a solsticial festival. *Before Muster*, they would say, as though the stars in their orbits turned round on it. *After Muster, the evenings draw in early. We shall wed before Muster. By Muster, he'll be in his grave.*

If midsummer haying was their summer feast, then Muster Day marked their penitential season. It was followed by a week of hectic preparation, as the women began their holiday baking and fussing: using up expensive cone sugar for pumpkin pie and mince tarts, sending the men out after wild turkies and deer, sprinkling clean new sand on their floors and sweeping it into painstaking patterns – a wheat sheaf border, a vine of grape leaves, or a chain of ivy and pine.

Then came three days of fasting and scanty meals of brown bread or Indian pudding and milk.

At last, with children and grandchildren, aunts, uncles, cousins, and old friends arriving from up and down the river, there was the annual day of Thanksgiving decreed by the Congress, the climacteric of their year. Families gathered at the Meeting House for five or six hours of preaching and singing, and for marriages and christenings that might otherwise have to be put off till spring. And on Thanksgiving night came the great annual ball in the assembly room at the back of Lamb's Inn.

But it was different this year. Because of the rebellion, Congress had set no fixed day for Thanksgiving. Though they still bit their lips to make them red and tucked tiny lavender pillows into their bodies, even the young girls were solemn and tense. Whatever they did, they must do despite troubles. Within the week, their men might be at war again.

The paper dollars Congress had issued to pay the Continental army were worthless and hard coin almost nonexistent, but the General Court in Boston levied more and more taxes to pay off the huge war debts – and taxes could only be paid in silver. For the yeoman farmers and small craftsmen, it was a vicious circle that narrowed and narrowed; foreclosures were rampant and the debtors' jails filled to bursting.

Most men drew the line at armed rebellion and refused

to act without a general popular vote. But at midsummer some of the hardest pressed – Regulators, they called themselves – had exploded after a debt-ridden farmer was shot down in irons for defying the sheriff and the court.

A number of these hotheads were arrested and dragged back to Salcombe for trial, and three men selected at random to be hanged as examples. The last and the youngest of the three was Jonathan Markham, the miller's wild-hearted son.

But two nights before the hanging, a band of Regulators dressed in Indian feathers and masks made of grain sacks had burnt Salcombe Jail and courthouse and set all the debtors and prisoners free. No one had seen Jonathan since, nor even had word of him.

From time to time, an emaciated, fever-ravaged corpse was found and brought into the village, and each time old Henry Markham brushed his ancient tie-wig, hitched up his oxen and went to see if this latest poor soul might be his youngest son. At dusk he would return, blank-eyed and stumbling, to find Julia waiting in the door of the stable.

'Husband?' would come her voice from the dark.

'Not yet, Mother,' he would tell her, and trudge past her to unyoke the oxen.

Hannah paused on the farmhouse doorstep and glanced down the hill at the high road. Though it was still barely light, a half-dozen mounted men were passing; at the head of them, his musket cradled in the crook of his arm with the bayonet already fixed, rode a tall man in a dun-colored greatcoat, with no hat on his head and curling brown hair tied back at his nape. He turned his black horse sharply up the path to Two Mills and Hannah knew him at once, not so much by sight as by a flood of nervous chills along her spine.

Marcus Tapp, High Sheriff of Sussex County, rode with a crew of rowdies and ruffians, most of them wanted for crimes that would be winked at so long as they did what they were bid. But today he left his men patrolling the high road and came on alone, very straight in the saddle, almost one with the horse.

Young Ethan Berge, red-haired, freckled, and not yet fifteen, threw down another bundle of willow saplings for the hired girls. 'Oh ho, Kitty!' he cried. 'Here's old Tapp, come to hang you and Susan for a-making of candles!'

'Hush! Mistress Sally will hear you!' whispered Kitty, peeping out from under her ruffled cap at a fair-haired young woman who sat idle on the wellcurb.

But if she heard, Jonathan Markham's wife did not mind. She stood up and walked to the edge of the yard, her grey cloak wrapped close around her and her blue eyes fixed upon the tall, lean figure of Marcus Tapp. Sally Jewell had been less than eighteen when Johnnie got her with child and was put-upon to marry her. Even now she was not twenty, and her mind was seldom on her work.

'He's a handsome creature, is he not?' Sally said as Susan passed her with a sapling of wicks.

'Oh how can you say so?' gasped the hired girl. 'They do say he's a devil indeed!'

But Sally only laughed. 'Why, I may admire even the Devil on horseback, if he keep so good a seat as that!'

Aunt Julia Markham came out of the barn with the large tin chest in which they would lay down the candles to ripen, too intent upon her task to notice the rider's approach. 'Where, may I ask, is Black Tirzah this morning?' she demanded. 'Sally, did I not send you a week since to bargain for her labor? I warrant you went gadding instead!'

The sheriff's horse wore many harness brasses that rang against each other like bells as he rode into the yard and dismounted. The old woman looked up at the sound, her gooseberry eyes staring and her long nose wrinkled as if she had smelt rotten meat.

'*You*, sir!' She dipped the end of her stirring stick into the fire. The tallow on it caught with a roar and blazed up, and she swung it like a weapon before her. 'Run, boy, fetch Husband from the mill! Kitty! Susan! Into the house and bar my doors behind you!'

Hannah's favorite aunt was over sixty, horse-faced and dumpling-shaped, but she had a voice you could hear halfway to Halifax, and when she trumpeted an order, she was seldom ignored. The servant girls scurried and young Ethan took off running.

But Marcus Tapp only smiled. He stretched out an arm as the boy passed, and Ethan went down hard on his backside in the half-frozen mud. 'No need to trouble the miller, old woman,' the sheriff said. 'You may pull in your horns.'

Tapp's eyes scanned the yard, missing nothing – the fire, the pails of tallow and bayberry, the grey-cloaked girl. Strange eyes, they were, so pale they seemed in daylight to have no color at all, glass eyes that the world passed through without effect, to be recorded by the raw ends of his nerves.

Some would have called him a libertine, but in fact he was so selective as to be almost ascetic in his pleasures. Oh, he took a certain pride in successful and challenging bedding, as he did in the killing of equals; but Marcus Tapp did not love and he did not hate. At five-and-forty, he had carefully scraped himself clean of all passions, so that if he should die – it was bound to come suddenly and soon to a mercenary soldier – not a shred of him would be left behind to betray him, invested in any living thing.

And Sally was right. He *was* a handsome creature, sleek and bold and strong.

'Very well, sir.' Julia doused the burning stick in the water bucket by the wellcurb. 'Then state your business and be gone from my house.'

But Tapp strode instead to where Hannah was working, calmly tying more wicks to the dipping saplings. 'My business is with you, Mistress Gypsy.' He smiled and made her a mocking half-bow. 'Shall we go into the house?'

The midwife did not look up from her work. 'You can have nothing to say that needs walls to conceal it.'

'Indeed? Well, then. You attended some two days past an old woman named Esther Jory?'

'The mother of Mrs Hewins? I did.'

'For what ill did you medicine her?' Tapp's gaze was unnerving.

'Why, she'd broke her arm in a fall!' cried Julia, who had been Rufford's chief midwife herself before Hannah's time. 'The whole village heard of it. Lady Jory's had fits this year past. With the last one, she tumbled from her basket chair and fell down on the turnspit. It's only God's mercy she kept from the fire!'

'His mercy has limits, it seems.' Marcus Tapp smiled. 'No doubt you heard the passing bell.'

Hannah glanced at her aunt, then back at the sheriff. 'So Lady Jory is dead,' she said softly. 'I am sorry for it.'

'You may soon be sorrier. Dr Samuel Clinch has petitioned the Magistrate's Court to bring charges against you. Now that the old biddy's dead, they are of even greater—'

'What charges?' Julia's voice rang like a gong in the cold air. 'If Clinch brings them, why does he not come here to speak them himself? Hah! I warrant his servant, Black Caesar, could not rouse him from whatever doxy he fell down with after last night's hunt!'

Tapp ignored the old lady, his pale eyes fixed on Hannah and a smile of mild amusement on his face. 'Clinch vouches you interfere with his enlightened prescribing and dispense your own medicines instead,' he told her.

Hannah raised an eyebrow, but no more. 'And what else, sir?'

'He accuses you of drunkenness in your watchings.'

'Drunkenness?' Julia exploded. 'That old rumpot?'

'Aunt! Let him finish.' Hannah turned back to Marcus Tapp. 'And what else?'

'Lewd conduct.'

'With old Lady Jory, sir? Or Mrs Hewins?'

He looked her up and down. 'Mrs Hewins did not give you a belly that hikes up your petticoat a full two inches from your boots. I must say, it becomes you. Most breeding women look like drabs. His Lordship Josselyn consents to marry you this time, I hear.'

Hannah bit her lip. 'Is that why you came yourself instead of sending the constable? To offer your blessing on the banns?'

'I don't trust your constable, madam. McGregor's a thick-headed Scotchman.' Tapp leaned a fraction of an inch towards her. 'Besides, Gypsy, yours and mine is a sporting contest, though you did stick a toasting fork in me last summer. Pray, allow me to take some pleasure in setting eyes on you now and again.'

'So long as your hands do not follow them.' Hannah met

his stare. 'But surely Mr Clinch's imagination is not satisfied with such paltry charges. Or had he some help in contriving better?'

Tapp drew a paper from inside his greatcoat, carefully folded and stamped with the seal of the Magistrate's Court. 'This letter charges you with wrongful prescribing,' he said. 'Shall I read it out to you?'

'I need no letter to tell the intentions of Samuel Clinch. He has made such charges twice before. They have never been founded. I wonder Magistrate Siwall bothers to act upon them now, when he has so much else of import to concern him.' Tapp's scrutiny was too much for her at last and Hannah pushed back her hair under the kerchief. 'What says Mrs Hewins to all this? She was present and saw what occurred.'

'Oh, you women stick to one another, especially when you're broody. She won't hear a word against you. But the coroner will cut open the guts at noon today, and then we shall see.'

Julia's cheeks were red, and not with the heat of the dipping fire. 'But Sam Clinch *is* the coroner! What justice is that?'

'Just or not, it is law. At noon today, in his surgery. Be there if you like.' Tapp turned back to Hannah. 'Should evidence be found that your prescribings interfered with the efficacy of the – what's it called? This damned elixir Clinch swears by?'

'Laudanum, do you mean?'

'That's it, laudanum. Devil take it, let's have it in plain English. If your weeds and his potions crossed paths and the old woman died of it, you will be charged with murder-by-mischance.' He smiled. 'It's not a hanging crime like your cousin's, but it'll keep you long enough in my jail to do your groaning there in what – six months? Five? I'd enjoy that – six good months of your company.'

Hannah did not reply and Marcus Tapp turned on his heel to be gone. But before he could mount his horse, Sally ran up to him. Her grey cloak was pushed back so as to show her fair hair to a better advantage, and her cheeks were flushed. 'Oh, sir,' she said, holding a fine linen handkerchief up to her eyes. 'Have you no word if my husband is yet living?'

'You're the traitor's wife?'

The long blond lashes gave the sheriff an enticing flutter. 'I am that unhappy creature, sir,' Sally said.

Hannah's eyes sought the patience of heaven. It was enough to make your back teeth grind!

The kerchief drifted down from Sally's hand exactly at Tapp's feet, and he took it up and sniffed it. For a moment he paused, his fingertips teasing her palm. 'I've heard no word of your husband,' he said, 'but I make no doubt we shall find him. Whether he lives or not, it is nothing to me.'

Marcus Tapp took up his reins and swung easily into the saddle, then urged his big black onto the steep downhill path.

Inside most things human, there lives a buried self that balances always on a narrow ledge between passion and mind and stubborn endurance. As Hannah Trevor watched Sheriff Tapp's horse skid down the steep slope of the hill, she felt that frail ledge start to crumble beneath her and the self that had so long sustained her begin a long, slow, strange descent.

'The Devil on horseback,' she heard herself murmur.

Marcus Tapp looked back at her and laughed.

THREE

The Lowly Position of a Widow, or The Mooncalf and the Chit

Once Tapp had gone, Julia shook Hannah hard by the shoulders. 'Go at once and tell Daniel!' she commanded. 'He will see that Clinch does not have it all his own way!'

'It's Muster Day, Aunt. Major Josselyn is no doubt as busy as we are.'

Hannah restored the subtle formality of his title; they were not married *yet*, after all. 'Besides, Clinch only wants to humble me in public,' she went on, 'and then he will burst like a boiling-bubble.' She paused and sniffed the air, then sniffed again. 'And now we speak of boiling – unless my nose mistakes it, the tallow is cooked halfway to burning in that pot.'

'Kitty!' cried Julia, as the hired girls came warily out of the house again. 'Find me another stirring stick! Susan, go fetch us the rest of the pails from the barn. Sharp, now! Run!'

Susan darted across the dooryard, head down and petticoats slapping the snow-dusted mud. In a moment there came a small thump, followed by a shrill, childish howl: 'Ahahahahaoooooooo!!!'

Little Peter Markham, Jonathan's two-year-old son, had been pulling the heads off a few frost-browned purple asters that still bloomed in the shelter of the barn. Suddenly deflected by Susan's flight, he careened into the outer leg of the kettle's tripod and fell face-down, wailing at the top of his lungs, with the hem of his long homespun gown not an inch from the fire.

'Sally!' cried Aunt Julia. 'What are you about, to leave the child untended?'

But in a minute, the problem was solved – or seemed to be. At the edge of the yard near the woodpile, Hannah's eight-year-old daughter Jennet had been feeding cheese rinds to Arthur, her big one-eared ginger tomcat. Now, seeing Peter's tears, she darted to where he sat wailing and picked him up in her arms.

Jennet sat down cross-legged in the dooryard, oblivious of snow and mud, and began to rock the baby as though he were one of the handkerchief dolls Hannah made her. The little girl's mouth hung open and her wide, brandy-colored eyes were almost shut, and with each motion she made a low sound, like nothing the women in the yard had heard before. It might have been the snow clouds moaning, or the half-frozen river below them singing the death-song of its year.

'Ahnnnn. Ahnnnn. Ahnnnn.'

Until midsummer Hannah had believed her daughter entirely deaf and mute, but now the envelope of Jennet's silence seemed to open at odd intervals. What the little girl heard or *when* she heard, nobody knew. But sometimes, as now, strange sounds would come from her, each one amazing and no two exactly the same.

'Shuuuu,' Jennet crooned to the baby. 'Shuuuu.'

*I have no more words than you, but I see you and touch you.
Feel how my hands are steady and warm on your backbone. See
how my eyes come inside you and know you, and make you free
of yourself.*

Little Peter stopped his wailing and began to play with
Jennet's long red-brown braids, and Hannah warmed with
pride as she watched.

'Get away!' In the blink of an eye, Sally flew across the
yard to snatch her son away. 'I won't have her touch him! I
won't have her conjuring gibberish over him! You ought to
have her locked away!'

Because Jennet had no real language, some in the village
said she was possessed. A mooncalf, they called her, and the
sniggering brats in the back lanes threw mud and stones at
her.

Once, in Boston, Hannah had seen a travelling circus
with a child – a boy of twelve or thirteen – in a wooden cage
on wheels, pulled by a white mule. He was deaf and blind,
scarcely aware of what manner of world he was in. His milky
blue eyes rolled upwards, visionary and blank, but when you
spoke to him, some secret chord seemed to strike deep in his
mind, beyond sight or hearing or the sense of touch. His
mouth would open and his fingers would curve around thin
air as though they sought its strings to play upon.

A thing of wild dreams, he was, if any could reach
them. A gentle thing wasted, kept locked in a box. *Oh, my
Flower,* Hannah thought as Jennet found her hand and clung
onto it. *If ever they lock you away, I will come after and find
you, though I must come from the grave.*

Determined and furious, she led the little girl to where
Sally was still trying to quiet the wailing baby. 'Madam,' she

said, 'I fear your troubles make you unjust, as well as coy in the presence of sheriffs. But, come. We have much to make us sisters. Take my daughter's hand, and I will take yours.'

Sally's pretty face was sullen, and when she replied she was careful to keep her voice too low for her mother-in-law to hear. 'Mistress Muck,' she snapped. 'I, be a sister to Josselyn's leavings?'

Hannah knew well enough that her impending marriage had not made the village gossips forget her. If anything, it had fueled them with resentment: *Lady Josselyn*, they might even be expected to call her, as they had always called Daniel's dead wife.

After James's departure, alone at last and still mourning her three dead children, Hannah had selected the quiet, war-damaged Englishman who worked at Quaid's Forge to father her another child – a free child, born of her own choice. Daniel Josselyn was penniless then, disinherited and racked by a turncoat's shame, in need of her comfort. Better still, he had a wife back in London and Hannah need not fear he would force her to marry him once she was pregnant; she need not love him, obey his whims, nor be bound to his will.

So, then. Six weeks' bedding and it was done.

They had met by stealth in those days, keeping clear of the Night Watch – in Daniel's loft room at the Forge, or in the upper floor of her uncle's mill, on a pallet of old quilts among the grain sacks and the coils of rope. Near sugaring time, it had been, when she sent him away, early March, the air with a deceptive softness to it so that they opened the mill shutters and quenched the single candle in order to lie side by side and look up at the stars.

His lovemaking had always been subtle, the play of his imagination often amazing her. Where she herself was bold and forthright, Daniel approached her so gradually, with such intense concentration, that Hannah was sometimes startled to find he had already entered her, grew greater within her own body, almost fused himself to her. Then the warm gift of his seed pulsing deep and steady, so that she laughed aloud with an animal's sudden delight.

'I've fallen pregnant,' she had announced on one such night.

He said nothing, only lay very still. Then at last he got up, his dark army cloak wrapped around him like deep, fluid shadow, and left her for a bit as he often did, to rummage about in the mill office below, cadging a pipe of her uncle's tobacco. She could smell the ripe darkness of smoke on his body when he slipped between the quilts again and kissed the two small spots he was fond of, the twin hollows at the base of her neck where her shoulders began. Her magic, he called them, a talisman against the bad dreams that never quite left him.

'So, my heart. You are with child as you wanted.'

He sounded slightly distant, but his good hand laid itself quietly on her belly, letting her feel its steady warmth. The other hand, the left, was missing two fingers, an atrocity of war. He never touched her with it uninvited. Never slept until she slept. Never looked at his own face in a mirror or a pond of still water or the bottom of an empty glass.

He knew he might lose her to this child, this imperative woman-self she had made him assert for her: *I am Hannah Trevor, and I own myself. I can bear anything, everything. Alone.*

'You know I have feared this,' he said. 'This child you were so eager to make.'

Hannah did not reply at once. What she had felt these past months was no more, she counselled herself, than a passing compassion for him. Yes, she could let him go now and feel nothing. Not a flicker of regret.

As though he had read her thoughts, Daniel drew away from her and got up again, his fair English skin very pale in the thin spring dark. He had small freckles sprinkled all across his back and shoulders. One night at the Forge she had made him lie still while she counted them, and he sang 'Fathom the Bowl' at the top of his lungs to taunt the nosy neighbors.

One hundred and one. One hundred and two. One hundred and three perfect freckles. I could find my way by them at night, like the constellations, she had said.

Now Hannah got up, the quilt gathered about her. She went to stand by the open window, glad of the cold edge still buried under the softness of the air. *I do not love him. I will not. Not I.*

'Why, what have you feared, sir?' she said, taunting him. 'Have you never lain with a pregnant woman before? They say we give greater pleasure so.'

'Damn you. Don't talk like a whore.'

Daniel's voice was barely loud enough to hear. Through the open shutters came the sound of sleigh bells, some farmer out to guard his sugar buckets from black bears and thieves. Hannah forced herself to cut an inch deeper, her voice grating and harsh.

'What else am I? Do I not tumble a man not my husband?'

He caught her hand and pulled her close. His eyes were too steady and she looked away from them, out at the sky.

'You knew I had a wife and could not wed you,' he said. 'But I will do you every other justice of a husband. Care for you, see you want for nothing, you and the child.'

'Keep me for a mistress, you mean.'

'You goad me on purpose!' Daniel breathed deep for control, then went on, determined. 'When the babe's born, you must name me its father and I will go to the court and claim it freely. It shall have my name.'

'So you may order its manner of life, I suppose, and its schooling, and take it to be a servant to your excellent wife when she comes?' Hannah fought free of his arms. 'My child does not want your fine name, nor do I!'

'It is *my* child too!'

'You have no proof of that, sir, and you will never have! I still had a husband in my bed no more than three months since, may God strike him. Perhaps it is Trevor's. Besides, if I couple so readily with you, why not with a half-dozen others?'

Daniel did not respond. He began to dress, that mad backwards way he had of pulling on his boots first, then his breeches. Another time she would have teased him. But now she was ashes and rock.

'I don't love you,' she said. 'It's all the use I had for you. The child is mine. Now leave me alone.'

Daniel stood up and threw his long cloak over one shoulder. 'Enough, then. Only hear what I say for once, and remember it. I won't crawl snuffling to your doorstep. But if you send to me, wherever I am I will come.'

A hundred and three freckles, she thought. Her fingers

reached out in the darkness between them, counting the air. He turned to leave and Hannah's resolve weakened.

'Where will you go?' she asked him.

'Back to the War. I'm good at killing, so they tell me.'

Daniel took a step towards the doorway. Then suddenly he spun on his heel and came back to her. His head bent very low and he lifted up first one of her hands, then another. She felt his mouth brush her palms, barely touching at first, the rough scrape of his two days' beard and then the faint suction, the adhesion that lifted her flesh and drew it inside him, tasting it as he did the skin of her breasts when he kissed them.

'I am the ghost of you, Hannah,' he whispered. 'You'll never be free of me. That is what love is, if you like it or not.'

'Such a hoyden as you, in his dead wife's bed,' hissed Sally, and Hannah's memories blew away like so many dry leaves. 'Why, I could die with laughing!' the girl went on in an undertone. 'I am better than you are, and one day soon you shall know it! You shall all know it!'

Feeling Julia's eyes upon her from across the farmyard, Sally bent and kissed little Jennet's cheek sweetly, then Hannah's, a modest smile on her face. 'A kind kiss in return, Niece,' commanded Julia. 'Do not be grudging!'

The girl smelt of cornflour powder and rosewater, like the crust of a Banbury tart, but Hannah smiled and complied, her stomach churning.

'If ever you trouble my daughter again,' she whispered, 'I will come in the night and singe your eyebrows off with a candle, so help me, and truss you like a Christmas goose!'

She returned mildly to her work, keeping Jennet close

by her. The tallow was ready, and with a practiced hand Julia dipped the ten lengths of tow quickly, then lifted them again. The thin coat of grease set fast in the cold air, and Hannah ran her thumb and index finger the length of each wick to straighten it before it was too hard to mold. The five hundred candles would be dipped forty or fifty times before they were thick enough to use.

Sally made no move to help, but Julia's temper would bear no more indulgence. 'Come girl,' she commanded. 'We're a pair of hands short without Tirzah. Bring me the rest of the bayberry here.'

Sally did as she was told, but she lingered by the dipping kettle. Suddenly she covered her face with her hands and burst into tears. Hannah broke the wick she was smoothing and swore under her breath.

'There now, Puss, whatever's the matter?' said Julia, one arm around her sobbing daughter-in-law.

'I – I had hoped to go to Great Meadow,' blubbered the girl. 'I prayed all the night that one of the men come for Muster might carry some word of my dearest Johnnie. Oh, please, Mother Markham, may not I go?'

Julia shook her head. 'Husband cannot take you, they are spiking the last raft of logs upstream. And surely you would fear to be alone among so many men, my dear, with the sheriff prowling.'

Sally stamped her small, scuffed boot. 'You would not hinder Hannah from going. She is everything to you and I am nothing. I am ordered about like a scullion!'

Julia was not inclined to coddle anyone and she had never liked Sally, but the girl's father was too poor to keep her. So for Jonathan's sake, here at Two Mills she and the baby must stay.

'You are my daughter now,' said the old lady kindly, 'and as welcome to me as any of my own. But you must know—'

The girl pointed at Hannah. 'If I am your daughter, why is it *she* who keeps the keys to the clock and the linen chest and the pewter dresser, and not I?'

Julia bristled. 'I suppose I need not explain my managing. I am yet the mistress of this house!'

'I want Hannah's keys,' said Sally. 'I want the place next my father-in-law, where she now sits at table. I am a married woman, and she is only a penniless widow, kept here at your charity. She must sit lower than I, with Kitty and Susan at the foot of the table, and walk behind me when we go in to church on Sunday. I will have my proper place in this house! It is owed to my husband and my son.'

Julia stared into the kettle, her mouth set and her eyes brimming. If he lived and was pardoned at last, Jonathan would one day inherit Two Mills from his father. And Julia's own place in the house would then depend almost entirely upon Sally's good will.

As for Hannah, she would be no better than a servant if she stayed here under Sally's rule, and Jennet even worse. Their entire worldly goods consisted of an old rocking chair with a hole in its caning, four shillings in savings, and a wooden chest full of quilts stitched from hand-me-downs and scraps. Even if she had not at last admitted that she loved Daniel, Hannah would have been obliged to marry him – or someone – before very long.

Obligation. The word slapped her in the face.

She unfastened the household keys from her skirt and dropped them at the girl's feet. 'Have them, then,' she said, 'and the sooner the better. Learn to shoulder the extra work you will have when I'm gone.'

But, as usual, work was the last thing on Sally Markham's mind.

'Ethan!' she cried to the choreboy, who had begun to rake up dry cornstalks against the north wall of the barn. 'Saddle me Mistress Markham's old raggedy pony! I shall go to the Muster. If anyone summon Mrs Trevor to a birthing, I suppose she may walk!'

FOUR

The Blind Fist of Power

PRONOUNCEMENT OF SENTENCE UPON
JONATHAN ELIJAH MARKHAM, TRAITOR AND FELON
RUFUS PENNY, TRAITOR AND FELON
FREDERICK O'NEAL, TRAITOR AND FELON
ISSUED THIS TWENTY-THIRD DAY OF SEPTEMBER,
1786
COURT OF HIGH CRIMES, SALCOMBE,
COUNTY OF SUSSEX,
PROVINCE OF MAINE
THE HONORABLE JUSTICES QUINCY, PROCTOR,
AND RANDOLPH
MARCUS TAPP, SHERIFF
MR BERIAH HONEYFORD, CLERK

MR JUSTICE QUINCY: Rise, prisoners at the bar, and face
your accusors.

*Here the Prisoners Penny and O'Neal did rise. The Prisoner
Markham attempted to do so, but fell back again upon
the bench.*

MR JUSTICE RANDOLPH: Confound it, sir! On your feet,
your rogue!

CLERK: There is fever in the cells, Master Randolph.
The prisoner is lately taken with it. He cannot stand
without assistance.

QUINCY: Then assist him, Mr Honeyford. We are not monsters here.

MARKHAM: I am well enough to stand. I want none of your pity.

The Prisoner Markham did rise with difficulty, but gave signs of collapse. Sheriff Tapp did grip him by the arm and support him.

TAPP: I don't fancy holding this fool up till you've finished palavering! Mr Clerk, fetch a chair!

MR JUSTICE PROCTOR: Just so. Hem. Now then. Prisoners, you are Rufus Penny, Frederick O'Neal, and Jonathan Markham?

PENNY: You know well enough who we are!

PROCTER: Order must be observed! We must have due process!

MARKHAM: Was it due process when Sheriff Tapp ordered chains put upon George Anson, though his only crime was having too little hard coin to answer his tax?

RANDOLPH: What's this, eh? Janson? Who the deuce is Janson? Eh?

MARKHAM: Was it order when magistrate Siwall shot down that same George Anson with the chains still upon him, in the sight of his wife and his children? Was it order that she now runs mad and must be locked alway?

RANDOLPH: Eh, sir? Eh? What's he say, Jack? I do not comprehend him. The villain don't talk plain English!

QUINCY: He suffered some injury, Bertie. His mouth was spoilt in his capture. He does not speak clear.

At this there arose a disturbance in the Court, divers men rising from their benches and shouting, as witness: 'Sheriff Tapp did knock out his teeth!' or 'Siwall must hang and to

hell with all judges!' or 'Justice for Anson and Markham!
Justice for all laboring men!'

PROCTER: They are a mob! They will lay hands upon us!
Sheriff Tapp, clear the Court!

TAPP: There are near three hundred men in this room,
Mr Procter. Shall I shoot them or slice them?

RANDOLPH: What's he say, Jack? Confound the feller,
what's he say?

QUINCY: I think you are in contempt, Mr Tapp.

TAPP: I won't give my liver to save your piss-ant dignity
of office. If that is contempt, you may have it so.

PROCTER: (*to the spectators*) Gentlemen, gentlemen! You
are citizens of a free republic, not brawling ruffians!
Let us have order in this court!

Here several white-headed fellows gave signal to the Mob to
content Itself, vidalicet, one Enoch Luckett, yeoman, and one
Jacob Crutch, yeoman and cooper. The Great Disruption was
quelled.

RANDOLPH: Well, now! That's more like it! Let 'em keep
their places, the dogs!

QUINCY: Will the prisoners now state their names?

PENNY: I – I'm Rufus Penny. My wife's in the court. If I
could—

O'NEAL: Rufe! Don't whine for 'em, damn you!

QUINCY: Who are you, sir?

O'NEAL: I? Why, I am God's monkey, Master Justice.

PROCTER: Blasphemy will not help you! And you sir, are
Jonathan Markham?

MARKHAM: It is a good name, and my father's lawful
giving.

MR JUSTICE RANDOLPH: Hah! Father, does he say? If the

whoreson had taught you some humility before your betters, you would not stand here now!

MARKHAM: I see friends here, and enemies. I see none of my betters in this room.

MR JUSTICE QUINCY: Prisoners, you stand before the Bar of Justice as before the Throne of God.

The Justices did all three put on the Black Cap, to signify a Mortal Judgement against the Accused.

QUINCY: Master Clerk, read the charges and the verdicts thereupon.

CLERK: Assault upon the Person of one Gabriel Bent, Collector of Property Taxes for the County of Sussex. Guilty. Wanton Destruction by Fire of the Rightful Property of Divers Citizens. Guilty. Spreading Sedition and inciting Rebellion and the Destruction of Property among the Peaceful Citizens of this County and of these United States against its lawful Governors. Guilty. High Treason in bearing Arms against its Representatives, Sheriffs, and Constables in the course of their Lawful Protection of Property. Guilty. So say you, Justices?

JUSTICES: So say we all.

QUINCY: Prisoners, for these crimes and others not specified, you are hereby sentenced to be hanged upon Salcombe Common at noon on the twenty-ninth day of September of this present year, and your bodies to be caged thereafter in iron wickets and left for the space of twelve months to hang in plain sight upon the Public Gibbet, as example to others who claim the right of assault upon liberty and property and of resistance to lawful authority by force-of-arms.

There fell a Great Silence upon the Court. Some Females and

Old Folk might be heard to shed tears at the Great Sins of the Condemned, and to exhort their Repentance.

PROCTER: Prisoners, have you anything more to say before you are taken down?

PENNY: We— We must hang, do you say? For *property*?

O'NEAL: We burnt some haystacks, that's all! Christ God, we've killed no one!

PENNY: We stole nothing, not a farthing! We broke open old Ike Hobart's mercantile, for he was charging three times the fair price for his salt and molasses and he would not take barter. But we left goods in exchange! Good corn meal and a barrel of salt pork!

MARKHAM: Rufe. Let it be. They don't speak the same tongue as we do.

PENNY: We tarred and feathered old Bent, the taxman, and he was back to his work in a fortnight! We did no mortal harm!

O'NEAL: Jesus. I'm a black sinner. I don't want to die. Not yet. Not yet.

RANDOLPH: What's the other knave say? You've been prating all the morning, you young puppy! What have you to say now, eh? Eh?

MARKHAM: I am tired and sick of the lot of you. I want to sit down, I – am –

Here the Prisoner Markham collapsed in the well of the court and fell to shivering from his great fear of the Just Sentence pronounced upon him. Mistress Trevor, the Prisoner's Cousin, with his old father, Master Markham of Rufford, did attempt to give him comfort, but they were prevented for their safety by the Sheriff's men. The Prisoners were removed to the cells and a Clergyman, Mr Simon

Whitfield, was brought in to them, after which they all three did confess their Dreadful Crimes and humbly beg Mercy of God and did crave Pardon most abjectly of the Governor and the General Court.

This same Pardon was sued-for by their Friends and Connections, and was shortly denied by the Governor, with the advice of the General Court of the State of Massachusetts, Boston, Master William Royallton-Smith presiding.

FIVE

Warrant for the Capture and Arrest of
Jonathan Markham,
Escaped Traitor and Felon
Hamilton Siwall, Magistrate
Court of Common Pleas, Rufford,
County of Sussex
Marcus Tapp, Sheriff
Lachlan McGregor, Constable
27 September 1786

THIS BOLD TRAITOR AND FELON is not yet one-and-twenty, well made though slender, with black hair and a fair complexion. In resisting the Representatives of a Lawful Authority, he caused his front teeth to be broken out, and bears a sabre scar on his Left Temple. Before his escape, he feigned the Ill Effects of a Putrid Fever, to excite sympathy from his Keepers that they might relax their guard. He is fled with his Fellow-Traitors, Penny and O'Neal, whose Corpses have lately been found in the Western Forests, and it is likely this Desperate and Recalcitrant Villain has taken their Lives to save his Own.

LET ALL CITIZENS BE ADVISED that if any Man or Woman have knowledge of the whereabouts of this Traitor, or if any give him Shelter and Succour, or if any provide him the means to remain beyond reach of the Dread Sentence upon him, that Person shall suffer Two Hundred strokes of the Sheriff's Lash and a Term of Imprisonment not less than a Twelve month, at Hard Labor for the People's Good.

SIX

The Man in the Uniform

'Now, then! Halt, sir, and let me inspect you!'

As he had done from his boyhood in Herefordshire, Major Daniel Josselyn – now three-and-forty and in full officer's uniform of the Continental Army – obeyed the imperious voice of his great-aunt Sibylla. He stood smartly to attention in the half-empty library of his fine manor house and saluted her, the thumb and fingers of his right hand barely tweaking the brim of his cockaded black hat.

When his wife Charlotte was alive, he had worn a leather glove on his mangled left hand to protect her from the sight of the stumps, which distressed her. After four years of slow decline, Charlotte had died in the summer. But Daniel still wore the glove.

Without it he felt skinless, as though his bones were exposed. Inside them, muffled and caged, was the thing that still burned in him, deeper than his distrust of God or himself. It cut and slashed him as fire does and left him silent and raw, restless at times and unable to sleep until daylight – and sometimes not even then.

Few men who had lived through the War had escaped these slow torments. They lived deep in the muscles and the blood and the bones, flooding the mind with self-disgust and paralyzing the will without warning. It was more than bad memory. Sometimes it was the lack of any clear memory at all.

Now that he and Hannah were free to marry, Daniel coveted more than ever the simple dreams of happy men. The laying of a certain stone to corner a garden wall. The putting-out of candles in cold rooms, the flickering light on the faces of children he might claim. The locking of house doors against wolves, against thieves. The mending of a roof against the snow.

And Christmas. For years he had missed the fine holidays of his childhood at his grandfather's estate near the border of Wales – the great log fires, the trip in the sledge to cut holly and mistletoe from the oak grove on the slope of Little Ben, the heavy spiced smells of roast beef and mincemeat pie and plum pudding and punch. And last of all, more precious than all, the high, thin voice of a small boy who slipped out alone into the Christ's Eve darkness to sing by himself to the bright, frosty stars.

But no one kept such Christmases here, and the boy he had been was long dead. Daniel paced the floor and did not sleep, for how could he risk such vain, peaceful dreaming? Was he not in uniform again?

He could not remember ever making a conscious decision to resign his commission in Burgoyne's army and join the Americans. He recalled writing some words on a half-sheet of paper, how he had had to stop once and sharpen the point of his pen with pumice, how the ink was poor and smelled of blackcurrants and blotted every other word.

The last few of those words he remembered quite clearly: *Our most sacred duty on earth is to die at some peace with ourselves.*

He recalled leaving his red coat behind, stealing another, brown and three sizes too large for him. Then riding, running, risking a crawl across half-frozen river ice. Hiding in haystacks, barns, henhouses, sties. 'Which side are you on?' they would ask with a pistol at his ear when they found him half-starved in the straw. 'Are you Tory or Patriot? Where do you stand? On which side?'

After Saratoga, after Webb's Ford, he could not remember thinking more than once or twice of freedom in the abstract, and he cared nothing any longer for fine words or politics. 'Our side,' he would say when they asked him, and they would give him food and sleep.

Now a new war was brewing, and once again Daniel Josselyn was caught in the middle.

Which uniform do you wear now? the burnt wound of his memory demanded. *Silk breeches or homespun? Rich man or poor man? Which side are you on?*

'You have underslept again, Nephew,' said his great-aunt, frowning as she studied his features.

Daniel's was a wide face, though chiselled, the cheek-bones high and sharp. The nose was long, sloping, hooked by an old break, and the hair red-brown, touched with grey here and there, now, and worn longish, untied, drifting soft around his temples and over his forehead. He was more or less clean-shaven today in honor of the Muster, but he preferred an unfashionable workaday stubble of beard and moustache that grew out always a shade or two darker than his hair.

It was chiefly her nephew's eyes that disturbed Lady Sibylla, however. They were hooded, deep auburn like very good brandy, and they seldom fixed themselves directly on anyone. This morning – as on most mornings of late – they were adorned by dark smudges of weariness, and the eyelids were puffy with strain. She made the little clucking noise with her tongue that had terrified him as a boy. It meant disapproval, and when Sibylla disapproved, the earth trembled.

'The circles under those two eyes would serve for a lunar eclipse, sir,' she said with a sniff.

He smiled. 'I went hunting deer very late with Josh Lamb and McGregor, the constable. Wretched sport, I'm afraid.'

But Sibylla would not be put off. 'Indeed? Pray then, what beast do you hunt when you pace these corridors night after night? Wild bears, is it, or tigers?'

In the front hall, the clock struck half-past seven; maneuvers would begin at nine o'clock. Daniel clicked his boot heels smartly and swept the old lady a bow, his blue-black cloak brushing the polished oak boards of the library flooring. 'I must go,' he said, 'but you have yet time for a final inspection. Will I do, do you think? Shall I dazzle the troops?'

Sibylla looked down her nose at him. 'Your stockings droop something shocking at the back,' she said. 'But I believe my good brother your grandsire, were he living, would not altogether disapprove that your coat is not red.'

At nearly eighty, Lady Sibylla Josselyn herself dressed with great elegance and – as she did everything – entirely to suit her own whims. This morning she wore a gown of greenish-bronze taffeta fit for the salons of Paris, her heap of carefully powdered curls topped with a purple turban and a white ostrich plume.

Even her eyes were gaudy, thought Daniel. They had a curious quality of picking up the colors around them, like the scales of fishes or the eyes of certain birds. At the moment, they were sparked with a disconcerting green. He looked away, impatient to be gone, but she glared around the nearly empty library and whacked her gold-headed stick on the carpetless floor till the room echoed.

'You have changed the subject, boy, but you shall not escape me so neatly! My dear brother charged me to see to the health of your soul, and by Harry, you make a Herculean labor of it! Look about you, sir! Why, you will offer Mrs Trevor a household as bare as a plate of old bones!'

He had had the room stripped of its finery and hung with new paper from Boston, very plain and pale. Charlotte's harp and spinet had been taken away and placed in a small back parlor, her embroidered cushions and footstools and firescreens and china ornaments packed into trunks. Much of the stylish Boston furniture in the other rooms had been crated and stored, and as each piecrust table and damask lolling chair disappeared, Daniel felt lighter in body, as if he had been living for years at the mercy of things.

The empty library, especially, pleased him. Only his rows of books remained, and his plain pine writing desk and chair. By day, he opened the high casements that faced Two Mills farm on the opposite bank and let in the cold autumn air, his eye always alert for a glimpse of Hannah's cardinal-red cloak against the gloom of the river and the dark woods beyond. By night he sat up very late, pulling books from his shelves at random and reading a page of Livy or Herodotus, a chapter of *Gulliver's Travels* or *Tom Jones* or *Pilgrim's Progress*, and watching for the swinging arc of her lantern as she made her way home in the dark.

When he needed to rest, he brought blankets and slept where he felt he was nearest her, already wed to her and clean of the past. Often he lay here in this emptied, fireless room, his books scattered around him, chaste and dreamless as a monk.

Sometimes when he woke, he would find himself in some other half-empty room, or nested warm next to Yeoman in the stable, or wrapped in his greatcoat on the cold bluff, by the ruined lookout post they called Rook's Nest. Even in the War, even after, in the worst of Charlotte's illnesses, he had never before walked in his sleep. Why he did so now, when he should have been happy and peaceful, Daniel asked himself a thousand times a day. Something long buried was working its way to the surface, something he must shed like an old dead skin to come new to the rest of his life and the promise of marriage.

But he did not know what. He emptied another room and read Ovid's *Metamorphoses* till dawn.

Only his dead wife's bedchamber he left untouched, the door locked except to the housekeeper, Mrs Twig, who dusted and polished it fervently, and aired the delicate silk gowns and pelisses to keep them as fresh as the last day they were worn.

'You cannot erase Charlotte's handprint on you with a bit of fresh paint and a scrubbing.' His aunt laid a thin, papery hand on his shoulder. 'You have been twice to her grave within a month. Was it to beg absolution?'

Sibylla's eyes had lost all their color. They were black now, like jet beads on a fan, thought Daniel. From out in the yard, he could hear the deep bass voice of John English, his steward. There were others, too, excited and angry.

But Sibylla ignored them, her voice suddenly soft. 'Do not carry the dead on your shoulder, my dear boy,' she said. 'Believe me, for I've reason to know it. They will crush you in time, if you do.'

He only smiled. 'My dearest Aunt. Do not trouble for the health of my soul. Mrs Trevor may do as she likes with it – and with this place – if we wed.'

'*If?*' Sibylla stared. 'Do you mean to discard her, like that puppy Jem Siwall's poor trollop?'

The magistrate's rake of a son had put a bastard into one of the kitchenmaids at Burnt Hill Manor, and she was promptly sent packing. According to Twig's formidable network of gossips, Molly Bacon was now pleasuring sailors in Wybrow, at a shilling and ninepence a throw.

Someone was pounding on the hall door now, fists banging the hard oak like hammers. But Sibylla would not be put off. 'Answer me, sir!' she demanded. 'Will you wed Mrs Trevor at Christmas or will you not?'

Daniel met her eyes. 'I would marry her this hour, if I might.'

The banging on the door grew even more insistent, the voices louder. 'Major Josselyn! We must speak to you, sir! At once!'

There was a rustling of skirts and a crackling of starched aprons, and the piggy eyes of Mrs Arabella Twig, the house-keeper, peered around the doorway, followed by a head of greenish-brown curls under a lace cap with lappets that hung down on either side of her plump face like a spaniel's ears.

'Oh, sir!' she cried, 'here's Mr Hobart and Lawyer Napier to see you, with Dr Cyrus Kent and the other Selectmen.

And Magistrate Siwall, too. And he says he will never go home till you see him!' Twig paused for breath and a cloud of lavender-scented cornflour rose up like a spectre from between her remarkable paste-white bosoms. 'I am informed, sir, on excellent authority,' she continued, in the low purring tone she reserved for her master, 'that Siwall and Dr Sam Clinch were the worse for drink at last night's hunt. And this morning—'

'That will do, Mrs Twig,' Daniel said curtly. The window frames were fairly rattling as the pounding and shouting continued on the doorstep. 'Show these hooligans in.'

'Here, sir?' The housekeeper twitched him a nervous smile and looked around the empty room. 'Now, in the second parlor there is yet chairs enough.'

'I said, show them in,' he repeated. 'Then ask Williams to fetch me a chair for my aunt, if you please, and a cushion. That is all we require.'

Twig dropped a crackling curtsy and in another moment the visitors filed in, gaping about them at the state of the room, cocked hats in hand and jackboots clumping. The boot boy brought Sibylla's chair, and from it, with her scientist's curiosity, she took stock of the town bigwigs as if they were so many native plants for her botanical collection, to be stuck down with pins to a page.

Isaiah Hobart, General Merchant and Ship's Chandler. A thick stem and a sparse reddish foliage, growing mainly about the ears. Lives well and likes it, but bends with every wind.

Thomas Napier, Lawyer. Branches bowed and scrawny, foliage ill-powdered horsehair, much bagged at the sides. A good old fellow enough, but so cautious he is surely a danger when afraid.

Cyrus Kent, Physician and Surgeon. A handsome plant and

a vain one, not long rooted here. Half-educated at excellent schools, possessing more ideals in theory than in fact. But he sometimes cuts, I hear, without reason, for the power that comes from the knife.

Erastus Cain, Rope-spinner. Short and bushy, with a trunk like a ship's cable. Bristles of hemp pop out of him everywhere, as though he might harvest himself and supply his own spinning. I do not trust such an overgrown plant.

Silvanus Whitney. A poor specimen, not likely to flourish. Ink on his chin and ink in his pockets. And, I warrant you, ink in his soul.

Hamilton Siwall, Esquire, Land Merchant, Moneylender, Magistrate and Representative to General Court. Ah, now. Here is the article. A reaching, ambitious plant that takes what ground it will. A ruddy face tending to choler, lank, brownish foliage drawn back across his bald pate and tied with a black velvet ribbon. A buyer and seller of men, but no judge of them, though a magistrate he may be.

And what is this? A weed, to be sure! A sprout of poison ivy! Robert Inskip, the great Siwall's bailiff. A pair of eyes like a rat in a woodpile, and fingers that have dipped into more than one pocket, surely.

Daniel frowned at the sight of the bailiff. Squeezer Inskip, they called him, a slippery fellow much disliked in the village. He was not a selectman like the others, he had no official standing; aside from his constant slavering over Siwall, he could have no business here.

'Williams!' Josselyn said, raising his voice only slightly. The boot boy stuck his head around the door. 'Show Mr Inskip to a chair in the hall if you please.' Siwall scowled, but Squeezer only grinned and bobbed a bow as he went.

Daniel took up his officer's small-sword from the writing

desk. It was an old weapon, a gift from his first commander in India. The blade was blued steel, double-honed, and the pommel ended in a silver wolf's head. He slipped it into the loop on his sword belt, then turned back to his visitors.

'I will hear you, sirs,' he said somewhat curtly. 'But be quick if you please. As you know, the training begins in something over an hour and I have much to attend.'

' 'Tis account of that we've come, Major,' said Erastus Cain the rope-maker. 'The Muster, I mean. Now, sir, we be all propertied men of the town like yourself—'

But Siwall was much too impatient for polite perorations. 'Josselyn, you command the militia, near five hundred men from here to the coast! We need their protection and we will have it, by God!'

At this oath Daniel glanced at Sibylla, who sat at her ease. Taking out an enamelled box, she laid a pinch of snuff along the curve of her forefinger and inhaled it with a mighty snort.

Siwall jerked round at the sound. 'Ah. Yes. Excuse me – I forget myself, madam,' he mumbled. 'But I'm a blunt fellow and these are bloody dangerous times.'

'And I am a soldier, Mr Siwall,' said Josselyn quietly. 'I will do nothing until I have direct orders from Colonel Scribner at Salcombe.'

'I *know* you, sir!' cried the magistrate. 'You follow orders only so long as they suit you! What we want to find out is, which side is your vagabond conscience on now?'

Sibylla's cane whacked the floorboards at her feet. 'This stick has thumped better blackguards than you, sir! My nephew is too much the gentleman to thrash you in my presence, but I shall very soon do it myself!'

Daniel's hand lay lightly on the hilt of his sword. 'I know

Mr Siwall perhaps better than he imagines, and my memory is as good as his own. If he cares to discuss matters of conscience in public, I should be glad to oblige him on some other occasion. But just now I have no more time to spare you, sirs. Mrs Twig will show you out.'

'Taunt *me* with conscience! You – You dare not defame me with such – such cheap insinuations!' Hamilton Siwall's broad back collided with the bookshelf and several small, leather-bound volumes clattered down to the floor. He was almost beside himself. 'My history is open for all here to know!' he cried.

'What Siwall means, Major,' said fusty old Lawyer Napier hastily, 'is – ahem – once they're assembled, will you keep the militia in muster and defend the sitting of the Debtor's Court tomorrow?'

The burning of the courthouse at Salcombe had delayed the prosecution of debtors for nearly a month, and these plump merchants were all losing money. So the court, with Siwall and two other judges, would sit at Rufford Meeting House instead, as soon as the training exercises ended.

'Surely, sir, after recent events,' old Napier went on, 'you cannot fail to appreciate the dreadful apprehension—'

Dr Kent interrupted him. 'I myself was inclined to pity these farmers' distresses, Major. But they've gone too far now, surely you admit that. Young Markham must be caught and hanged, and the rest taught a lesson.'

Siwall's fist banged on the top of Daniel's desk. 'Have you not read the papers from London, man? These rebels make us the laughing-stock of Europe! If it goes on, we'll have no hope of restoring trade and paying our war debts to the French. The Debtors' Courts *must* sit unmolested, if we are to have sound government and peace!'

Daniel's eyebrow lifted a quarter-inch. 'As you know, I too am owed substantial amounts, Mr Siwall. I confess, I have never quite comprehended how a man may pay his debts while he is locked in a prison. But you put me almost in a mind to find out.'

Siwall's face was set and angry, but he made no reply to this. Old Napier's eyes narrowed and he spat into the end of his stock-tie, cleared his throat again, and took another tack.

'As you are aware, Major, the Continental government has no funds for the payment of soldiers. But Governor Bowdoin and other gentlemen in Boston have given gold by subscription to raise a force-at-arms against these rebels, and we propose to follow suit.'

Daniel turned his back on them. 'Ah. A private army that will do as rich men tell it.'

'That is harsh, sir. We have no intention—'

'I have friends near Stockbridge, Mr Napier. They write me that the rebel farmer Shackley was recently taken by this army you so admire. They went to search his home, and when they did not find him, they grew somewhat impatient. His wife is slashed across the left breast with a bayonet, and his ten-year-old son is now missing an eye. As for Shackley, they found him alone, thirty or more against one. They slashed the tendon of Job Shackley's knee from behind with a broadsword. He will never walk upright again.'

'Let him be hanged, then, if he cannot walk upright! Chaos and Anarchy!' cried Silvanus Whitney, the printer. His rhetoric was as rumbustious as his newspaper pieces. 'Defend the Infant Republic!'

Siwall broke in again, his voice a raw growl. 'Look here, Josselyn. You know these men in the militia and they'll follow you, whichever way you go. It's in your own interest to side with us and we'll make it worth your while!'

Daniel's eyes were fixed on the high, curtainless window. He could just make out a bright speck of scarlet moving slowly along the opposite bank towards the forest. Hannah, bound for some birthing? Nearly five months with child, alone and afoot? –

He scarcely cared what he said now. He was furious – with Hannah's stubborn independence, with his uniform, with the ice and the mud, with these men who distracted him from that small, wandering spot of crimson red.

'When Master Siwall and I were partners,' he said, turning to face them, 'he did as he liked with his share of our holdings. He sold cutover land that wouldn't grow a decent cabbage to poor men fresh from the army who'd have bought a tombstone in order to find an hour's peace under it.' His eyes raked his one-time friend. 'These militiamen are not idle ruffians, Mr Siwall. They are honest farmers and tradesmen who went into debt to you to purchase their own ruin. And now you would "make it worth my while" to order them into a war for your defense? Leave my house, sir. I think you are mad.'

Siwall's face was bright crimson. 'No, sir! I demand you do your duty!'

'My duty? Or your bidding?'

Daniel was not to be bullied, but Hamilton Siwall gave no ground. 'Every man in this room pays his taxes to outfit and train that militia!' he shouted. 'All here are selectmen and we have cast votes on the matter!'

'So has the town meeting. The majority voted to take no sides either way.' Daniel's eyes sought Siwall's and probed them. There was something else, something no one was saying. 'Why do you fear these men so suddenly?' he asked. 'There has been no new trouble since the summer.'

The magistrate snorted. 'You call the burning of Salcombe jail nothing?'

'It did not trouble you overmuch until today.' Josselyn searched the tense faces around him. 'What has happened? Is there fresh news from Boston?'

Lawyer Napier's bony hands twisted and untwisted the facings of his coat. 'Nothing untoward has yet occurred, Major. But with so many men in the town for Muster, all armed and their loyalties unknown – We must know where you stand, you see. The militia, that is.'

Daniel stood at attention, his back very straight and his eyes glazed with irritation. He could no longer see Hannah through the window, she had gone too far and even her red cloak did not show through the trees.

'At present,' he told Napier stiffly, 'the militia stand as neutral. But if a general county convention should be held during Muster, as I have heard talk among my men—'

Siwall's fists were clenched, his florid face suddenly pale. 'Damn their conventions and damn you, sir! You will do as you're bloody well told!'

'And if I do not?' Daniel's fingers closed on his sword.

'If you do not, sir,' cried Hamilton Siwall, 'then by God's eyes I shall see you are hanged for a traitor, along with your rascally friends!'

SEVEN

Redoubtable's Voyage

The selectmen had not yet arrived at Mapleton Grange when a canvas-topped wagon drew up to Henry Markham's mill. It paused, then started up the steep slope towards the busy farmyard, the two big shire horses that pulled it stamping and steaming in the cold. 'Hard a-port, Neptune! Mermaid, trim your bowlines!' cried the driver.

Master Dick Dancer, chapman and peddler, had never sailed before the mast, but in his boyhood he had thought of little else. He talked like a sailor and thought like a sailor, and when he slept, he snored like a sailor. He was sun-browned and round-faced and bald-headed, with a shape like a pudding-basin above his meridian and a bow-legged clothes-peg below. Every spring, Dick and his father and daughter set out from Portsmouth or Boston in their creaky old red-and-blue wagon; Redoubtable, he called it, for its tar-blackened canvas had come from a ship of that name.

Like most peddlers' wagons, Redoubtable's sides were built up of a series of boxes inside and out, like cupboards, their sizes depending on the merchandise they held.

Saucepots! cried one in bright yellow. *Yard goods*, intoned a very large box in baritone purple. *Salt*, murmured a third box, adorned with the likeness of a stiff and rather crusty lady – Lot's reluctant wife.

'Land-ho, Reminder!' cried Dick, as the wagon lumbered into the yard at Two Mills. 'Redoubtable's ready to dock, father! On deck, if you please!'

A pair of bright blue eyes peeped nervously out of the hooped canvas doorway, surrounded by a face so brown and wrinkled it might have been one of the fallen leaves that strewed the path. The Reverend Moses Dancer had never obtained any living and had never preached a sermon in his life, but at his ordination – so Dick's famous story went – he had vowed to give up strong drink, and had kept his vow so faithfully that a certain brother parson was long ago moved to point him out from the pulpit as 'a Mortal Reminder of the Evils of Grog.'

So he was called to this day. The Reminder wore a clergyman's white bob wig, into which were stuck two pairs of sharp steel knitting needles with a half-finished stocking dangling from them, along with a bobbin of bright green yarn.

'Ladies on the quayside, Father, a-dipping of candles,' said Dick in a soft, kindly voice. 'Merchandise, sir, if you please!'

The old man popped back into the wagon, then popped out again, this time wearing a soft felt hat. It had a tall crown that sank down in the middle, and a flat round brim hung all round the edge with notions – red and yellow ribbons, strings of brass and pewter buttons, and reels of many-colored thread. Into the hatband he had stuck papers of pins and new steel needles and stork-handled brass scissors and thimbles, all in order of price.

In the center of the crown, like a fine lady in a lolling chair, lay a fashion-baby – a wooden doll intricately dressed in the latest Boston styles, this morning a fine peacock silk with tiny embroidered festoons of flowers in purple, green, and gold.

Thus weighted, the soft brim of the hat hung down around old Moses Dancer's face, nearly hiding him. He had lived so many years in this shadow of merchandise, clinging on like a cobweb, that when he spoke it was with a cobweb's soft voice.

'Six-and-nine, sir,' he ciphered unsteadily. 'Add five and carry the two. Interest quarterly, Dick, my dear boy. At seasonable rates.' Then he sighed. 'Such a cry, was it not, Dick? Such a terrible wail in the woods.'

The peddler looked around at his father's face and found tears there, in danger of clouding the merchandise. 'Jemima, my dove!' Dick called out, leaning into the wagon. 'The dear old chap's a-sobbering again!'

The woman who climbed out to perch between them on the wagon seat was no more than thirty, but she looked forty-five at the least. Most grow into age with the world's heavy weather, but some few are born to it, and the peddler's daughter Jemima was one.

She had crisp black hair tucked up under a starched white lawn cap that was carefully rigged with a little crackling bowknot just under her chin. Her bones were sharp and her mouth was thin and her features were faded, as though she had been scrubbed until they almost disappeared. Only her eyes were still young and would die young; they were large and round and shining, deep blue and never at rest.

She wore, as she always did, a many-colored cloak made of a quilt. Its pattern was Mrs Washington's Garden, each tiny hexagon carefully stitched of bits of salvaged wools and calicoes, and even some velvets and silks. They were old clothes given her by women at whose houses her father's wagon dropped anchor, but the colors glowed chestnut and cranberry and gentian-blue, and Jemima had worked them with careful embroidery inside the patches – stars and flowers and animals that seemed to run and dance as she moved, and all done in tiny crossed stitches, counted thread-over-thread. The doll's clothes, too, were her work, sewn with twenty running stitches to the inch and never a knot to be seen, back or front. She had travelled on Redoubtable only since her mother's death at the end of the War – so Dick told all his customers – and they would smile at the thought of old Dick Dancer with a wife, and think what strange fruit that unlikely union had borne him. For deep under her sour, fitful manners, Miss Jemima was honest and kind.

'Why, you naughty Reminder!' she cried. 'You've been a-reading of them wretched old books again, that I forbid you!' Jemima gave the old man's knee three sharp smacks with her palm, as though she were slapping bread dough that had been let to rise too high. 'What a wicked Reminder it is, to go slipping away on the sly among pages! Racketing and tinkering his poor brains just to defy me! Take down your knitting, you devilish creature, and keep to your work!'

The old parson did as he was told. He extracted the needles and began to work round the green stocking, glancing now and again at his granddaughter as if he feared she might fly away. Tears had begun to run down Jemima's own cheeks as they often did, falling unchecked upon the patches of her cloak. They made no sound and gave no warning, and what she wept for, she herself did not know.

'Where is she?' whispered the old man. 'Where has she gone, Dick? Where does she wander?'

Indeed, Jemina hardly seemed aware of them or of the farmyard they were entering. Her blue eyes were glazed and her hands locked down tight in her lap.

'Ah,' said her father. 'She's a woman and a baffler, old chap. Her mother was a woman and a baffler before her. 'Tis the burden of sex in this world.'

The peddler took his father's cobweb hand in his own two sturdy ones and patted it carefully, as though it might crumble to dust. Then he drew his bottle-green coat even closer around him, pulled down his old tricorne to shelter his ears from Jemima's soft sobbing, and brought Redoubtable safe into port.

'You're welcome back, Dick! Miss Jemima! Come down, ma'am, you and your grandsire! How are you, Moses? I say now, Mother, have you not a cup of tea and a piece of cornbread to spare for old friends?'

Stirred by the slight fall of snow in the night, Hannah's uncle, Henry Markham, had been helping the millhand lash together the autumn's last rafts of sawn boards. It should have been Jonathan working there by his side, and all the morning the old miller had missed him; indeed, he had thought of little else but his youngest son for nearly four months.

Still, he took heart at the sight of Dick Dancer's wagon, like a piece of the old days that had not yet crumbled away. Henry trotted almost merrily uphill to greet his friends and when he saw them, a broad smile drove trouble for an instant from his face.

Almost as soon as the wagon pulled into the dooryard, Jennet began to jitter about near the brightly painted cargo cupboards. Her hands were making some motion or other – a new word, no doubt, in the Indian finger-talk Daniel was slowly teaching her, but meaningless to Hannah. She and Jenny had other ways of speech that needed neither fingers nor tongues.

'Hush, Flower, don't be pesky,' she said, and drew her daughter close against her, her fingers stroking the little girl's soft red-brown hair.

Before the new child came into her, Hannah would have let Jenny jump up, catch arms round her neck, and lock her small, strong legs tight behind her mother's back. Those days were gone now, of course, until after the birth, but Jennet did not understand it. She had seen kittens born, and lambs and piglets, but so far as she knew that cumbersome process had no connection with her own existence. She might have been dropped from a tree like a walnut, hard and perfect and always herself.

Her world was unique and her mind was a labyrinth, only seeming to converge with the grown-ups' when it met familiar shapes or bright colors; it was really for Jenny's sake that Hannah clung to the old scarlet cloak and wore a skirt of the same shade in summer. The sharp smell of lye soap, the flavor of horehound, the angle of light through the bed curtains at morning, the heat of the flannel-wrapped soapstone that warmed their feet at night – such things reached into her silence and found her. Through them, Jennet heard the world speak, and they marked her way in it.

Her mother's warm, willing body was another such landmark, but suddenly that landmark had a mind of its own. Jennet reached up to be cuddled, her legs already crouching to jump. 'No!' Hannah said sharply, and stepped back from her, hands pushing her away. The little girl stared, her mouth open wide and her breath coming in great gasps.

Wrong, she thought angrily. *She is not my friend now. I hate her. She is wrong.*

'Give me your hand, my love,' Hannah said, and reached for her. But Jenny clamped her arms down to her sides and turned her back.

I am invisible now. I can disappear whenever I like.

Henry Markham frowned. Not the first time the child had been willful of late, and it wasn't like her – at least not with Hannah. But he was too glad to see old friends to worry overmuch. 'Come in and have a pipe with me, Dick!' he said, smiling. 'What's the news from upcountry?'

The peddler jumped down with a bounce. 'Why,' he replied, 'here's a strange business, this very morning. A puzzler, that's what it is! We was just a-weighing anchor from Drewel's place when—'

'*He* only heard, sir, but I *saw* her!' The Mortal Reminder was not to be hindered.

'Now, Father—' Dick coaxed him.

But the old fellow stood upon the wagon seat like a parson in a pulpit, all the merchandise on his hat brim shivering and his hands still at work on his knitting. 'I saw her stand there, as pale as a flame in the air! Pure as scorn, with a crown of light upon her!' His voice was shrill and dry, like old sticks scraping a window pane. 'Life! Life!' he cried. 'Eternal life! Interest compounded! Purl two and knit to the end!'

'He's beside himself, poor old chap,' murmured Henry.

Dick lifted his father down from the wagon and the tiny old man peered round the place, studying the river, the dark woods that rose on low hills to the west, and the heavy clouds gathering eastward. Finally he crouched down and began to scratch some lines on the snow-dusted mud of the dooryard with his knitting needle.

'Oh, he's a worrisome old child,' muttered Miss Jemima, wiping her eyes. She climbed down cautiously, stepping with small, painful steps. 'I wish I had never laid eyes on him. Sobbering and ciphering at all hours, and not a scrap of pity on my nerves!'

The Reminder's knitting needle had drawn out a map in what remained of the snow. It seemed to show the eastern edge of the forest, north of the Trace – the narrow logging road – at the foot of Chine Ridge. Henry peered down at the scratchings, then glanced at Hannah. 'I know that spot,' he said. 'That's west of Josiah Bridge's old sugar bush.'

Hannah knelt down beside the old parson; she could feel his slight body tremble slightly, as though the wind blew through his bones. 'Who have you seen, sir?' she asked him gently. 'Are you sure it was a woman? What sort of cry was it she made?'

'Oh, a long cry and a deep one, ma'am,' he said. 'A borning cry, it was, though what comes of such a birth, I know not, nor any mortal man.'

'Borning? A woman in travail, do you mean?' Hannah looked up at Jemima. 'You must have heard, Jemima. *Could* it be such?'

'What have I to do with borning?' snapped the peddler's daughter, and tied two more knots in the bowlines of her cap. 'Am I courted or wedded or bedded? I heard nothing! And I shouldn't admit if I did!'

Jennet had returned to her fidgeting, tugging at the latches of the large cargo boxes. Catching sight of her, Jemima smacked the deaf child's hand, kissed the top of her head, and disappeared into the wagon. In a moment they could hear her sobbing and shifting the merchandise about.

Dick shook his head. "'Tis the visions, you know. Poor girl wasn't built for 'em. Her ma wasn't built for 'em, and *she* broke up early. But dear Father sees, you know, with the Everlasting Lens, that's his strength and his burden.' He paused and took a puff of the long-stemmed clay pipe Henry offered. 'Male or female, I know not, nor borning nor dying. Only 'twas a terrible cry we did hear. Just the one, mind. It came but once, and then no more.'

'I know three or four women with child in the home-steads thereabouts,' said Hannah. 'Martha Newcomb. Susannah Penny. If one of them ventured too far and mis-carried, or if her time came on her suddenly – Oh, and there's Beulah Wynant, too, I'd forgot her, and Mrs Kersey! How early was it? Was it yet full day?'

'Dark, my dear. Clouds this morning, couldn't steer by the stars.' Dick smoked again and considered. 'But a cloudy sky bears its own light before sunrise. I seen there was a tree fallen, so I stood ashore to shift it, and 'twas then we heard the cry.'

Henry's face was set and his eyes would not come to rest except on the map in the snow. 'Was it never a *man's* voice, Dick? A *young* man's?'

The peddler looked away; he knew the old miller was thinking of Johnnie. 'Whatever it was, 'twas in a sore state. There was a great hunt last night, you know, and I helped Amos Drewel bring his cows into stable, for he said those town fellows would wing a spinning wheel if you left it defenseless, they take such a precious poor aim.'

'Someone wounded by mischance, you think?' said Henry.

'Well, I got wondering, so I walked round the place near an hour just in case.' Dick shook his head. 'Vanished, sir. Into the air.'

'You saw no branches broken?' Hannah asked him. 'Nor any foot-marks? But surely there were more cries. Perhaps you did not hear.'

'My ears are keen, Mrs Trevor, though I'm getting on a bit. But I heard nothing. As it grew light, I marked a broken branch or two. But I put it down to the hunters, a-beating after deer.' Dancer reached into his coat and brought out a small book with a homemade red cloth cover. 'Only I come across this, ma'am. Lying dropped in the meadow by Sable Brook, some ways from where we heard the cries.'

She took it from him. The red cloth had frayed and begun to come unstuck and the pages were caked with mud. Hannah opened the cover carefully. 'Why it's an almanac, and six – almost seven years old now. *Tom Tearaway's Calendar of the Year 1780, or The Farmer's Frugal Year*.' She looked up at Dick Dancer. 'Not one of your father's books?'

'No, my dear. I know all his cargo.' Dick took off his tricorne and rubbed the five or six remaining sandy hairs that veiled his bald head. 'The voice *was* high and shrill, Father's right about that. But what would a lass be doing alone in those woods by night?'

'I don't know, Dick, but I mean to find out.' Hannah got to her feet. 'Kitty! Fetch me my cloak and my basket, dear! And that bunch of lady's mantle from the stillroom, and some comfrey and flax!'

'Niece! Whatever are you thinking of?' Aunt Julia stood in the doorway, a pitcher of steaming spiced cider in her hands for their guests. 'What is this nonsense, girl?' she trumpeted. 'On foot, at your time, and into the woods? I forbid you!'

'Not far in, dear Aunt. Only to Sable Brook.' Hannah tried to catch Jenny and kiss her good-bye, but the little girl wriggled away. She was still angry, her small face set in a frown.

'Keep her out of Sally's reach, Aunt, please,' Hannah said. 'I must see to my women, and I cannot say but I may be gone a day or two, if a borning has come before its time.'

'But that fool Clinch and his humbugging charges!' Julia cried. 'Oh, I shall despair in a minute! At least take a pair of mitts against the cold, girl. And promise you will go across to the Grange for the loan of old Twig's speckled mare!'

'Very well, Aunt, I promise,' Hannah told her.

But she knew in her soul she would not.

EIGHT

The Dead in the Air

It was Hannah Trevor's favorite season to venture into the Outward, this time of late autumn when the winter had not yet begun in earnest and the harvest lay ripe in the barns and ricks. It was fragile and quiet, subtly shaded and secret – a time between times, rich and dormant and sweet.

As if she had planned it so, it was also the season when Hannah's daughter had been born, an autumn child with hair the burnished russet of the oaks. Jennet Trevor – so they still called her, for even once they were wed, the American law would not let Daniel adopt his own bastard – would turn eight years old tomorrow.

The fallen leaves of red maples and ashes and hickories lay thick and sodden on the Trace, the dusting of snow that had fallen in the night almost melted. The branches were chaste and clean, except for the bittersweet that hung its burnt-orange clusters like a woman's fancy earrings from their dark, jagged limbs. Only the oaks kept their leaves, and here and there a splatter of crimson clung to a tangle of creeper or a sumac bush. Among the leafless thickets of high-bush cranberry, the white heads of late foam-flowers bobbed shyly, and the purplish asters had faded almost to the same color as the pungent smoke that hung in the air. Hannah drew a deep breath of it; some farmer was burning the stubble from his cornfield to leave it ready for the plough again in spring.

Beyond Daniel's manor, Chine Ridge was dark with virgin spruces and pines and firs, the higher slopes of Jade's Mountain already blanketed with white. Now, before the snow made them vanish, the small things of the forest grew briefly visible, and Hannah treasured them up like the patches of some magical quilt – the many colors of mosses, green, grey, orange, even pale turquoise; the dapple-grey alders; the pale dry swale grass; and the red-brown of the shaggy larches.

In spite of her concern for the women in her charge – and for her cousin – she felt happier here, almost her old self again, free and at ease.

But when she passed the crimson flag at the end of Flynn's lane, her secret delight in the journey came to an abrupt halt. It meant another sheriff's auction and another bankrupt for the debtors' courts. Flynn's place, Amos Drewel's, Thomas Whittemore's – most hereabouts were to be sold soon for taxes, except Oliver Kersey's and old Josiah Bridge's, and Simon Penny's, which lay an hour's walk west along the Trace. Their debts were paid for the moment, but even for them, it could not be long if the General Court did not relent.

Hannah turned in at the Kerseys' lane and made her way through the orchard and past the small fenced graveyard; country folk preferred to keep their lost loved ones near them, laid close in their own land. When they lost a farm, they lost more than their living. They lost their dead as well.

A few chickens were scratching in the barnyard as the midwife walked up the narrow path to the house. It was small and square, with only a loft and a lean-to aside from the single main room, built of upright logs in the old-fashioned manner and well chinked with hard, whitened clay.

'Leah!' Hannah called out as she knocked on the heavy oaken door. 'It's Mrs Trevor, my dear, come to see how you are faring.' There was no answer. She peered in through the small window, but it was too dark inside to see anything. 'Leah?' she called again. 'Mr Kersey?'

There was a rattling noise; one of the shutters was blowing loose in the wind and someone had tacked a piece of paper onto it, already once written on, the words scrawled heavily over the old, faded letters.

GONE TO MUSTER, it said.

'For the love of God, Hannah! Where are you going?'

She was just at the end of the Kerseys' lane again and about to go on to Mrs Penny's house when Daniel rode breakneck up beside her. He jerked the bridle harder than he meant to and the animal's eyes rolled. But Yeoman was a soldier's horse, trained not to rear at sudden stops; his master dismounted and patted the sorrel's broad flank.

'Whose child's borning this time?' Daniel forced himself to match her slow pace. 'If you'd sent to the Grange and told me—'

'I thought you'd be playing at soldiers,' Hannah said curtly, looking his uniform up and down with a chilly eye.

It was a bait and he knew it. But he did not rise to it. 'I saw you pass,' he said, 'and it's yet three-quarters of an hour till roll call and first muster. If I'm delayed, Josh Lamb or McGregor will order the drill in my stead.' Daniel glanced at her sidewise, suddenly shy now that he was with her at last. 'Where are you going, my dear?' he asked her again.

'Not far.'

Hannah had already convinced herself she dared not tell him about the cry the peddler and his father had heard. Daniel would feel he must stay to protect her, and she would not *be* protected, especially by him. Besides, without reason she felt he must somehow be changed by his uniform, she could scarcely abide the sight of it now.

He *was* changed, of course. Time and brewing war and his wife's death had darkened his mind and uprooted old memories. But if Mrs Trevor had only been able to see and admit it, she herself had changed fully as much. After the fever deaths of her two daughters, Susannah and Martha, and her little son Benjamin, she had had nothing left, cared for nothing. War, when it came, meant only that her husband James was too worried about his own safety and the chance of a profit from smuggling to bother his leftover wife anymore.

But that was before Daniel, before Jennet. It is easy to be bold when you have none but yourself to consider: a strange kind of freedom, but freedom it had been. Now, all of a sudden, Hannah Trevor had a great deal too much to lose to be heartfree. She felt haltered, caged in by the very things she most desired. And she clawed for her life at the bars.

'What ails your aunt's old pony?' asked Daniel. 'You should not be afoot here, and alone.'

'Small matter to *you* where I am, sir. You have not called at my door in a fortnight, nor so much as sent me word.'

Daniel winced, remembering their last meeting at the husking. She had snapped at him like a terrier, and the kinder he was, the harder she snapped. He had given her these last two weeks without him, hoping his absence would calm her. But from what he could hear, it had not.

'The excise man was holding up a cargo of our ships' masts at the Head, claiming we couldn't send them to Calais in an English frigate,' he told her. His voice was uncertain, as if he did not quite believe it himself.

'But you did not *only* go to Wybrow Head. You went to Gull's Isle,' she said, her voice a little too loud in the stillness of the woods. 'You went to visit Charlotte's grave. It would seem you still have a wife after all, and she claims you far deeper than I.'

Daniel's eyes closed, letting his silence fall safely around him. It had been a petty, spiteful, unkind taunt, and Hannah was bitterly ashamed of it as soon as it was said. She wanted to touch him, to ask his pardon.

But she did neither. For a long time they walked on in silence, Daniel leading the horse by his reins.

'I saw to the headstone,' he said at last. 'If they're not properly set, they tilt in these gales and fall down in a season. I returned only three days ago.'

'And did not bestir yourself to come to me even then.'

'Your servant said you were from home!' Daniel spun in his tracks with exasperation. 'Besides, Madam, you were as prickly as a thistle the last time I saw you! I see you cannot be civil even now.'

Hannah's two hands lifted, then fell to her sides again. 'Daniel,' she said. 'I did not intend . . .'

But he strode on ahead of her now, picking his way along the rutted trail. You could see the heavy, fresh tracks of the peddler's wagon, cut deep in the half-frozen mud, a few footprints beside it – most likely Miss Jemima's or Dick's, Hannah thought.

'I'm your husband, or as good as,' Daniel said at last. He stopped, turning back to confront her. 'In God's name, what have I done to anger you?'

'Nothing,' she said softly. 'You've done nothing. Perhaps . . .'

'Say it.'

'It's not you, Daniel. Truly. Only I can't seem to support the idea of being – so much loved.'

A long silence. On a big oak near the path, a squirrel barked and scolded. A pair of ravens cried to each other in a thicket.

'So much married, you mean.' He braced himself. 'Do you wish me to release you?'

'No! I don't know! I *do* love you! Only—'

'Hannah, look at me. Let me see your face!'

He took hold of her and pushed the hood of the cloak back so he could study her. Her dark eyes gazed at him steadily, and she put up a fingertip to touch his cheek. 'Your eyes are shadowed,' she said.

'I was out late with the hunt.' He paused, drew a breath. 'Dearest heart, listen. Counting this one that's inside you, I've fathered three children, and never yet held a living babe of mine. I'm pig-ignorant of babies. And of women when they're—'

'Broody?' It was Marcus Tapp's sour word she rapped out at him.

'Christ! Don't prickle so!' Daniel drew a breath to gain

patience. 'When they're with child, I would have said. But if there's anything the matter, if you want for anything—'

He stared down at his boots and she thought how young he looked in spite of his weariness, how shy and afraid when he spoke of these matters of birth.

'I scarcely saw Charlotte in those months she was pregnant,' he said, very softly. 'I think she was ashamed of what she carried, as though I had dirtied her. When I spoke, she would not answer at all, or else snap at me.'

'As I do.'

'Much worse. Daggers and knives. In her mind, I think she had already begun to be ill, even before the child died. I think *she* wanted to die, Hannah. At least since I disappointed all her hopes of me. She married the third son of Lord Bensbridge and found herself lumbered with a turncoat farmer instead. I was her husband, what other escape did she have from me but dying?'

And what subtler means of punishment, thought Hannah.

'Oh, I have blamed Dr Clinch for what happened,' Daniel went on, 'but unhappy as Charlotte was—'

'Your *child* need not have died, sir! Clinch killed it! He's a rumpot and a fool,' said Hannah sharply, 'and I will hear no mitigation of him!'

Samuel Clinch was a barber-surgeon of the old school, handy mainly at the sawing-off of arms and legs, or at blistering, purging, cupping and bleeding. When Daniel's first child had proved to be a difficult birth, Clinch had refused Hannah's advice in turning it safely and mangled both mother and son beyond repair with his forceps. In the end, he had cut off the dead baby's head and arms to get it out of Charlotte's body, and bled her almost to death.

That terrible memory was all Daniel Josselyn knew of

the business of birth, all he could have known. Had not Hannah, too, pushed him aside?

'I don't want to marry you only to make you unhappy like Charlotte,' he told her now. 'And if there's anything wrong, you must promise not to hide yourself away as she did, and let it come upon me unawares.'

Hannah took his two hands and laid them on her belly, low down, nearly level with her hips. 'There,' she said. 'Can you feel? He is still very small, and rides deep inside me. When I walk, when I work – he can scarcely feel it yet, nor I him. Later, when he sits higher in me and grows great, then he will squirm and kick all day and all night. Then I must do lighter work and be quieter.'

Daniel smiled. 'You? Quiet? Do eggs grow on trees?'

She laughed in spite of herself. 'You tease me, sir, and then you complain when I prickle.'

Suddenly he put his arms round her and pulled her close against him, wanting her to feel the shape of him and know that he was not his uniform, to remember how deep he belonged to her – the fragile cage of his ribs, the long bones of his thighs, the smooth plane of his back, and the rising hardness of his sex that urged itself against her even now, so that she almost believed he would take her where she stood.

'Don't fuss over me, my love,' she whispered, 'I am well and strong. Why, I gave birth to Jenny on my two feet, holding on to a bedpost, and only lay down once it was done.'

'Eight years ago tomorrow.' Daniel tried to think where he had been this day eight years ago, but he could not. 'Marry me now,' he said.

His voice was very low, and the cries of the ravens had grown louder, joined by a greater flock, all persistent and furious. *A deer*, he thought. *Some fool wounded a deer last night and it has died in the brush there. The ravens are eating a deer.*

'Marry me now,' he said again. 'Tomorrow, for Jenny's birthday gift.'

Hannah extracted herself from his embrace. 'But who would pray over us, a dog-collared scarecrow? There is no new parson in the town since Master Gwynn died, and the banns are not yet read.'

'Banns be hanged! There are preachers aplenty now, in town to watch the Muster. We'll have one of them.'

'No, sir, Christmas is soon enough, if I am not to come to you unprovided. The sewing alone – ' She walked a few steps on, away from him. 'Besides, I can't leave my aunt with Jonathan still not found.'

'You give me excuses, not reasons.' Daniel stared at a fallen tree beside the path. An extinguished torch from the hunt lay beside it, the stems of the cattails trodden into the half-frozen mud.

Suddenly a pair of ravens swooped down screeching, wings whirring, so close Hannah could feel a cold current of air as they passed. 'Those birds are mad!' she cried.

There were tears in her voice and she had to escape them. She pulled the hood of her cloak over her hair again and plunged into the undergrowth towards the circling birds.

'Hannah!' he cried, and crashed after her. In a moment, she was out of sight, but he could hear her moving, pushing aside the bare branches as she went.

It was very still, a great weight of silence that bore down upon Daniel, making him fight for every breath. A lone raven, unwilling to give way, circled over the alder grove again. From the fringe of blackberry canes at the edge of the trees, he caught sight of Hannah, saw her take a step, then another.

'Ah,' she cried softly, and fell with a thump to the ground.

Daniel dived through the thicket to reach her. 'Let me lift you,' he said.

'No.' She was searching the leaves with her fingers. 'I tripped over something, just here, at the edge of these bushes, and—'

Hannah's words were cut off like a candlewick. She got to her feet, staring down at the ground in the tangle of bushes, both her hands laid above the unborn child as if she would hide him.

'The dead in the air,' she whispered.

It was an old wives' tale, he remembered it from his childhood. *On the morning of first snowfall, the dead are alive in the air.*

Then he saw it, just as Hannah had done a moment before. The pointed toe of an old boot sticking up from the drift of leaves. 'Get away,' he told her. 'Go back into the clearing and wait for me.'

Daniel's tone was not to be questioned, but she seemed not to hear him, only stood there, her body rocking a little from side to side. She knew death of all kinds too well to be afraid or superstitious. But she braced herself against it, still shielding the child with her hands.

'Surely not Johnnie,' she whispered, 'not with such boots.'

The toe that stuck up from the leaves was caked with dried mud, but the worn leather was well polished and supple even in the cold. The wooden heel was near two inches high and badly run over; it had been painted bright red in the latest London fashion, though the boots were far from new.

I know him, Hannah thought. *I know a man who wears such ridiculous boots.*

The fact of it reached her from a great distance, one thread of a ravelling that chance had flung at the mind. Her eyes lost focus on the thing at her feet and she caught at the stray patches of memory.

He steps in horse droppings and tracks them into the kitchens poor women have scrubbed on their knees. He kicks his servant with that same polished toe.

'Give me room,' Daniel said, and began to hack away the interlacing branches with his sword.

Little by little, like a figure walking out of a thick fog or a sandstorm, the body of the dead man emerged from the leaves. He lay on his back, the scrubby alder branches carefully woven together to conceal him. Wet leaves had been gathered by armfuls and poured in upon him, red maples and chokecherries and yellow alders that lay thick on the ground.

Daniel went down on his knees to paw the rest of the leaves away, and Hannah began to help. The corpse was not Jonathan, that much was clear. The belly was bloated, swollen with drink under a grease-stained blue damask waistcoat. When Daniel removed the pale kidskin gloves, the man's hands were age-spotted, the knuckles knotted and rheumatic, the nails dirty and chewed-upon.

Still Hannah's mind shuffled the random scraps. *I know those hands. I know a man who chews his nails and spits the parings on the floor.*

There was a bullet hole just above the eighth waistcoat button – by the look of the puncture, a clean shot that had been meant to finish him. But there was no more blood on the wound than would have been left in the surface of the skin. The man had been already dead when the shot struck him.

Hannah looked away from the belly wound, forcing herself to go on with her inventory, her quilting of fragments into patterns. The breeches were cream-colored satin, old and much-stained, and the coat was a balding brown velvet. When they pushed more of the leaves away, a paper stuck out of the waistcoat, and Daniel took it and knelt there, reading a singsong rhyme aloud.

But Hannah did not hear it. *I know a man with such a coat*, she thought. *He spills rum punch upon it and beats his servant for letting it be spoilt.*

As they pushed back more and more of the branches and leaves, they could see that one of the boots had been pulled off and heavy grease smeared on the worn yellow stocking, tallow such as the hunters had used on their torches – or women made candles from. The sole of the stocking was charred black in several places, as though someone had tried over and over to strike a spark and failed to make it catch.

'They meant to burn him,' Hannah whispered. 'His feet.' In the War, it was a thing raiding parties had done to spies, to make them give up information. It was how you used traitors. But what use was it to torture the dead?

Daniel felt his nerves clutch and the great muscle of his chest contract. He had been here before, surely, kneeling by this same unkindled corpse, in these same leaves, to calculate this same nightmare. Or to cause it, to complete it? He could not remember enough to be sure.

'Christ,' he said. Then he said it again, stammering, his tongue unable to stop. 'Christchristchristchrist. What have I done?'

He began to shake, his whole body convulsing. Years seemed to pass, reeling backwards, to end nowhere. He felt Hannah touch him, but he shook her away, not wanting her kindness.

He was at war again, and that was the way of soldiers. You bathed yourself clean in the tenderness of random strangers, like swimming in cold water. But to what was deeply loved, you grew harsh, protecting the wound at the heart.

Daniel saw a hand move – his own left hand, it was, though he scarcely believed it, scarcely recognized the two short stumps like vestigial gills inside his glove. It reached out of itself and pulled away the last of the leaves that hid the corpse's face.

But there was no face, only the husk of one. The ears were intact, almost perfect; the chin and the lower lip dangled obscenely, and the jagged bones of the temples still stood like the shell of a house hit by cannon. The nose, the brow, the eyes, the cap of the skull – they were dark clotted blood mixed with the pinkish-grey scramble of brains, the ooze of spoilt eyes and the sharp, powder-burned slivers that once had been jawbone, cheekbones, the rubbery cartilage of the nose.

This, too, was somehow familiar, a part of the same buried pattern. But he could not think now, could not will himself to reason or to remember.

I want to live, he thought. *I want to belong to the living. I must beat these dead away.*

But the huge dead were too much for him. Like a muster of ghosts, all his battles returned to him, places muddled with people, with nameless faces, eyes, voices, words spoken in pain, anger, desire. Small horrors jumbled in with the large.

Webb's Ford. Golderville. Taunton Bridge. Elm Creek. Staley's Barn.

Three women hanged from an apple tree in full blossom. One was dead. One ran mad. One I sheltered awhile.

An old man shot dead, lying dead in the leaves with his feet burnt. Everywhere the stink of slow burning, in the eyes, in the mouth, a taste like corruption that lingers through sleep.

My soul is forfeit, all souls are smoke. I have death in my heart now, and my blood carries it like a poison. I am, I will always be, to blame.

'What have I done?' he said again, his mouth barely open. 'What have I done?'

Daniel felt Hannah pull at him, and it seemed he heard her voice from a great distance. Something struck him, but he did not realize it was her own clenched fists. They smashed into him once, twice, three times, four, like hammers, trying to rouse him. but he only looked down at himself, kneeling there by the dead man, like a picture badly smeared onto canvas.

Then he grew very cold, shivering with it, and the deep cold restored him. Daniel rolled over onto all fours, crawled away from the dead, and lay there in the leaves, his body convulsed with shuddering. Hannah said nothing, simply lay down beside him, her own body stretched the length of his, drawing him close to her.

I am safe only in her, he thought. *I sleep in her like the child.*

When at last he grew quiet, she took off his stock-tie, went to the little trickle they called Sable Brook, and brought the wet cloth to wipe his face and hands. He opened his eyes and watched her touching him, stroking his arms and his throat, laying her face against him. She put her cool, wet palms on his cheekbones and left them there, sweet and quiet, a long-missing part of his own body restored.

She would, he knew, have done the same for a man she had never met till that moment, and the purity of her impartial tenderness filled him with pride. 'My heart,' he said, and laid his face against her.

'Where have you come back from?' she said. 'Was it the same place you go in your dreams?'

'I don't know.' Daniel drew away and got up. 'You must think me a fool or a lunatic.'

Yet he knew she did not. He moved cautiously, like a man coming slowly awake after fever. In a moment he left her and turned back to the dead man, thinking himself alone. But Hannah followed him, her skirt rustling the leaves. He clung to the sound of it, like the wind in one familiar tree he had loved as a child.

Now Daniel noticed what he had overlooked in the frenzy of uncovering the body. An object hung from an alder branch above the dead man's left temple, half-covered with leaves they had displaced in rooting out the corpse. He picked it off, holding it gingerly by its tail – a powdered wig, torn almost in half by the musket ball.

'I must know him,' Hannah said, and crouched down by the body. She winced and moved aside, feeling once again in the wet leaves for something.

'What is it?' Daniel asked her.

'A button. I didn't see it till I knelt on it.' She handed it over and he peered at it, scarcely seeing. It was pewter, a uniform button. Everyone lost them, they came off easily, the metal shanks cutting the thread like the teeth of a saw.

But the dead man was not dressed for the Muster, and all Daniel's own buttons were firmly in place.

'When they bent over to burn him,' she said, 'the button was lost from a coat or a greatcoat. It's not a waistcoat button, it's too large. Perhaps the boot came away when they dragged him. The stocking was wet with the snow and would not burn.'

Hannah's voice was expressionless, her figure tensed with concentration. Only her hands began to move. They played lightly along the blood-splattered shoulder and forearm. Even in the long-dead, she seemed able to find some remnant of living, some source of pain that must be shared to be healed.

She lifted up the two stiffened hands in her own. 'I know that ring,' she said.

There was nothing unusual about it. It was a wedding band of cheap gold, much worn, engraved with a garland of acanthus leaves and a single initial: the letter C.

In that instant Daniel Josselyn, too, saw the ring and remembered it – the flash of brassy gold above the bleeding basin as the old man bent huffing and snorting over Charlotte's blood-soaked bed, prating of Science while Black Caesar, his servant, carried the mangled parts of the dead child away in a bucket.

'God's heart,' he said softly. 'It's Clinch.'

NINE

Muster Day

'Owen! Set down, sir! Sure, this cannot be an army! Have you carried me off to the moon?'

Lady Sibylla Josselyn gave three sharp raps with her cane on the roof of her black-lacquered sedan chair and it drew to a sudden halt at the edge of the sea of men, horses, dogs, tents and spectators that crowded the Training Ground at Great Meadow.

No one paid it much heed, for the old dowager's elegant chair had become a familiar sight these last few months. Still, it occasioned some glances, for it was more commodious than most and as gaudy as she was – curtained with red silk damask, its sides embellished with peacocks in jade green and scarlet, its periwigged bearers, faithful Jenks and Owen, in livery of striped red and gold. Like Dick Dancer's wagon, the sedan chair had a name; Hobble, Sibylla called it, for without it, her rheumatic old limbs would have forced her to do so.

And forced she would not be.

The footmen settled the chair with scarcely a wobble,

near where a number of horses were tethered to a loosely-stretched rope. One animal in particular caught the old lady's eye. Hannah Trevor's shaggy pony, it could be no other. Nearby stood a fine red box coach with an elaborate shield on its door, the crest an eagle and snake.

Sibylla knew it at once. Hamilton Siwall's coach, she had seen it this morning in the yard at the Grange. Her brow arched and her upper lip curled. That rumbustious rascal! Come, no doubt, to plague Daniel again with his bullying. A snake and an eagle, indeed!

But where was the fellow himself? Come to that, where was Daniel? She peered out between Hobble's curtains, a pair of smoked spectacles held up before her on a long gilded wand. 'Jenks!' she cried. 'Scan the field, sir! Do you spy out my nephew?'

'No, ma'am. I heard one say as he passed us that Major Josselyn was too late for the calling of roll,' the servant replied.

'My nephew, truant? Hah! He would not show such a lack of discipline to this assembly of clodpoles! Surely he must be—'

Sibylla was suddenly distracted by a flutter of movement inside the box coach, followed by a soft feminine laugh. She settled the lenses of her lorgnette closer to her nose and craned her long neck a bit more.

A bit of tea-colored lace. A flounce of foolish pink ribbon – a most common color. A faint scent of lavender upon the air. Or is it rosemary?

A woman in old Siwall's coach! But not his chilly wife, I vow. That laugh was warm, and willing. And young. Why, the prating old hypocrite has some mistress besides his pocketbook after all!

Still, perhaps it was only the black sheep son, Jem, and his new-married Boston lady. As the old lady watched, a man's broad hand pulled the green sailcloth shade across the window. The girl's laugh sounded again, and the man's, too, soon followed by a low moan and a soft cry, quickly smothered.

Sibylla smiled. Coupling, at such a time of morning? And in such a place? A bold pair, whoever they were!

Great Meadow was really the flat top of a hill that rose high above the south bank of the river, spreading out to some four or five acres of common grazing land. At one end was the arsenal, built during the French and Indian wars sixty years ago but still kept up, its huge logs carefully chinked. It held powder and shot, small arms, and three small cannon, two brass six-pounders and an eight-inch howitzer – not much good in a pitched battle, but practical. It fired grapeshot, or if you had none, then rusty nails, gravel, broken dishes. Even old carriage bolts would do.

As usual on training days, sentries had been posted at all four corners of the building, their guns at half-ease. Three wore blue coats faced with red, the regular artillery uniform. The fourth wore a long fringed buckskin shirt tied round the waist with a red sash of some sort, and all had plain grey homespun breeches instead of white or buff.

Near a cluster of infantry tents, a boy was beating a snare drum and Blind Patrick played 'Portland Fancy' on his fife. Farther up the field, a trumpet sounded, and somewhere a bagpipe droned.

Most on the meadow today were infantry, five companies in all, from up and down the Manitac. Foot soldiers had never been uniformed even in the War, and they looked as though they were out to do their morning milking, not to practice the manual of arms.

There was only one company of cavalry, dressed in blue coats with white facings and the high riding boots of gentlemen. A trumpet blared nearer-by and one of the officers began to perform sword exercise on horseback, his blade flashing through all the nine ancient cuts handed down since the Romans.

'To reap!' he cried. His sword slashed the air as though it were ripe wheat. 'To sow!' A back-handed cut from the left. 'To thresh! To mow!'

Target practice was going on nearby for the regulars, but the elite riflemen did not bother with such elementary business. They were an expert and independent lot, and they dressed to suit the country, the weather, and themselves. A number wore green from head to toe, others buckskin breeches and loincloths in the Indian fashion. In deference to the trace of snow that had fallen in the night, one or two wore the winter uniform of white shirts and white breeches, and soft brain-tanned moccasins that let them move without a footfall in the woods.

Some had brought their Indian wives and set up a haphazard camp at the top of the hill, dogs snapping and yowling and half-breed children squabbling, the bright trade-goods calicoes of the women's skirts far outshining the plain homespuns of the farmers' wives.

Where there were so many men there would always be a travelling madam with a weary whore or two, and a gaming wagon where the dice rolled all night long. And likewise, where there were women there would be tradesmen, and gypsies selling love potions and reading palms. A half-dozen peddlers' wagons – Redoubtable among them – made a little high street of merchandise stalls near the farmers' carts.

'Sea salt from Rogue's Island!' cried Dick Dancer. 'Fine fresh salt!'

'Shawls! Spanish shawls!'

'Song sheets and ballads, miss, penny apiece! Broadsides and mazes! Fair Rosamund's Bower and the Tinker's Retreat!'

A young woman in a grey cloak came picking her way across the muddy field to stroll among the huddle of tradesmen and travelling scoundrels, her lace cap fluttering and her skirts lifted to keep them from the mud. She paused beside a caravan covered with brightly painted wood; a fortune teller's wagon, it was, with a wide-open eye on the side.

'Love potions, miss! Philtres and charms, and a future as bright as a shilling!'

Sally Markham looked about her nervously, then climbed up the bright blue wooden steps into the cart and pulled the door shut behind her. By the cook fire, an old man played on a fiddle and a young girl began to sing, low-voiced and urgent.

> I once had gold and silver,
> And love without end,
> I'd a sweet bridal bower,
> And one valiant friend
> Now my wealth it is lost,
> And my friend he is false,
> And my bower, it is burning,
> 'Tis turning to ash.

At the far end of the field the engineers had built up a

precarious barricade of logs piled as high as a house. Two squadrons of foot armed with make-believe muskets were scrambling, shoving, shouting and brawling for possession of the summit, one side wearing red armbands, the other white.

'Reds! To the left flank, you rogues! Stap me, but you're a damn sight quicker to get your elbows onto my bar-counter of an evening! Not that way, Pettingill, you great yob! To the left, I said! Ha, ha, ha!'

Josh Lamb, the big, round-faced innkeeper who commanded the red squadron, doubled over with laughter, but his feet were planted like tree roots and his bemused eyes recorded every flaw and wasted chance. He was Daniel's second-in-command, resplendent this morning in a plain blue homespun coat with rusty gold captain's epaulettes sewn to the shoulders by his dearest Dolly.

'Ach, ya squill-eyed buggers! Wiggins! That's a gun in your hands, not a shovel of cow shit! Aim at the fucking bastard, man, and make believe you can shoot!'

This last accent was thick Scots and the voice was that of Captain Lachlan McGregor, village constable, blacksmith and farrier; he was in perfect artillery uniform today – if you took no mind of his plaid and his bonnet – and he commanded the Whites. McGregor was in charge of the arsenal, too, and the firing of the cannon that would put an end to each day's training and signal the start of serious business – drinking, cards, brawling, and a shivering tumble with some willing lass by the watchfires on the hillside.

A cheer went up from the Reds as they reached the summit of the barricade. A White clambered up beside him and knocked him down, and two more Reds tackled the treacherous White. Two sergeants tried to break up the brawl, but it was hopeless.

'John!' called McGregor to one of them, a shaggy, middle-aged man in a farmer's leather jerkin and an old cavalry coat. 'Where the hell's Josselyn? It's gone half-past nine.'

Daniel's steward and bailiff, today *Sergeant* John English, smashed a work-hardened fist into the eye of one of the Reds and looked up. 'He rode out near an hour before me. Said he'd come as soon as he was able.'

'Able, you say?' Josh Lamb shot a look at McGregor. 'What's got into him lately? He said me scarce a word last night, after we came in from the hunt.'

'He'll be here, all right,' said Oliver Kersey, the other sergeant. He was a taciturn fellow of almost fifty, dressed in the winter uniform of the riflemen, white breeches and coat, and long Indian leggings that would have ended in snowshoes, were he fighting in the woods.

Leah Kersey's husband was broad-chested and not very tall, but tenacious and somewhat forbidding, with a lantern jaw, a mane of dark curling hair and heavy jutting brows already gone grey. Without warning, he ploughed his elbow into a White's ribcage and the air went out of the man with a huff.

'Whatever ails Daniel, he'll weather it,' said Josh. 'Perhaps if Hannah stops her shilly-shallying over the wedding. Let my Dolly have a word in her ear, she'll soon see sense!'

'Ach,' grumbled McGregor, 'it's always the women. Marry them or no, they play the devil with a man's peace of mind!'

But by quarter past ten, Sibylla, too, had begun to worry in earnest. Jenks and Owen had set down her chair at the crest of the hill near the peddlers' vans, where she could observe every nuance of the scene below, to the music of the merchandisers' cries.

'Ribbons and laces!'

'Stewpots, saucepots, two shillings each!'

One of the dogs from the Indian camp, a brown bitch, had been prowling under the wagons, sniffing for scraps from the cook fires. When she reached Redoubtable, she began to bark in earnest, jumping up to claw and snap, then backing off again, her teeth out and her yelping wild and frantic. Growling and jerking the thong with her teeth, the bitch jumped again and again at one particular spot on the wagon box, the door of the cupboard labelled Yard Goods.

'Why, there is His Honor at last, ma'am!' cried Owen suddenly, pointing down to the field. 'Major Josselyn is come!'

The old lady sighed with relief. 'Your arm, sir!' she demanded, and was helped out, her ostrich plume tossed like a sail in the wind. 'Confound the boy!' Sibylla muttered, clicking her tongue. 'What does he mean by it? Sitting that spavined mare of old Biddy Twig's instead of his own proper horse, and bare-throated like a stableboy!'

'He has been locked away too long with his dead, ma'am, like my dearest Jemima.' The unexpected voice of the Mortal Reminder was soft as the drifting of ashes in Sibylla's ear, and the hand that laid itself upon her arm was dry and light, like paper long since burned away. 'See!' he murmured. 'Their mark is upon him. The dead have touched his heart.'

She had not heard old Moses Dancer's footfalls approach her and though his thin chest moved in and out, she could not hear him draw breath. But no one on earth could have been less inclined to superstition than Lady Sibylla. 'By the look of that hat, sir, you are some travelling tradesman,' she said, peering down her long nose. 'But I have no humor for haggling. What are you and what do you do here?'

He smiled up at her gently. 'Why, I should have been God's chimneysweep,' he said, 'only none would employ me. Merchandise, dear lady, false merchandise will be the finish of us all. Currency counterfeit. Interest compounded. Hire and salary. Seven and sixpence, and carry the two.'

The fight between the Reds and the Whites had spread now, and infected one or two of the riflemen as well; most of the armbands were lying on the brown, trampled grass before the barricade, all order forgotten in the nervous relief of the brawl. For months, they had done little but work and fret and fend off the tax collector. Here, for a few hours, they felt like men again – or was it boys?

A weedy little fellow in a blanket cloak and a pair of worn leather breeches lay flat on his back in the grass, feet kicking and nose spouting blood, while two big farmers sat on him and pummeled him.

'Get off!' roared John English, dragging the larger of the two bullies off the little man on the ground. 'Away, I tell you, do you mean to murder him?'

A weasel-faced fellow of forty-odd and a gap-toothed lummox with a mane of greasy blond hair had been lounging against the barricade – watching but taking no part in the fray.

'Wybrow men?' asked Josh, glancing at them sidewise.

'Sheriff's men,' muttered Oliver Kersey. 'God damn their eyes.'

His fun interrupted, one big farmer took a good-natured

poke at Mr English; the bailiff dodged, grabbed hold of the second bully and crashed the pair of them together like two oxen that resisted the yoke.

'Look-ye, Tully,' whined the weasel to his lumpish comrade. 'His Lordship's old bear can still manage a couple of ploughboys, at that.'

John English said nothing, only let the two bullies fall and gave a hand-up to the little man with the bloody nose. 'Name?' he demanded.

'Newcomb, Sergeant, sir. Lorenzo Newcomb.'

'You hear that, Ketchell?' the greasy-haired lummox called Tully lounged over to the little man and stood sizing him up. 'I mind a Lorenzo Newcomb from up by Chine Ridge. Dirt-grubbing fool with six snot-nosed brats and a missus that drops 'em like rabbits.'

'Oh, aye,' replied the weasel called Ketchell. 'I had her once, in the bushes by Triler's Bog. Tits like a breed-sow, she's got.'

Newcomb lunged, but John English restrained him. 'What do you want here?' he demanded of the sheriff's men.

'Why, we come out sniffing debtors, old bear.' Tully ambled nearer. 'New jail's built now at Salcombe, and we need no warrant to take 'em. Might as well have this one to start with, though he be but a runt.'

'You'll pay hell if you try grabbing a one of us!' The bigger of the two farmers, a fat-faced fellow with the red-and-blue checked shirt of a Bridgewater man, sprang to his feet at the mention of debtors' jail, all thought of the brawl forgotten. The Regulators were thick on the ground at that stretch of the river, and they stuck together when they must. 'Take one of us to that jail, they'll take fifty,' he said. 'Scarce a man here that doesn't owe part of his tax yet unpaid.'

'Aye, let 'em try to take us!' said his friend. 'Come and get me, ye splay-footed bastards!' He spat on his hands and wiped them on his breeches, feet planted and fists clenched for another fight.

'No man will be taken by force from this field.'

Daniel's voice rang clear as he cantered up beside them on the chubby, foolish little mare. He spoke calmly and quietly, as always, but there was not a man for fifty yards who failed to hear every word he said.

''Tention!' roared John English, and the men assumed almost the look of an army at last.

'Sergeant, see these fellows escorted from the meadow.' Josselyn was pure soldier now. 'The Debtors' Court will not sit until tomorrow, and so long as the General Muster lasts, the civil law must wait.'

'And once Muster is ended?'

This time the voice was neither Ketchell's nor Tully's. It was Marcus Tapp's. He stepped out from behind the forgotten barricade, hatless and cloakless in the cold. And as though Tapp were not enough, Hamilton Siwall and another man – grey-haired and well dressed, with a double-caped greatcoat in the latest Paris style – bore down upon them, hot-foot across the field from the officers' tent. Daniel's teeth set tight, but he did not dismount, only looked down at the sheriff.

'Once the Muster is dismissed, Mr Tapp,' he said, 'I have no military authority and the law must take its course.'

'But it may not be dismissed until Doomsday if you choose?'

'If I see reason for extending the time beyond tomorrow noon,' Daniel replied, 'I shall do so. But the orders here are of my giving. And just now, I regret I must order you and your men from this ground.'

'You, sir! Josselyn!' Siwall and the grey-haired man huffed up beside them, and Daniel studied them, memorizing faces and postures, judging the cost of cloaks, wigs, waist-coats, rings. *Boston money*, he thought. *So then, Siwall will not pay for his rich-man's army by himself.*

Hamilton Siwall's florid face was angry, but determined. 'You were absent from roll call! One letter from my son's father-in-law, here, to your fine Colonel Scribner at Sal-combe, and we shall have you removed from your command!'

So that was the fellow. Master Royallton-Smith of the General Court, whose daughter had brought five thousand pounds hard silver in dowry to fatten young Jem's empty purse.

But *this* was what the marriage had really been meant for, surely. Back-scratching. String-pulling. Influence. The consolidation of Ham Siwall's power in the legislature. Even a seat in the Confederation Congress, if things went well.

Since the killing of George Anson in summer, however, it was no longer simple ambition that drove Hamilton Siwall. His pride was mixed with fear, now, and it seemed to be goaded by Daniel's calm containment, by his knowledge of Siwall's shady dealings. By his very existence, indeed.

You could see it even as the magistrate blustered and bullied – how the eyes were too wide and the vein pounded hard in the temple and the side of the neck; how the vessels in the red face had burst under the skin and made blotches; how the lips remained open when he did not speak, and the breath sometimes caught in his throat and made him gasp. If Siwall coveted more and more power these days, it was more for a safe wall to hide behind than for ambition's sake.

There were still moments when Josselyn regretted their feud. They had soldiered together, he and the two brothers, Artemas and Hamilton Siwall, along with Josh Lamb and the Markhams' dead son, Eben. Ham had been transferred to some other regiment after Saratoga, and they had only seen him again after Yorktown, when they stumbled home to Rufford by twos and threes to find him already building his power.

Artie Siwall went mad after Webb's Ford and was dead now; it had been for his sake that Daniel had taken Ham for his partner in the Bristol Company's thriving new trade in timber, furs, and homestead lands. But mere prosperity was never enough for Hamilton Siwall.

'We shall have you court-martialled, Josselyn!' he huffed.

'Then write your letter, Mr Siwall, by all means.' Daniel turned away and his voice rose slightly, asserting command. 'Sergeant Kersey!' he said.

'Sir!'

'Why were these infantry brawling?'

'High spirits, sir.'

'Then lower them with a double march around the perimeter, Mr Kersey. Full kit and rifles, at the run. Oh, yes, and escort these gentlemen to the visitors' camp, if you please. Sirs, I must ask you to join the other civilians at the top of the hill.'

'Come, Siwall. Don't make a rumpus,' said William Royallton-Smith. He was not many years older than Daniel, a sober fellow, his face heavily lined with responsibility. Not a fool, but too easily made one by those who could play upon his good opinion of himself.

'No, William! I won't be put off!' Siwall shook free of him and his voice rose to a shout again. 'Why, the man's uniform looks as though he had slept in it! Have you nothing to say for yourself, Major? Where is your hat, sir? Where is your officer's cloak?'

Daniel's eyes travelled past them, down the brow of the hill to the village that lay like a child's wooden puzzle below them, the river at its foot already slushy here and there with early ice. A figure in a scarlet riding hood was moving slowly across the snow-dusted common, leading a big sorrel horse they all knew was Daniel's. Behind Yeoman, an Indian travois hastily made of willow poles left heavy tracks on the grass.

They had wrapped the body as decently as they could, but the dead man's single red-heeled boot could be plainly seen even at this distance, bouncing with every step of the horse.

'My cloak is there, sir, should you wish to inspect it,' Daniel told Siwall quietly. 'On its way to the constable's office with the body of Samuel Clinch.'

TEN

The Lay of the Land, or On Which Side Their Bread Was Buttered

It was a noble notion, the equality of men. But these yeoman farmers are unlearnt, and a prey to gossip and passion. Why, even their petitions of protest are vastly ill-spelt!

No, no. We must have a rational government, removed from the whims of the mob and alive to the interests of property.

Draw closer, friend. I would be circumspect. We've set business afoot in the Confederation. George Washington shall be crowned King of America! Or if he will not, we have sent to Prince Henry of Prussia. One king's as good as another, so long as he be sound on the questions of property and trade.

I, a Tory? God forbid, sir! Why, I would not have an *English* king again for all the world!

—*William Royallton-Smith, Shipbuilder,*
Moderator of the General Court, Boston,
Father-in-law of Jem Siwall

There be no more slaves in these parts now. But I was one time house-slave to a great man in Boston, when I was but a boy. He learnt me from his own books, and when I knowed enough to need freeing bad, so I bled out the want of it like sweat from my body, then he tells me I am already free, that the law has made me so.

'Go, Caesar,' he says to me. 'Try yourself. You have as good a brain as the Governor General, and no man is free unless he takes his fortune in his hands and feels himself equal to any man else.'

He was kind, that old master. But because he was rich, he talked easy of freedom. He never carried no burden that was heavier than the sterling in his pockets to drag his soul down.

Only I am a poor man and I must work, and whatever may be in my brain, my skin is still black and my lips, they be thick, and my feet walk heavy with my father's chains on them, and my grandfather's. Every rich man, every proud man that sees me, he sees them invisible chains, and I am his slave for the taking, brain or no brain. And so I will always be.

To be free is a circle that has no tail to it. It spins and it spins, and hope spins with it. Only sometime it comes smash, like a wheel in the mud.

And them spokes – oh, they be sharp in the heart.
> —*Caesar Daylight, servant to Samuel Clinch*

I have been wed near twenty-five years to my Joshua, and though we have no child nor any hope of one now, I am in his heart and he in mine, so mixed up together I scarce know where he ends and I begin.

But Jonathan is my own little brother, that I nursed with

a rag soaked in warm milk, and taught him how to fly kites and play conkers. And if they send out the militia against the Regulators, my Joshua must ride against Johnnie, and how shall my heart divide itself in two unless it break?

I lie awake in the nights, now, and hear the clock strike and the Night Watch call out the dark hours, and I do not lie so warm upon Joshua's breast as I was wont, for fear I shall be no more at home there.

When I ask what he will do, Husband makes me no answer, only takes out his fiddle and plays me Gentle Robin, as he used to before we were wed.

—*Dolly Lamb, wife of Joshua Lamb, Lamb's Inn and Ordinary,*
daughter of Henry and Julia Markham

Liberty, the Rights of Man – it's all gas and dumplings. Get power and keep it, see, that's the real ticket.

You must build power solid, like a brick wall. Once a man's outside it, there's no foothold and no future. You may climb till you're blue, but you'll never get over the top.

Oh, they might make Washington king and Dan Josselyn general, if he lets them. But such men are the old sort, they're like maidens in a whorehouse. They're not where power lives these days, poor things. No matter who sits on the throne of America, it's Siwall and his like that will rule. And I mean to be one of them.

Not the decent, see, nor the honest. But the sly and the hard.

—*Erastus Cain, Rope-spinner*

I'm an Englishman born, I came here from Warwickshire back in the Sixties. I'd no love for the king and I fought for a time under Washington. He's a spry old cock and a heart of gold, like Daniel Josselyn.

But, stap me, they are rich men, like the lordships at home were, and every lord with a dozen arse-polishers, and each one of them with a dozen lackeys, and each of the lackeys thinks himself better than me. And in between, truth is lost. Men are wasted, who are more than other men may buy.

If we have freedom here, it is only the freedom to kiss different arses. John Adams is a rich man. And Franklin and Jefferson and all the rest – why, even the poorest is richer than me, and his riches buy him a voice among them that will call him their equals.

But the poor are ever mute and dumb. We are like ghosts to them, we may pass by and be trampled and our wives with us, and our cries never heard but to say of us, 'Hark to that ignorant, no-account rabble. We shall bring them to heel by-and-by.'

—*Oliver Kersey, Farmer, Sable Brook*

Ignorant, restless desperadoes, without conscience or principles, have led a deluded multitude to follow their standard, under pretence of grievances which have no existence but in their imaginations . . . Luxury and extravagance both in furniture and dress had pervaded all orders of our countrymen and women, and was hastening fast to sap their independence by involving every class of citizens in distress and accumulating debts upon them which they were unable to discharge. Vanity was becoming a more powerful principle than patriotism . . .

You will be so kind as to present my love to Miss Jefferson, compliments to the Marquis and his lady . . . The little balance which you stated in a former Letter in my favour, when an opportunity offers I should like to have in Black Lace at about 8 or 9 Livres per Yard.

—*Letter of Mistress Abigail Adams, London, to Thomas Jefferson, Esquire, Paris, 1787, regarding the Rebellion in Massachusetts and a Certain Sum to Purchase Paris Goods*

ELEVEN

Piecing the Evidence: In the Matter of Samuel Clinch

Item the First

One Leather Hunting Pouch, deerskin worked with trade beads and thread, a design of tendrils and human figures in reds, purples, blues and greens, the figures chalk-white. Inside the same, as follows:

> *One small mirror, much clouded.*
> *One stub of wax candle.*
> *Seven lead balls, poorly cast and scarce fit for a musket.*
> *One cob pipe with remains of tobacco.*
> *One tinder-box containing flint and steel.*
> *Fifty pound seven shilling in coin.*

Item the Second

Button. Pewter, much tarnished, of the size for a greatcoat or uniform coat. Upon it engraved the Ensign of the Twelfth

Battalion, Massachusetts Artillery, with a Skull and Crossed-bones, as below.

Note: This button was found by Mrs Hannah Trevor among the leaves where the Corpse was first encountered and presented to Constable McGregor. It was first thought to have come from the uniform of Major Daniel Josselyn, who discovered the body, but upon examination it was recalled that his regiment was not the Twelfth but the Seventh.

ITEM THE THIRD

Sheet of paper. Foolscap as from a child's copy book. Hand ruled, and jagged at one edge, as having been torn from its stitching. The writing upon it performed with a plummet of lead badly sharpened and in two different hands.

On the first side, in a square unpracticed hand, as follows:
Rosepath Tabby Monks Belt

On the second, in a man's Italian hand, a verse:

> Here lyeth One who lived by Taking,
> Who used the Poor to Tears and Breaking.

> *Cold may he lie, his Greed Confounded,*
> *His Death the Hope of them he Hounded.*

Note: This foolscap sheet, folded, was found in the dead man's breast pocket by Major Josselyn when the corpse was discovered.

Deceased's body being much damaged and there being no doubt of his manner of dying, no dissection was ordered by Sheriff Marcus Tapp.

TWELVE

How the Dead Fool Grew Wise

It took six of Daniel's militiamen to carry the body of Samuel Clinch into Lannie McGregor's Forge and lay it out on the work-table, as nine-year-old Robbie tumbled the last of his father's half-finished hinges and pot hooks and horseshoes onto the stone-paved floor to make room.

The smith's house was built onto his shop and the kitchen door stood half-open, but Hannah did not go inside at once. A pale sun broke through the clouds and she sat down on the rough bench in the dooryard to hoard it, pushing back the hood of her cloak and closing her eyelids to take the healing light inside her for the child.

One by one, like funeral mutes to a widow, the amateur soldiers in their ragtag uniforms murmured their pious sentiments and went quietly past her, back to the Muster. On the common beyond, a small crowd of civilians had gathered; for the most part their voices were lowered, but now and then a phrase escaped their control and crashed against the bright cold.

'Sheriff's men!' shrilled a woman. 'Raw-dealing bastards! Don't mind who they kill!'

'Anson the Martyr!' someone else shouted, and a cheer broke the air. 'Indemnity and liberty! A pardon for Jonathan Markham! The Cause! Hurrah the Cause!'

'What easy fools they are, Sarah,' said a woman's voice from the open door of the house. 'I would rid the world of them all, if I could.' Her voice was thick-napped as velvet, and there was something opaque and foggy about it, all but lost in a mist.

When Hannah got up to see who had spoken, she found Leah Kersey there. Not surprising, for weaver-women like Mrs Kersey and Susannah Penny and the blacksmith's wife Sarah conferred on their projects and traded their pattern-grids constantly, working out new fashions and ways of threading their warps.

Hannah had spoken to Leah only a few times, but she had grown strangely fond of her – a quiet young woman who must have married very young indeed. Even now she did not look much past Sally's age, and her face had not grown weary and sullen from hard work on her husband's farm as Sally's was sure to in time. There was a distance about Mrs Kersey, an invulnerability, as if nothing ever quite touched her.

Well, perhaps it was only a mask against troubles, thought Hannah. Leah Kersey had lost a child last year and two to miscarriage the year before that; for all the midwife's efforts to protect her and help her, new life seemed unwilling to grow in her beyond the space of three or four months.

But then, most women lost one or two children during their bearing years, and so far this one still inside little Leah seemed healthy enough. Pray God, thought Hannah, she would carry it to term.

Like most Outward homesteaders, Oliver Kersey did not take his wife very often away from their cottage, but he treated her gently – at least when there was anyone else about. Perhaps he feared her with young fellows her own age, and so kept her close. She *was* handsome, in spite of her paleness, and like many country husbands, he was almost old enough to be her father.

'Oh my dear, you must be very cold,' said Sarah as Hannah came in at the door. 'I was just coming to call you. Look, Leah has set me a new pattern on the loom, and it's coming up nicely. Flame in the Forest, it's called. Is it not fine?'

Indeed, it was a striking pattern, a double-wide border of dark indigo followed by another of crimson-and-white, in a figure that swelled like the heart of a flame, then narrowed, blending back to the same rich shade of deep blue.

'Why, it's lovely,' Hannah exclaimed. 'And the colors are bold, too. Will you not set me the same pattern when you come to us after Thanksgiving, Leah? What a beautiful shawl it would make!'

'That'll be a hard trick, won't it?' Sarah smiled at Kersey's young wife and winked at Hannah. 'Poor little creature, her mind's a sieve now she's pregnant, just like mine is.'

Leah laughed, a soft, throaty sound. 'I've misplaced the grid, that's all. Husband rifles my pages and carts them away. But I can work it out again, from counting the threads in what's already finished.'

McGregor's wife perched herself somewhat awkwardly on the corner settle beside Mrs Kersey, bracing her hip and her back with one hand. On her wedding day, Sarah had been seven months with child, and it could not be a week more till her confinement.

Not that anyone called Sarah a slut as they often did Mrs Trevor, not once she was wed to her Scotsman. There had been some mumblings about her, and about Leah Kersey, too, as there were about Susannah Penny or any of the other women who fell pregnant when their men were out of the way or locked in debtors' jail. But they were no more than mumblings. The old biddies might count off the forty weeks on their fingers, but the tally was seldom exact. So long as you bowed to convention and were sensibly married, old Twig and her army of gossips let the business go.

Hannah's trouble had always been that she did *not* bow, but Leah Kersey did – on the surface, at least. She wore a modest white cap over her fair, wispy hair, a careful kerchief tucked decently into the neck of her gown, and when you spoke to her, her eyes – wintry grey-blue and very large in her finely chiselled face – were likely to fix themselves at something invisible just beyond you.

But whatever she saw there, she did not seem to approve it. Leah Kersey's demeanor might be mild-mannered and gentle, but her mind was strong and she judged life for herself, that was plain.

'You look far spent, Mrs Trevor,' she said quietly. There was an odd hesitance in her speech, almost a stammer, as though she thought out every word before it was spoken. 'This day has been hard on you. Come, do sit down.'

'Surely you don't mourn for old Clinch, Hannah? Do you?' Sarah busied herself with the teapot. 'The whole town has heard of it, it's a terrible crime, to be sure. But—'

'Mourn him? No.' Hannah took up a spindle and twisted the yarn round her finger. *Rather fear him*, she thought. *More dead than I ever did living.* 'Nothing ails me but a long day and this heavy, damp weather. I will be better when Major Josselyn has come.'

Suddenly Leah Kersey got up and went to Hannah where she stood near the fire. The girl's slight body was much swollen with the child now, and her balance gave way a little where she stood, as though the world turned on its axis inside her. *Twins*, thought the midwife, and bit her lip to keep from saying so. One child was dangerous enough to a woman with a history of miscarriage, but two at once could be deadly.

'You *will* be with me when my time comes?' the girl murmured. 'I trust you. You won't go away from here once you're married?'

She gripped Hannah's wrist hard; there were scars there and Leah seemed to know them by instinct and to seek them out. During the War, alone and despairing, Hannah Trevor had cut herself and tried to die.

'We are all sisters at such times, are we not?' said Sarah.

She came to slip one arm through Mrs Kersey's and the other through Hannah's own, and for a moment the three women clung to each other. Hannah felt stronger for their nearness, and for the fingers that still held very tight to her wrist.

We are a world to ourselves, she thought, *we who wait to bear children. No one else knows us, how the color of sky through a tree makes us weep in the morning. How the taste of a plum is as sharp as a knife and cuts our tongues and makes our teeth ache. How the tide of mere living rises inside us and drowns us sometimes, so that we struggle and scream and grow angry as I do with Daniel, or weep through the night and pray to die before another day grows old.*

'Husband sets great store by the child,' Sarah McGregor murmured.

'And do you not set store by it, too?' asked Hannah.

'I – want it. And do not want it.' The blacksmith's wife glanced over at Leah, her eyes lowered, her voice very soft. 'I was wild by myself, before he found me and kept me. But I was strong in my body. Stronger than here.'

'Men do not know us,' Mrs Kersey said suddenly. 'They cannot bear it, what we are in ourselves. The things we have done. The things we must do.'

Hannah freed her hand from the girl's strong grip. 'I have done terrors in my time,' she whispered. 'I will do them again, if need be.'

'I know,' replied Leah. 'It is why I can trust you. I have seen it sometimes, in your eyes.'

'Shall I stir up the fire, Dada?'

Young Robbie bounded along at his father's side as Daniel and McGregor strode into the Forge. Hearing them, Hannah came in quietly through the connecting door to the room where the dead man lay, but Sarah and her friend kept to their weaving and did not follow.

'Nay, lad,' said the smith. 'Never mind fire. Dead men stink if you warm 'em.'

'But can't I just see him? Please!'

The Scotsman ruffled his son's dark hair. 'Away, you idle callant! If you've no chores, I can scout you some out!'

But Robbie insisted. 'I want to see him, Da!'

The boy puffed out his chest, stuck out his lower lip in a pout, and began to prance about the room. ' "You, sir!" ' he cried – a fair imitation of old Clinch in high dudgeon.

' "Where is my wig-powder, Caesar you knave? Where is my silver tooth-pick that I got from the Governor! I shall fetch you a boot in the breeches, you black jack-a-knapes!" '

Without warning, Lachlan McGregor's great hand shot out and connected with the boy's temple. Robbie landed with a crash at the foot of the deflated bellows. 'Don't scorn a dead fool, boy,' his father commanded. 'Nor mock at a servant. I have been one myself before now.'

'I didn't mean harm, Dada,' murmured the boy.

'I know.' Lannie scooped up his son and embraced him, as suddenly tender as he had just been harsh. 'There, now,' he said. 'There's clean hay to be forked in the stalls. And mind you give old Smoke that fine bone Mother saved him!'

'Yes, sir,' said Robbie, and went quietly out.

Lachlan McGregor was a big, ugly fellow, built like a brown bear. His teeth were bad, as most men's were at nearly fifty; his nose was thick and ended in a sort of knob; and his brows – oddly dark for his coloring – were so heavy they seemed to smash down his light brown eyes all the way to his cheekbones. Today, his plaid caught with a brass pin at his shoulder and his broadsword clanking, he looked as much like a Highland cattle thief as a constable.

When Robbie was safely gone, McGregor closed the heavy oak door of the forge and barred it. 'I've no time for pussyfooting, Daniel,' he said. 'Did you crop the old bastard last night, or did you not?'

Josselyn let his hand lie upon Hannah's. 'There were two dozen fellows in those woods, and every one with a rifle or a musket. Why ask me?'

'Your case is particular, and if I don't ask it, Tapp will! You forbid Clinch your property. You threatened more than once to horsewhip him if he crossed you.' The Scotsman's voice grew hoarse. 'He hacked apart your only son, man. That's cause enough, by Christ.'

'It was an accident of birth and it's four years past. If I meant to kill him, why wait so long?'

'Accident be damned! Besides, your lady died of the business but four *months* since.'

'But you were all three together last night, Lannie!' cried Hannah. 'You and Daniel and Joshua. Surely *you* know he could have done no murder!'

'Nay. None of us fancies hunting in packs like these sugar-tit townsmen.' The constable's eyes were steady and cool. 'Once we got to the Trace, we went our ways.'

'And met at Blackthorne Falls after.' Daniel's voice assumed the calm formality that always sheltered him under attack. 'That's a good four miles north of where we found him this morning, and across the river besides. It would take an hour each way even to ride it, and we didn't go out on horseback. I should reckon nearer three each way to walk. Or did I fly on a broom, do you think?'

McGregor frowned. 'You say true. So old Clinch must be shot on the south bank and humped away over the river on foot or by boat. Or else—'

'Or else someone on foot must wade through the river,' said Hannah, 'find Clinch among a score of other men in the dark, shoot him, drag him out of the way – there are scrape marks, Lannie, on his back where they moved him.' She paused. 'And then finish their work.'

'So you think it was not planned?'

'How could it be? No one knew where Clinch went, except—'

'Except them that went with him.' McGregor scratched

his shaggy head. 'But who did the burning, and why? Burn him or bury him, Clinch was sure to be missed.'

'I think he was not burned in an effort to hide him,' she said.

'But what for, then? To burn only his feet? Ach, it's a mad business.' McGregor shook his head and scowled.

'Part of it, yes,' Hannah said thoughtfully. 'The burning does speak of madness. Clinch's own flint and steel wasn't used, so some other must have been fetched. Or carried along. A torch, perhaps. Or a candle.'

Daniel considered. 'The range of the shot was close, to do so much damage. Someone came upon him by chance, saw him, crouched down and fired. The bullet struck from below, when he was almost straight above the barrel.'

'And then vengeance came back later, calm and determined, and burned him?' Hannah could not make sense of it.

'And left him an epitaph.' McGregor unfolded the paper they had found in Clinch's coat pocket and studied the writing. 'I can fathom leaving the verse there. It's like capping the curse on him, same as the burning. But this other writing? Rosepath? Tabby? Monks belt? What babble is that, now?'

'Your own Sarah could tell you.' Hannah looked over the big Scotsman's shoulder at the paper. 'They are weaving patterns, very common ones. I have been teaching Jennet to weave plain tabby. We use it for backgrounds, before the colored weft is put in. Rosepath is a diamond pattern, and monks belt is rectangles joined onto squares.'

'So, then. It must be a weaver.' McGregor did not look best pleased with the possibility. 'And the hand is a woman's.'

'It is no clear proof,' Hannah said. 'Every woman has a

loom whose husband is able to buy one or build one, and these are simple patterns.'

'So it means nothing.' Daniel was calm, giving no sign of the strange, intense emotion she had seen in him that morning.

'The *names* of the patterns mean nothing,' she said, 'nor the fact that the page is writ on both sides. Paper is scarce, and every letter comes double-scribed, written and cross-written in the other direction.' Hannah paused, moving a little about the chilly room. 'But the two sides of the paper together may add up to something – the woman's hand there, and an epitaph well written in a man's fine hand on the other side.'

'Aye, and a sharp-witted verse it is, too,' said McGregor. 'He's no fool, this fellow. And he bears a long grudge. So we seek out a poet, do you fancy?'

Hannah's mind sorted people like colored scraps for a quilt. 'A parson, perhaps?'

'Or a stonecarver,' Josselyn considered. 'Though not many in Rufford can afford more than a board with the name burnt into it, or a plain wooden cross. Besides, there are no monumental masons hereabouts that I have ever heard of. The nearest is in Wybrow.'

'Then let us keep to what we know,' she said. 'He is a man with a settled life. A careful wife who owns a loom to weave his shirts and breeches on. She's not so educated as he is – look, see the handwriting. But then, few women are.'

Daniel paced back and forth. 'You think they compassed it together? Conspired in it, a man and wife?'

She considered. 'It may be. Someone brought the tallow to smear on him, surely. That speaks a home nearby, does it not?'

Josselyn stared down at his gloved hands, then locked them behind his back. 'Not necessarily. Servants always bring tallow to a hunt, to dip more torches when the first are burnt out.'

'You are thinking of Caesar?' Hannah frowned.

'I scarce know what I'm thinking.'

Daniel could not remove the sight from his mind – the burnt cloth, the smell of singed flesh. Even the dangling wig. It was like double vision, the past imposing itself on the present, two terrors jumbled together. Still he had no clear notion where the earlier memory came from, nor from how long ago.

Hannah thought again of the cry old Reverend Dancer had heard before daybreak. A woman's cry and a pale shape. A woman come back to see to the body? To take her private vengeance upon it?

A man, after all, would surely have found such vengeance trivial. No, the burning was a woman's deed, some ghost of the past like that haunting Daniel – a mad thing that seems like perfect sense to a troubling mind.

Painstakingly, Hannah tried to construct it, laying one piece to the next and color upon color, like the pattern she had been piecing for her wedding quilt or the borders she had seen on Sarah's loom.

A bridge of dark blue and a fire of crimson. Threads of indigo that climb to a licking flame of deep scarlet.

Bridges Burning. A Flame in the Forest.

What must I do now? the woman thinks. She is not guilty. Not afraid. Only sensible, practical under her anger. But her memory catches her. Something tears at her, some loss too often suffered, or too long suppressed.

Stern, she is. Strong-willed. Methodical. How else has she lived all these years but by piling the days on each other, clinging on to the details of living to keep herself whole?

She fetches tallow, and flint and steel from her own hearth, perhaps even brings coals in the long-handled firebox. But there has been snow in the night, while she waited her chance. His stockings are too wet, and the leaves are sodden and will not serve for kindling. Her fire dies out time after time.

Her vengeance is stolen. She cries out, shrill, furious. That single sharp cry, and no more.

Suddenly she hears wagon wheels in the dark. The peddler's singing, perhaps. The old man saying his sums as he knits.

She breaks from the thicket and comes face-to-face with him, old Moses Dancer looking out at the back of the wagon. The gleam of his candle lights her up like a pale, perfect flame.

And then she is gone.

Hannah shivered and pulled her cloak closer. It could only be one of her women, that she traipsed to for birthings and saw through the fevers of children and husbands and the deaths of old parents. Sable Brook was near to the town and she went there often. Most were Siwall's debtors. And Clinch was Siwall's henchman.

Susannah Penny, she thought. Bess Whittemore. Mrs Drewel. Leah Kersey. Jane Flynn. My sisters. How shall I turn on them and rend them?

She shook herself free of it, determined; it was patterns upon pattern, the pieces still jumbled. Daniel was studying her face and she looked away, unable to conceal her forebodings from him.

But he said nothing, only drew back the cloak from Clinch's body. 'Can a dissection tell us anything more of it, do you think?' he asked her.

'Perhaps,' she said, and then was silent.

'Well,' said McGregor, 'the business passes me, I admit that. And whose button is this that you found there, from the Twelfth Massachusetts? Most men around here are the Seventh, not the Twelfth. That's up near the Hampshire border, eh, Daniel, not away here in Maine? And the fifty-pound hard coin in his scrip? The last time Sam Clinch had fifty pound to spare, he was still sucking titty for breakfast!'

Hannah did not tell them yet of the almanac, nor of the Reminder's vision. The old man was fragile and could not bear the sort of questioning Marcus Tapp was known to give, and besides, the book might have tumbled from anyone's pocket who rode that way. She needed time alone with it, to study its pages with her sensible spectacles firm on her nose.

And she needed time alone with Daniel, too. Though her heart never doubted him, her probing mind hesitated to tell even McGregor of his strange collapse in the woods, how his usual soldierly calm had deserted him. How he had murmured over and over, *What have I done? Christ. What have I done?*

'I'm settled myself you've done nothing amiss, Dan,' the constable continued. 'But I fear there'll be hell to pay. The old fool was Siwall's bellwether.'

'Oh, Clinch is a fool no more, Lannie,' Josselyn said quietly. 'He will be a fine, wise fellow now he is dead, and a paragon of honor.'

But McGregor shook his shaggy head. 'Have a care, man, and leave off philosophy. You're caught in the midst of their squabble with these debtors, and Hannah has risk enough herself.'

'What? What risk is this?' Josselyn spun on his heel, staring at her. 'What have you kept from me?'

'Only Sam Clinch's palavering,' Hannah replied.

McGregor would not let it go. 'Before he died, Clinch charged your lass with mispractice, Dan,' he said. 'If the evidence proves, she'll be cried for wrongful death and put away. And even if it doesn't prove, they may say she connived in the shooting to save her own skin from the charge.'

Daniel stared at Hannah, his voice so quiet and cold it could scarcely be heard. 'How dare you say nothing of this to me, madam? Am I really so little worth to you as that?'

Even if we marry, she will always be alone, he thought. *And so will I. It is the burden of freedom, and I cannot have her less than free.*

She reached for his hand but he could not give it yet. Still he was proud of her loneness, that she set her teeth at the world and would not fear it for any man's raging.

'I thought it nothing to trouble over,' she told him. 'Now that Clinch is gone, Dr Kent will perform the dissection, and he is well schooled. I did nothing amiss.'

'You don't trust *me*, but you put great faith in that smug capon!' Josselyn was ready to explode. 'Oh, his clothes are cleaner and he wipes his mouth with a linen napkin. But he's as much in Siwall's camp as Clinch ever was, and he'll do as he's told!'

He might have said more, gone too far into anger ever to turn back. But just then they heard horses outside, and the wheels of a carriage. McGregor unlatched the door and in a moment Marcus Tapp entered, Siwall not far behind him.

With them was Mrs Lavinia Clinch, accompanied by one of her five indistinguishable daughters. All were faded, overdressed, twittering creatures, who had nicknames like cage-birds and never seemed to wed.

Their mother was shaped like a tree trunk, just as wooden and thick enough around to testify to at least sixty winters. You could not find where her bosom ended and her waist began, nor be certain she possessed a pair of legs at all beneath the long, loose wrapper she had come away in.

'Where is that rascal my husband?' Madam Clinch demanded, looking around the blacksmith's shop with furious, yellow-brown eyes. She stared past the corpse on the table as though it were invisible.

Siwall took off his elegant hat before the muffled shape of the dead man, then glanced round the room at the others. If his own danger from the farmers had frightened him and weighed down upon him, this unexpected death seemed to make him resolved. His red face was almost pale and he moved with solemn deliberation.

It was only when he looked in Daniel's direction that the fear rose in him and his breathing grew hoarse and quick. 'I think we must say a word of prayer,' he murmured. 'Must we not?'

'Let his soul quiver another ten minutes, sir, before you shove it back-arse into heaven.' Marcus Tapp took the arm of the doctor's wife and hustled her over to the table where the body lay. 'Come, madam. Here is your husband. Say so before these witnesses and you may go home.'

But the lady only stared. 'Why, this is some package, Master Sheriff! Some bundle!'

Mrs Clinch turned away with a scoff, but the pale daughter drew back Daniel's cloak a bit from the corpse's feet. 'Boots, Mama,' she whispered. 'Pa's boots!'

Lavinia sniffed. 'Boots may be purloined, my dear Chirrup. Never forget it, child. All men are false.'

The sheriff's patience was at an end; he snatched away the cloak with one sharp jerk. 'Is this your husband, Madam Hackbones? Or is it not?'

Chirrup fell down in a limp heap on the floor, but her mother gave no sign of distress, and she certainly did not seem to mourn. In the face of such terrible ruin, she seemed mildly irritated, nothing more.

She looked the battered shell of her husband up and down, from top to toe. 'Those be Clinch's boots,' she said. 'I shall not quibble upon *them*. And that be his wedding ring, the match of this same that weighs on my finger. But that, sir, is as much as I will say.' She nudged the trembling girl with her foot. 'Come, come, Chirrup. You will dirty your stockings. They were ten pence apiece.'

'But ma'am,' spluttered Siwall. 'You must identify his remains before justice can be done him!'

'Rubbish, sir! Justice? Why, I'll be no more than sat down to my supper when in he will stumble yet living, ten pounds out-of-pocket and a-stinking of rum! Clinch has tricked me in such wise before, and I know his sly ways. Oh, Black Caesar will root him out yet, good fellow, and bring him home again. Mark my word if he don't!'

Madam Clinch made for the door, then stood motionless, her hand upon the latch as though it had frozen there, her invisible feet rooted down to the stones of the floor.

'He – He will stumble in,' she said again. 'Clinch will – Caesar will—'

For a long moment, she made no sound at all except for the slight gasp of her breathing and the sound of lace against silk on the bosom of her gown.

Then they heard a low growl, such a sound as a cat makes when it is cornered by dogs in an alley. Hannah had heard it before in the chests of the dying, the life in them caught there and anxious to be gone.

But never in a living woman. Never till now.

At last the growl turned to a dry, choking sob, and Lavinia Clinch's ungainly body seemed to contract, to grow smaller, even younger. She was a girl again, as though she had shed forty years of desolate marriage in a single instant.

She turned back from the door and stared at the others. 'Dead,' she whispered. 'The fool's dead, by my word.'

'She will fall!' cried Hannah. 'Fetch a chair!'

Between them, they eased the doctor's wife into a rush-bottomed rocker from the smith's parlor. Chirrup – her real name was Charity – knelt before her mother, moving the chair back and forth, back and forth as you might rock a child in a cradle, her head in the woman's broad lap.

'We are ruined, my dearest girl,' murmured the mother. 'He spent all and saved nothing. From the day of my betrothal, he deceived me, and now he has destroyed me. I am paupered and you are betrayed.'

The constable's wife had come now and stood stroking back the old woman's disordered hair, and Leah could be heard in the kitchen, rummaging for some of McGregor's Scotch whisky to help revive her.

'Run, Charity,' Hannah commanded. 'We will stay with your mother. Go and fetch your father's servant. Caesar will know what is best to be done for her relief.'

But the girl only looked up, her eyes streaming. 'Why, ma'am, that I cannot! When Caesar did not come to fill Pa's bath this morning, I sent our maid out to fetch him, but they are all run away in the night! Black Caesar is not to be found in the town, nor Tirzah, nor none of his family!'

'So then! There is your murderer, Master Sheriff!' the magistrate said with relief. 'The black man has done for him, and fled in the night. No wonder this good lady fears for her future. No doubt we will find Clinch's money-box robbed!'

Tapp shot a glance at Daniel, then at Hannah.

'A pity, Gypsy,' he said. 'I had such great hopes of welcoming your gallant paramour, here, to my jail.' He shrugged, a smile playing round his harsh, handsome features. 'But all things come, they say, to him who waits. And who knows? I may yet have you in his stead.'

THIRTEEN

Piecing the Evidence: What a Rumpussing Noodle He Was

LETTER OF SAMUEL CLINCH, PHYSICIAN AND
SURGEON, TO MAJOR DANIEL JOSSELYN
WRITTEN FROM RUFFORD, COUNTY OF SUSSEX,
PROVINCE OF MAINE,
THE FIFTEENTH OF DECEMBER, THE YEAR 1782

My dear Sir, etc.

I write to express my condolence, etc., on the lamentable death of your infant son on Friday week. We are Christians I trust, and God's will be done, don't you know. Anyhow, your Lady Wife's a young filly and no doubt you'll get others on her. Or if not, then upon some other, what? You must be a man, sir, and take your pleasure as a man does, and a bastard ain't so bad if the gal be sensible, you know, and keep to her proper place once the business is done.

I ain't sentimental and you are a soldier, so I make no doubt we see things much the same.

I shall overlook the clout I received with the bleeding-basin in your presence at the hands of Midwife Trevor, that piece of *impertinence whom you neither reproved nor repressed. I shall overlook also the mention of horsewhips at present. Only choler ain't healthy, Major. I should recommend a sound bleeding once a fortnight and a dose of Tedham's Elixir to settle the brain.*

For my part in the matter, my conscience is clear, sir. I applied the latest methods of Science and the Principles of Enlightened Delivery according to the Best Minds of Medical Practice, and if Mrs Trevor had kept to her place and not thwarted me, your son might now be alive. These country midwives are no more skilled than a witch with a broomstick, with their pawings and strokings! What does a woman know of such matters? Can she spell, sir? Can she read and write and cipher Latin like a man?

No, she cannot! Women are soft for our pleasures, but they ain't got the brains of a sheep where Science and babies is concerned!

With all due respect, etc., etc.
 Yours as he findeth you,
 Samuel Clinch

Post Scriptum
I had taken no liquor on the night in question, to which cause my servant Black Caesar will gladly attest in answer to all allegations, or if he do not I shall peel his hide! Besides, my forceps were clean enough, by Christ, whatever that impudent doxy may say!

P.P.S. You will find enclosed my bill-of-hand at ten pound, twelve shillings and sixpence, for your Lady's successful delivery. I trust she is sufficient recovered by now to receive my salutations and best regards, etc., etc.

FOURTEEN

Piecing the Evidence:
How the Womenfolk Spoke
of the Dead

QUESTION: How long did you know Doctor Clinch, ma'am?

ANSWER: Why, nearly so long as I have been a wife to Mr Siwall. Master Clinch was ship's surgeon on the *Daedalus* when we set sail from Dover in 1768 to come here. And before that, we knew him in Ramsgate.

Q: Knew him well?

A: If one wishes to rise in society, Master Constable, it is wise to know everyone slightly, to nod to. But not to know anyone well.

Q: And your husband craved to rise, did he?

A: Husband considers it his Christian duty to puff up to an eminence, sir, for the Glory of Heaven, and so do I the same!

Q: Being bowed-to and scraped-to? Pranking about like a lord? I wonder he didn't take the king's side in the war, then, and wear the red coat instead of the blue.

A: My husband, a Tory? God forbid, sir! He is as true a patriot as ever walked!

Q: Did you come to Maine straightaway? It was very wild then.

A: I fear it has seen scant improvement. Husband left me and my dearest boy near two years with my sister in Boston, while he built himself up a situation.

Q: Oh, aye. He meddled with smuggling to build himself up, did he not?

A: Smuggling, sir? My husband is a respectable land merchant and a solicitor, he has no need of such palterings! Smugglers are very low fellows, not at all to his taste.

Q: Indeed not. Did Master Clinch come to the Manitac country with him?

A: I believe be bought out his ship's papers, and when the War came, he entered the Army, as my dear husband did.

Q: Rebel or Royal?

A: Doctor Clinch spoke loud against Tories, sir.

Q: That was not what I asked. Ah, to the devil with it. Did your husband lend him the money to set himself up here? Has he lent him money since? Has he paid the man bribes for his service?

A: Money and business are never the concern of a woman, sir. It would be a presumption to meddle with things that are best left to men.

Q: So you know nothing of Mr Siwall's finances? How his own debts are fiddled? How he spends and saves and so on? Nor those of Dr Clinch?

A: My husband is no gambler, Mr McGregor. He would never risk the comfort and sustaining of our mutual station here. That is all I need know of his business. I know him. He has plenty, and spends free.

Q: But Clinch, now. What did you think to Dr Clinch? As a man, I mean.

A: Why, that he spat to excess, and farted at table when there was a dish of cucumber pickle or a radish to be had. But a sound enough fellow. A blessing, no doubt, to the poor when they find themselves ailing.

Q: And a blessing to women?

A: If you mean his little amours, does not every man have them? It is excellent physick. I think nothing of that.

Q: Does your husband take any such – physick?

A: He does his duty to me, sir. Twice a week, as he has done since he wed me. That is more than enough, I am sure.

> —*Mrs Honoria Siwall, wife of Hamilton Siwall, mother of Jeremy Siwall, Burnt Hill Manor, North Bank*

Old Clinch and Ham Siwall, they comes here to the Bush yester-evening. Well, no, Lannie. I'm a liar, for Siwall would never come in, only waited outside in the dark, as if I wasn't to know who it was, and got Clinch to bespeak me. A gentleman, Clinch says it was, a stranger to the town, name of Nathan Jenkins. An old friend, he says.

Well, I can tell a dog from a duck, even by moonlight! I should know Siwall's shape in the dark, for haven't I grappled him by half a dozen other names before?

But I let him keep to his games, for men is strange in what rouses them best. Some takes to blows and some must stroke and tickle and knead me in the flanks like a new-leavened loaf. For the most part, I favor a fellow that's brisk at his business, and so Siwall is.

I went with them as far as the millpond, with old Siwall a-tailing behind like a shadow, and I laid down on the bank there and pleasured him. And Black Caesar, he waited and watched in the shadows, and I heard him sing Blackbirds and Thrushes, and The Trees They Do Grow High.

'I love you,' Siwall says when he's into me, over and over, as though I was somebody. And when he is finished, he leaves me two shillings and a hank of blue ribbon. Can you fancy? Only I seen him give Clinch full fifty pound, the old pimp!

And I may say, his boy Jem wasn't the only one humping poor Molly Bacon, neither, and when Siwall turned her out he give her thirty pounds sterling to quiet her tongue and not to tell Jem and his Ma.

—*Patsy Innes, Barmaid, the Red Bush tavern*

Now, Constable-dear, you knows me and you knows that lying slut Patsy Innes, and I trust you will credit me when I say she could not be with no Nathan Jenkins. For I seen her last night go upstairs with Jack Strut, the second mate on the Belle Fleur, and unless Patsy can fly, she never come down again till 'twas broad day.

And I have myself pleasured this Nate Jenkins four or five time in the winter of last year, though he will never have candles to see me by. But, there now. Some fellows is odd.

—*Bella McKee, Barmaid, the Red Bush*

'Tis the duty of every Christian to speak well of the departed, to be sure. But I will say this. I come here with Mistress Siwall from Boston in '72, and in those days old Clinch was a hanger-on and a gobbler-up and a carouser, and nothing more.

Only him and Master went away to the War, and Clinch was a surgeon of a company – I forget which one, but it don't matter, does it? – and when they came back, things were other than they had been before.

Oh, Sam Clinch still does what Master asks of him in small matters, and what that may be I will not repeat, for it's no worse than most menfolk, whatever their wives say of them by daylight.

But there's a fear in Master Siwall when Clinch sits at his table a-drinking and joking aloud. I have seen it and I know it. And what Clinch asks, Master gives him, and next week back he comes with his hand out for more.

—Mrs *Marjorie Kemp, Housekeeper, Burnt Hill*

FIFTEEN

Apple Parings

'I cannot be spared from my men any longer,' Daniel said as they left the smithy. 'But I must speak to you, Hannah. They close up this business too soon and too handily, now they have Caesar to blame it on. No questionings. No dissection of Clinch's body. Tapp knows more than he says, and I mislike his eyes when he looks at you.'

Already Marcus Tapp had sent out some of his men in search of Black Caesar. But the sheriff himself remained at the Forge, lounging by the doorway, his pale, bemused eyes fixed on Hannah's straight, stubborn back.

'I must witness Mrs Jory's dissection at noon,' she said. 'But I will come after, and bring Flower to see the parade.' On Muster Day, there was always a grand march along the high street at one o'clock, when the cannon was lugged out of the arsenal and fired across the river as a memorial salute. 'Jenny will like to see you in your fancy dress,' Hannah told him with a smile.

But Daniel's mouth was set in a downward curve of worry and his eyes were still angry. 'The officers dine at Lamb's Inn when the business is over,' he said. 'Wait for me there, and I will find you.'

By then, he thought, it might already be too late. There would be speeches made at the review parade. If Royallton-Smith brought some bad news, if the General Court still balked at redressing the grievances of the rebels, these debt-ridden farmers might go off like a cannon and do some rash deed that could never be mended.

And now there was this dangerous business of Clinch.

Siwall and his friends would blame it on sedition and anarchy, of course, and twist it to serve themselves. If they found Caesar, he would not be gently treated, for servants who killed their masters were still guilty of petit treason under Massachusetts law. Murderers of that sort did not merely take life, they attacked the rule of one class over another, just as these rebel farmers did, and that could not be borne. For petit treason, you were not merely hanged; if the Court so decided, they might burn you alive.

Burning. A great broad pit and the stench of flesh. This is hell, someone said, and we are the devil. Bodies tipped in by moonlight, by torchlight. Someone playing a bagpipe. 'The Boatman of Skye.' A woman's scream. One scream and no more, as the fire caught them.

Daniel's eyes closed and behind them the darkness was shot with red and gold. 'Hannah,' he began, 'I cannot remember—'

But he said no more. What was there to tell her? Fragments? Dim shapes and half-summoned scents and sounds?

In the dooryard, the sheriff's men were removing Clinch's body, spitting and swearing as they heaved it into an oxcart and creaked away towards old Hosea Sly's ferry, which would still make a week or two of crossings from Lamb's Inn dock before the ice closed in.

Daniel mounted Yeoman and was about to ride away, when suddenly Hannah seized the bridle to keep him with her. So strange, he seemed. Almost disconnected, drifting as he had been when they first met, near nine years ago now.

I have held him away from me too long, she thought, *and now I have almost lost him. I will have him back. I will not be alone.*

'I do not believe Black Caesar a murderer,' she said aloud. 'Do you?'

Daniel shrugged. 'He's a clever fellow, and his master used him ill enough all these years. Perhaps he could no longer bear it.'

'In anger, yes, he might have struck out. But the burning? He is not mad.'

'And I am. Is that what you mean?' He stared straight ahead, hands fiddling with the reins. 'Do you think I have not felt your eyes on me since this morning, doubting me? I don't blame you. I behaved like a mad thing out there in the woods, I know that. But – I cannot explain.'

Surely Daniel Josselyn was no stranger to killing, and he could be cruel if need be. Hannah was almost certain he had taken the life of Isaiah Squeer, an old enemy of hers, in the Outward forests, for the sake of her honor.

But the killing of a man from ambush – that was not in Daniel, of that she was certain. 'You could not do to any man all that was done to Sam Clinch,' she told him.

'You're sure of that, are you?'

'I am sure of *you*, my dear,' Hannah said.

And yet, as Daniel rode away up the high street, she saw not a friend, not a lover, not even a husband. Oh, she did not see a murderer, because she did not wish to see one. What Hannah Trevor saw was an unsteady piece that would not fit into any pattern her desperate stitchings could contrive.

'Missus!'

Someone tugged at Hannah's sleeve, jarring her out of her troublesome thoughts. One of Phinney Rugg's army of cheeky, lank-haired offspring stood at her elbow, grinning and tossing a penny from hand to hand.

'His Honor, old Magistrate Face-ache, says you're to see Missus Clinch don't want for nothing and he'll pay you the trouble in silver,' the boy told her. 'When he gets round to it, you know.'

Hannah's brow arched a bit with irritation. But when she glanced in Siwall's direction, she found him watching her. His expression was still placid, not full of anger as it so often was. But there was something else, a kind of containment. A coldness she had never glimpsed in him before. It frightened her more than his anger, and she knew she must find out its cause.

'Say I will go to Mrs Clinch's house at once,' she told Phinney's boy, and turned the nose of Mrs Twig's speckled mare towards the docks.

Hosea Sly's ferry was a flat, railed barge with a rope to guide it from bank to bank and a long pole to propel it. He had been ferryman here almost forty years, and what he didn't know about most people in Rufford wasn't worth knowing.

Hannah gave him his farthing and dismounted, leaning

against the warm shape of the mare to steady herself from the drag and sway of the current. In her fourth month, the morning queasiness had almost stopped so long as she stayed on dry land, but the ferry crossings brought it back with a vengeance. She set her mouth tight and took great deep breaths of the damp November air.

It had grown steadily colder all day, a stiff north-east wind snapping the guy-rope as the old man pushed off for the North Bank, where the doctor's house stood in a small grove of larches and pines. Now and then a few drops of slushy rain fell, then stopped, then fell again.

Hannah drew her cloak close around her, feeling better for the cold and the promise of winter in spite of the drizzle. From the bluff above, where Great Meadow spread out, she could hear the staccato sound of rifle fire and the music of a fife.

'A sorry business, this of Dr Clinch,' she said to the bargee.

'Who's sorry? Not me!' Sly rubbed a grimy fist across his grey stubble of beard and chuckled, his deep voice rumbling. 'Fair old stoat, he was. Bastards up and down the river, like spittin' out pips from a wormy apple!' He lowered his voice as they neared the North Bank docks. 'As for his dying—See here, Clinch knowed too much, didn't he? Oh, it's nothing to me, I don't give a rat's tit for the pair of 'em!'

Hannah nodded. 'No, of course not.'

'Only Siwall didn't get where he's got without turning a corner or two in the dark. You ask old Squeezer Inskip, that bailiff of his. And such things gets knowed-of, and knowed-of means paid-off, don't it? Faugh! Damn him, how else you think Sam Clinch kept out of debtors' jail all these years?'

*

The house of Dr Clinch and his family, grandly named Longleat, was little more than a two-story saltbox like the Markhams', but brick-faced and with a half-dozen ells and corners and dormers built onto it of weathered grey boards. One such addition was a large, square space jutting out from the west wall, with its own entrance and a sign that read 'Samuel Clinch, Esquire, Physician and Surgeon, By Appointment at Ten Shillings, Cash.'

Hannah had been inside the place often enough, as the requisite female observer at dissections. But today she avoided the surgery door and went instead to the kitchen at the back, where she had never ventured before.

'State business prompt! State business!' cried a raucous voice. Three steps led down from ground level through a narrow passage to the dimly lit kitchen, and at the bottom, on a shoulder-high wooden perch, sat a large blue, red and green parrot, peering out into the stairwell. 'Begone! Begone!' he shrilled.

'Pagan, you naughty old rogue! Hush your squawks, or I'll cook you for supper! The way *she* wolfs her victuals, she wouldn't know parrot from pheasant, nor pork from pussycat!'

This particular voice was human and female, with a permanent cold in its nose, and it belonged, Hannah knew, to Mrs Betsey Skowser, the Clinches' housekeeper and cook. Bella Twig at the Grange; Marjorie Kemp who kept house at Burnt Hill, the Siwall's manor; and blowsy old Betsey Skowser here at Longleat – that gossipy triumvirate had long since shattered Hannah's good name beyond repair, and many others besides.

And here they sat now, three simpering, broad-bottomed crones with pans of apples in their laps and paring knives in their hands. Change-work, the women called it – today's cidering or rug-braiding or apple-drying here, tomorrow's at the Grange and the day after at Burnt Hill. It was practical, efficient, and most of all, it was the perfect way to spread the local news.

Hannah pricked up her ears and put on her spectacles to get a better look. The old women sat by the hearth in a semicircle, the flames making their stout figures seem to jitter and dance and tinting their faces with reddish light, as though they were three witches at a homely sabbath.

Mrs Kemp's voracious eyes narrowed and her fingers turned and turned an apple, removing the peel in one long, continuous strip. All of a sudden she picked up the paring and tossed it over her left shoulder onto the floor behind her chair. 'There, Belle,' she said. '*You* must read it this time. 'Tis your turn, by rights.'

Mrs Twig hoisted herself off the settle and toddled to where the paring lay, skirts crackling and lappets flapping. How an apple peeling fell was usually taken to spell out some letter of the alphabet, as a prophecy of who would be next to marry or next to die – all according to how you interpreted its crooked shape.

'An F, I think, my dear.' Twig peered down at the shrivelling paring, turning her head this way and that to get the look of it from many angles. 'Yes, sure 'tis the letter F!'

Mrs Skowser put her panful of apples onto the floor and went to bend over the omen herself.

'Aaoooow!' she wailed. 'If ever there *was* a S, that there *is* a S! 'Tis the hand of Providence! S for Samuel! S for Slaughter! S for Situation! Whatever shall I do for a new situation? *She's* got no money for housekeepers! *She* cannot pay!'

'Begone!' screeched the parrot. 'Begone, you dolt! Begone!'

Betsey sank down upon the settle, a limp puddle of black bombazine and black net cap. Her arms waved and flailed and her feet kicked at the baseboard, while her bosom heaved and spluttered and heaved again.

'There, there!' crooned Marjorie Kemp. 'He's white-robed and in glory by now.'

Hannah bit her tongue at the picture of Sam Clinch white-robed, in glory or anywhere else. But the old woman's shrieks became wilder and wilder.

'Why, she will have herself in a fit, like old Lady Jory!' whispered Twig. 'I think we must send for Dr Kent, Madge, do not you?'

Betsey Skowser choked on a sob and her breath would not come for a moment. Her red cheeks turned purple and her eyes rolled.

'She will die!' cried the terrified Twig, twisting her apron into a clothes-rope. 'She will strangle! Oh, I know she will die!'

'If she dies of such nonsense, she deserves to.' Hannah came down the last stair and into the room. 'Is there brandy in the house?'

Twig and Mrs Kemp stared at her as though Pagan the parrot had somehow changed his shape and grown a cardinal cloak and hood.

'S for Sam! S for Skowser! S for Sweetheart! Whatever shall I do without my sweet old Sam?' Mrs Skowser still raved.

'What ails you? Do I speak Hindu?' Hannah marched past the two gawping biddies. 'Strong spirits, I tell you, and quickly!'

Twig went to a cluttered dresser on the far wall and returned with a bottle of gin, already more than half empty. Winking furiously, she handed it to Hannah, bobbing a somewhat resentful curtsey.

'Take her arms and hold them down!' They hesitated, but Hannah could not long be resisted when she had a patient in charge. 'Do you want her to choke herself with hysterics? Hold her arms down! At once!'

This time the two old women obeyed, and Hannah gripped Betsey Skowser's bulbous nose between her thumb and forefinger and pinched it shut. The toothless mouth opened like a trap door, gasping for air, and the midwife poured a sound swig of gin down the broad red funnel of throat.

She let go her grip and stepped back, and a split-second later gin erupted like a fountain from the nose and sprayed out the mouth. Betsey began to cough, and they pounded on her back until at last she was quiet.

'Well, then. Wipe her face,' said Hannah.

'You're better now, ain't you, Bess?' Marjorie Kemp scrubbed at the red, foolish, gin-sodden countenance.

'Hunh! Better is as better finds!' Betsey scowled at Hannah. 'And 'twas a shameful waste of Dutch gin, to be sure, for the state of things in this house is such, I shall wait long for a sup when next required.' She sniffed and wiped her eyes again. 'But better Madge, yes. I have done my proper mourning for him now.'

'And how is your mistress?' asked Hannah. 'I am sent to see Madam Clinch wants for no comfortable medicines.'

'Oh, *she's* comfortable, all right! *She's* a-licking up the crumbs of my fine beefsteak pudding, ain't she, and feeding on gingerbread and pears! *She's* in her parlor with them dustballs her daughters, a-pulling the bell for me to wear out my poor trotters in waiting on them all!'

'But where are the other servants? Where is Lucy, and Ruth, who scrubs the pots? Where is Tirzah?'

'Lucy and Ruth be gone to Great Meadow, the hussies, to flirt with them officers, and as for Black Tirzah, she may fry in hell with that savage, her husband! I never trust black folk and foreigns, nor them that's clubfooted neither, nor them with the squint. Nor them that's too tall! And red-haired folk, neither. Red hair's unnatural, ain't it? Judas, they say, had red hair.'

It was hopeless to expect any sensible answer; Hannah tried a less direct path. 'Caesar went to the hunt with his master last night, did he not? At what time did they leave?'

'Why, Master Clinch dined at Burnt Hill with us, Mrs Trevor dear,' put in Marjorie Kemp. 'At half-past seven, prompt, for I sent up the port and sugared walnuts for the gentlemen at gone nine. 'Twas Caesar himself took it up, we being short of a maid since that slut Molly Bacon's turned off to drabbing.' She shivered. 'Oh, to think that black rascal took his meal in the kitchen with me and poor little Mercy, and plotting every mouthful of the time! It's a wonder we weren't all poisoned in our beds!'

Only one point concerned Hannah. 'So then. They left for the woods – before ten, would you say?'

''Twas nearer half-past when I sent out the stirrup cup of hot rum-and-butter to the stableyard,' Mrs Kemp told her.

'Stirrup cup? They *rode* to the hunt?' Now it was Hannah who stared.

'Why, ma'am!' Twig sounded amused. 'It's near five mile to the woods, and no gentleman would go so far afoot!'

She was right, of course. Most townsmen were foot-spoilt and not accustomed to walking much distance. At the yearly hunts, some went upriver by boat, but most came on horseback, leaving their animals to graze in some farmer's clearing with a groom to tend them till they were wanted for the trip back to town.

Hannah's mouth was set and angry. 'Did Major Josselyn ride, too, then?'

Mrs Twig's eyes opened wide. 'To be sure, Mrs Trevor! I saw him myself, ride out upon Yeoman, for I'd sent Thankful to the springhouse and—'

'Very well!'

Hannah could hear no more. Her face felt fevered, and it was not from the heat of the fire. *Trust me*, Daniel had told her, and all the while he had lied! His whole defense against the suspicion of killing Sam Clinch was founded on the time it had taken a man on foot to move from one place to the other in the woods. But he had not *been* on foot.

What have I done? His words reeled through her head till she felt sick and giddy, far worse than her pregnancy could ever have made her. *What have I done? Christ. What have I done?*

'At what hour did he leave?' she said, her voice sharp-edged with fear and betrayal, while at the same time the guilt of doubting Daniel smashed against her and made her feel for a place on the settle beside Mrs Skowser.

Bella Twig considered. 'It could not have been later than half-past seven when he rode out, for I thought as I saw him, "Poor good man, he does not stay at table long enough these days to surfeit a cage-bird with crumbs!" I thought he meant to go and call for Mr Lamb at the inn, but he took the westward turning and rode at once towards the woods by himself. I supposed he would meet the other two gentlemen there.'

'Did you see him return?'

'No, ma'am, for I took Lady Sibylla her posset of milk-punch, and I went to my bed at half after nine. Early abed, late a-dying. Twig, when he lived, made it ever his rule.'

Somewhere a bell rang. In a moment it rang again, insistent.

'Oh, blast her!' said Mrs Skowser. 'You go, Belle, will you? I ain't my legs under me proper just yet.'

Twig sailed crackling away and Marjorie Kemp got up to stir a pot of stew that simmered on the hob.

Hannah took one of Betsey Skowser's pale, puffy hands between her own strong slender ones, still sun-browned from the summer's work. 'Please do not think me prying,' she said. 'But you were more than a servant in this house at one time, were you not?'

'We was all young once, mistress, though we wasn't all lucky as you are. I wheedled no lordship to wed me, once I was rid of old Skowser. I done as best as I could and kept my name in the town.' The old woman looked Hannah over and snuffled resentfully. 'And *I* bore no bastards, neither. I seen to it I should not, and Sam seen to it, too, if you take my meaning.'

'Did you know Mr Siwall in those days?'

'Know *him*? Nobody knowed him, only Sam. Nobody knows him yet, woman nor man, nor never will. You may ask Madge Kemp if they do.'

Hannah let go of the housekeeper's hand and stood up, pacing from one end of the black-and-white painted floorcloth to the other, thinking of what the old bargee had told her. *Things gets knowed-of, and knowed-of means paid-off, don't it?*

'Did Dr Clinch ever give you to think he might have any hold over Siwall?' she asked suddenly. 'Some secret that might do him harm in the town?'

The old woman wiped a drop from the end of her nose with her apron. ' "We shall soon be pigs in clover, old Bess." That's what he said to me. "Investments pay handsome if you're patient," he says. "We shall soon be pigs in clover, and you'll have a gold spoon to stir up your tea." '

'When did he say this?' Hannah stopped in her tracks. 'How long ago?'

'Oh, more than a fortnight since, after Master Jem and his lady come back to Burnt Hill from Boston. They was bid to dinner, Sam and *her* was, and *she* come stamping back alone like a Barbary Tartar. So I sits up late for him, knowing he'd come see his old Bess.' She rocked herself gently back and forth on the settle, the parched wood creaking under her weight. 'We was comfortable together, him and me. Oh, I don't mean bedding and cuddling. That's long gone now. But we *talked* comfortable and we *was* comfortable. "Bess, girl," he says, "you can still make me happy. You're a one in a million," he says.'

Hannah stared into the fire, thinking of Daniel. 'Did he love you, do you think? Enough to tell you the truth if you asked it?'

'Why, bless you, a sensible woman don't look for the truth! And as to loving, that ends soon enough.' Mrs Skowser wiped her eyes with her kerchief and her pink-rimmed eyes met Hannah's. 'A little kind comfort that's gone in the blink of an eyelash, that's all you may hope for this side of your tombstone. Oh, you may look at me crosswise. But it will end the same for you.'

SIXTEEN

Ashes and Lies

Two ramshackle one-room cottages attached by a shared chimney-piece huddled against a bare bluff at the back of Dr Clinch's stables. From the look of them, they were built of the boards Noah had left from the Ark; the roof of one house had been neatly repaired and patched with tar, but the other had only an old piece of sailcloth tacked across it to keep out the worst of the rain. Each had a loft under the eaves for sleeping, and a lean-to byre built against the outer wall for the storage of hay or the stabling of animals. A small milk cow, barely bigger than a nanny goat, lowed mournfully from the stable of the better-kept house, and a few hens scratched in the dirt of a small garden patch, its dry corn-stalks now shocked and tied and the pumpkin and citron and cucumber vines piled up for banking.

Both cottages belonged to Sam Clinch; they were let out by the month at the exorbitant price of twelve shillings – little enough, at that, when compared to the size of the late doctor's debts at horse-racing, dominoes, ninepins and whist. The more down-at-heel place had once housed a spinster who had died of the canker a year ago or more; it had stood empty since, and the landlord had not seen fit to invest in repairs – or had nothing to spend on them.

The other cottage, kept up by the sweat of its tenants, was home to Black Caesar, his wife Tirzah, and their two sons and three daughters. Hannah had delivered the last of these children on a clean pallet of quilts by that same mud-and-wattle hearth a year ago, a fine son called Justice.

But no smoke came from Tirzah's chimney today.

The path from Betsey Skowser's kitchen door led past the stables, then narrowed, rounding the garden. Hannah had left Twig's mare at the mounting block with her basket of simples hooked over the saddlehorn, intending to ride back to the Grange and leave the animal there.

But she felt she could not bear to go to Daniel's manor now, with the burden of his lies and her own suspicions weighing heavy upon her. As she lifted her basket from the mare's saddle, her reason labored as always to make sane patterns out of leftover scraps that seemed nothing but mad.

Ride Yeoman to the woods and tether him in some thicket. Then come back to the Grange on foot, quietly. But why, if he did not plan some secret deed? And how should he leave such a fine horse to be stolen or got-at by wolves?

Hannah sighed. Unless Daniel Josselyn was two men in one body, or Samuel Clinch was far more than the blustering ass she had always believed him, nothing about this strange business made sense.

'Mrs Trevor!'

The midwife looked up, startled. A slender young man of near thirty – though he scarcely looked twenty – stood near the path to Caesar's cottage, fiddling with the reins of a big dappled horse.

'Felt obliged to come, you know.' Jem Siwall's brown hair fell over his eyes and he raked his fingers through it nervously. 'Only damme, I can't summon the bottle to pay my respects to his lady.' He smiled, a sudden flash of white teeth. 'Taught me dancing, she did. Bit of a shock, ain't it, eh? Madam Clinch, dancing? But Pa disapproved and old Ma couldn't foot a reel if it was a ticket to heaven.'

There was a heavy volley from the target-shooters on the meadow above them, the sound so near Hannah cringed at it involuntarily. A steep, rocky path almost overgrown with wild currant bushes led straight up from behind Caesar's cottage to the eastern end of the field, a shortcut used by the town urchins to catch a closer glimpse of the Muster than could be had from the spectators' camp.

Jem Siwall, too, frowned at the burst of firing, and stared down at his boots. 'They say old Clinch was burnt,' he murmured. He glanced up at Hannah, then away again quickly, embarrassed. 'Feet, and so on. That right?'

'It is,' she said. 'But whoever attempted it was not successful, or had too little skill with a flint.'

Siwall's son shook his head. 'Burn a man that way. Torture the dead. Savage business.'

'You are thinking of Caesar?'

As they called Jennet a mooncalf, there were many like old Betsey Skowser who called black folk savages. But Jem only smiled. 'Good old Caesar, a savage! Why, damme, no man I know has a better eye for a trotting-horse, and his taste in cravats gets the better of mine!'

Still, his sharp-boned face, so like his mother's, was worried and intent, betraying more concentration than

Hannah had ever seen in it before. 'Who told you of Clinch?' she asked him. 'Your father? Or Mr Tapp, perhaps?'

'Ha! He don't waste his time on the likes of me, ma'am, he saves all his talents for Pa. If Tapp said magistrates could fly, poor old Pa'd be up on the roof in a twink, flapping his wings and crying cock-a-doodle.' He gave a soft laugh. 'No, I've too little money to be worth tinkering with.'

'But surely, your wife's dowry?'

Jem's eyes closed. 'I must earn that, they tell me. Grandsons, and so on. I call it devilish hard.' From what Hannah had seen of Harriet Siwall, hard it would be, and no mistake. 'Seems Pa and old Royallton-Smith made a bargain and neglected to tell me,' he went on. 'I won't see a farthing till I'm five-and-forty.'

He landed a resounding kick against the stable wall. His eyes opened, staring straight ahead of him toward the beaten-silver ribbon of the Manitac at the foot of the rise. 'Never trust me, Mrs Trevor,' he said suddenly. 'I'm a wet-leg and a liar and my word ain't worth spit when I've nothing to lose.'

'In what way, sir?'

'In the way of confidences. I'm resolved not to keep 'em from now on. It's all pounding and grinding in this world, you know. Hammer and anvil. If you ain't inclined to be the second, then you must learn to be the first and pound down like sixty, and take what you want when you want it. And so I shall, by the Lord!'

Hannah would not be deflected. 'Did you go yourself to the hunt last night? What do you know of all this?'

Jem's toe ground in the half-frozen mud. 'Take a word of advice, ma'am. Don't ask too many questions. Old Pa measures the world like a counting house, he don't understand you and he don't understand Dan Josselyn. Says you've no proper feeling for profit and loss.'

Since the War, it was all getting and spending to Siwall and his friends. In the Outward, his clearing crews went through the forests like locusts, sparing nothing. If the trunks were straight, the trees were cut clean for ships' masts or lumber. If not, they were girdled; cleared land brought more money, and the crews chopped shallow circles of bark from the walnuts and pines, hacking deeper into the oaks and sycamores.

Making a deadening, they called it. In a month, the leaves began to fall. In a year, great branches crashed down in the storms. The mink and marten and ermine forsook the place. Vermin moved in, rats' claws scuttling under the bare fallen limbs. Weeds grew higher than houses, poison ivy and oak tangled the pathways.

In two years, the bare, jagged tree trunks stood up, grey as an army of dispossessed spirits, the growing world shamed and defeated and lost. Old men passing these graveyards murmured their prayers and grieved quietly. Some ancient thing once whole had been subtly cracked, a bond owed to the earth. Once it was gone, you could do what you liked with the land – buy, spend, use, pillage, possess. *A free market*, they said. *Free trade*.

But under the feet of these takers and fakers, the crack slowly widened. For once made, there was only one way to clear off a deadening, in trees or in men.

Fire, thought Hannah, and her hands clutched one another for balance. *The refiner's fire. The war that will burn out the weasels and rats.*

'Pa's shaking in his boots, ma'am,' said Jem Siwall. 'If the militia should go with the rebels and Josselyn leads them against the Court—'

'He will let no harm come to your father, Jem.'

The boy shook his head. 'Pa won't risk it. He will have Major Josselyn out of the way. He's afraid of him.'

'But why?' she cried. 'What has he to fear from Daniel?'

'Owes him money, I expect, that's what it usually comes to. Don't know, though. Pa's secrets ain't all in his moneybox.'

Hannah's breath caught in her throat. There was shouting from the field above them, and another volley of shots. 'Jem,' she said. 'I must ask you – Did Dr Clinch have some hold on your father?'

'Hold?' He considered. 'Damned if I know. Old Caesar would, though. Nothing about Clinch he don't know.'

'Then I must find Black Caesar and speak to him.'

Jem paused for a minute, deciding some private question he did not choose to tell her. 'Oh, devil take me!' he said. 'Come along, ma'am, and see what I've found.'

Still leading his horse, he turned round on the path and Hannah followed him, her cloak catching at the bushes. When they reached it, Jem Siwall pushed open the door of Caesar's cottage with his riding crop.

The pounded dirt floor was dug down six inches below the level of the ground outside; it was very dark in the single room, and very cold. The fire was long burned out, and not even the tentative sunlight that fell now and then from the heavy clouds entered, for there was no window glass and the shutters were pulled tight.

But in the light from the open door, Hannah saw Black Tirzah and knew her. She was a handsome creature, tall and full-breasted, with skin the rich shade of good sorghum, a deep golden brown. She wore a plain homespun gown and a cloak of felted brown wool, and her hair was tied in a striped turban of huckaback, one end hanging loose beside her face. There was a silver ring in each ear, and around her long, dark throat she wore a necklace of five silver shillings strung onto a leather braid – her dower-gift from Caesar when they wed.

She crouched beside the cold hearth, sifting the ashes and singing softly, the strong voice rising and falling like a lullaby, very deep in her throat. 'God Jesus, deliver him. God Jesus, carry him safe.'

Tirzah bared her forearms and rubbed them with ashes, then arched her body backwards and smeared both arms against her cheeks. A knife blade flashed in the gloom, lifted above her, and more ashes fell from it, sifting down on her heart.

'Oh my dear,' said Hannah quietly. 'I am sorry to see you so stricken. And Caesar, how is he?'

The black woman looked up, her eyes huge and gleaming. 'Liar!' she spat at Jem Siwall. 'He says if I come, he will tell nobody!'

'I met her in Cade's Lane, ma'am,' Jem told Hannah. 'Hiding in back of the icehouse and Tapp's men not a hundred yards away up the hill. But I didn't see Black Caesar anyplace about.'

'Where is your husband, Tirzah?' Hannah came closer. 'You must take me to Caesar! Perhaps I can help him.'

'My man, he comes crying in the night and says we go hide,' the black woman told her. 'Says they have his neck broke in a rope if we don't. Only I think how them children be cold all winter, without I come here one time more for a bundle. So he lets me go.' She pointed a finger. 'And *this liar*, he says I be safe!'

She stooped and gathered a fistful of ashes and threw them in Jem's face. He stood very still, his eyes watering, head bowed against the charge.

'You misjudge him, Tirzah,' said Hannah. She took up a corner of her cloak and wiped the boy's face with it, thinking of Johnnie, how she had done such things for him as a child. They had been boys together, he and Jemmy, gone fishing and frogging together, and wenching, too, when they grew old enough.

Is it I who misjudge Jem? Hannah asked herself. *Do I trust him for Johnnie's sake, because I miss him and fear for him?* She let her cloak fall again and Jem rubbed his arm across his eyes.

'I think you be good woman, lady,' said Tirzah, watching her with wide, solemn eyes. 'But I can't speak where my man be. I slit my tongue before I do.'

Hannah took her arm. 'Come, make up your bundle and I will help you.' She turned to the boy. 'Jem, go into the house now and pay your condolences. They have surely seen your horse in the yard.'

Young Siwall glanced at Black Tirzah, then back at the midwife. He took Hannah's hand in his own. 'Mind yourself, Mrs Trevor, and tell Josselyn to do the same. And do not think too bitter of me if – if—'

'If what, Jem?'

'Oh well. Never mind.' He grinned. 'What would the old biddies talk of, eh, if not for you and me to give them fodder?'

He went quietly out, closing the door behind him, and in a moment Hannah heard the crunch of his boots on the rocky path by the garden. Tirzah's tall shape moved quickly and quietly about the dark room, rolling up one of the pallet beds with a few articles of clothing inside it.

'I must go, lady,' she said at last. 'He waits for me.'

Hannah spoke from the doorway. 'Caesar didn't kill Mr Clinch. Did he?'

'No, mistress.'

'Tirzah, how did Caesar come to work for the doctor? Where did he meet him?'

'Portsmouth, I think. Somewhere by there. Clinch got plenty money them times, after the War. But he don't keep it long. Don't keep nothing long.'

Suddenly there was another burst of rifle fire, very loud and near, and men's voices, the pounding of booted feet along the path. 'There he is!' someone shouted. 'In the yard!'

'Jesus Lord!' cried Tirzah.

'No, there! Over there!'

The cottage door crashed open, shattered by the stock of a musket. Hannah snatched up the iron poker from the hearth, as Marcus Tapp's deputy, the big ox named Tully, lunged into the room, and Tirzah crouched, moaning softly, the knife once again in her hand. Tully took a step and she slashed at him, quick as a cat, her breath coming in shallow painful gasps.

'You want taming, bitch,' he growled. A little blood seeped through his coat sleeve and he took another step towards her where she hunched in the near-dark little room.

More feet ran past, down the path from the meadow. 'There he is!' Marcus Tapp's deep voice shouted. 'On the roof!'

Through the open door Hannah could see men in the dooryard; some were in uniform from the Muster – Sergeant

156

Kersey and Amos Drewel and two or three others. But most of them were Tapp's.

Twig and her friends were huddled in the ell of the kitchen, and the elder Siwall was there, too, in the porch of Clinch's surgery, the doctor's wooden-faced wife by his side. She was blank-eyed and stolid, but her hands clutched and unclutched the wrinkled black silk of her skirt, and her grey hair fell unpinned from under a black lace cap.

'Fire, you bastards!' somebody shouted. 'He's well in range now, the black villain! Fire!'

'No!' Kersey shouted. 'For God's sake, let him be heard!'

Hannah tried to run past Tully, but he snatched at her, caught her so close against him she could scarcely breathe for the stink of ale and pickled onions. 'I shall spew in a minute,' she said through clenched teeth. 'I have no stomach for this huddling. Let me go!'

Taking her chance, Tirzah ran past them, out into the yard. But the big deputy didn't follow her. His mouth found Hannah's and she felt a sharp pain in her milk-swollen breast as he clutched at it, his other hand fumbling with her skirts. The poker was still in her hand and she struck backwards and down, hitting his kneecap a sharp crack.

Tully let her go with an oath and bent double, clutching his knee. Hannah pulled her skirts free and ran, slamming the door on his curses. 'Caesar!' she heard Madam Clinch cry, and the chaos and shouting ended all at once.

Sam Clinch's handsome black servant stood on the sagging roof of the empty cottage, balancing precariously on the ridgepole. He had discarded the foolish powdered wig his master had forced upon him; his hair was clipped close to his head, so that the shape of his skull could be clearly seen – a high forehead, curving proudly back and down. He might almost have been carved from a bole of mahogany, except for his wide brown eyes and the mouth that flashed white when he smiled. Whenever Hannah thought of Black Caesar, it was that knowing smile she remembered, exchanged with her so many times behind his master's back in confidence, while the old doctor snorted and huffed.

But Caesar was not smiling now. One musket ball had struck him and a second had grazed him; he bled from the shoulder, and there was a deep bloody gouge in his scalp.

'What monkey tricks are you up to, sir?' Lavinia Clinch made her way through the garden, holding her silken skirts clear of the mud. 'My husband's bath is not filled and he is not yet properly shaven!'

The men stared at her, stepping aside as she passed, their eyes lowered.

'Your master is yet sleeping,' she called up to Caesar. 'I have seen him there, but he wants for clean linen and his hair is much disarranged. Do your duty, sir, or he will beat you when he wakes! He is not so soft as I am.'

The black man looked down at her. 'She is broken,' he said gently. 'Take her away from this place.'

'Who's got a good hank of hemp?' someone shouted.

'Here!' Cain the rope-maker took down a new hank from the horn of his saddle.

In the stableyard, one of Tapp's men threw the rope over the bare branch of a chestnut tree and when he let it fall free, there was a noose at the end. At the foot of the cottage, in the skeletal garden, Tirzah rocked back and forth on her knees.

'Climb up, damn you!' cried someone. 'Bring him down!'

'No! That old roof won't bear us!'

Two muskets were primed, the bullets seated with a single smooth thrust of the rods.

'Wing him, but don't kill him! Be a waste of good rope!'

'Hold your fire, you bloody-minded fools, and let Caesar speak for himself!' shouted Oliver Kersey. 'For the love of God, have we not trouble enough?'

Hannah pushed her way through the crowd and looked up at the spot where Caesar balanced. 'What is your name, sir?' She spoke very loudly, so everyone in the place could hear her. But for a moment Caesar only stared, not comprehending.

'We have witnesses,' she insisted. 'Do you hear me? Tell them your name.'

The black man shook himself, dazed, beginning to understand her. When she and Clinch met at some bedside, he had observed Hannah's methods often enough to recognize them now. Whenever she asked unwed girls to name the fathers of their bastards at borning, it was just such a tone she always used.

What is your name, girl? Who is the father? Will you swear it on the health of your soul?

'My name be called Caesar Daylight, lady,' he said.

'Caesar Daylight, did you murder your master?'

'This is no court of law!' Siwall stepped into the yard from the doorway. 'Some – some innocent man may be injured! He may swear to anything, speak any slander, with no Testament before him and no clerk to record it! Mr Tapp, take that woman away from here at once!'

But the sheriff made no move. He leaned against a fence rail, a long-barreled dueling pistol in his hand. Up on the roof, Caesar's foot slipped a few inches, the half-rotted shingles crumbling beneath him and clattering to the ground.

'Quickly!' Hannah shouted again. 'Did you murder Dr Samuel Clinch?'

'Not I! I come upon him in the dark, lying dead by the path.'

'On the path? Not hidden in a thicket?'

'No, lady. On the path, he was then.'

'Do you swear on the health of your soul?'

'On my soul and my children's!'

'Have you any idea who killed him?'

Caesar looked around at the faces before him, then at Tirzah. For a moment he focused on Siwall. 'I don't know, lady,' he said softly. 'Only I did not kill any man. Not since the War.'

'Let him climb down, then, if he has done no murder, and face justice!' demanded Siwall. His red face was ashen and his hands were locked tight together to stop them from shaking. 'If he's nothing to fear, why run away from the law?'

One or two men among the militia laughed softly; it was an absurd contradiction. Innocence would not protect the black man, nor any other man, and all of them knew it. Caesar's eyes could see nothing but the noose and the chestnut tree. He looked down at Hannah and smiled then, the old smile at a secret joke.

'God Jesus, help him,' Tirzah moaned. 'God Jesus, lift him.'

For a moment he paused, as though he were memorizing the shape of his wife to take with him. His face turned up to catch the wind, and he took a deep breath of it.

'I will come down,' Caesar said.

His arms spread wide and he laughed, a deep laugh that seemed to come from the empty belly of the world and fill it up again with scorn. Then he jumped with both feet onto the wretched old sailcloth that covered the hole in the roof. It tore away under him and he crashed down, rotten timbers and broken shingles raining down around him.

'JEEEEEEEEEESUUUSSS!!' cried Tirzah, and the knife flashed in her hands. Before anyone could stop her, she had slashed one dark forearm, then the other.

Hannah sank down beside her, and Mrs Twig – though she had no great stomach for the sight of blood – came trotting over at double time to help.

Tapp plunged into the ruins, some of his men after him. 'Not dead, but his neck's broke!' one of them cried.

Then a gun was fired, a single shot from the sheriff's pistol. Above them in Great Meadow, a trumpet blew the retreat.

When Tapp's men emerged from the ruin of the house, they carried Black Caesar between them. His head hung crazily, at a sharp angle from his shoulders, and there was a small hole in his forehead where the sheriff's bullet had finished him, clean and precise.

There was no sign of young Jem; his horse was gone from the dooryard. But his father looked relieved, more like his usual blustering self.

'That settles it, eh?' he said to the sheriff. 'No greater admission of guilt than self-murder. The business is closed.'

'There are still questions—'

'I tell you, sir, the business is closed!'

Marcus Tapp's eyes were pale and cold. 'If that's what you want, I will say it,' he said in a monotone. 'But if any man here believes it, he's as big a damned fool as the black.'

He spat onto the ground at Siwall's feet and turned away,

pausing only to look down at Tirzah. She was unconscious now, and the women were struggling to bind up her slashed arms. 'Will she live to be questioned?' he said.

'The cuts are not deep. She is strong.' Hannah glanced up at him. 'You did Caesar a kindness, did you not? With your bullet. I should thank you for that.'

'A pox on your kindness,' the sheriff growled back at her, and stalked away out of the yard.

SEVENTEEN

Piecing the Evidence:

Inquiry into the Guilt of Caesar Daylight
Statement of Tirzah Daylight, known as
Black Tirzah
Lachlan McGregor, Constable
Peter Fellingham, Clerk

QUESTION: Lie still, there's no need to bestir yourself. Can you hear me, what I say?

TIRZAH: Where is my children gone? Where you take them children?

Q: Your sprouts are here at the inn, girl, down in Dolly's kitchen being petted blue by the maids. Lay you down, now, before you start in to bleed again! Fool thing to do, cutting yourself like that. What did you mean by it?

T: What a woman can't no way save, she must bleed for.

Q: The way of your folk, is it?

T: My mother's way. She was Indian slave, Cree, from Canada. What they do with my man now he be dead?

Q: He's buried decent, never fear me for that. Only not in the churchyard, mind.

T: They lay him in the cold ground? Ay-ahhhh! Ay-ahhhh!

Q: For the love of Christ, don't keen so!

163

T: How will his spirit live if his body is put in a box in the ground? You must dig him up and burn him!

Q: Christ. Not me!

T: Fire burn out the black from his skin and the slave-taste from his mouth! Fire make him free, so he find me again, and his children! You must do this!

Q: There's laws in these things, and I broke nigh a dozen just burying him on the quiet! You must answer my questions now, or worse than me may come asking instead.

T: I will not talk to that sheriff!

Q: Hunh! No fear of that. Mr Tapp's not much interested, it seems, in who killed Dr Clinch, and Siwall's closed up the whole business like a coverlid over a dunghill. But what's underneath it, that's what I want to know. Did Caesar go to the woods last night with his master?

T: Caesar must go. When Master be drunk, he goes lost, don't come home three days, maybe four. Only last night Master will not have Caesar close by.

Q: But Caesar was packing Clinch's musket, wasn't he? Surely—

T: Master says, stay back from me. Says he's sick of the sight of my Caesar. Stay by my horse, he says.

Q: Something he didn't want Caesar to see? Did he often try to hide things away like that?

T: Master has woman, Caesar knows it, he waits by the house gate. Master plays cards, Caesar must count up the losings.

Q: But last night he'd not have him about, eh? So, then, Clinch carried the musket himself to the hunt?

T: No, sir. He didn't have no gun, only torch to light him. Caesar keeps the gun.

Q: Was the drink on Clinch? Where was he going?

T: Drink is always on him some. Caesar waits by the horses in Bard's pasture till Master goes in amongst them trees by the brook. Then he follows. But after awhile, he can't see Master no more. He hears him once, call out 'Caesar, you black bastard, where are you?' And then no more.

Q: Did he hear no shot? No cries?

T: Many shots. Many lights. Many men crying out.

Q: What did Caesar do then? Did he stay in the woods?

T: It is snowing, but he walks a long time, looking. There is logs piled up and he crosses the river on them.

Q: All right. Go on.

T: Caesar comes out of the woods above Blackthorne Creek, and he still cannot find Master. He knows it is bad. The snow tells him, and the dark birds that wake too soon. So he goes back in them woods again, clear past Flynn's place. A big oak tree with roots coming out of the ground. A path. On the path is Master.

Q: Shot dead?

T: Yes, sir, Caesar knows they will say him a murderer. So he comes to get me, and I go away to the woods with him, and them children with us, and if I had not been a fool of a woman and pined for my hearthfire and what things I left lonesome beside it, my Caesar would be here living and not in a box in the ground. Ay-ahh. Ay-ahh. Ay-ahh.

Q: Hush, now. He will fight his way in that world as he did in this. But – when you went back to the woods with Caesar to hide, was the body still there? Did he show it you?

A: It is gone from the path. Caesar finds it close by there, in some trees, and he puts more leaves on top to hide it, so they don't find it before we be gone far away.

Q: Was the body— Ah, to hell with it, I can't put it in pretty posies. Had somebody tried to set him afire? Smeared his feet with tallow?

T: Caesar drags him. I do not look then, only gather the leaves for Caesar. I smell fire and tallow-grease, but there is the torch on the ground.

Q: Was it morning? Was it full light?

T: Dark when we leave here. Near morning when we get to them deep trees. Not so dark as the night-time, but not light.

Q: Did you not see a wagon? Nor hear a voice cry out?

T: No wagon. No voice. We go quick and hide in Berge's sugar shack. Then we come back here.

Q: All right. But I must ask you this, Tirzah. When you saw him lying dead there, did you never try to free the spirit of your Master by fire?

T: Oh, no sir. A stone will not burn and go free.

EIGHTEEN

Piecing the Evidence:

I, Hamilton Siwall, do give and depose that Dr Samuel Clinch did dine at my table on the night of 5 November and did ride to the hunt with me after, and with my friend, Master Royallton-Smith and my bailiff, Mr Inskip. And we took with us my servant, Ned Bottoms, and Dr Clinch's servant, Black Caesar, to see to our weapons and light us a way with torches. Dr Clinch did not remain with us, preferring to hunt in the deeper parts of the woods nearer to Chine Ridge, where he said the game was better come by. And he sent back his servant, Black Caesar, to stay with the horses, for he said the fellow was grown fierce of late and he did not trust him so far in the forest, with no other man by to observe what he did. And I was all that night with my two friends a-hunting deer, and we took six, and two of them fine, racked bucks. And when we came back to our horses we found Black Caesar gone, and Dr Clinch nowhere to be seen.

*

I, Robert Inskip, do say as how Dr Clinch was a trusting fool to keep that black devil by him, and it don't surprise me a tick that he done the man in. I did keep with my fellows, for I'm never at ease in them woods there. It's thick with thieves and Regulators, and many do blame me for turning their debts to the sheriff, though it be nobody's fault but their own if they want what they cannot pay for! But as to Black Caesar, I seen him turned back when he followed after his master, and told off to keep by the horses. And afterward I seen him on the path to Blackthorne Falls, though he did not see me, God be praised! and he held Clinch's musket still a-smoking there in his hands, and the eyes bugging out of his head with his guilt. And if that don't spell murder, I don't know what does!

I, Neddy Bottoms, do swear I know nothing of Clinch's doings at the hunt, nor of Caesar's. I carried a torch for Master Siwall and his friends all the night, and a bucket of tallow to freshen it, and when we come back to the horses, Caesar was no more waiting there as Clinch bid him when we took our leave.

Only I do say this. Clinch came drunk to the dinner and he left three good sheets to the wind, and I heard him say as how he was a rich man from this night forward, and others could lump it for all their high rank.

I was told off to speak ill of poor Caesar, and they give me a shilling to say he done murder. Well, now, I took their shilling, for I'm a poor chap like all the rest. But I shall say as I like. Caesar taught me to write my name and do sums, and I care not if I'm sacked for it, he would never kill no man that did not threaten his own life or his babes or his woman, and that's the God's truth!

NINETEEN

The Mooncalf's Revenge

Once her mother was out of sight on the path to the forest that morning, Jennet Trevor tried to forget her anger at grownups. She even determined to resist the great fascination of the many small cupboards in Dick Dancer's wagon, and set about doing her daily chores.

Of course, she had all the usual tasks of eight-year-old girl children – setting out the knives and spoons for meals; drying the everyday wooden plates once they were scoured with sand and teazels; and gathering eggs from the gaggle of nervous hens, who seemed calmed by her silence and yielded up their treasures with far less flapping than for anyone else. There was also her daily visit to Daniel at the Grange to learn sign-talk, and the simple weaving Hannah had been trying to teach her, and learning to spin yarn with the little drop-spindle, and quilting a scrap-muslin petticoat for her new cornhusk doll.

But such things were imposed upon her by the speaking world of grownups, and they were not the important matters of Jennet's life. Denied all but the most penetrating of sounds

– or those like her mother's voice, so often repeated that they seemed to grow from her own blood and bones – she guided herself by color and light and form. Denied verbal advice, she arrived at her own scale of relative values; denied speech, she expressed herself in action so independent it would have put George Washington to shame.

Pattern, the steady order of things, was of greatest importance, and each morning she kept to her own round of duties, invisible to everyone but herself. They gave her something solid to venture from – whenever and wherever she chose.

Soft friend wants following.

It was the first item of her daily agenda. Arthur the cat came winding round her skirts while she gathered the eggs every morning and away they would go, the one-eared tomcat marching ahead, his orange-striped tail like a banner curled over his back. The procession most often ended in some corner of the barn or the shelter of the lilac hedge, where the cat would slide down his mistress's foot and lie purring, all four feet in the air to present her his gift of the day. A dead rabbit, two or three unlucky mice, sometimes a squirrel or a mole or a possum – Arthur's nights always yielded some trophy.

Next, open the secret door and then close it.

Against the corner of the woodpile, Henry Markham and Daniel had built her a sort of playhouse, carefully piling up split logs at angles against the main stack until they made low roofless walls. The little girl had only to move one small log to enter. Once inside, she could pull it shut behind her and disappear.

Aside from an old rickety hobbyhorse and the new cornhusk doll, Jennet cared very little for toys. Instead, she would snap up some small worthless object and hoard it for a day or two – carrying it against her thigh in the embroidered pocket her mother had made her, feeling the shape and the weight of it, taking it out now and then to gauge the subtlest tint of its colors against those her mind heard with such clarity, rather than saw.

When Hannah undressed her at night, she would discover these odd things and reclaim them. But now that the playhouse was built, Jenny's pocket was only for transport. At the end of each day, she would empty it onto the ground at the farthest corner of the tiny log house, behind a wall of flat stones she had made.

An oriole's feather, and another from a mourning dove that had drowned in the rain barrel last summer. A fine silver snuffbox she had taken from Lady Sibylla's dressing table on one of her visits, for the way it reflected the light. Six long, sticky cones from the red pines that grew by the mill pond, for their sharp, clean scent – it came to her sometimes when the wind was northerly, and made her restless, like a cat after nightfall.

And last of all, seven buttons of various sizes – one pewter, two brass, and four red-and-blue painted clay.

'Jennet! Where are you, child?'

Jenny could not make the low buzzing of the servant girls into words, but Aunt Julia's voice reached her ears like a sharp crack of thunder. She looked up from her hoard, her small face turned up to the clouds.

'I'll go look in the playhouse,' offered Kitty and marched into the yard.

When she saw the third girl coming, Jennet opened her mouth in a silent giggle. *I will hide from Silly-boots and make her cry.*

Taking only the time to put Sibylla's snuffbox into her pocket, she slipped out of the playhouse and into the barn. Up the ladder she went, and into the hayloft. Jennet liked being high up, and the loft was almost as good as climbing the big ash tree by the house. From here, you could see everything, even the gardens of Mapleton Grange.

Man-friend, she thought, catching sight of Daniel there. He was climbing up onto Yeoman's back! Jennet shook with excitement.

Man-friend would come now, and lift her up onto his big horse, and hold her against him with his arm tight around her, and she would squirm and tickle him to feel the sound of his laughing that rang up and down in his chest.

But nothing was right today, nothing was as it had always been. Hannah had pushed her back, Sally had snatched Peter away from her. Now Silly-boots did not take her across for her lessons. And Daniel did not cross at the ford to come for her.

He rode towards the great trees instead, the same way her mother had gone. When you rode to the trees, it got dark and cold, and there were strange birds that did not come near to the village, and moose and porcupines and tiny shy shrews that peered out of the leaves underfoot.

Jennet loved the woods because there it did not seem to matter if she could not talk as other humans could, and sometimes she slipped away and went there, and only came back when she chose. Years before, when she was smaller, on an autumn afternoon of gusty north-east wind that made the red maple leaves blow in skittish crowds along the paths, she had caught the sharp scent of the white pines and run away by herself, deep into the Outward.

She had been happy enough for a while, but when it

began to grow dark she was hungry. She sat down all alone by a path and waited, and finally a thick man came walking. He picked her up in his arms and carried her to a house. It was not so big as Aunt Julia's, and there was a woman with very light hair in a braid down her back. Jennet had slept there, on a pallet of woven rag rugs by the fire. Next morning the man brought her as far back as the sheep meadow, but he would not come nearer than that.

When she got back, she had had to drink gallons of horrid catnip tea and have a bath in the shallow tub at the workroom hearth and her hair washed with lye soap and rubbed with rosemary leaves. They kissed her and fussed over her, but nothing seemed wrong with her, and Jennet could not tell them about the stranger who had found her and sheltered her, nor the woman who had rocked her as if she were still a baby – though she had been almost four!

Of the woman she had known in the woods, Jennet recalled only a brightness, the fine pale hair loose in the firelight. She hardly remembered the strange man either; she might have seen him a dozen times since and not known him. But when she closed her eyes she could feel how his hands had been hard and calloused across the palms and how the buttons of his waistcoat pushed into her shoulder when she rode in his arms.

One of these small pewter buttons she had pulled off and kept, her greatest treasure because it meant a part of her life no one knew about, not even Hannah. Her private universe, which she kept polished very bright.

Thinking of it now, she felt warmed by her secret, and she made two fists and crossed her arms over her chest. *Affection*, it meant, a sign Daniel had taught her. Whenever she made it, her father would pick her up and kiss her and hide his eyes against her neck.

She made that sign, too, his special sign. It meant *father*, but Jennet had no notion of fathers or mothers. Relationships were all equal, none dependent on others, none subservient. To her, the sign only meant *Daniel. The-man-who-loves.*

'Jenny! Jennet!' Aunt Julia was calling again.

'She's not in the playhouse,' cried Kitty, leaning over the half-high log walls. 'I'll look in the hay loft.'

'Never mind,' the old lady told her. 'She can't have gone far. Why, see there, that fool cat of hers is still in the yard! Come in now, and help with the breakfast. Mr Dancer must leave soon for the Muster, to set up his stall.'

Now Silly-boots will come to the loft, and I will go hide in the wash house, thought the child. But suddenly the game was over. Kitty went back into the house and closed the door.

No one sees me. They look through me and leave me and do not want me. I will teach them a lesson, these grownups. Arthur and I will go back to the woods and find my other friends and live there with them.

But first, I will have my revenge on that Pie-face, the one who has taken our pony away.

Her small chin in the air and her mouth pursed with determination, Jennet climbed down the ladder and made her way to Arthur's latest victim, a fine fat mouse with its head munched neatly off. She took it up by the tail and put it into her pocket with the silver snuffbox.

Then into the house she went, through the workroom and up the back stairs. In the kitchen beyond, where the others were still at their breakfast, Henry Markham heard the familiar clatter of her boots and the occasional stumble as she tripped on her half-undone bootlaces.

'There, Mother,' he said with a smile. 'There's our lamb back again, all over her sulk.'

Once upstairs, Jennet trotted along to the room that was Sally's and opened the big cedar-lined chest at the foot of the bed. She laid the prize mouse in the exact center of Pie-face's Sunday-best gown, closed the lid again, and put back the rag rug that had covered it.

That would fix her. Jennet's mouth opened wide in silent delight, and her shoulders shook with laughter. Then she went down the stairs again, the front stairs this time.

But somebody stood by the clock in the hall; it was Sally herself, come back again! How had she come? There was no pony in the yard, and she had not come into the kitchen with the others.

Jennet ducked into the parlor and peered out through the crack in the door, as Sally took a bright brass key and put it in a hole at the base of the clock. A little door opened. *A playhouse*, thought Jenny. *Open the door and close it.*

Sally lifted out a tin box and put something from it into her pocket, and then stowed the box away again and closed the little door. Walking on the points of her feet so her heels would not touch the floor, as though she were dancing, she went out the front door that none of the family ever used.

Nobody but Jennet knew Pie-face had been there. That was a secret for you! That was a prize almost as good as the pewter button!

Sally ran tiptoe down the path between the bare lilac bushes, and across to the wash house at the edge of the yard.

A slender man with a black coat had a horse tied there; he took something from her and kissed her. Then he lifted her up on the back of the horse and rode away with her, back towards the town.

Jennet was disappointed that Sally had not found the mouse yet; even revenge was not as sweet as it should be today. But the other secret pleased her almost as much, that she had seen what none of the grownups had.

Little Peter was toddling about the workroom in his standing-stool, and she paused on her way outside to feed him a bit of molasses on the tip of her finger. She spread a slice of warm cornbread with more of the sweet, sticky stuff and went out with it, pleased with herself and ready to enjoy a consoling reward.

But the peddler's wagon still stood in the yard, as tempting as the Tree of Good and Evil. Something about it had annoyed Jennet from its very arrival, nagging at her like a bothersome fly. Now she went to the cupboards and tried all the doors again, but she was no good at knots and she could not untie the latchstrings.

She made another sign, her left hand at a shallow angle over the right. *Hide*, it meant. *Hiding place*.

The two huge dray horses, Neptune and Mermaid, munched peaceably at their nosebags of oats, and Jennet circled around them, stroking their great flanks and murmuring softly to herself.

'Naahh. Naahh. Naahh.'

'Who's that?' a voice whispered hoarsely. 'Hannah?'

The deaf child did not really hear, but she caught the familiar shape of this last word. 'Annh-ahhh,' she said.

Arthur the cat leaped lightly up onto the wagon seat and began to pace back and forth, mewing his hunting call. In a moment he disappeared inside the wagon, and in another moment, Jennet had followed him.

It was dim under the canvas, but she could see a rope hammock strung from two poles set into the wagon-bed, a wicker trunk and another of hammered tin tied up with leather straps, a small table with a workbox and a tallow candle upon it, a rocking chair, and some rolls of bedding. Pots and pans, baskets, hanks of ribbon and lace, and strings of black licorice hung from the hoops that supported the canvas, and a tiny finch burbled and danced in a white-washed wicker cage.

There were more of the goods boxes, too, lining the walls like so many windowseats, and this time the little girl could not resist them. She tried one and then the other, till she found one unlatched. She knelt down before it and lifted the lid.

But before she could look inside, a pair of strong arms pushed her down onto the wagon-bed, and some great weight came on top of her. A hand stroked her hair kindly and warm breath touched the back of her neck.

'Jenny,' someone said, and she seemed to hear something of it, the hard slash of the J and the smashed sound of -ny. 'Little Jenny. Why, God Christ! She makes sounds!'

'I thought you said she was mute!'

'I didn't know, did I? Jesus, don't hurt her!'

'What shall we do?' Jennet heard their voices only as more buzzing, like a gnat that had flown in at her ear and could not get out again. 'We can't take her with us. God knows what may happen.'

'Let me take her into the house then. No one here will betray us.'

'No, you fool! What about Dancer? Peddlers will sell anything for half a crown, including us.'

'Devil take it! I guess you're right. The Cause comes first. Here, then, give me that quilt.'

Something dry and grey came down over Jennet. The light went away and the ground was gone, and still the weight pressed her down and down, flat on her belly, and would not let her move. She struggled and heaved, determined to find Arthur.

'Hellfire! She bit me!'

'Here! I've got her! Bring up that quilt, boy!'

Jennet was caught by the heels and she hung upside down for a moment, arms flailing and braids dragging the wagon-bed, a piece of flossy wool quilt batting over her mouth for a gag. Strangely, this circumstance quelled her fear rather than fed it.

I am straight and they are all upside-down! The very idea delighted her. If not for the gag, she would have laughed out loud.

She could see only the feet of her captors. The smaller one wore clogs with wooden soles and stiff cowhide tops, but the other had on a gentleman's black leather pumps, old and worn, but with long kidskin leggings to cover his stockings. Sherryvallies, they were called, and they laced up the sides like the tight bodices Hannah had worn until lately. Woman-friend did not wear them now, she had grown too fat and wore a loose short-gown instead of a bodice.

But the sight of the hooks and laces made Jenny want to cry again. She tried to open her mouth, but the batting prevented her. 'Aannnhhh!' she croaked. The sound went back down her throat and she swallowed it and began to cough.

'Take that rag away! She'll strangle!'

'If she makes another of those yelps, we'll *all* strangle!'

They wrapped her in the quilt and tied it close around her, leaving only enough open space at the top for her to breathe. Once this was done, a hand reached inside the cocoon and pulled out the gag and she sank her teeth once again into somebody's finger. Jennet tried to cry out again, but the quilt was too thick and the batting stuck out through the tears in the cover and muffled what sound she produced.

Someone picked her up and carried her; they put her in a small space where it was colder than inside the wagon. But she lay on something very soft, like a bed.

A crack, she thought. *I must find where the daylight has gone*. She struggled and squirmed, trying to see out. But it was no use. She began to cry silently, her mouth drooling onto the dusty old quilt she was wrapped in, her small body shaking.

Then the wagon started to move. She could feel it rocking from side to side, jarring as it struck rocks or bounced over ruts. It went on for a long time, Jennet did not know how long. The bouncing threw her back and forth against the sides of her box, but the layers of old quilt protected her.

When the moving stopped, she had ended her crying. What use was it, anyway? It only made her head ache and her nose feel thick and sore. The old quilt tasted of salt from her tears, and of molasses. The one who had caught her had accidentally wrapped up the piece of cornbread she had been carrying, sweet and sticky and smashed against her gown. She felt for it now, bending her head down and licking it up with her quick, sudden tongue, the way a bird pecks at an apple.

They are silly and faithless, she thought as the wagon

carried her farther and farther from Two Mills. *Man-friend. Woman-friend. Soft-friend. All gone.*

But I am what I am.

I do not trust anyone. I will go where I must go. I will have no more friends in this world.

TWENTY

Piecing the Evidence:

RESULTS OF THE DISSECTION PERFORMED UPON THE
BODY OF MRS ESTHER ELIZABETH JORY,
NEE WHITBY, 6 NOVEMBER 1786
RUFFORD TOWNSHIP, MAINE, UPPER
MASSACHUSETTS

The age of the lady being very great, the lights, or lungs, were found to be much congested with phlegm and the heart somewhat enlarged. The veins were narrowed and brittle, and the brain showed the signs of much recent damage, as from seizure or stroke. Upon the legs, arms and breast were many deep burns from a fall upon the hearthfire, not yet healed but insufficient to be the single cause of death. Once removed, the poultices upon them were found to be of simples, as comfrey, plantain, and coltsfoot, all known to be sovereign for burns.

We opine that deceased did expire of a failure of blood to the brain, due to great age and infirmity. Laudanum tincture was given by the late Dr Clinch to ease pain, and the burns were poulticed by the Midwife, according to the homely level of her skill. There is no harm to either such treatment, nor might their combining have caused the deceased any harm.

To this we do give and subscribe as true.
     —*Cyrus Kent, Acting Coroner and Surgeon*
      Lachlan McGregor, Constable
       Hannah Trevor, Witness

TWENTY-ONE

Lost and Found

'Well, at least you are free of the charge of mispractice,' sighed Aunt Julia. 'Thank Heaven for small blessings! But how is poor Tirzah?'

'As you might think. Very ill, but not from the cuts. They will heal soon enough.' Hannah stopped in the mudroom to take off her cloak, then came into the workroom.

'God send she doesn't run mad, like poor Polly Anson.' Julia shook her head sadly. 'And Caesar's children? What has become of them?'

'Dolly will keep them all at the inn, for I told McGregor he must not bring them to Sarah. She is too near her time.'

'It's a bothersome business, this manning-and-womaning,' came a voice from the settle. 'I would not do it for a mine of gold!'

Jemima Dancer had not gone with the wagon to Great Meadow. She would have nothing to do with the crying of merchandise or the taking of money. When she was forced to handle a coin, she threw it down on the counterboard as though it burnt her fingers.

Just now, she was busying herself with a basket of quilt pieces, snipping them up into careful triangles and squares for the wedding quilt, Bridges Burning. In the frame was another, of blue and white hexagons. China Dish, it was called, and Hannah sat down to it gratefully and took up her needle, stealing a few precious moments of calm.

'You will change your mind, Jemima,' she said with a smile, 'when you come upon someone to love you.'

'Love me? Pah! What do I care for love? I have my silly old child,' she murmured. 'He's a great nuisance, and sometimes I must punish him sore and threaten to lock him away. But he's a sharp old child, for all that. He can see in the dark, better than ever poor Dick can.'

'You must not call your father by his Christian name, child!' Julia's gooseberry eyes were shocked. 'It's not seemly.'

'I had a mother once, but she's long dead. I had a sister, I think, but they squandered her. I have no father that I remember. And if I *had* one, I wouldn't tell who!'

Jemima's mouth snapped shut with a click of small, sharp teeth. Hannah and Julia changed looks and the old lady shook her head sadly.

'You're sure the Court has no mind to quibble with your practice, Hannah? I saw Lady Jory myself not a week since, and I will testify if need be,' offered Julia, gratefully changing the subject.

The midwife put on her spectacles and began to run a row of tiny stitches a spare quarter inch from the edge of a patch. 'It was a foolish business from the start. The whole village knew Esther Jory would not last the year out. What puzzles me is why Siwall even bothered to issue the charge, let alone send his sheriff with such an empty threat.'

'Clinch has made ignorant charges before, you said so yourself.'

'Siwall always *issued* the charges, but once he heard my defense, he took them no further. Why press so hard now, when the court is overburdened and the magistrates fear for their lives?'

'Perhaps he did it to protect Clinch's reputation in the town.'

It was true that Cyrus Kent had not found the heavy dose of laudanum in any way at fault for the old lady's death. In absolving Hannah, he had also absolved Dr Clinch.

'But why?' Hannah pondered aloud. 'Why should Siwall care so much for Sam Clinch's good name? What reputation *had* he?'

No, her mind answered. *All the reputation is Siwall's. What he did, he did for some hold Clinch has had upon him.*

'Plaguing and nattering,' muttered Jemima. 'Nipping and snapping! A man is more worrisome than a sore tooth, and harder to be rid of!'

The mudroom door opened again, and Sally came in. Her eyes were very bright and her cheeks flushed. 'It's raining,' she said, and went to the fire to warm herself for a moment.

Julia glanced at her. 'You could have been twice and back to the town in the time it has taken you. Come, help me to break all these eggs for the Training Cake.' Eggs were very small at this time of year, not so big as a robin's egg; it took three to make up the volume of one, and breaking thirty eggs was a slow, finicking job.

'I must go up and change my gown, Mother Markham. I wet my gown crossing the river,' Sally told her.

'On the ferry?'

Julia looked up and frowned at her. The girl had never forded a river on horseback in her life, except when she rode pillion with Jonathan. Sally laughed and tossed a stick onto the fire.

'It was— The – the rain wet my skirt,' she said, 'and I shall take cold unless I change. Hannah may break up the eggs; she has nothing to do.'

Sally went lightly up the back stairs and Julia drew a deep breath, her nostrils flaring. 'A few sprinkles, and she calls it a rain!'

Hannah made no comment, only laid down her needle and set to work with the eggs. But her aunt drew near and put an arm round her shoulders.

'About the household keys, my dear,' Julia said in a low voice, half-ashamed. 'I would not have taken them from you for the world, except—'

'Never mind, Aunt.' Hannah planted a kiss on the old woman's forehead. 'I shouldn't want them much longer in any case.'

But why does Sally want them so much, she thought, *and so suddenly, when she cannot be bothered with anything else about the house?*

Why, why, why. Could she never stop asking it? That one word was what kept her from Daniel, kept her from probing his motives and doubting her future. If he had *ridden* to the woods, if he had lied to McGregor—

'Well,' Julia said, 'at the least, there's no way they may tangle you in Clinch's death. You were home before six last evening, and in your bed with our sweet lamb beside you by half-past eight. I saw you there myself, when I came in to put out that rascally cat.'

Henry Markham sat in his favorite old bent-willow

rocker among the clutter of washboilers and candlemolds, with little Peter playing at his feet. Above them, the bunches of drying flax and the strings of dried pumpkin and apples and pears swayed gently, as the smoke of the old man's clay pipe curled up with the draught.

'Our Sally can speak for you, too, that you did not steal out after,' he said. 'She stays up all hours, that one, working them mazes she dotes on.'

It was true that Sally had still been bent over a candle at the kitchen table, all her concentration focused upon one of the silly paper puzzles they sold for a penny at Hobart's. Every two or three days she went off to the village and came back with some such fiddle, instead of minding her son as she ought to, and saving her pence.

''Tis a strange business,' Uncle Henry went on. 'Clinch was a pompous old pisspot that nobody liked and everybody needed, one time or another. But you don't go about taking aim at a pisspot and blowing it to kingdom-come, do you? And as for this burning—' He took a deep pull on his pipe. 'What's Dan make of it all?'

'I fear for him, Uncle.' Hannah lost a piece of shell into the eggs she was breaking and began to fish for it. 'They've said nothing yet, and Siwall shuts up the whole business too quickly. But Tapp is not satisfied Caesar murdered his master, and Daniel grudged Clinch with reason.'

'Now, girl. Half the village grudges Clinch with reason.'

'But Daniel was there last night, at the hunt, and there's no one to say he was with them when Clinch was shot, not even Josh.'

'Why, I will say so!' cried Jemima.

She stood up too quickly and the pile of cut quilt pieces fell in an avalanche of brown and crimson and green onto the sanded floor. Then suddenly she grew very still, like Lot's wife on the cupboard marked *Salt*. Her eyes were wide and moist and very blue, bottomless as some parts of the ocean were said to be, where ships fell away and were lost.

'He is a kind heart,' she whispered, 'and a healer and binder. They will pound him to pieces and sell him for grist.'

Hannah was almost afraid to move nearer. '*Did* you see Daniel last night? How come you to know him, Jemima?'

Twig saw to all the peddlers who came to the Grange, and when Charlotte was living, they had been turned curtly away.

'What need have I to know him at all?' the peddler's daughter replied. 'I shall *say* he was there, and that's that!'

'You would not lie to the Court, my dear?' asked Julia, aghast.

The strange tears had begun to stream down Jemima's face now. They seemed to have no effect and proceed from no cause, like rain from a clear sky that makes nobody wet. She did not sniffle nor sob, and betrayed no emotion aside from the usual irritation that made her small boots crunch the sand on the floor and kick the spilt quilt pieces about.

'What I know I know,' she said. 'And what I say when I'm troubled and haggled by stubborn old babies and sheriffs is no lying at all, to be sure!'

She sat down again with a thud on the bench and took up her scissors. Untying the strings of her cap, she held them out before her, snipped them off even, and then tied them up again, with even more knots than before.

Hannah was robbed of the chance to ask any more questions. There was a sudden gust of cold air from the mudroom, and young Ethan, the choreboy, burst into the room, with the two hired girls close behind him.

'I ran down to the mill,' he gasped, 'and she's not there, and Susan's been all through the attic and Kitty's just come from the loft, and there's no sign of her! No place! And I run halfway to Cove Bridge on the high road, and there's no sight of anyone, upstream nor down!'

'Calm down, lad,' ordered Henry. 'Get your breath and then say what you're babbling about.'

'Why, the moonca—!' Ethan gulped, catching his blunder. 'Jennet, I mean! She's been all morning sulking and so we left her to herself in that playhouse of hers, and now she's gone off! There's nothing but a pile of old buttons and trash.'

'But she came in while we sat at our meal, before Mr Dancer and his father left for Great Meadow!' Julia insisted. 'I heard her myself. Look there, Arthur's curled up by the fire. She must surely be somewhere about.'

'Oh no, ma'am, we've looked everywhere!' Kitty wailed. 'Jennet's run away to the woods again, the poor little mite!'

On Great Meadow, they had set out long tables for the men near the arsenal. The officers would dine at Lamb's Inn itself, but the common soldiers ate here at Daniel's expense, and the meal was always the best Josh's capable wife could provide.

Hannah's cousin Dolly had worked for the better part of a fortnight and recruited a dozen young girls from the town to assist her. They were joined by some of the wives who had come in from the farms with their husbands. Oliver Kersey's Leah was there, her sweet face placid and gentle as always, and Mrs Bridge and Hattie Bunce and Mrs Whittemore, and Simon Penny's pregnant wife, Susannah, and Ethan Berge's sister, Nabby, and his mother, Louisa, and little Mercy Lewis from Burnt Hill and Thankful Warren from the Grange, all rushing back and forth from the cook tent and the half-dozen open fires.

Now and then the girls' eyes would light on some particular face and their cheeks, already pink from the cook fires, would turn a shade pinker, and the dishes they carried would tremble a bit, as they helped to lay out the huge platters of corned beef, chicken and dumplings, and boiled pork and mutton, and the great steaming bowls of turnips, carrots, cabbage, and red beets. There were plates of hot biscuits, too, and cornbread and stacks of sliced barley bread, freshly baked in the ovens at Lamb's Inn that morning, and mounds of fresh-churned butter stamped on the tops with a wheatsheaf, and bowls of applesauce and ripe pears and pickled eggs and onions and cucumber relish, and great stacks of gingerbread, rich with currants and spices, made a week since and properly aged in Dolly's stillroom, then cut in squares and stacked up one on the other till they rose in a sweet fragrant tower at the center of each table. There *had* to be gingerbread, or the old saying would be proven a liar: *I pledged my love with gingerbread, / And after Muster I was wed.*

'It's a feast for a king, my love,' said Josh, squeezing his wife's arm as she passed him. 'Not a woman but you from here to Boston could manage all this and look fresh as a new apple tart.'

'Tart, am I?' Dolly laughed and shoved a piece of the gingerbread into his mouth.

McGregor had been given leave from the Muster to go about his constable's duties in the matter of Dr Clinch, but Daniel had gathered the rest of his officers and their sergeants, mounted and in good order, at the end of the tables in plain sight of the men.

Sergeant Kersey gave a signal and the drummer boy rattled his snare. Men rushed for the tables, took their places in order of rank, and stood at attention.

Daniel took off his tricorne. 'God sweeten this food to our use and this day's labor to our peace and protection.'

'Amen,' they all mumbled.

'And thank the Lord for a short-winded preacher!' cried someone.

'Three cheers for Mistress Lamb and her ladies, and the fine dinner they've brought!'

The hurrahs went up and died away to a clatter of plates and mugs and carving knives. Nabby and Mercy began to go round the tables pouring out the traditional stoup of rum for each man, and at the end of the table a fiddler, a Bridgewater man, set bow to string, and Blind Patrick took up his penny-whistle. 'Winds of Morning', they struck up, and after a verse or two, a fine, deep, bass voice began to sing along.

'What though your cannon raze our towns / And tumble down our houses . . .'

Others joined in, beating time with fists and tin mugs.

'We'll fight like devils, blood and bones, / For children and for spouses!'

The chorus was almost a roar now, every man joining in, and most of the women, too. It was an old marching tune from the War, and Daniel began to sing with them on the chorus, his clear baritone rising to catch the higher notes.

'Blow ye winds of morning, blow ye winds high-ho / Blow ye winds of morning, and blow, boys, blow!'

They gave a cheer and a round of applause. Thinking

the song at an end, the men pitched into their food. But the same deep voice began another verse, this time with words they had not heard before.

> For freedom we may fight and die,
> But money fears no gun, sirs.
> A rich man rides and owns our hides,
> And makes a poor man run, sirs.

This time there was no chorus. Nobody spoke and few even swallowed. A commotion began at the end of the table. Someone was handing along branches of white pine, and many cut off sprigs with their jack knives and stuck them into their hatbands.

'Mr English.' Daniel spoke softly. 'Are your guards posted at the bounds?'

'They are, sir.'

'Double them, John. Quietly. Don't make a fuss. And pick men you can trust.'

John English turned his horse for the edge of the field where the sentry posts lay.

'That was a fine song, to be sure.' Daniel urged Yeoman closer to the table. 'But who is the singer?'

A surly boy of seventeen or eighteen slipped his arm through that of dark-eyed Nabby Berge. He was broad-shouldered and heavy-armed – a farmer's son, to judge by his leather-topped wooden clogs. His hair was lank and brown and fell over his forehead, and his eyes were cold and grey and sullen.

'Climb down off that gelding, Major,' he demanded, 'and then ask us again whose song it was.'

'Aye. Stephen's right, by Harry!' somebody shouted. 'Let him climb down and stand level with us, man to man!'

The angry boy was Stephen Anson, eldest son of the man Siwall had shot in the summer. *George Anson, the martyr of Rufford* – that's what they were calling his father all up and down the river these days. Stephen had joined the Regulators soon after, and he seldom ventured out of the woods now for fear of arrest.

The cries rose thicker and angrier.

'Let his fucking lordship get off his fine horse!'

'Aye! Rich men rides and owns our hides!'

'Damns our hides, you mean!'

'Stand down, Major, if you're one of us! Stand down off that horse!'

Josh Lamb – Captain Lamb, now, every inch of him – dug his heels into the sides of his own brown mare and rode up to stand even with Yeoman. 'They've been brawling all morning,' he murmured, 'and this news about Clinch and Black Caesar has them nerved. There's no telling which direction they'll go.'

But Daniel stood down, stroking Yeoman's nose and patting his neck to quiet his jitters. A hush fell over the men. One or two nodded, satisfied he was with them – or at least too afraid of their numbers to say so.

'My friends,' Daniel said, 'I'm the same sorry fellow on foot or on horseback. But I'm not afraid to make a fool of myself with a bit of a song, either. Your fiddle once more, sir, if you please.'

The fiddler struck up and Daniel Josselyn stood to attention, very straight, his hands clasped behind his back and well away from his weapons. His voice was clear and strong,

the words so steady you might never have known he was
making them up as he went.

> *For freedom still you'd fight and kill,*
> *And nobly spend your lives, sirs.*
> *But once you're dead, who'll buy the bread,*
> *For children and for wives, sir?*

He stopped singing. For a moment it was very still on
the meadow.

'Dan's about got the right of it, I reckon,' somebody
muttered.

'Aye. Overhasty falls headfirst in the midden!' cried
another, and they broke into half-hearted laughter.

Some noise erupted at the bounds, the sentry shouting
and a woman's voice answering back. In the Indian camp,
the dogs set up a yelping and in a moment an oxcart came
rumbling over the hill, with John English riding beside it.

Daniel caught a glimpse of Hannah's red cloak and was
pleased. So, then, she had come here to find him and not
waited till after dress parade.

'Your meal's getting cold, now,' he told the men with a
laugh. 'No woman likes to see food go to waste. Fall to, or
she'll take it out on you later, you mark my words!'

The tension was ended. Blind Patrick the fife-player
struck up 'London Lancers'. One or two latecomers began to
fill their plates and the girls resumed their serving of rum, as
Dolly came out of the cook tent with another plateful of
biscuits.

'I'll have one of those while they're hot,' said a man's
voice beside her. 'Long time since I've tasted those butter
biscuits of yours, sister.'

The plate crashed to the ground and Dolly turned on him, staring.

'Oh my sweet Johnnie!' she cried, and threw her arms round her youngest brother's neck and wept.

TWENTY-TWO

Wildheart

Jonathan Markham was dressed in a gentleman's black coat, the sleeves somewhat too long for him, and buff breeches that bagged down over his knees. On his feet were a pair of fine black leather slippers, with sherryvallies laced over his stockings almost to the knee. His black hair was neatly combed and tied with a ribbon, and he wore spectacles and a sober black tricorne with a cockade of blue.

But aside from his voice, even his fond sister would scarcely have known him. He was very thin, his high cheekbones so sharp it seemed they must poke through the pale skin. At odd moments, when he should have been heedful, his black eyes stared straight ahead and did not focus, still betraying a trace of jail-fever.

His mouth had been smashed with Tapp's rifle butt and it dragged sharply downward at the corner so that he could not open it properly, and when he spoke you could see the jagged stumps of five front teeth. There was a scar on his temple, too, a deep gouge that had healed well enough but left an inch-wide brownish-red track from his ear to the hinge of his jaw.

'You're so thin, my love,' Dolly whispered, and wept softly against his shoulder. 'Oh, I'm glad you've come home.'

At the tables, the long lines of men said nothing that might be heard or repeated. Some stared at their plates. A handful quietly withdrew and came to stand beside Jonathan. But most watched, moist-eyed and sorry, thinking it might as well have been a brother or a son of theirs.

Again the branches of white pine came round, and more men took sprigs for their hatbands, or laid them next to their plates, undecided as yet where they stood. Simon Penny, whose brother Rufus had been condemned with Jonathan and had been broken out only to die of the fever, came over to shake young Markham's hand and embrace him.

At the top of the hill, Daniel could just see Henry's oxcart, with the old fellow driving and Hannah beside him, as it followed John English to the huddle of peddlers' stalls and creaked to a halt. Had they heard some warning of Jonathan's arrival? Surely not, or they would have come straight here to the mess tents instead.

'Damn fool boy,' muttered Josh Lamb, scowling fiercely. 'Does he mean to get himself hanged?'

'He's been here all the morning,' said Oliver Kersey, the taciturn sergeant. 'Or at least the last hour or so. I spotted him with the Bridgewater Regulars and again with the Snaresbrook lot. Took him for some bailiff or other, in those fancy clothes.'

'Why the hell stand out in the open now, when there's officers about?' Josh rubbed his hand across his eyes.

'Militia officers aren't sheriffs,' said Kersey.

'I shall have to arrest him.' Daniel's voice was grim. 'He's left me no choice.'

'Arrest? But they won't have it, man! Look at them, they've made a hero of him! And besides—'

Daniel knew what Josh had left unsaid. *Besides, Hannah will never forgive you. If you take him, your future is gone.* But he could not do otherwise than risk it.

'There are near seven hundred people on this field, Josh,' he said, 'counting the women. If I don't place him under military arrest, Tapp will come up here and take him soon enough, or try to. We'll have a real battleground instead of a toy one, and wives and children in the middle of it. I must have time to get as many of them clear of this field as I can.'

'And if they take him after?' Josh looked down at his boots.

Josselyn's face was set in deep lines of worry. 'I will do what I can,' he said.

There was shouting from the civilians' camp, and the sound of women's voices, shrill and upset. 'Mr Kersey, ride up and see to that rumpus,' Daniel told him. 'Mrs Trevor's up there, and the miller is with her, I think. Tell them the boy is here. Quick as you can.'

The thick-shouldered sergeant paused only to glance round for his own young wife. 'I'll keep an eye on your lady,' said Daniel gently, 'if you will keep an eye on mine.' As usual, Kersey said nothing in reply, he narrowed his eyes in a frown and saluted, slapped the flank of his horse, and rode away up the hill.

'We must have a vote, friends!' Johnnie was saying. Somebody had cleared a place for him and he stood on the table where everyone could see his face and the damage the sheriff had done him. 'There are enough men here for a fair vote of the county, if we call a convention! Will you fight for the government, right or wrong? Or will you march with me tomorrow to close down the Debtors' Court?'

'By God, it'd tickle me pink to see old Siwall tarred and feathered,' said one burly man with a missing ear.

There was a roar of laughter at this, but Nate Berge, Ethan's father, didn't join in it. He was a sober, well-respected man with a good farm and no debts that anyone knew of. But his daughter had been promised to young Stephen Anson since Christmas, and Polly, Stephen's mad mother, was kept locked in an old cowhouse at the edge of Berges' woods.

'I've two brothers in the Debtors' Jail down at Wybrow,' Nate said. 'So I took my old dory and rowed down to see they wasn't ailing. But the jailer's bitch of a wife, she wouldn't let me in. No more visitors for debtors, she says. By the governor's order.'

He stared at the sprig of white pine on the table before him, then looked up at his wife and his daughter.

'And I'm wondering now what more they will take by the governor's order. They have taxed my land and my beasts and the glass in my windows. I am expected to pay in hard coin though no man has hard coin to pay *me*, and when Siwall's wife rides past in her carriage, she puts a kerchief to her nose like I was a cow-pat to be drove over, because I sweat for a living as her man does not.'

Slowly, with great deliberation, Nathan Berge put the pine in his hatband and emptied his tin mug of rum.

'I don't hold with more killing,' he said. 'But if we don't stand for ourselves and our place on the earth, no one else will stand for us. Lock out the judges as peaceful as we can, I say, till the General Court sees sense.'

'Nate's right! We done it in the War, and we can do it again!'

There was a cheer and a burst of applause. When it had died away, Ralph Bunce got up to speak – a moderate little man, a church deacon. 'Suppose I should join you,' he said. 'Who would lead us?'

'Why, Johnnie Markham!' someone shouted, and a cheer went up.

'Down with the judges and sheriffs! The Regulators and freedom!'

'The Cause! The Cause!' they cried.

Through all this, Daniel had remained silent, but Josh Lamb could not hold his tongue any longer. 'You mad Yankee fools!' he shouted. 'You'll face governor's troops, and that means artillery, cannon, maybe cavalry. Can you dig a redoubt or throw up a breastwork? Do you know how to place a howitzer so the loose shot won't fall short and be wasted? Johnnie Markham don't, that I can say for a fact!'

Jonathan jumped down from his tabletop platform and walked to where Daniel was standing. 'He's right, Dan. I am not fit to lead them. None here has the skill for it, only you. Will you help us, in the name of the Cause?'

'Josselyn shall lead us!' someone cried.

There were more shouts, pro and con. Then they died away into a tense, expectant silence, waiting his answer.

'I am a retired officer of the Continental Army,' Daniel told them. 'I am commissioned to lead this militia in war and to train it in peace. Nothing more. And nothing less.'

He spoke very slowly and very clearly, so that even the women who huddled together in the cook tent heard every letter of every word he said.

'I believe many here have been hard-used,' Josselyn

continued. 'But until I am removed from this post by Colonel Scribner, or tender my resignation in writing to Fort Hendly at Salcombe, my only choice is to defend the court and its judges and to support the law of the land. It is my word, and if I had given it to you instead of the government, I should keep it just as true. Captain Lamb!'

'Sir!'

'Mr Markham is a wanted felon. Escort him to the officers' tent and post your guards.'

A sound moved along the tables from man to man, a hollow roar like north wind down a chimney flue. 'Betrayed!' someone cried.

'You bastard,' hissed Johnnie. 'You promised to help me.'

'Damn your eyes, I did help you, and this is how you repay me!' Daniel spoke through clenched teeth now, his voice audible only to Jonathan. 'You used me to come here and trump up your war, but you won't use me twice!'

Young Anson lunged at him, but Daniel caught the boy like a sack of meal and threw him back onto the tabletop, sprawling across the gingerbread tray.

'He can't arrest us all!' Stephen screeched. 'He's one of *them*, a rich bastard like Siwall! He cares nothing for the Cause. Burn them, I say! Burn them all down!'

Stephen Anson was furious, his eyes mad and his hand on one of the carving knives they had left in the mutton. He made war on shame and scorn and loss, and saw them even where they were not. It was a disease in him now, and his son and his son's sons would inherit it.

'Listen to me,' Daniel said. He stood very still at the end of the table, his palms flat on the wood, his voice perfectly steady. 'All of you, listen. If I don't arrest Jonathan Markham, the sheriff will. There's a prison and two hundred lashes waiting for any that helps him. Which of you wants them? You, Bunce? Or you, Corporal Berge?'

Nobody answered. He looked from one of his men to the other, eyes raking the long table.

'Once they get their hands on him,' Daniel went on, 'how long do you think they will wait to prove sentence? There's a rope on the gibbet down there in the common, and a wicket waiting to lock up his bones when they've done. He's safe under guard here. So long as Muster lasts, Tapp can't interfere with it. That is the law.'

'We'll fight off the sheriff, then!' cried Phineas Rugg. 'They won't take him, by God!'

'But they may take one or two of you, and kill some of your women. And what will you use for shot and powder?'

'Why, there's powder aplenty in the arsenal there, and cannon, too!'

'That'd fix 'em! Turn the howitzer on 'em!'

Daniel's eyes closed for an instant, then opened. 'If you break open that arsenal, it's high treason. General Washington has no sympathy with your cause. He will send Continental Regulars against you. Where will you winter? Who will provision you? What will you wear on your feet once those boot soles rot through from the snow? It's colder here than it is in Pennsylvania. You were at Valley Forge, weren't you, Whittemore? And you, Stinson?'

'It's true,' said Thomas Whittemore. He was a debtor, a jailmate of Johnnie's, and the fever had left him silent and pale and remote. No one had heard him speak a word since he came home, not until this moment.

'I read it in the Boston papers at Lamb's,' he went on, 'how George Washington says we are villains and the enemies of freedom. Only I've got me a cousin in Virginia, and he says General Washington owes taxes himself and cannot pay all, and Tom Jefferson, too, for he spends like a king these days over in France. But there's no taxman comes and drags *them* off to die in the straw of some prison, for though all men be equal, there's some that's more equal than others. And I am not one of them. I am not one. I am—'

Tears streamed down poor Whittemore's cheeks and his wife, Bess, came to stand by him, shamefaced and quiet. 'Hush now, Tom, my love,' she said. 'Let us go home in peace.'

Nathan Berge walked over to Daniel. 'What you say makes sense, sir. We all know that. But you see we are pushed long past sense.'

'Josselyn must lead us!' cried one of the Bridgewater men. 'Up the Regulators!'

'The Cause!'

Somebody began to bang the table with his tin plate and the others took up the cry, till it crashed on Daniel's ears like the ring of McGregor's hammer on the anvil at the Forge. 'Josselyn! Josselyn and freedom!'

They had believed the dream of liberty all these years, lived on it, kept themselves alive by its fraudulent glimmer, and even now they could not quite accept that it had never been meant to apply to them. The poor, the plain, the inelegant – it was not for them that flags were waved and grand words uttered. They were mooncalves, to be locked in their cages of toil.

And Daniel, too, was a prisoner. He stared down at himself in the ridiculous uniform. A few pewter buttons, a cocked hat. A pair of stockings that drooped at the back, and the world slipped away, hope slipped away. And Hannah with it, perhaps.

All these years I have dreamed her, he thought. *I have dreamed, and am dead.*

'Will you lead us, Dan?' Joshua stood at his elbow.

'You as well, my friend?' He had not expected it from Josh.

The innkeeper wiped his eyes with the back of his hand. 'They are my friends, Daniel.'

And I am not. Josselyn didn't say it, but he knew the truth of it. All those years of war when he had fought at their sides, and after, as he cleared brush with them, ploughed with them, mowed the fields with them in summer – it was all nothing now. In spite of it all, he was still an Englishman, a lord's son, a rich man, an officer, an alien.

But Daniel did not refuse them, not yet. They were in no mood to be gainsaid. 'Take your vote properly,' he told them, 'and then come and tell me. I shall think on the matter tonight, and tomorrow at final assembly I will give you my decision.'

Josh drew up and saluted. "Tention!' he shouted, and one by one, the men at the long tables obeyed.

But Daniel was not finished with Johnnie. 'Dr Samuel Clinch was found this morning,' he said, 'shot dead in the woods, from ambush as it seemed. Did you kill him?'

Jonathan gulped. 'I – thought he was killed by Black Caesar. What reason would I have to—'

'He might have happened upon you. Recognized you.'

'I didn't kill him, Daniel. I swear on my heart's blood.'

'As you swore you would go to your father today, and not come into the town?'

'I didn't kill Clinch! I never killed a man in all my life! Get me a Bible, I will swear it!'

'Was it Regulators?'

'How the devil should I know?'

'They're your friends. You speak for them.'

'My friends are farmers and tradesmen, they don't hide in the bushes and cut down old men. We want justice, that's all—'

'Save your sermons. Did you hear nothing last night after I left you?' Daniel's gaze did not flicker.

'In the night I heard nothing.' Jonathan looked away.

'And this morning, just before daybreak? When you were hid in the peddler's wagon? What did you hear and see then?'

The boy bit his lip, troubled. 'After we'd pulled away from Drewel's, I was stuffed into a basket trunk, and Stephen in a goods cupboard. But I heard a shrill cry.'

'Man's? Woman's?'

'A woman's. A single cry, like something tearing to pieces. I took it for that mad daughter of Dick Dancer's, she's as wild as a marmot. In and out of the wagon every quarter hour, and talking to herself all the time. There was the cry, and then I felt the wagon lurch when she jumped down.'

'And you did not venture out to see what the trouble was?'

'How could I? The old man was there in the wagon, knitting away. He'd quenched the candle when the cry came, but I could still hear his needles clatter, and that counting he does as he works.'

'He did not climb down himself?'

'Maybe. I didn't see, did I? And he's light as a feather, you'd feel nothing. Once the candle was out and the mad girl gone, he gave a shout. Then the wagon pulled up for a time, that's all I know.'

'What did he say? Any word you made sense of?'

'It sounded like "sheep". If that makes any sense to you.'

'Sheep?' Daniel played with the word in his mind, but it made no sense to him.

'Aye,' Johnnie said. 'Sheep. And then he began to mumble.'

'That's all you know of it?'

'Only that Dancer jumped down and went crying in the woods for his daughter. I heard him call to her. Then in a while she came back in the wagon again, and I heard the old chap praying over the broken in spirit, and her bawling. She weeps like a fountain, that one. When she's not throwing things.' Jonathan looked up at Daniel. 'I didn't kill Clinch, Dan. If that's why you took me, you must let me go!'

Daniel studied the young man's face for a moment, then turned away. 'Take Mr Markham to my tent, Captain,' he said again, 'and post your guards. Good ones. And give him some food. He looks as if he could use it.'

'And if the sheriff comes for me while you're all away prancing and marching?' Jonathan's dark eyes scanned the field, still angry.

'So long as I remain in command here and you do not leave the bounds,' Daniel assured him, 'Mr Tapp has no authority to take you, and I think he is not fool enough to attempt it. If I am wrong, our sentries will resist him.'

He turned back to his soldiers. 'Gentlemen, the review parade,' he said. 'We are already behind-hand. Our sweethearts are waiting to see us swagger and strut. I trust you would not disappoint them?'

'*Fall in!*' ordered Josh, and the fife struck up. 'Yankee Doodle' as the column of silent, worried men began to form.

TWENTY-THREE

The Hammer of God

'Your little one stowed away in Redoubtable's hold, my dear? Well now, I don't think so.' Dick Dancer wrapped a packet of needles in a twist of paper and handed it to a farmer's wife. 'Still, let's have a look.'

He peered into the wagonbox, and Hannah would have climbed up to follow him. But in a moment he was out again.

'My Jemima's been in one of her passions, Mrs Trevor,' he declared, 'and she's pitched the cargo about some. When she's taken by the passions, she's no patience with merchandise and she gives it no quarter. You may step in and look for yourself, ma'am. But other than pitching, I see nothing amiss.'

'And no sign of the child?' John English, who had escorted them from the sentry post, looked nearly as worried as Hannah and her uncle.

'Have you opened all of these cupboards this morning, Dick?' Henry Markham was poking about with the latches.

'Why – no. Some goods we sets out and some we leaves back till it's called for. Reminder, sir! Haul to, if you please!'

The old man came trotting over from the fortune teller's wagon nearby, munching on a roll of hot meat and cabbage. 'Aye, Dick? What's wanted?'

'My Jennet is gone from Two Mills, Mr Dancer,' Hannah told him, 'and we can think of nothing but that she's hidden herself in your wagon and been carried here by chance.'

'Red hair in plaits, Pa,' said Dick. 'Stands no higher than your elbow. Come now, brisk, sir! Have you seen her?'

The Reminder blinked. 'I've seen an old lady with eyes like a black bird. She sat in a throne on two poles, and she asked who I was. But she bought nothing and sold nothing. I think she was not of this world.'

'Pa! Red plaits, Pa! No cap! Boots undone!'

The old fellow considered. 'I've seen a young woman with a face like a fury. I've seen a boy with knives in his eyes and another with distances, oceans and continents. But no children. The world runs very short these days of children. They are here and then gone.'

Sergeant Kersey rode up and dismounted. He gave Hannah a salute, his sober face bearing no discernible expression.

'Major's compliments, Mrs Trevor, ma'am. I'm to see that all's well with you.' He glanced at Henry, then back at Hannah. 'Mr Markham, sir. I must say that your son's come back. He's below in the camp. You may see him if you care to come down.'

'What?' Henry Markham stared, as though he had not heard. 'Wh-what?'

'Your son, sir. He's below in the—'

'Alive?' The miller stumbled and fell against the side of the wagon.

'Here, Uncle!' Hannah reached for the old man, but he

was too heavy, she could not hold him. Henry crumpled, his hands stretched out before him and the left one clenched hard, the fingers jerking and jumping.

'Wh-where is Mother?' he said. 'What have they done with Mo-moth—'

His right eye was focused but the left stared straight ahead, and there was a more violent jerking now, a convulsion of the nerves and muscles all down the left side of face and his body.

'It's a stroke!' Hannah cried. 'Fetch my aunt to him, someone, quickly! And Dr Kent, he must come. Hold him steady now! Please! Quickly!'

She prised open the tightly pursed lips to see that he did not bite down on his tongue. But such a seizure was beyond the midwife's skill; it was out of her province and she knew it. Her hands shook as she loosened his collar. She had never seen such sheer terror as she saw in the stricken man's eyes.

'Give him a swig of this, my dear,' Dick told her, and produced his clandestine flask.

Hannah held it to Henry's lips, but he could not swallow, could not even try. He stared up at her unseeing, the rum dribbling down his chin untasted. He tried to speak again, but the sound was like Jennet's strange noises, half-strangled and senseless to everyone but himself.

And yet he knew what was happening to him. His eyes spoke it: *Death. This is death.*

'How bad is it?' Dick knelt down by the midwife's side.

'Bad enough,' she whispered. 'But he cannot lie here, the ground is cold and damp. Please, can you not put him into the oxcart? I will take him where Jonathan is.'

*

Of all this commotion, Jennet Trevor heard nothing.

She had lain in the cupboard marked *Yard Goods* for more than two hours, wrapped up in Jemima's old quilt. For awhile, she had made a game of it, thinking what she would do to get her own back on them when they came to let her out. She had wriggled about and at last managed to get her mouth free of the quilt; once or twice she had whooped out the loudest wail she could, and still nobody came to get her. (In fact, nobody could have heard her over the cries of the vendors, and the trumpets and the firing of rifles on the target range nearby.)

But Jennet heard only the silence that caged her, tangled with murmurs and mumblings, rocked by nameless rhythms, cracked open by high-pitched whines and the crashes of thunder that were gunfire. She kept squirming about until one eye could see out through a hole in the quilt. She tried to get her arms free as well, but she could not, and at last she fell asleep. When she woke, she thought at first she might be in her playhouse.

But nothing was right. She was still not at home, and Arthur was missing, and Hannah was not there. She had stopped pouting now and she missed her mother. Even if you couldn't jump up on her, she was warm and close in the bed, and she always smelled like the cold water she washed in. People who could hear and speak might say that cold water had no fragrance, but Jennet knew better. Hannah's smell was clean and new, like fresh-cut melon in summer, very ripe and sweet.

'Annhhh-ahhhh,' she said softly, and hid her face in the quilt. But it only smelled of dust.

She missed Daniel, too. He had a different smell, a spice smell, like sycamore leaves, or Uncle Henry's tobacco. And a taste. When he carried her, she sometimes put his coat buttons in her mouth and sucked at them. Once she had bitten one off, as she had when the man in the forest carried her, and taken it to hide in her pocket. They were both with the other buttons now, in her playhouse hoard – one wooden, painted plain black; the other pewter with signs on it like the ones Hannah tried to teach her with the pen and ink.

Jennet was lonely and bored and sticky all over with molasses, and she began to be more than a little afraid. It was very dark in the cupboard, only a slit of light around each edge of the drop-leaf door that opened out into the world where Hannah and Arthur and Daniel must be.

You will not shut me out, she thought, and her small face drew into a scowl, brows lowered, chin thrust out. Hannah's chin, it was, and it would not be hampered. *I will not let you shut me out of the world.*

Jennet tried shoving the door with her shoulder, but the latch was too sound and the door was too heavy.

There was a small door, just her size, in the wall of the parlor at home, a secret way to get down to the cellar. To open that door, you had to kick it, hard, with your boot. Very well, then. She would kick her way through this door, too. On her knees, with her head down on the soft heap of calico and cambrick beneath her, Jennet worked herself round till her feet touched the wood of the little cupboard door.

Thump.

Not hard enough. Use the heels.

Thump! Thump! Thump! Thump!

Disappointed, Jennet began to cry again, silently, tasting the salt of her tears on the dusty old quilt. But she did not stop kicking.

Thump! Thump! Thump! Thump! Thump! Thump!

'What was that?' Hannah looked up at Dick Dancer. The seizure had eased at last and they were lifting Henry's helpless shape into the oxcart.

'I heard nothing,' the peddler told her.

Thump!

'There! It comes from inside the wagon, I'm sure it does!' Hannah climbed up onto the seat and peered in, but there was no sign of the child.

Thump! Thump! Thump!

'Jennet!' she cried.

'Why, that is God's hammer,' said the Reminder. 'I have heard it all the morning, making ploughshares of swords.'

'Let's have these cupboards open! Quick, now! All of them!' John English began to unfasten the goods-boxes all along the side of the wagon, while Dick unlocked those under the canvas himself.

Thump!

'Here!' cried Hannah. 'The piece goods cupboard!' She fumbled with the knotted latchstring, swearing under her breath at Dick Dancer's everlasting sailor's knots. The thumping stopped all of a sudden and she heard the wild, precious cry.

'Annnnhhhh-ahhhhhhh!'

The cupboard door gave way and out spilled a squirming, kicking, wailing object, wrapped up in an old quilt that had lumps of matted wool batting sticking out of it in a dozen places. It was tied tight around her with the narrow thongs Mr Dancer used to tie down his canvas wagon cover.

John English cut them and out she rolled, sticky and red-faced and furious. But sticky or not, Hannah gathered her close, and in a moment Jennet's arms had stopped flailing and locked themselves close around her mother's neck.

'She's well?' Kersey asked softly. 'No hurt is done her?'

'None I can see.' Hannah stood up, smoothing Jenny's hair and settling her crumpled gown. 'Take my uncle now. He must be seen to. We will follow you down to the camp.'

Sergeant English rode on ahead and Hannah untangled herself from her daughter, meaning to ride with her uncle in the back of the cart. But Jennet would not be pushed away this time. She held out her arms to her mother, mouth gaping open and feet stamping with impatience.

Hannah would almost have risked picking her up. But Oliver Kersey would not have it.

'Here, now,' he said. 'You mustn't lift her. Let me.' He scooped the little girl up and hoisted her onto his shoulders just as Daniel often did, her legs hooked under his armpits and her hands clutching the buttons on his coat and twisting them fiercely, as they climbed onto the oxcart and began the steep journey downhill to the camp.

'Thoughtless fool! Idiot!'

A moment before, Julia Markham had held her son tight, his face smashed to her broad bosom. Now her strong right hand suddenly connected with Jonathan's face, so hard that he staggered where he stood and reached out for the tent pole to keep from falling. Before he could steady himself, she slapped him again.

'Look there at your father! Could you not have sent word to him? If you cared too little for us, you have still a wife and a son to be thought of. Or have you forgot them in the pleasure of rousing up wars?'

'How could I write to you?' he cried. 'If Tapp heard of it, he'd have locked up the lot of you in my stead, till I came to turn myself in.'

But his mother would hear no excuses. 'So now you come back like a sneak-thief,' Julia said, 'in a suit of stolen clothes!'

'I do not steal!'

Jonathan sat down on a camp stool beside the cot where they had laid Henry Markham, and the sight of his stricken father subdued the boy's defensive anger. Hannah and Dolly had taken off the old man's wig and his coat, and he seemed very old indeed now, and very tired, worn down almost to nothing. 'Does he hear us?' Johnnie looked up at Hannah.

'I think so. His eyes open now and then. He hears something.'

'But will he know me?'

'Perhaps later.'

'He will die.' Julia would not come near to the cot. 'He will break his promise that he made me.' She stood very straight, scarcely breathing. 'Faithless. Faithless. He said he would never die before me, and now there he lies.'

'Come, Ma.' Dolly had tried to make her mother sit down, but Julia would not. 'Don't take on so,' she soothed. 'It gives Dada no comfort.'

'Yes.' This last Julia understood. 'That is true, we must do what we may for him. What says the doctor?'

Hannah left Henry's side and went to take her aunt's hand. Dr Kent had left a bottle of laudanum, with instructions to give it every two hours at least. But so close upon Lady Jory's dying, it could only seem like a death sentence to Julia now, and Hannah said nothing of it.

Besides, she did not trust the stuff. She thrust it into her pocket and left it there for safekeeping.

'Kent thinks the stroke is not so bad, Aunt,' she said. 'Only one eye is blind, the left one.'

'Why, there Ma! Hosea Sly has had but the one eye these twenty years,' Dolly said, 'and he still keeps a-going.'

'And my uncle's left arm may be something stiff.' Kent had presumed it from the length of the seizure, but Hannah was almost sure she had seen Henry's fingers close on the blanket and open again when they put him to bed. It was a hopeful sign.

But Julia could not risk hope upon so slight a ground. 'Not so bad?' she cried. 'Can a one-armed miller cut boards and grind flour? He is proud, he will rather die than be helpless. Winter is coming, and our firewood not yet in, and we owe Siwall a debt of near seventy pound, and Daniel more yet! Every penny will be a nail in Husband's coffin!'

'Joshua and Daniel will both help you,' Hannah told her. 'I will help you. You will not be left friendless.'

'Yes.' The old lady sat down and put her face in her hands. 'I must beg charity now.' Julia looked up at Jonathan. 'I had a son once, and I thought he would turn out a comfort. But he is gone.'

'I am here, Mama,' said the young man, and took a step towards her. 'Come, let me hold you.'

But she only stared. 'I do not know you, sir. I have no living sons in this place.'

'Ma, you mustn't say such things!' Dolly was stunned and pale.

'She is right.' Johnnie's body slid down from the stool to the ground, now, his dark head drooping till it almost touched his knees. 'I have used everyone ill. Pa. Sally. Daniel. Even Jenny.'

'So it was *you* that locked her away in the wagon?' In spite of her anger, Hannah was relieved it had been nothing worse.

'We feared she'd make a ruckus,' the boy told her, 'and we thought she'd be safe with old Dick. Saw his wagon tied up at Drewels' last night and hid ourselves away in it. Easy enough, till Jenny stumbled across us this morning at the Mills.'

As though she had discerned the spoken shape of her own name, Jennet looked up. The child had been sitting at Daniel's map table, eating bread and cold pork and applesauce, but now she came over to Jonathan and laid her two hands on his sharp-boned face. Inside Johnnie Markham, under the damage and the brashness and the boyish self-interest and the fanatical pride, there was something that drew Jennet Trevor, some wild sameness they both recognized.

'See,' he said, 'she doesn't grudge me.' He pulled Jennet against him and kissed her, and for a moment she lay still in his arms. 'I'm glad she has learned to make noise.'

'You were *there*? At the Mills, in Dick's wagon? And you didn't so much as show yourself to Dada?' Dolly could only stare. 'Oh Johnnie, that was ill done! How could you just go away again and say nothing? Your wife was there! Your own son!'

'The Cause!' he said. 'I peered out when we left the woods and I saw Tapp ride away from the Mills on the high road! I couldn't be sure he hadn't left one of his fellows behind to wait for me, could I? And besides, it was too much risk to you, all of you!'

Hannah stalked over to face him. 'And what about Daniel? You said you had used Daniel ill. What did you mean, boy?'

'I'm no boy! Don't call me that!'

'When you think less of yourself and more of them that love you, I shall be happy to call you a man. What have you to do with Daniel?'

'To do with him? He betrayed me, I'm under guard because of him and now I shall hang, that's what I have to do with him! I trusted him, he swore he wouldn't give me away to the sheriff. He brought me these clothes to the woods.'

'Brought them? When?'

'Last night, before the hunt. I've been living with the old Dutchman up at Fort Holland off and on. I sent a message to Daniel by one of the half-breeds that I meant to come home for Thanksgiving, that I'd wait in the woods just beyond Berge's place, and he must bring me some clothes so I wouldn't be known.'

'But you came here instead to preach sedition to a lot of poor fools!'

'It's not sedition! It's freedom! We fought for freedom, but we get only scorn and worthless money and debts and foreclosures—'

'*You* fought for freedom? You were still playing marbles and pitch-farthing when they went off to war! Now you've roused them to another such, and put my husband in the middle of it!'

Jonathan's eyes were cold and they made Hannah shiver to look at them.

'Husband?' he said. '*You'll* never have a husband! You're

an end in yourself, and you don't love anything you can't make or manage. And you call *me* selfish? Go home and look in a glass, Hannah Trevor. God help you. You're the most selfish creature I know.'

TWENTY-FOUR

Secrets and Swords

The column assembled at the end of the high street, just beyond the village in a farmer's field known as Dabb's Mead.

First came the artillery, two brass six-pounders and their tumbrils, and the eight-inch howitzer pulled by four big shire horses, their manes and tails braided with red-and-blue ribbons, followed by companies from Bridgewater, Saybrook, Pownalby and Rye, as well as the Rufford and Salcombe men. Beyond them were the riflemen, white-coated and green-coated, not fond of drilling and marching in general but taking a special pride in it today.

McGregor had rejoined his company, riding his old chestnut mare Lizzie, who sported a fine spray of white goosefeathers in her bridle and a plaid thrown over her saddle. A piper, Ewan Campbell from Saybrook, began to work his bellows, and behind him the bugle of the Light Infantry from Wybrow sounded the All-at-Arms.

After them came the cavalry, their horses braided and ribboned, some caparisoned with homemade buntings of red, white and blue. Each company had its own flag, some green, some yellow, some blue, and some crimson, depending on the dyes the local wives had had to hand. Horses neighed and danced, dogs barked, trumpets blew, and sergeants shouted, practicing the drills they would do before the reviewing stand and the crowds in the common.

'Left foot, I said! Left face! Right face! Make your square! Again!'

Last of all came the infantry, the plainclothes soldiers they called the String-Beaners. The sprigs of pine were most apparent here, stuck in almost every man's tricorne. But there were plenty to be seen even among the cavalry, by tradition the aristocracy of the army.

'Form up, you lot of tree toads!' cried Sergeant Kersey.

Though he himself wore the winter white, he was attached to the green-uniformed riflemen, the group they called Haggar's Company. In the War, expert riflemen had been shuffled about from division to division as they were needed, ranking here and there and impossible to attach to any local group. They had only a broad regimental distinction – the Sixth Massachusetts, say, or the Tenth Pennsylvania – and the name of their commander, who was elected by vote among them.

Daniel sat on Yeoman's back, a drummer boy at either side and two flags – one the American and one the Commonwealth of Massachusetts – snapping out in the cold wind behind him.

'Mr English! Strike up the fife!' he called out.

'Aye, sir! What tune?'

' "The White Cockade," Sergeant.' Daniel turned to the boys. 'Can you manage that one, Aaron?'

The tow-headed grandson of Mr Teazle, the old sexton, grinned and saluted with his drumstick. Daniel drew his sword and raised it. There was a rattle of the tinny snares and the men pulled into formation.

'*FORWARD!*' cried John English, and the order was carried all down the column, to the last String-Beaner with patches on his breeches and pine in his moth-eaten hat.

'Set Hobble down just there, Jenks,' ordered Lady Sibylla. 'By the forge. Yes, that will do nicely. We shall have an excellent vantage.'

She peered round the village square, now crowded with wives and daughters and mothers decked out in their Sunday gowns, old white-headed fellows with bits of the uniforms they had worn in the French and Indian War, and children like a surging, shouting, shoving sea around the vendors of cider, apple tarts, candied quinces, spruce beer, and gingerbread men. Sibylla was fascinated by a fellow with a barrow full of kegs who was handing out tin mugs to his customers.

'What is that oaf selling?' she asked her servant.

'I believe it is known as gin-sling, my lady. Soldiers' grog and molasses.' Jenks winked at Owen.

'Go and fetch me a cannikin, and some of their gingerbread.' Sibylla peered through her eyeglass. 'Who is that, Jenks? The woman in the red cloak, there – is it not Mrs Trevor?'

'It appears so, my lady. And her daughter with her. Do you wish to join them?' He began to raise the bearing poles.

'In the midst of those hobbledehoys? No, no! Go and fetch her to me here, Owen.' The old lady reconsidered. 'Or better still, *ask* her to come to me. Say I am feeble and require her advice.'

This time Owen winked at Jenks. 'Then shall I not fetch

Dr Kent, ma'am? And send word to Major Josselyn that you
are ill?'

'Don't prattle like a booby, sir! I haven't felt so well since
I was a girl of seventy! Oh – and bring *two* cannikins of the
grog.'

Hannah had already seen Hobble from across the common,
a small absurd island of imperturbable elegance plumped
down in the yard of the Forge amongst old sleigh runners,
piles of scrap iron, cordwood for stoking, and the fragrant
leavings of countless nervous horses.

Keeping a firm hold on Jennet's small hand, the midwife
followed Owen through the crowd that lined the high street.
The dignitaries had already assembled on the reviewing
stand. Magistrate Siwall was there, of course, and Jem's
father-in-law, the dignified Mr Royallton-Smith, as well as
the new town moderator, Isaiah Hobart, and all the Selectmen. The great folk of the other towns along the river sat
at the back, and a flock of periwigged parsons, like so many
blackbirds, lined up in the foremost row.

At the edge of the platform, Sheriff Marcus Tapp stood
quite alone, his dull brown greatcoat wrapped close around
him and his head bent. He seemed to be studying a thick
sheaf of papers, very official, with a wax seal dangling from
them on a wide black ribbon.

'Lady Josselyn.' Hannah drew even with Hobbie's curtained side window and made a quick reverence to Sibylla.
'I am told you are ill.'

'That was only a ruse, my dear, to draw you to me. A
great age makes the truth more often expendable.' The old
lady's eyes were very black in her white-powdered face, like

two specks of soot on a tablecloth. 'I was hoping for news of your uncle,' she said. 'I hear at the inn he is sorely stricken.'

'My aunt and some of the menfolk have taken him home,' Hannah told her.

Jennet had already dived into the sedan chair, for Daniel's great-aunt had quickly become a particular favorite – thanks largely to her taste for gaudy clothes and bright jewelry. The child clambered up onto Lady Sibylla's lap and began to finger her ear-drops; they were garnets set in filigree silver, very fine.

'No, Jenny,' said Hannah softly. She took the child's hand away from the jewels and held it, then turned back to Sibylla. 'I thank you for your kind inquiring, madam, but I fear you must excuse us now. The parade is beginning and Jennet is eager to see – '

'Her father.' It was a challenge.

Hannah's chin lifted an inch. 'So he is,' she said.

'And when, pray, shall Jennet's father be your husband? In my lifetime? In hers?'

'That, madam, is his concern and mine. Come, Jenny.' Determined to make her escape, Hannah tugged gently at her daughter's hand.

But just then Owen arrived with the two cannikins of gin-sling and a half-dozen gingerbreads wrapped in greasy brown paper. And what child of eight, after all, could be expected to resist anything baked in the shape of a prancing horse, with black currants for hooves and a saddle and bridle of icing sugar?

Sibylla laughed at the child's eager face. 'You'll go nowhere till she's gobbled that up, my dear. Besides, you ought not be huffish. I am fond of my nephew, and that gives me the privilege of hectoring you a little, for his sake.'

Hannah accepted the mug of drink and stepped into the sedan chair, taking Jennet onto her own lap. *Take no strong drink.* She sniffed at the mug, sighed, and nibbled a currant from the gingerbread instead.

But Sibylla wasted no more time. 'I am told Daniel has arrested your cousin. Is that so?'

'It is. I am sure he means—'

'Then why does that handsome brigand of a sheriff not go and take the boy to prison? Look at him! He might be out picnicking, the rascal, for all the haste he displays!'

It was true. Tapp seemed unconcerned, he merely went on studying his papers, turning the pages over and over. And now, of all times, when Daniel and most of his men were away from Great Meadow and he might come upon a garrison scarcely manned and a guard ill-prepared to resist him? Indeed, it was not like Marcus Tapp to miss such a chance.

He is waiting his time, thought Hannah. *He knows something we do not, some blow he will strike unawares.*

But it might only be that he could not act till the Muster was ended. Yes, surely that was it. With all these folk in the town, he would not risk upheavals.

'Events follow very hot upon one another's tails this day,' the old lady went on. 'Clinch found dead in the woods. Then the black fellow, Caesar. It *was* self-murder, was it?'

'Siwall calls it so.'

'But you do not believe Caesar was guilty.'

'He denied it. His wife denies it.'

Sibylla's eyelids fluttered and the eyes took on a glint of gold. 'Mr Siwall is an impatient fellow. Prays to excess, I believe. I never could abide a God-botherer.' The old lady drank from her mug. 'Such a man, with a need to seem pious while he lines his pockets – has he no weakness to be played upon? Sentences may be commuted, and a bit of judicious blackmail seldom comes amiss.'

Hannah studied Lady Sibylla's features. They were sharpened by age and fragility, but they were very like Daniel's – the same long hooked nose, the same broad forehead. Even the eyes had mellowed now and taken on the brandy color that was his. In spite of the armor of rational cynicism and the faint condescension she wore like a mask, there was often a glint of real pain in them, and real sweetness.

'There was a woman in Siwall's coach at the Muster this morning,' she told Hannah. 'A young thing. Silly and giggling. And a man with her. Has Siwall a mistress, then?'

'If he has,' Hannah said slowly, 'no one has ever known of it.'

Sibylla laughed softly. 'Oh, never fear. If there is a mistress, someone knows.'

Nobody knowed him but Sam, Mrs Skowser had said. *Nobody knows him now.* And what was it old Sly had been hinting at? *Such things gets knowed-of, and knowed-of means paid-off. How else has Sam Clinch kept out of debtors' jail all these years?*

Pigs in clover, Clinch had told Betsey Skowser. *We shall soon be pigs in clover, my Bess.* And that fifty pounds in Clinch's hunting pouch – was it only a guarantee of better things to come? Why had Clinch made Caesar stay behind once they got to the woods? To meet Siwall, perhaps, and take greater payment, enough of a portion of Jem's new wife's dowry to put him in clover for good?

Hannah's mind was racing, but she forced it to a halt. She must be slow and methodical. The truth was somewhere, hidden like a faulty seam among torn scraps. Blackmail was part of the pattern, she was almost sure of it. And not of the tame sort Sibylla had in mind.

'Is there none you might question?' Daniel's great-aunt opened her snuffbox – her second best – and tapped out a pinch of the fragrant black stuff along the edge of her forefinger. 'His lady, perhaps? You have a way of making women trust you, I have observed.'

'Oh, no. Madam Siwall would never confide in me. She is very proud.'

'Hunh!' Sibylla took in the snuff with a shrill whistle. 'We shall see about that, in due time!'

'There *is* someone,' Hannah said. 'Siwall's daughter-in-law. But—'

'Speak to her, then. Find some pretext.' Sibylla snapped her snuffbox shut and took Hannah's hand in her own. 'I fear few things on earth, Mrs Trevor. But I fear this man Siwall, for my nephew's sake. I observed him this morning – a secretive creature under his bluster, who has lived too long with a bad conscience. When Daniel speaks, Siwall seems to feel the ground go from under him. I do not know why. And my nephew's own mind is too clouded to perceive it, he speaks poniards to the fellow without knowing it.' She paused, sipping at her drink. 'Daniel is not himself since Lottie's death. He does not sleep, and he wanders.'

'He still mourns her.' Hannah did not meet Sibylla's gaze. 'It is right that he should.'

'It is deeper than mourning.' The old lady let go of the midwife's hand and sat very still, her gnarled fingers picking at the piece of gingerbread in her lap. 'We all have our devils and our ghosts, of course. For the most part, they hone us and keep our edges clean. Only this business, this new war of theirs—'

'Surely you do not believe Tapp can trump up a charge against Daniel?'

'It is not what Tapp will do that concerns me, my dear Hannah.' It was the first time Sibylla had called the midwife by her Christian name. 'It is Daniel. He is too much alone, and he wears himself hard. Bitter hard.' She reached out and drew Jennet against her, the wrinkled hands stroking and stroking the little girl's hair, their gold rings gleaming. 'He speaks of going west to the French territories, where he might adopt the child and give her his name.'

'Would you not disapprove?' Hannah asked her. 'Such a child, born as Jennet was, to bear the name of your great family?'

'Hah! If all the lords whose great-grandsires were born on the wrong side the blanket were cast out tomorrow, there would be empty palaces all over Europe! Besides, I'm fond of the child, she's a clever little minx.' Sibylla slipped her hand into Jennet's pocket. 'Ho! I thought as much.' She pulled out the silver snuffbox.

Hannah stared. 'She stole it from you?'

'Oh, she takes some trinket now and then for a plaything. In time she returns them.'

'Bright things attract her, but I must take care to teach her better. It is hard, with such a child.'

'And the next one?' The old lady peered down at Hannah's softly swelling figure through her long-handled lens. 'Will you delay this marriage till it is born without a name as well?' She paused, studying the midwife's face. 'Oh my dear. You are not the only woman ever to fear being wed.'

'I do not fear!'

Sibylla laughed. 'Hah! What a familiar ring that lie has! I have told it to myself these sixty summers, since I was old enough to know what men kept in their breeches. Oh, but the winters, dear Hannah. The winters are cold at my age.'

Hannah did not reply at once, only looked away down the high street. The regimental band – mostly men too old or too maimed by the War for the marching and drilling – was tuning up at the foot of the reviewing stand. In the distance, she could hear the sound of the fifes and the bagpipe playing 'The White Cockade', and the drums rattling the approach of the column.

'I *am* a selfish creature,' she said softly. 'It is true.'

Jennet was all but asleep, now, and the old lady began to rock her gently, making the chair creak like the bent willow rocker at home.

'What we want most in the world, we fear most.' Sibylla's eyes flickered open, a glint of deep blue like the heart of a flame at their centers. 'Hannah – why do you think I never chose to wed?'

'I – don't know. You are a very clever woman. I supposed you had not met your equal.'

'I met him. And, oh, how I struggled! Bedding was perfectly rational. Excellent exercise. But love? It was the stuff of fictions, all those Pamelas and Clarissas and Sophias. Gingerbread women, and just as sickly sweet. I denied and denied, till at last it broke upon me. To confuse love with romance is as bad as confusing one's god with religion. The foolish corruptions of the one do not erase the existence of the other. Unless the mind is utterly perverse.'

'You accepted his love, then?'

'And returned it. But I still could not marry.' Sibylla laughed softly. 'I had been alone so long I mistook it for freedom. And I could not give the habit up.'

Hannah laid a hand on the old lady's silken sleeve. 'You speak of your friend, Mr Franklin?'

But there was no time to answer. A cheer went up from the crowd, followed by a riffle of applause. Then the column came into view at last, with Daniel riding at the head of it, his sword raised in salute to the spectators.

Sibylla's soot-black eyes did not leave him. 'Do not abandon him, Hannah,' she whispered. 'Freedom's a cold country to live in forever. I don't wish to welcome you there.'

TWENTY-FIVE

Bad News Is Come to Town

'Friends! Let us pray!'

The maneuvers and marching had finished. The column, still in company order, stood at ease before the reviewing stand as George Greenleaf, the parson from Saybrook, rose to give the invocation before the speeches began.

'O God,' he intoned, 'from whom all good counsel and all just deeds do proceed, grant unto thy servants that peace which the world cannot know, which is the peace of a heart that renounceth all anger and false pride, all resentment of lawful power— '

There was a grumbling from the soldiers and a few hisses from the civilians in the crowd. 'Siwall's bought you, too, has he, Parson?' somebody shouted.

' —and to accept all trials,' the old man continued, 'all poverty, all sufferings, as chastisements of God for the purification of our immortal souls.' Here the parson paused, his face very pale, and glanced down at the people he had once thought he knew. 'Let us strive to obey all laws— ' he tried to go on.

'All *just* laws, you mean!' someone shouted.

Mr Greenleaf drew a deep breath and forged on to the finish, all the words pouring out in a rush. ' —and to live in peace and accord with all men. In the name of Jesus Christ our Lord, Amen!'

He was afraid, and they knew it. As the old parson sat down hurriedly next to Lawyer Napier, there was a groundswell of movement among the spectators, and from where she stood in the yard of McGregor's smithy, Hannah could see that someone was passing out half-rotten apples and hickory nuts and old heads of cabbage left too late in the gardens, brown and slimy from the frost.

But Hamilton Siwall did not choose to notice. 'Gentlemen,' he began. 'And – er – ladies. After such a stirring display of martial prowess, and in the presence of the great flags of our hard-won republic and of our Commonwealth of Massachusetts, it is—'

'We are Maine men!' cried a voice from the outskirts. 'The devil take Massachusetts!'

Siwall cleared his throat again. 'It is my privilege to address you as your representative to the General Court, and to speak of certain decisions—'

'Freedom's a rich man's swindle!' cried Stephen Anson, and spat at the magistrate's feet.

'That is not true!' cried Siwall. 'We of the Court are not rich men.'

This raised a roar of laughter.

'Will they issue new paper money that's sound?' shouted young Anson. 'My father would not have left his debts unpaid, if the taxman had not held out for silver!'

'Unless paper is backed by gold or silver, new money will be no more good than the old Continentals you have now.'

Siwall tried to be patient and rational, but it was not his nature. 'The government is bankrupt. If—'

'Send the bloody government to debtors' jail then! That's where you put me!'

'Now, fellows! We are sensible men!' cried steady Nate Berge. He turned back to Siwall. 'Will you and your sheriffs lock up the debtors' courts so we may live and our wives and babes may not hunger and freeze in the winter, or will you not?'

'Debts must be paid, sir.' Royallton-Smith stepped up to join his friend at the podium. A good man, intelligent and well-meaning.

But a man who had never laid down to bed at night with his muscles so sore they would not let him sleep, nor had to lie cold and lonely for months and years, for fear his woman might breed him another mouth he could not feed. An ignorant man, therefore, who had never been poor. And yet, knowing nothing of most of their lives and even less of their chances of dying, William Royallton-Smith assumed himself their superior.

'If our merchants are not paid in silver,' he said, with infuriating patience, 'trade will cease. No other country will take our currency.'

'Then they're a damn sight wiser than I was! I took it for army pay and trusted it was sound!' somebody yelled out.

'Listen to me. Try to understand.' Smith spoke not to equals, but to recalcitrant children. 'If we have no trade, we cannot pay our war debts to the French. Their soldiers were promised pensions and—'

At first the men in Daniel's column had stood silent, maintaining their discipline. Now they began to shout with the others: 'The hell with the French! Let them take a peck of turnips for their pensions, that's what I'm paid in!'

Royallton-Smith mopped his face with a lace-edged kerchief. 'You don't understand. Be guided by those who have studied the matter. If there is no foreign trade, local prices will go up. You will not be able to buy the necessities, let alone the luxuries you now enjoy!'

'There he stands, farting into blue silk breeches and telling us of our luxuries!'

'Who the hell is he? He ain't a Rufford man. He ain't even from Maine!'

'This is Master Royallton-Smith of the General Court,' Siwall said with a self-satisfied smirk. 'He has come to bring news of certain recent measures—'

'Hah! Here's what we think of the General Court and its bloody measures!'

A rotten apple whirled above the crowd and struck the magistrate full in the chest, making a brown spot on his pale yellow damask waistcoat. More apples followed. Then half a cabbage, and a rain of nuts as hard as rocks. Siwall and Smith ducked and dodged and the row of black-coated ministers fled from the platform.

Hannah saw Daniel stride over to Josh and McGregor, his captains, and speak to them in an undertone. Then he turned to the sergeants, John English and Kersey, and gave an order.

'Present arms!' shouted Josh.

Some in the column straightened up, their weapons at the ready, but most were beyond all orders. They were men, now, not toy soldiers. The fruit flew thick and fast.

'Enough!' Marcus Tapp pushed his way along the platform and came to stand beside Siwall and Smith.

At the edges of the crowd, almost in unison, two dozen men – none of them in militia uniform – primed their rifles and raised them to their shoulders, trained upon the wives and children in the crowd. They were cold-eyed men, woodsmen and half-breeds and brigands from out of the forests.

Mercenaries thought Hannah. Tapp must have gone into the Outward and paid the sheriff's shilling to any man with a gun who would take it. Her body shuddered as though a blow had struck her, and Hannah looked away. If there was anything that would provoke them to war, it was this cruel stroke.

A private, one of the String-Beaners, ran up to her and saluted. 'Major says, get the womenfolk and the little 'uns inside, ma'am!'

But there was no time. Tapp had already begun to speak. The hammers of two dozen rifles were pulled back with a sound like a single heavy bolt slipping home. There was a rumbling from the crowd, a low roar like the fast current of the river when it was swollen with too much rain. Then silence.

'I am come to read you the latest decrees of the General Court.' Tapp unrolled the sheaf of papers, glanced at it, then tossed it aside. 'Let us have it plain. There's a new Militia Act. Any officer or common soldier who joins with the rebels or helps them, or so much as speaks up for them when the rum's on him, will be court-martialled and shot. If any common soldier does an act of rebellion while he's under muster, his commander will be held as guilty as he is, and court-martialled for treason.'

The sheriff's empty eyes sought out Daniel above the heads of the crowd, and the men stared at their commander. But Josselyn did not blink.

Lachlan McGregor's huge shape loomed up from among them. 'If I choose to let the bloat of pride out of your guts with my dirk, Master Sheriff, the guilt of it's mine, not Dan Josselyn's. To take that from me is to take my free will. And that's God's business, Mr Tapp. Not yours, nor any bastard's that walks.'

'As of this day, my business is whatever I say it is.' Tapp's pale eyes remained focused on Daniel. 'Ten days ago the General Court passed a Riot Act.'

The very words stunned the crowd. At the beginning of the War, the British had imposed a Riot Act upon them. It had made power a law unto itself and left them no defense against it. But these were not the king's officials; they were neighbors, freely elected as equals – or so the story went.

Now, looking up at the platform, the truth had come home to these folk, and they could see the future stretch away before them, no different from the past. Rich men elected other rich men and they scratched one another's backs like sleek cats and did not understand why poor men resented them, and any who resisted the growth of their power were labelled as traitors and fools. So it would be under governors and presidents, as it had been under kings and popes and caesars.

Take what you are given. Give gladly whatever we choose to take away.

'If more than twelve armed men gather in public,' Marcus Tapp went on, 'that is a riot, and my men will put it down as they may.'

Josh Lamb could be silent no longer. He pointed at the sheriff's new men, their rifles still shouldered. 'Twelve of us is a riot. But what is twelve of *them*?'

Tapp smiled. 'A superior force, Master Landlord.' He

went on with his recital. 'Dead or alive, if you are found guilty of riot, all your lands and goods are forfeit, and you'll have forty stripes and a year in my jail if you're caught.'

Here he took up the paper and read from it rapidly.

'The writ of habeas corpus is hereby suspended in this Commonwealth. Any person suspected of being unfriendly to the powers of government shall be arrested and jailed, and may be held without trial. Any person speaking ill of the government shall be denounced, arrested and jailed. Any house may be broken into without warrant. Any person may be seized at the sheriff's discretion and kept without charge.'

For a long moment, nobody spoke. Here and there a dog barked and the meeting house bell clanged softly in the wind. All across the crowded common, women clutched their children against them, and the vendors withdrew into the doorways of shops and houses, wishing they had never come.

A young woman near the front had been suckling a little girl of two, and the breast of her gown was wet with milk. Noticing the spot, she drew her shawl across it, her eyes lowered. 'We are plain folk, sir,' she said in a clear voice. 'What does the words mean, if you please? Habie – Habie – us what?'

This time Royallton-Smith replied. 'It means you must live quietly and mind your own work, my dear, that is all, and speak no ill of your betters.'

She looked up at him. 'But if any mislike me or my man, he may report me a traitor whether I speak or not, as they did to the Tories in the War?'

Smith shook his head, smiling. 'No, no. This is not the same as the Tory hunts, not at all. Those men were known villains, the servants of an alien king. Besides, no one will report you if you keep at home and do nothing amiss.'

There was a stir at the far end of the high street, and the scream of a horse. Men's voices shouted and a musket went off, then another.

In a few more seconds, three men rode into sight. Two were Tapp's men, and the third was a young man in uniform, very pale and wide-eyed. Hannah recognized him, one of the sentries who had been pacing back and forth on duty outside the tent where Johnnie was held in arrest. She got up from the bench and moved forward, into the crowd near the high street.

Behind the sentry's terrified horse, half-dragged by the ropes round his waist and his neck, stumbled Jonathan Markham. He was barefoot in the cold; one of the deputies, a French half-breed called Le Duc, wore the gentleman's slippers now, the kidskin sherryvallies laced absurdly over buckskin leggings. The other wore his coat and hat, the blue-cockaded tricorne perched atop a head of black hair greased with bear fat and braided on either side of his swarthy face.

They had beaten their prisoner, most likely for the sheer fun of it. Jonathan's right eye was already so swollen that it bore no resemblance to an eye at all. Blood streamed from his nose, and whenever they dragged on the rope he cried out from the pain.

'Major Josselyn!' Tapp stepped down from the platform and the crowd parted for him.

'I am here, Master Sheriff.' Daniel did not move from where he stood with Josh Lamb and McGregor.

'You arrested this man at the camp, did you not?'

'He is wanted as a felon. It was my duty to place him under military arrest, and I did so.'

'But he is a civilian,' Tapp said, 'and he is no longer within the militia encampment. Your sentry has brought him.'

'And your men have brought my sentry. Against his will, as it appears.' Daniel glanced at the two ruffians and the pale-faced young private not a foot from their guns. There was a dark bruise on his temple and a cut at the corner of his mouth that still bled slightly.

'You will not deny that the jurisdiction is now mine, under the Riot Act powers?' asked the sheriff.

'It would seem that whatever you wish to take is yours.' Josselyn looked around him at the faces of his men, then at those of the women. 'Mr Tapp, you have given these people one martyr already,' he said in a low voice. 'If you give them another, you will drive them beyond hope, and without it there is nothing to lose, and no chance of peace. Take the boy to your jail if you must. But do not hang him. It will seem you are *asking* for war.'

'You're a man of capital letters, aren't you, Major? Peace. Hope. Justice, too, I expect, eh? And Honor?' Tapp's pale eyes stared blindly, as though he might see through Daniel's flesh to the bones, and through the bones to the heart that smashed against them like a wild thing caught in a cage. 'Peace is a dream, man,' he said. 'And if you can find hope in this world, then God make you free of it. That is, if you can find a trace of *Him*.'

'If I ordered these men to take the boy, they would do it.' Daniel spoke with more certainty than he felt.

The sheriff laughed softly. 'With guns trained on their

women? I think not. Besides, where would your honor be then?'

Tapp stepped back and stood to attention. 'Under the powers of the Riot Act, I ask you as commander of this militia to hand over the prisoner Markham for summary punishment by the civil law.'

Hannah pushed her way through the crowd, trying to reach Daniel. Her breath came shallow and there was a catch in her side. She tore at the clasp of her cloak, but it would not give way.

In a minute I shall strangle, she thought. *Like Johnnie. Like my Johnnie. Dear God, don't let him die.*

What came next she remembered in flashes, as dark corners are glimpsed in a flicker of candlelight that flares and is suddenly snuffed.

The gibbet, the old gallows at the far end of the common. Three or four little boys playing hangman, laughing and squealing, unaware of what is coming. The guns of the deputies are aimed at them, at their mothers.

Daniel's stillness, his body giving no sign he still breathes. He looks from one of the primed guns to another. Then he walks up to Marcus Tapp. Unfastens his sword belt and lets it fall to the ground. Tears the officer's gold bars from his shoulders and drops them. Turns on his heel and walks away through the column of men.

Josh does the same, and the sergeants, John English and Kersey, and half a dozen of the rest. But Lachlan McGregor does not, cannot, his constable's oath like a fire in his belly.

Hannah sinks, her muscles gone out of control like her uncle's. She feels again the sense of inexorable fall. As she slips downward, hands try to catch her, to claim her, to keep her from crashing apart. But they cannot. Sarah McGregor bends over her, and in a moment Daniel is there. He is lifting her, hiding his face in her breast. She can feel him sobbing; like most men of his class, he is not afraid of tears.

But they come silent and dry from him now, like retching when the stomach is empty, uprooting memory, tearing pain out of him he scarcely knew was there.

'Put me down,' she says, hoping to soothe him. 'My love. My own love.'

But he will not. Cannot. He stands in the cold wind, holding her so tight, so hard, that her arms and legs ache from his grip.

'By order of the Court of High Crimes, Salcombe,' Tapp's deep voice intones, 'County of Sussex, Province of Maine, Commonwealth of Massachusetts, on the twenty-third day of September last, and by the powers vested in me by the Riot Act, I order the execution of Jonathan Elijah Markham, Traitor and Felon duly convicted, to proceed under public witness at this same hour.'

Dolly Lamb cries out, a shrill scream, and she runs a few steps. But Josh stops her, holds her steady. With the guns trained on their women, the silent men can do nothing more now, only watch and remember, keep every word, every image sharp as a honed blade in their minds to feed their rage upon, once it is done.

The snare drum begins to roll. The old minister, Mr Greenleaf, is praying over Johnnie. 'Almighty and everlasting God, have mercy on this Thy wretched and contrite servant and grant peace to this soul.'

'Set me down,' Hannah says, sharper this time. 'I must be on my feet, Daniel. Please.'

Now he obeys her, but he keeps his arm round her, pulling her close as much for his own sake as hers.

Johnnie stumbles, a rope round his chest and another binding his hands. Past the column of soldiers. Past the reviewing stand. Through the silent crowd that parts as they pass.

Someone begins to sing, a young girl's voice, the ballad singer from the meadow.

Bad news is come to town, bad news is carried,
Bad news is whispered round, my love is married.
As I was pondering, I fell a-weeping,
They stole my love away while I lay sleeping.

'Have you any last words?' Royallton-Smith still needs to think of himself as a generous fellow.

Jonathan looks out across the crowd, catches sight of Hannah's red cloak in the distance. 'The Cause,' he says. Then he stops for a moment. 'Christ,' he murmurs. 'Tell my son—'

But he is no longer anyone's father, nor anyone's cousin, nor anyone's son. It is too late to let him live now. He is already dead.

They put him up then, a stool under his feet and the noose round his neck. A light drizzle has begun to fall again, a thin veil of mist that will turn to rain after dark, and then to snow.

'Un!' cries Tapp's straggly half-French deputy. 'Deux! Trois!'

They kick the stool away and Jonathan's body jerks, his

feet swimming, his hands clutching the air. 'Freeeedoooom!' somebody cries, a long shrill shout. But the voice chokes on it.

Jonathan's body jolts one last time, and Hannah's jolts with it in spite of Daniel's strong arm that clamps her tight against him. Then the boy hangs limp, finished, finally at rest.

'Ayieeeeeeeeeeeeeeeee!'

Somewhere in the crowd a woman screams. One scream and no more. It is the same cry Dick Dancer heard just before dawn, it can be no other. She is here with them, watching.

Daniel has heard it before, it is part of the image Clinch's body has begun to bring back to him. A single, shrill cry, like a wild creature mourning its mate.

But Hannah scarcely perceives the shrill sound, and where it comes from, what woman's throat is torn loose with it, no one can say because no one is looking. There is only one human thing on Rufford Common now and it hangs from the gibbet.

All the living are ghosts of themselves.

Daniel feels Hannah's fingers pry his hand loose from around her. It is not easy. He has grown into her flesh and together they make a wall against the bitter dominion of dying.

But at last she frees herself. She picks up his sword where it lies on the ground and walks into the crowd with it. She hears his feet moving a few paces behind her and turns, shakes her head at him. This is her honor and she is fierce in defense of it.

He feels his roots begin to bleed. He lets her go, but she

still carries him beside her, inside her. Hears his voice in her ear, warning softly.

Do not stumble, my heart. Do not try to lift more than a lone thing can carry.

She walks carefully, as though the ground were rolling under her feet, but her back is very straight and her eyes are clear and dry. As she moves towards the gallows and the strangled shell that hangs from it, other women follow. Susannah Penny. Dolly Lamb. Bess Whittemore. Nabby Berge. Most of them Hannah does not know, and they are women who never saw Johnnie until this hour. Some are trailed by small children, others carry toddlers on their arms. Many are with child, some greater than others, nearer their time. Leah Kersey is there, and Sarah McGregor. Even Lady Sibylla walks with them, leaning hard on her cane.

One by one, the sheriff's wild-eyed deputies lower their rifles. Against this, bullets are no defense.

Someone puts up the stool again and Hannah climbs onto it, side by side with her cousin's dead body as though both had been hanged. The others gather around her to keep her from falling, and some support Jonathan's heavy dead weight, clutching his legs and putting their hands up to catch him.

Hannah slashes the rope with Daniel's sword and the body comes down among them. One or two of the strong old men, Henry's friends, lend their muscles, and they lay the boy down and Sarah takes off the noose from his neck.

Though it is not much past two, the day seems to be fading, darkening towards evening. Dolly is sobbing, great tearing sobs that will never be comforted. She takes off her cloak and would cover her brother.

But Hannah pushes it away. She bends over Jonathan's battered body and her hands linger above him, fingertips closing the staring eyes, stroking the dark hair from the forehead. She cuts his arms free of their bonds and holds his dead hands to her, then lays them down at his sides.

This is her work in the world, to reconcile living and dying. To wash away fear and shame and loneliness with a touch the dead must somehow feel where they stand watching, invisible, behind their window of clouded glass.

For a moment she lays her head down on her cousin's chest, her arms close around him. Listening for something. Some truth that explains him, what living has made of him. At last she lifts up her head.

'Waste,' she says, and the word passes through the crowd like a cold wind.

Daniel hears it, and so does Hamilton Siwall. Where he stands at the podium, William Royallton-Smith hears it and begins to pray, but his hands will not fold themselves and his voice is too soft to be heard.

'I will take him home now, to his mother,' says Hannah very clearly.

They had meant to leave Johnnie hanging, caged in the iron wicket as a grisly warning to the rebels. It was the sentence of the court. But no one steps up to resist her.

Even Marcus Tapp says nothing, only watches, his features without expression and his eyes like ice. Josh and some of the other men carry Jonathan's body to a cart and it moves slowly away across the common, with Daniel driving and Hannah beside him, as the ballad singer's voice begins again and young Aaron gives a roll of his drums.

THE BURNING BRIDE

Bad news is come to town, bad news is carried,
Some say my love is dead, some say he's married.
As I was pondering, I fell a-weeping.
They stole my love away while I lay sleeping.

TWENTY-SIX

Piecing the Evidence: On the Nature of Marriage

From the day of steady, slanting rain when he had stumbled upon her, scarcely alive and not yet fully a woman in years, Sheba's husband had known she was somehow uprooted from human connection, cast loose on the universe as he himself had been since his youth.

He anchored himself in her, swallowed her whole so she lay like a stone in his body to keep him from drifting.

Back in England, he had been indentured to a monumental mason who carved lambs and urns and foolish heavy-lidded angels, and set verses on gentlemen's tombs. The boy had a skill for such singsonging rhymes and the old fellow took to him in a humorous kind of way.

Whenever the vicar's daughter walked by the shop with her basket, the apprentice would stop his work of polishing the marble with emery and watch her.

'So you fancy Miss Snippet, do you?' The old mason held

his sides and laughed fit to burst. 'Why she'd no more take you than the Man in the Moon!'

But the boy knew he was more than he looked like. His hands had a skill with the marble, and under them the stolid faces of angels and maidens and sleeping gentlemen took on a sweetness, so that they almost seemed to live and to weep.

As he tapped with the chisel, forming the perfect round of a cheek or the curve of a finger, he imagined the sardonic verses he would put on the glassy marble and the pink and grey granite.

> Here lies old Samson Peter, third Squire of that Name.
> He tumbled Black Betsey and fancied a Game.
> If his use of the Poor is rewarded by Heaven,
> He'll be frying in Hell till the Cock crows Eleven.

Words took on a power for him; the sharper, the more cutting he made them, the more secret comfort they gave him. He read every book he could come by, sat up late squandering candles, practiced his use of a pen until he could manage a fine hand.

But by day he lugged slabs for the mason and felt his muscles bulge and his body thicken, pinning him down to a fate he could not hope to escape. When he stripped for the bath, he looked down at himself and wept in despair for the sake of the vicar's fair-haired daughter.

What a gentle thing she was. How he would treasure her, once they were wed, and protect her, and see that she wanted for nothing. He felt his searching heart leave him and go into her slight body, looking for the same shelter it had found in his books.

One day, passing the shop with her little giggling maid

at her side, the vicar's daughter dropped her handkerchief in the pathway and the boy ran out and snatched it up to return to her. With a perfunctory nod, she received it, then walked on with her nose in the air.

'You had better have this, Honor,' she said to the servant in a shrill voice that was plainly meant for the boy to hear. 'I could not bear it to touch me, now it's been handled by that coarse, lumpish thing!'

All thought of the future, of the world and of women, left him entirely; he wasted no candles and read no more books. When his indenture was up, he left England and came to America, determined to change his profession, to make use of his mind. But in Boston the rich merchants wanting a clerk or a secretary would look him up and down and sneer at his homespun breeches and his wooden-soled clogs.

'Gad, sir,' they would tell him, 'I am not in the habit of taking in boys off the roads to make free with my household! There's an inn down the way, generally wanting a swabbie. From the look of you, you'll do much better there.'

So instead he did odd jobs, connecting with no one, drifting for years from place to place, going for days and weeks without speaking to anyone. If a man used him ill or angered him, he would write it out in angry verses, a gravemaker's vengeance:

> *Here sleeps greedy Frederick Guys,*
> *Who'd steal the pennies from your eyes.*
> *May worms invade his pocketbook*
> *And gobble all the gold he took.*

St Peter, guard your gateway well!
If Guys get in, 'twill stink like Hell!

When they came back from the woods on the night of the shooting, he sat up a long time making the verse for Clinch's tombstone. He went back to the woods with it, dragged the body out of the path into the thicket and hung the old man's wig on the branch.

Not noticing the button he had lost from his greatcoat, he came back to the cottage to find that Sheba had left the bed to him and laid herself down by the fire. They had once had an old dog, Buster, that slept there on the hearthrug. Sometimes in her sleep she would reach out to stroke it, though it was nearly four years dead.

Anything she had ever lost remained with her, a tactile shape with sharp edges. Any lover she had ever slept with still slept with her. Any child she had ever conceived still waited for birth in her womb.

There had been five children in the seven years of their joining, all miscarried before the sixth month. Four were buried in a small fenced yard at the back of the orchard, in little boxes of rough-hewn pine boards he had built for them. The first child they had left behind in another cold forest, wrapped in Sheba's second-best skirt and buried by the side of some track.

When they came here to Maine, he began to cut stones again, secretly, telling none in the village. He took a sledge to Jade's Mountain and brought back slabs of the fine Maine granite; working far into the night, he cut gravestones, tiny plinths that stuck up through the snow.

Each time he had made her give names to these scarcely formed wastlings before he would bury them. 'Human things must have names,' he would whisper, and kneel down before Sheba to take her swollen nipple into his own mouth, drawing off the useless milk that made her ache till she wept. 'You would not leave our children nameless when God raises them at the Day of Judgment?'

'God? He will not raise them,' she told him. 'He died when my father was hanged.'

Except for the story her body had told him, it was all Sheba's husband knew of her history. He was afraid to know more.

Once he had hidden Clinch's body, a great weariness came over the man, but he did not sleep. He felt no remorse for what he had done, after Sheba had forgiven him. He cared for nothing but her, and the part of himself where he kept her hidden.

The snow was still falling outside, very fine and dry so that it did not pile up on the ground. But it made a soft light in the cold, dark little cottage, through the panes of ill-gotten glass.

His eyes flickered open and he saw that Sheba was naked once more, like a column of light in the dark. She turned sidewise to show him the swell of her body, how fragile she was, the sad, sweet droop of her breasts.

'Was it him?' The man's voice was low and rough, like unpolished granite. 'Did *he* give you that belly? Old Clinch, that I killed?'

He saw everything now with a terrible clarity – the debtors' prison, the fire, the sleek smug men of the town. When they took her, they had taken him, too, raped and abandoned him. One by one, he listed them over. *Siwall*.

Josselyn. Cain. Hobart. Napier. Inskip. Tapp. McGregor. Lamb. Clinch.

'No,' she said, very soft. 'He was not the one.'

She sat down on the bedside and he saw her move above him. She unfastened his breeches and slipped her cold hands inside them, feeling the coarse dark hairs at the bend of his hips, and below them the comfort she had craved ever since he came home from the prison. She bent her mouth to it, her hot tongue flickering down the slope of his belly, then dancing away again, teasing him. 'You are the world to me,' she said. 'The child could never be his. He does not want it. It is yours if I say it is yours.'

It was true that she loved her husband, to madness and beyond it. He was her only living child.

'Whose is it?' he demanded. His sex was hard and stiff, he could see the shadow it cast, like a ghost on the wall. He ached for her so that it was sharp in his voice, sickle-edged.

But he would not be satisfied.

'Did he take you by force, my soul?' he asked her. He reached out a hand to her face, suddenly gentle. 'He came upon you unawares, is that not the truth of it? In the orchard or the stable, while they had me locked away?'

'I love you,' she said. 'Do not ask me again.'

She lifted his hand to her breast and he could no longer bear it.

'Christ, Sheba,' he said. He drew her down onto the bed and held her, very close, her swollen body a bridge between them. 'I cannot!' he wailed, the need of her like a wound in him. 'I will hurt you. The child, the child.'

Already he had begun to love it, to imagine it his own and to smother it.

Beside him, Sheba's body arched in slow rhythmic movements, like groundswell, and he felt her tongue on him again, lambent and warm. His seed spilled out of him suddenly, onto the bedclothes between them, unstoppable, no longer needing to enter her. Her body was an irrelevance to his own. His whole being travelled inside her like the child in her womb, all his sins and his ghosts and his furies.

This is what marriage is, he thought. *To be two inside one.*

She relaxed and he held her against him, satisfied and whole at last. He kissed her hair, her throat, her breasts, more for her sake than his – or so he thought. For a long time they lay quiet. Soon morning would come and the dead would be found, the first blow he had struck for their honor.

'He was beautiful,' she said suddenly. A lie, perhaps, but it pleased her. Some part of her despised him for loving her, knew she must leave him or be smothered to death. It was too much for her, he wanted too much. 'He was strong,' she went on, 'his long limbs. Beautiful in his body. But how I hated him, for all that.' Her voice was low and dazed, as if she spoke in her sleep. 'How I hate you all, with your sweetmeats and laces and your stroking and moaning.'

He pulled away and sat up on the edge of the bed. 'Hate me? Why, everything I do is for you. I have worked for you, gone into debt for you. When I lay in the prison, I did it for you!'

'Do not make me guilty of your failures.' She began to laugh, very soft, her whole body shaking with it. 'Besides, your debt is paid. I have paid it ten times over.'

He pulled away and sat up on the edge of the bed. 'What have you done?' he said. 'What do you mean? Paid? You are mad!'

Then slowly, like a nail being hammered into his brain, the truth of it reached him.

'Have you not wondered,' she said, 'while you sat so long pondering my belly and the wrong I have done you, why there is no sheriff's flag by our gatepost? Why Inskip has not come again asking for money, nor threatened to take you back to Debtors' Jail?'

He dragged her from the bed and took her by the shoulders. 'How? Tell me how my debt was paid!'

In his voice, Sheba could hear the hollow ring of madness. She slipped out of his grasp and her body was very still, as though he had carved her of the granite from Jade's Mountain.

'I worked as poor women must,' she said. 'On my back, with a great weight upon me. Like one of your stones.'

The man stumbled out of the cottage and fell down on his face in the snow. 'Lost!' he cried.

The trees in the forest bent low when they heard him, and the wolves and the foxes wept tears.

TWENTY-SEVEN

The Candle of the Wicked

The soldiers of Daniel's militia returned to Great Meadow by twos and threes for fear of the Riot Act, their comradeship broken. The peddlers and fortune tellers had all fled, and even the Indian women were breaking their camp and gathering their children for a hasty journey back to Fort Holland.

The sheriff's men were on guard at the arsenal, hauling the cannon back in and barring the doors, and all round the field Tapp had posted his own mercenary soldiers. They had long ago crossed the invisible line that divides men from brutes; it was their greatest value as fighting men, for they did not hesitate at any order, and could be relied upon to improvise with practiced skill when the need or opportunity for violence arose.

When they came to the field to take Johnnie, they had left two of the sentries bleeding and unconscious and knocked down the officers' tent and ridden their horses across it. The smaller tents of the militiamen were ruined as well; canvas was slashed and campaign chests split open with axes. Wheels had been pulled from wagons and gun carriages and broken, and horses driven off from the paddock.

The cook tent, too, was a shambles. One or two of the women who had helped lay out the dinner sat weeping in the ruins of platters and crocks and spoiled food. Mrs Whittemore had a black eye beginning to swell, and little Mercy Lewis's gown was torn at the shoulder and neck.

If the rebels had hoped to find provisions, ammunition, shelter, or transport still waiting here in the camp for the taking, they found themselves forestalled.

But the lack of a conscience in Tapp's bully-boys went hand-in-hand with an almost total lack of discipline. You might give them an order, but whether they obeyed it or not was their business; they had lived too long in the woods to fancy themselves as any man's soldiers, even Marcus Tapp's, and once they had coin in their pocket, they spent it as might be expected. Most had been drinking off and on since the morning, and one or two were already asleep on their feet.

The wind had begun to blow steadily, now, gusting into a north-east gale that carried the sharp teeth of the Atlantic along with it. Women huddled in wagons and children wailed to go home to their own warm hearthfires.

'Nor'easter,' the women shouted above the wind. The cannon had never been fired to signal the end of the Muster, but they had no commander and the word passed among them: go home now, find a safe place to weather, get out of the storm.

But the threatened farmers were not ready. They had one last task in mind.

Two straw targets had been left standing at the end of the rifle range, and someone had stuck up a piece of blue cloth on one, a piece of brown on the other, pulled very tight and fastened with thongs at the back. Beside these makeshift slates lay several pieces of charcoal, well burnt and hard, but easy to mark with.

'Blue for the rebels!' whispered Lorenzo Newcomb to his neighbor, and then walked away across the field towards the butts. Two others heard him and each went off in a different direction to tell someone else.

Nobody picked up a musket nor fixed a bayonet. Nobody shouted. They might have been going to Sunday meeting, so quiet did it seem on the field. The sheriff's drunken bullies lounged and joked with each other, already huddled down around watchfires though the day was far from gone.

'Brown for the court and the sheriff!' said Sam Wiggins as he passed by Fred Pettingill's wagon.

'Blue for our freedom!' murmured his friend, and passed the word to someone else.

Josh Lamb had been the first to make his mark, a clear line of black on the blue. After him, John English, Thomas Whittemore, Oliver Kersey, Nathaniel Berge, Simon Penny. Every one of them blue.

One man at a time strolled across in front of the targets, made his mark, then drifted away again. They returned to packing their wagons and drove off quietly, bound for the nearby houses of friends or for one of the inns to spend the night and wait out the heavy rain and snow they were certain would follow the north wind.

As for the women, they watched as the marks on the blue side grew thicker, so many, now, that the cloth was nearly covered with black.

'What is it, Si?' murmured Susannah Penny, perched on the wagon seat beside her husband. 'What's it mean, all them marks?'

'County convention,' he said. 'If the vote goes blue, we keep the militia in muster and march on Siwall's court tomorrow.'

'And if it goes brown?'

Simon's face was grim. 'Then they may hang me like Johnnie, for I can't go back on it now.'

Susannah's hand gripped his arm. 'Who will lead you?' she said.

'They'll ask Josselyn.'

'And if he will not?'

Simon Penny snapped the goad over the back of his off-ox, old Barleycorn. 'He must,' he said. 'Or else we are as good as lost.'

'I make it four hundred and fourteen blue, and a hundred and twelve brown,' said John English.

It was past six and full dark now, raining steadily, and he and Josh and Oliver Kersey were counting the marks on the piece of blue cloth, spread out on a table at Lamb's Inn. Black Tirzah's eldest daughter, Persia, a girl of thirteen or fourteen, was minding the counter for Dolly, who had taken Jennet home to Two Mills.

'Carried, by Christ!' Phinney Rugg stumbled over to their table unnoticed, and he did not trouble to disguise his delight.

Kersey grabbed him by the collar and shook him, glancing round the room for any of the sheriff's men who might have come in from the storm. 'Rugg, you little skiver! Keep your voice down and your mouth shut!'

'Me?' The little ferret face screwed up with drunken indignation. 'I'm a safe hand, Noll! You may trust me for the world!'

'Lock him up.' John English was a worrier by nature. 'You know that tongue of his when it's oiled with beer.'

But Joshua didn't fancy locking any man up against his will, and Phinney could get stroppy when he'd a bit too much taken. 'There's not a room to be had in this place tonight, not with the rain,' he said. 'Look there, he's out like a halfpenny candle already!'

'I'll take him on home,' said Kersey. He caught up his rifle from the corner and shoved his tricorne down hard on his head, then hustled Rugg out the door.

Once they were gone, John English sat down with a sigh and poured himself a pewter mug of Dolly's best cider, and another for Josh. At a motion from the innkeeper, the black girl, Persia, heated a poker at the hearth and came to plunge it into the two cannikins, till the cider bubbled and steamed.

'A good lass, that,' said John Lamb. 'I shall ask her to stay and help Doll in the kitchen, I fancy. And I can use one or two of Tirzah's boys about the place, too.'

'That's providing you still have a place to your name.' English sucked at his pipe and sipped gingerly at the hot cider. 'What Siwall didn't grab up from Tories or taxes, he'll get now by calling the lot of us traitors.'

'Well, he'd not make much profit from this place tonight,' the landlord replied.

The bar-parlor was unusually quiet – no singing nor playing at draughts or backgammon on the boards by the fire, and nobody calling out for Josh to play them a tune on his fiddle so the young ones might dance. The men sat in small knots at the tables and benches, most still in uniform, and the women kept nearest the fire.

Nate Berge was there, and his wife and daughter, and Dick Dancer, too. Some of the womenfolk had brought knitting or sewing or mending, and they spoke in soft voices among themselves. Jemima sat quietly for once, working a pattern in delicate crosses on the hem of a doll's nightdress, fine lawn and as white as milk, the stitches deep blue like her eyes.

Aunt Sibylla's two chairmen, Jenks and Owen, no longer in periwigs and livery, looked like a pair of sober brown sparrows where they sat reading the week-old Boston papers by the fire.

'We must have a practiced commander, John.' Josh Lamb spoke too low to be heard by the others. 'I'm not fit for it, maneuvers and all that – it's beyond me.' He hesitated. 'Will you ask Daniel? Or shall I?'

John English shook his head. 'He's hung up his sword and resigned his commission, or soon will. And by God, I don't blame him. I won't ask him. Not I.'

'But surely, when his neighbors need his good counsel—'

'Counsel's one thing. War's another.' John laid a big hardened hand on the innkeeper's arm. 'Besides, you heard the sheriff. One of us so much as sneezes the wrong way, and whoever commands us is as guilty as we are. Would you take the risk of that, with four or five hundred untrained farm boys mad as hell and ready to fire at anything in silk breeches?'

There was a noise at the door, and three men came in, shaking the rain from their cloaks and hats. Siwall and Royallton-Smith were followed – somewhat too eagerly, as usual – by Bob Inskip, Siwall's bailiff.

Squeezer Inskip was thick and grey-haired and slouching. He wore a fine woolen coat and a pair of good breeches – though they were not silk – but his shirt looked as though it had not been washed in a year and a day, and his neckcloth still bore the stains of his morning's porridge. His eyes were small and piggy and pink-edged behind a pair of thick spectacles, and his tongue always peeped out a bit between his teeth, as though he were squeezing it, too.

'He's got his nerve, I'll say that for him,' murmured Nate Berge to Tom Whittemore. 'Some in this room would just as soon carve old Squeezer for supper as look at him!'

'Landlord!' cried Siwall. 'Is the Salcombe coach late?'

Josh looked up, surprised. 'Why, it left an hour and a quarter since, and glad to be gone before nightfall in this weather!'

'I'm damned if it did! Well, then, let us have three good mugs of that hot cider!' said the magistrate. 'It's a cold, wretched night, and my friend Smith here has a long horse-back ride ahead of him, it would seem. Can you not wait till the morning, William? This weather will clear by then.'

'I must be in Salcombe the day after tomorrow, and I can manage to ride as far tonight as Beale's Inn, surely, storm or no storm.' Smith laughed ruefully. 'But a little fortification before I set off will never come amiss. A round for all these gentlemen by the fire! They will have a cold way home this night, too.'

It was a calculated effort at healing the breach the afternoon's sad business had widened. But no one stepped up to the counter. For a moment it grew very quiet, except for the ticking of the big clock in its black walnut case and the snap of the pine logs on the fire.

'You hold us damn cheap, Master General Court,'

somebody said. 'To think a bit of cider will buy us, after what you done this day.'

Siwall looked up. 'Who said that?' he demanded. 'Who spoke?'

But the men only stared at their hands on the tables.

Persia, who had been serving a group of Pownalby men in the corner, went quietly behind the wicket and poured out the drink from her pitcher. She heated it and took it to Siwall's table. But as she approached, Squeezer Inskip stuck out his big booted foot and tripped her up.

She cried out as the hot cider splashed her, and sprawled to the floor at their feet, and Inskip sniggered. 'Seems the black bitch takes after her sire, don't she?' he said. 'They neither one can keep their footing under the eyes of their betters.'

The men did not move. One or two set down mugs with a crash on the table. There was a hiss from Jemima, like a snake that is ready to strike.

Josh helped the black girl up, his eyes narrowed. 'Go in the kitchen, my dear,' he said gently. 'Put some butter on that burn, and then go up and see how your mother's faring, eh?'

Persia did as she was told and the landlord reached behind the bar for a mop. He began to clean up the mess of spilled cider, but Inskip was riding too high to stop now.

'Mr Siwall, here, bespoke us three mugs of your brew, Lamb!' he shouted. 'Mr Smith of the General Court has no time to spare for laggards and fools!'

'Then what's he doing in your company, y'old bugger?' growled Josh, and went on mopping. 'If you're in such a passion for cider, go fetch three mugs for yourself.'

'Why, Squeezer can't count to three, Joshua!' cried

Lorenzo Newcomb. His wife, Martha, who sat hunched over her knitting by the fire, looked up at the sound of his voice, wide-eyed and afraid. 'For didn't I pay him three times what I owed to his master,' her husband went on, 'and he swears I have not paid it once!'

'Aye, Renzo has the right of it!' said Ben Petherbridge.

'I paid him *four* times in one month, and he still says I'm behind in my debt!' another chimed in.

'And me!'

'We've most of us been two-timed! You just ask old Noll Kersey how *he* come into debt, he'll say the same!'

Smith looked around at the faces. 'What is this, Siwall? What are these men saying?'

'It's nonsense, William. Pay no heed to them.'

'You'll pay heed to us soon enough, Master Magistrate!' The Pownalby men had pine sprigs in the buttonholes of their waistcoats. 'When your court is closed down and your sheriff is helpless, then we shall see who's telling the truth and who isn't!'

'Be still,' somebody hissed, and the room fell silent again.

But Royallton-Smith had more on his mind than a blockaded courtroom. He stood up, a tall, dignified figure. A decent man who had begun to doubt his own dealings at last.

'You say you have paid to this man, Mr Inskip, the debts and the fair interest you owe to his master?' he asked them.

'I don't know about fair.' Again it was little Lorenzo Newcomb who spoke up first. 'But I owed thirty pound, sir, that I borrowed from Siwall last April to buy boards in at Markham's to put up my barn. I paid off two pound in May, and another two in June, and when Squeezer come back in

July for his money, he says I owe four, and twice the interest, for I never paid him nothing in June.'

'Do you not ask receipts of him? Had you no evidence in writing?'

'He might give me a bushel of paper, sir, but I cannot read writing. My Martha, she sets it all down in straight lines in a copybook, and when I pay, she makes a cross mark through 'em, though she can't read neither, nor write proper. But it was marked plain enough, and I showed it to Squeezer, and he said he would take it and show it to Siwall.'

'That was the last you seen of *that* book, I wager!' cried old Enoch Luckett.

'Is this true, Mr Inskip?' Smith turned to Squeezer.

'Why, no sir, it ain't true!' The bailiff's fat cheeks puffed out and then in again and his forehead shone with sweat. 'They're lying, as you might expect of a crew of spenders and wasters! What proof is a bunch of lines and crosses writ down on a page? Any fool can make crosses! I'm no thief, sir, and no two-timer, whatever they say!'

'Well, if you ain't, we know well enough who is!' someone shouted. Every eye in the place turned to Siwall.

'I will put up with this no longer!' The magistrate got up from the table and flung open the door, snatching up his cloak as he went.

'Mr Lamb, you will hear from the sheriff tomorrow!' he snapped. 'I have no doubt he will shut down this hotbed of insurrection and impose a curfew on the town. And as for the threats I have heard against the Debtors' Court—'

'You call it rebellion to declare you're a thief and a liar? Are you king, Mr Siwall?' asked John English.

'Or naught but God Almighty?' somebody shouted.

Inskip had backed away towards the door to the kitchen, but Smith stood his ground in the middle of the room.

'Siwall!' he said sharply. 'Come away from that door, sir! You owe me an answer. What have you done with the payments these men claim to have made to you?'

'Done?' Siwall's face was the color of brick. 'I have taken no more than just payment and interest for what they have owed me! They expect to live like gentry and have silk gowns for their women—'

'I have heard that stale argument before, sir. In my pride, I have even given it some credence. Now I begin to doubt but I have been nine parts a poor hoodwinked fool!'

The door blew shut with a crash and now it was Smith who took up his cloak. 'I must not be hasty to bring accusations,' he said. 'You have books in your office, Siwall, have you not?'

He turned to look for Inskip, but the bailiff had gone, slipped away through the kitchen. 'Where is your constable?' Smith said to the men. 'The Scotchman must lay hands on that rogue of a bailiff, and bring him to me at Burnt Hill. I will have a reckoning here!'

Hamilton Siwall was shaking with rage, but his breath came in the deep painful gulps of a man who fights for his life. 'You take great liberties, Smith. If you were not the father of my son's wife—'

'I fear I have married my poor daughter into a family of rascals, sir. But I pray you will yet prove me wrong.' Smith flung wide the door and stood for a moment, the light of the hearth and the candles behind him, and his tall frame did not give when the cold wind struck it.

The rain had begun to turn into sleet. From outside on the common, through the ice and the storm and the rising wind, came a shrill cry, like a woman in labor. One cry and no more.

'Aayiieeeeee!'

Then there was a muffled sound like the pop of a stick in the fire, faraway and half-drowned by the rattle of ice on the cobbles.

Smith's lean body buckled as though a spasm had struck him. There was another shot and he convulsed again, then fell heavily to the floor, blood streaming from a gaping wound in his throat and seeping slowly from another in his belly.

'Clear out!' someone shouted, and the men ran for their womenfolk. In less than a moment the parlor was empty, but for Siwall and John Lamb and Mr English, and the peddler and his daughter. Jemima hardly seemed to notice the dead man; she sat peaceably as though nothing had happened, still stitching away at her doll.

Joshua bent over the corpse and so did John English. But Siwall only gaped, open-mouthed, tearing at his stock-tie as though it would strangle him.

Smith had taken a shot that pierced his throat from front to back, and another in the guts to finish him. It was a thing they taught you in the army, and all woodsmen knew it. Shoot twice and be certain. Never leave a creature wounded, lest it claw you to pieces as soon as you turn your back.

'Same as old Clinch,' murmured the innkeeper.

'This needs the sound of a prayer.' John gave a shudder. 'Is your father here, Dick?'

'The Reminder's back at the Mills, sir. Thought he might do some good there.' The peddler stood crushing his hat to his bosom.

'Still, some word should be said for the dead,' Joshua murmured.

'Oh, bother you all!' Jemima stood up from the settle and came to where Smith's body lay, the fashion doll still cradled against her. 'Men may cipher and count and add up their moneyboxes. But women know how to serve the dead proper. You must send for some woman to come!'

'Why are *you* not a woman yourself, my dear?' said Josh softly.

Jemima walked around the body once, twice, three times. 'I was meant for one, sure. But I never growed into it. A woman must love and I can't love. A woman must bear and I daren't bear. A woman must die and I will not.' She bent down to the man's body and dipped her fingertip into his blood. 'See,' she said. 'See how it burns me? But the candle of the wicked shall soon be put out.'

Siwall made a sound, almost a sob, and she looked up at him. 'I know you of old. You are a dull, smoky candle,' she told him. 'You should have guttered long ago.'

She held up the doll to inspect it, planted a kiss on its forehead, then hurled it all of a sudden into the fire. With a low cry, Siwall suddenly bolted, crashing out into the night and the pelting ice.

But Jemima only stood on the hearthrug, her slight body turning in the light of the flames, the strange, motiveless tears streaming down her cheeks and the red glow of the fire reflecting upon them, so that her face seemed to burn like the small wooden doll on the grate.

'We have a little sister,' she said, 'and she hath no breasts: what shall we do for our sister?'

'Song of Solomon, that is,' murmured Joshua. 'The

bride's song. Preacher read it when me and my Dolly was wed.'

'If she be a wall, we will build upon her a palace of silver. If she be a door, we will cover her with fine boards of cedar. I am a wall. I am a door. I am a tower of ivory.' Jemima looked up. 'She is here. I have seen her. My foolish old child has seen her. Little sister is coming home again, and all the false prophets shall be quite cast down.'

TWENTY-EIGHT

The Journal of Hannah Trevor

6 November, the year 1786

Past nine in the night, a great storm from the north-east. The old ash in the dooryard is weighed heavy with ice and groans like a man in chains.

My Aunt fears for it as the last gasp of her living, for she planted it there as a bride.

I write at the bedside of my Uncle, who I thank God is yet senseless of the sorrow that is come upon his House.

I have seen my cousin hanged this day, that was like my own little brother, that I taught to sing Farmer in the Dell and carve Jack-o'-the-Lanterns at All Hallows' Eve. More cruel a death it was than most men would vouchsafe to a wolf or a weasel, and what Johnnie died for the gain of I know not, nor never shall in this world.

Now I see how the prison of power and arrogance grows tighter about us and is not to be broke by the bravest, for we carry it with us wherever we go. If we live, we must live as my

silent daughter speaks, in the deep of our minds, where no law
and no scorn and no master may reach us, excepting the Scourge
that is God's.

They will make a saint of Johnnie now as they did of George
Anson, but to have him so is to stifle the truth of him with foolish
painted rags. For the sake of himself he did much harm to many
that loved him, and it will not be soon ended, whether the cause
was good or not.

And I too have done harm to hold back from my dearest
heart, for I think now that some brief loving is all the freedom
there may be in this world.

If marriage be a bond, I am ready to bear it. If love be a
fire, I am already burnt.

Men ride this night with torches on both sides the river, so many
the Night Watch cannot challenge them. Some are sheriff's
men and some are Regulators, but all are blind when they ride
and war bites at their heels, and drives them as the wind drives
the sleet.

I thank God my love is not among them. He will not leave
me and sits now at this table with the candle between us, writing
a letter to resign his commission, which he will send as soon as it
is day. This he does for my sake and my daughter's, and for the
child's that is not born.

But his danger is not yet ended, nor mine with him. If the
men come to ask him, I fear he may yet be brought to lead them
against the Court and the Sheriff, for the winter is coming and
they know little of armies but the orders they follow. They are
his friends, and his good heart aches for their trouble.

Another such night may be the last we are granted together.
I am determined to marry as soon as may be.

My Uncle sleeps quiet without aid of the poppy. Have given hawthorn tea and all-heal, very scant, which seem to have good effect. I dare hope he is not so sorely stricken as was feared at the first. When I take his left hand in mine and squeeze it, I feel, I believe, some pressure returned by his fingers, and his left eyelid will flutter when I hold the candle near.

Dolly weeps beside Jonathan's corpse and will take no comfort, and my Aunt sits like stone and scarcely speaks, hearing only the wind in her tree. I thank God they have not to bear the false wailing of my cousin's wife, Sally, for after all her clamor over place in the house, she is gone off of a sudden this afternoon, to visit her mother at Cade's Bay, so she said. And her son left behind like loose hay from a haycart, poor mite, with a note pinned onto his gown.

I am weary and sick and afraid of the morrow, but I shall work some while on my quilt of Bridges Burning, piecing the blocks and laying out the pattern together. So my hands may give ease to my mind, and the beauty of simple making lay a healing leaf upon the heart.

I have not wept for my Cousin, and I shall not. But the child inside me mourns.

TWENTY-NINE

Piecing the Evidence: On the Nature of Freedom

LETTER OF DANIEL JOSSELYN, MAJOR, RUFFORD
AND WYBROW MILITIA, TO COLONEL EDWARD
SCRIBNER, COMMANDANT, SEVENTH REGIMENT,
FORT HENDLY, SALCOMBE, PROVINCE OF MAINE,
COMMONWEALTH OF MASSACHUSETTS
6 NOVEMBER 1786

My Dear Colonel,

It is with deep regret and great anguish of spirit that I must herewith resign my commission as commanding Officer of the Fourth, Fifth, Sixth, Eighth, and Tenth companies, Seventh Regiment, Commonwealth Militia. I beg you to believe that my decision has been reached after much deliberation, and is no token of my intent to serve any cause other than that of peace and justice among my neighbors.

But let me speak frankly, my dear Edward. You know me as well as any, and you know that I cannot dissemble. The government and the squires – I suppose I am one, though I still carry the title uneasily – call men rebels who are no more than decent, simple fellows pushed past endurance. They take no action in their own defense that was not taught them in the War by the same men who now call them traitors, and they do not comprehend on what grounds the tyranny of rich profiteers who close ranks against them is more to be borne than that of a king. There are some few hotheads amongst them, I grant you, but the cooler minds keep to a fair vote and have no wish to harm property or lives.

They want time, that is all, to dig themselves out of a hole.

And what else is freedom, my friend? Time to do honest work, and a decent night's sleep after, once the debts have been paid? And better memories than yours and mine, pray God.

But the law will not give them time, and their memories are like to be bitter indeed. I have seen as much this day, with the hanging of Jonathan Markham. It was sheer folly, a gesture of punishment to put fear into the poor they call rabble. It will put hate there instead, and more will die of it, sons after fathers and their sons again, if some redress is not made.

They have asked me to lead them and they will ask again, but I will not take sides in this business. I will not be used against them, nor by them against my own life and that of my dearest wife and children, call me coward who will.

For this reason, I resign my commission, and I hope you may comprehend and forgive me. My mind is clouded with fighting and my body is weary of wars, and no cause looks noble to me but a quiet life with my family round me.

If I cannot find such a life here, I am resolved to seek it farther west, in Pennsylvania or the Ohio country, or perhaps north, in French Canada. I can never go back to England, as you know. Perhaps a man ought not return to a place he carries so deep in his marrow, lest he gorge on it, and surfeit and die.

You and I used to say we were fighting for freedom, but I do not think we were such fools as to believe it, even then. Wars are for land and money and politics. But freedom is like true marriage, I think. It is a grace of the spirit that few ever attain, and the more we prate of it, the less we achieve it. It crumbles like a poorly kneaded loaf under the weight of selfishness and the intoxication of power, and no couple – no country, however benign – will ever be able to slice it and serve it up neat, without a crumb left behind.

The thing is to labor, my friend. To study the best receipts, and take time to set a new loaf and work it more carefully than the last one, and be better housewives than we ever were before.

With my sincere regrets, my dear Edward, in unaltered amity,

Daniel Josselyn, Esquire
Mapleton Grange Farm

Post Scriptum. As you see, my metaphors grow somewhat homely, now I am to wed again. Mistress Hannah will teach me to quilt, next, and make candles! Come to us at Christmas, and we shall show you a fine time, I promise you!

THIRTY

Lock and Key

Almost as soon as he had written it, Daniel crossed through the postscript of his letter to Edward Scribner. Foolish words, written as though the events of this day would be miraculously erased once he was free of command.

It was beyond him to hope for marriage now, with all Hannah's family troubles and the new war besides. And as for Christmas, that seemed like a fairy tale someone had long ago told him, a magical thing never known in the grey, waking world.

Since they brought Jonathan's body home, Hannah had said scarcely a word to him beyond the needed instructions, calmly spoken. The boy's body must be stripped and washed, and then dressed in clean linen, and Julia had driven them all from the kitchen while she bid this private farewell to the last child she had borne.

'He is too heavy for you,' Daniel had told her. 'Let me stay. Let me help you.' Though he knew he had done only what he had to, he needed to be forgiven.

'No,' Julia said. 'I must do this alone.' Her long, equine

face lifted and she looked up at Daniel. 'I was near too old for bearing when I carried him. But I begged God for another, and bamboozled poor Husband into it. There is – a sovereignty in it, men do not understand. When a woman is with child, she is a separate country and no man can rule her. Not even with love.' She glanced over at Hannah. 'It was – selfish. And now I am paid.'

Daniel lifted the old woman's hand to his lips and bent his head over it. Julia drew him against her for a moment and he could feel how her nerves were numbed and braced against what she must do.

'Now leave me to my boy,' she said. 'I must tend him this last time alone.'

Once Julia had finished, Daniel brought boards from the mill, and Jonathan's newly washed body was laid on the backs of two rush-bottomed chairs in the parlor. But still Hannah said little beyond the giving of orders.

The cows and the horse and the oxen must be seen to. Shutters must be closed and fastened. Enough wood must be brought in to last through the storm, and fresh water put in all the buckets in case the well froze over.

At last it was all done, all the orders carried out.

Then nothing. No questions. No counsel. No reproach from her.

Daniel folded his letter to Scribner and looked up. 'How is your uncle?' he asked her.

Hannah was holding a mirror to the sick man's lips. 'His breathing clouds more of the glass than before,' she told him.

'I think he improves. I have seen such cases sleep for two days or more, and wake with only slight damage. But I shall say nothing to Aunt for the present.'

'You are right.' He sealed the letter with a drop of greasy tallow from the candle, then sat staring into the flame. 'False hope is worse than none.'

Daniel got up and went to the settle where Jennet was sleeping, wrapped in quilts with the old cat nestled warm by her side. They had brought Henry's bed down here to the workroom for the sake of the fire, and this strange arrangement, added to her father's unaccustomed presence in the house and her own strange adventures that terrible day, had made the child restless and fretful. Hannah had brewed her a cup of linden-flower tea with honey, which Jennet liked for its sweet lemony flavor, and it had made her drowsy.

But they had not had the heart to pack her off to the cold bedchamber by herself. Even now she fought against sleep, her arms flinging off the quilts and her small feet thrashing as though some phantom dragged at her.

What had she seen that day that upset her? Daniel wondered. Not the hanging, Sibylla had made certain of that. Not the corpse. Kitty had kept her upstairs playing at cup-and-ball till the body was laid in the parlor.

Did Jennet perhaps *hear* the storm outside, or the ice striking the windows like gravel thrown by naughty boys? Did the wind call to her, and the quick-frozen river that cracked and groaned and stove in the dories like wickerwork?

Where are you? he thought, and though his hand lay on Jennet, his eyes were on Hannah. *Where do women go when their minds desert us and only their bodies remain? What frail bridge do they walk upon? What storms wash their hearts and keep them clean?*

'Unnnhhh,' Jennet breathed, her hands reaching out to catch at nothing. The small throat was tight and the sound seemed trapped inside her.

'Hush, my girl,' Daniel said, and bent down to kiss the child, her eyes and her cheeks and her fragile, laboring throat, and the hands that reached out to him, to someone. He caught them and held them, close against his chest.

The candle flame danced in a sudden draught, and he heard Hannah pour off the melted tallow into a pail, to keep the light from guttering. When the pail was full, they would add it to others and melt it again and make more candles, using it over and over, so that the flame of the first light, once kindled, never quite died away.

'I don't expect you to forgive me,' he said quietly. 'But you must talk to me, Hannah.'

'What shall I say?'

The light grew brighter behind him. When Daniel turned to look at her, she sat at her quilting frame, two candles burning in the sconces set into the wall at her back. On top of the nearly finished China Dish quilt she had spilled out new pieces, squares and triangles and hexagons of blue and brown and crimson, her fingers scattering them like jewels in the flickering light, wedding the two patterns together by chance, as the colors fell.

'I am to blame for Johnnie's death,' Daniel said, his voice scoured with weariness.

Her hands stopped and she clutched them together. 'This day has been a great harvest of dying. You cannot take blame for it all.'

But he continued, uncertain. 'I should never have listened to him. When I came back from Gull's Isle, I found Jean-le-Petit, the Dutchman's runner, waiting in my stableyard. Johnnie said I must meet him in the woods beyond Berge's place. Bring him clothes and a horse, so that he might come home.'

Her hands took up the work again. 'And you rode to meet him.'

'Yes, of course. How could I not?' Jennet reached out again in her sleep and Daniel took her up in his lap, her head on his shoulder. 'Last night, before the hunt set out, I took him the clothes as he asked, and an old pair of my aunt's spectacles so he might not be recognized. The horse I could not risk. My horses are all known hereabouts. I rode back by the crest road so I wouldn't be seen, and then I went on foot to meet Josh and McGregor.'

'You said nothing to me. You didn't show me his letter.'

'There was no letter,' he told her, 'only a message. Jean is a thief and a twister, he makes a virtue of horse-stealing. I couldn't tell but it was some scheme of his to rob me.'

'And once you had seen Johnnie? Could you not have told me then?'

'The men who had helped him ran a terrible risk, Hannah! Berge and Drewel and the others. I gave my word I would say nothing to anyone, and I thought Johnnie would be here with you next day.'

Daniel's face looked thin and drawn in the light from the candles, the dark shadows under his eyes like hollow caves. His long fingers lay on his daughter's face, stroking her cheek as though he played on some finely tuned instrument.

'He told me he only meant to come home,' he said very softly, 'for a visit, an hour or two with his son. I could not refuse him that.'

'No. You could not.'

Hannah left her work and drew closer. From the parlor

came the murmur of old Reverend Samuel Dancer's high tenor voice, speaking a psalm for the dead.

Out of the depths have I cried unto thee, O Lord.

'Johnnie swore he wouldn't chance setting foot in the village,' Daniel said. 'I forgot – how young he was. What it is to be young and still to believe in great causes. I was a fool, and now he's dead.'

If thou, Lord, shouldest mark iniquities, O Lord, who shall stand?

With the little girl nestled between them, Hannah came and sat on the settle beside him. Her hand reached up and laid itself against his face, so that when he spoke she felt the warmth of his breath as it passed through her fingers.

'When he came to the Muster,' Daniel continued, 'he left me no choice but to arrest him. If I had not—'

'I know,' she whispered, stroking his eyes closed. 'The blame is not yours. You didn't know of the Riot Act, what power the law let Tapp take upon himself.'

'You forgive me? For deceiving you, for not being plain with you?'

'Could I wed you this night if I did not?' she said.

His eyes opened, the lashes brushing her palms. A great limb crashed down from the old tree in the yard, with a sound like the smashing of glass as the thick coat of ice on the ground below broke with the weight of the bough. Her arms had slipped around him, but now he drew gently away.

'First I must tell you, Hannah,' he said. 'This morning, how I was in the woods when we found Clinch's body— God knows what you must have thought. There is some memory plagues me very like what we found. A man shot, older than Clinch, but—Some business of burning mixed into it. It was there even before this morning. Only it's in bits and pieces, so that—'

'Tell me after. It will be soon enough.' Hannah stood up, suddenly brisk and determined. 'Just now I am much engaged, sir. I must get my daughter to bed and then put on my wedding gown. An odd order of things, I do grant you. But heigh-ho. Life's a conundrum, take it at the best.'

Daniel's tired face broke into a grin. 'Oh, a wedding gown, by all means. That's providing you can still do up the buttons.'

'That gown cost five shillings dressmaking and my best piece of rose-colored wool, sir. I shall do up the buttons, all right.'

In the bed nearby, the sick man's breath came heavy and deep. In the cold parlor, the dead boy lay broken, with candles at his head and feet and the women keeping watch over him. And yet Hannah Trevor would do up her buttons, whatever they cost.

She bent to kiss Daniel and he pulled her close, Jenny's warm shape still snuggled between them.

'How proud,' he said. The words came half-strangled, like his daughter's. 'How proud I am of loving you.'

He kissed her deeply, letting her feel the ache and the joy in him.

'Only what shall we do for a preacher, in such weather and on such a night?' he said at last.

She smiled. 'The preacher is ready. Can you not hear him?'

I wait for the Lord, my soul doth wait, and in his word do I hope.

'Now, Hannah. Be sensible. The old fellow prays well enough. But he's almost as dotty as that granddaughter of his. How if it should not be legal? If he be not a preacher at all?'

'You are grown terrible scrupulous all of a sudden, Your Lordship! I regret we must cheat your great-aunt of the sight of us stood at the altar. But I can wait no longer, sir. Tonight you must take me or not.'

'Your memory fails you, Mrs Trevor,' Daniel Josselyn whispered. 'I took you long ago.'

Hannah paused only to lay a hand on her uncle's throat for a sense of his heartbeat and to wrap up the soapstone in flannel to warm Jennet's bed. Then, taking the candle, she led the way up the back stairs and Daniel followed her, the sleeping child in his arms.

It was a small, bare room with sloping ceilings and long windows that looked out towards the river and Mapleton Grange. He had been there briefly in summer, while her aunt and uncle slept next door – or pretended to. But now, to prepare for the winter, the red-checked bed curtains had been hung up again and white muslin draped across the windows, and on the walls Hannah's own quilts gave the room enough brightness and pattern to delight even her daughter, as well as added warmth.

She set the candle down on the table and peered out of the window. The sleet had almost stopped now, leaving a coating of ice nearly three inches deep on the low ground and a glistening sheen of an inch or so on the slopes.

The sluice and the mill pond gleamed bright silver in the strange stormlight, the low, racing clouds reflecting the whiteness of a snow that was already beginning, its flakes like small grains of white sand. It would coat the paths and the half-frozen river, hiding the treacherous ice underneath, but making it easier for riding horses and light sleighs or sledges to travel.

For men on foot, though, or for oxen and heavy wagons, it would still be hard labor indeed to get up the steep slope from the mill.

Well, at least they might have this one night's peace. Hannah drew back the bed curtains for Daniel to lay Jennet down. But Arthur, the old cat, had come padding up with them, and true to his custom, he was already installed in the middle of the bed.

'Away now, you old rascal!' Hannah tried to shoo him away with a slipper, but he only laid back his one good ear and gave a hiss and a growl, slapping at her with an angry paw. She held the candle higher. He was pawing at something in the bed and growling, backing off and pouncing, then purring with pleasure.

Daniel leaned over to look. 'Why, he's brought us a mouse for a wedding gift!'

'On my best quilt? Out! Out of there, and take your prize with you!'

Where Arthur was concerned, Jennet had a sixth sense, and she woke in Daniel's arms to the sight of her mother picking up the headless mouse by its half-eaten tail and flinging it into the slop bucket across the room.

The child's shoulders began to heave and her mouth fell open.

'Yes, that's right!' Hannah cried. 'Laugh, my little scamp! I know whose idea it was to let that cat make free of my bed!'

But Jennet was no longer laughing. She had begun to make signs now, the Indian fingertalk her father had taught her. The child's small hand wagged back and forth, back and forth, the index finger out and pointed downward.

'What is it? What's she saying?'

'I don't know,' Daniel frowned. 'It's nothing I've taught her.'

The little girl was squirming now, demanding to be set down. Once her boots hit the floor, she snatched up her mother's hand and began to pull at her, tugging her toward the door.

'Annnhh-ahhhh,' she said, and made the sign again.

Hannah shook her head in frustration. 'She wants to show me something. I don't doubt it's no more than a piece of old rock or a button. At this rate, we shall never be wed.'

'Annnhhh-ahh!'

Into the hall they went and along the dark passage to the front stairs, then clattering down the uncarpeted steps to the entry hall that separated parlor and kitchen. It was a narrow space, very cold and unlighted. Hannah disappeared for a moment into the kitchen, to return with a light.

'No, Flower, leave the clock alone!' Jennet was pulling and prying at the door to the weight box. 'What's she doing? She'll topple it in a minute!' Hannah cried.

She snatched the child up, but Jennet would not be satisfied. Again she made the sign, index finger pointing downward and hand moving back and forth.

'Why, it's not sign-talk at all.' Daniel smiled. 'She's aping the pendulum, that's all.'

'But she's never bothered about it before.'

It was true. There were clocks aplenty at the Grange, too, and Jennet seemed used to them, but tonight something was different. Something gnawed at her and plagued her, something like her father's buried memories, that she knew and could not say.

'Let me have that candle, my love.' Daniel held up the

light and ran his hand around the edge of the glass over the clockface. 'It was the weight box that seemed to upset her so. Have you the key to it?'

'Not anymore.' Hannah's heart skipped a beat, as she remembered Sally's words of that morning: *I will have the key to the clock and the pewter dresser. I am better than you, and one day soon you shall all know it.*

The door to the weight box creaked open under Daniel's hand. 'Why, here is the key,' he said. 'Still in the lock.'

But once the small door stood open, it was plain enough what was wrong. The small tin box of carefully saved shillings and pence that was Henry Markham's savings bank was empty of every last pence. Inside was a piece of paper, neatly folded but not sealed. Hannah felt for her spectacles and looked at it.

On the front was a strange, senseless design of black parallel lines. Broken lines met solid ones and crossed them, and others wound in and out of them. In the center was a picture of a heart pierced with an arrow. *True Love's Retreat*, they had printed at the top of the page.

'Why, it's one of Sally's fool mazes,' murmured Hannah.

'Turn the page over. There's writing on the back.'

It was Sally's round, childish hand, scribed with a quill that had not been sharpened in some time, and the ink had soaked into the soft paper, making it difficult to read.

How do you like your wedding gift, Mistress Hannah, that I left on your bolster? Your mooncalf gave me a dead thing for spite, and now I give it back for triumph. I am gone away and I shall laugh myself sick to think of your sour faces when you read this. You may make more money, but I must have something to buy fine things once we are in Boston, for I shall soon be a gentleman's lady and ride in a carriage and have more maids to wait upon me than ever Mistress Hannah Drab will have! It is little money enough and besides, it is owed me. Have I not had to bear with all your slights?

Hannah took off her spectacles and handed the paper to Daniel.

'Jennet must have seen her at work here,' she said. 'What shall I do, my love? It is all Uncle's savings, near forty pound. The tax is paid till the summer, but there is his debt to Siwall. And to you.'

'In an hour more I shall be his nephew. Do you think I would grudge him ten times forty pound?'

'But my aunt will grudge borrowing. She is bitter proud.'

'Then she must not hear of it till we have filled up the box again.' Daniel held the corner of Sally's smug letter to the candle flame and it caught and blazed up. 'A gentleman's lady, the girl said? What connections has Sally in Boston?'

Hannah was already more than certain. But as she watched the letter burn down to a charred bit of ash in the candlecup, her mind returned to what Lady Sibylla had told her: *I glimpsed a woman, a young thing. Silly and giggling. In Siwall's coach.*

All those trips to the village, to come back with nothing but a tuppenny paper puzzle. The fine laces and ribbons and kerchiefs Jonathan could never have afforded and would never have thought of. Why, the girl must have been meeting her lover almost since the day of his marriage to Harriet Royallton-Smith!

'She's gone off with Jem Siwall,' Hannah whispered. 'I saw him this morning. He tried to tell me, I think, but my mind was on Clinch.' She sank down on the visitors' bench by the foot of the stairs. 'What else have I seen this day and not seen? I am blind. Dear God. What will become of her?'

Jennet wandered back to the clock and began to grope in her pocket for something, but they were too preoccupied to pay her much heed.

'If you wish,' Daniel said, 'I will try to recover her. Make inquiries along the post road. Or go to Boston myself.'

'But you think it is useless?'

'I think— ' He drew Hannah close and put his forehead to hers. 'I think you cannot save all the foolish lost things in the world. But you wouldn't be Hannah Trevor if you didn't try.'

She leaned on him for a moment, considering. 'If Sally were dragged back, she would only find somebody else to run off with, perhaps a worse rascal than Jem. Who knows, they may even learn to steady each other if they have no choice. No. Best leave it alone.'

Daniel nodded. It was harsh, but sensible. 'I am sorry for her boy,' he said, 'but she did better to leave him here safe than to take him God knows where, that's certain.'

Jennet drew something out of her pocket and laid it inside the empty tin savings-box. Then she closed the lid and picked it up and shook it to feel it rattle. The clock struck ten and the deep sound reached into her silence and startled her.

'Nahhh!' she cried and ran to hide behind Daniel, the box still in her hands.

'What's she got in there now?' Hannah went to peer inside the box. 'What did I tell you? It's only a pewter button.'

Daniel took it up and examined it. For a time he was

silent, so far away from her that he might have been dreaming.

'Christ,' he whispered.

'What is it?'

'A uniform button,' he replied. 'See there, the skull and crossed bones? It's the Twelfth Massachusetts, the same as the button you knelt on by Clinch's body this morning.' Daniel swooped up his daughter and held her, so tight she could hardly get her breath.

'Whose is it? Where could she have got it?' A few thick threads were torn away and clung inside the shank, as though it had been pulled off by twisting, and Hannah examined them by the light of the candle.

Daniel rocked the child back and forth, trying to think. 'The Crossed-Boners were rifle troops. Ghostkillers, Burgoyne used to call them. They didn't fight by the rules of warfare. Shot from ambush, like Indians. And—'

He seemed suddenly remote. He set Jennet down again and put his hands to his face.

'My love, what ails you?' Hannah asked him.

'I hardly know. Something I remember and do not remember. A fight with a party of Tory raiders, I think. Perhaps they were not raiders. Perhaps *we* were the raiders. There was a woman I buried. A dead girl the soldiers had gotten with child and abandoned, so they said – and a dead man. Many men. Burning. This is hell and – and we are the devil. You – you are the world to me now.'

He was shaking, his head and his hands like a patient with palsy, and all the while trying to stop himself, to force back his control.

'Breathe deep, my dear.' Hannah took him by the hands and held him, hard. 'Deeper. That's right.'

'I'm sorry. I'm sorry. It comes on me mostly in sleep,' he said. 'Then I'm up half the night wandering, trying to fix on it. Only this morning, with Clinch, it came waking. As it did now.' He stared down at the button that lay clutched in his palm.

'Where were you, where was the battle?'

'I don't know. I don't even remember which side I was on.'

'And the dead girl? Who was she? What did she look like?'

'Young. She'd been beaten and hanged. There was a village. A wood. Some cold place, not much different from this. Even in spring, it was cold there.' He turned from Hannah and stared into the dim parlor where the old parson still murmured his psalms and the candles burned for the dead. 'The world smashed into bits, once I left you. I can't put it together again. Who I was. What I did then. It's like somebody else, and I only watch from a great distance.'

She took the button from him, puzzling over the design. 'Are there any of this regiment in your company?' she asked Daniel. 'The Crossed-Boners?'

'If there are, it will be in the Muster List, with the regimental histories. All the records are there.'

'Where is it, Daniel? We must see that list.'

'It was left in the officers' tent. Tapp must have it by now.'

Hannah knew she must calm him. 'Ah, well. Perhaps it means nothing, after all. Men shed their buttons like feathers in molting season. And Jenny picks up every bright thing she sets eyes on these days.'

'There's something else it may mean,' said Daniel grimly. 'She may have been with Sam Clinch's killer this morning, unwitting. A loose button. We delayed the column while I helped you to see to your uncle, she could have pulled it from a dozen uniforms then. Men she knew. Trusted. I saw her myself with Berge and his wife, and with Simon Penny.'

'But they are friends. Surely—'

'Such a man has no friends. He can't afford them. He knows where he lost that other button, the one you found by Clinch's body. The whole town's heard it talked of by now.'

Hannah stared down at the tarnished piece of pewter. 'You mean, if he thinks Jenny has this one, the mate of the other—'

Daniel nodded. 'Then he may come to claim it again.'

THIRTY-ONE

Bridges Burnt

'Wilt thou, Daniel Edmund Charles Josselyn, have this Woman to thy wedded wife, to live together after God's ordinance in the holy estate of Matrimony? Wilt thou love her, comfort her, honor, and keep her in sickness and in health; and, forsaking all others, keep thee only unto her, so long as ye both shall live?'

The Mortal Reminder stood with his back to the kitchen hearth, with Daniel and Hannah kneeling before him. The rite was Anglican, the same graceful and familiar words of the *Book of Common Prayer* Daniel had heard at his marriage to Charlotte. Who could have thought this frail old man would bind them now with a service that had been all but driven out of America with the exiled Tories?

'I will,' Daniel murmured.

Hannah looked almost girlish in the rose-colored gown Bertha Pinch, the hunchbacked seamstress, had cut and stitched for her – though the two lowest buttons had had to stay unfastened, after all. A length of fine cream-colored lace Daniel had sent for from Boston was thrown over her dark curls and framed her face and shoulders, and around her neck she wore a chain with a tiny silver locket on it, a gift from among her aunt's few treasures.

Julia stood up beside her, and Dolly, too, and behind them the hired girls watched, bright-eyed and sniffling. Beside Daniel, young Ethan Berge, still half-asleep, yawned and gulped and rubbed his eyes.

'Wilt thou, Lucy Hannah Rowlandson Trevor, have this Man to thy wedded husband, to live together after God's ordinance in the holy estate of Matrimony? Wilt thou love him, comfort him, honor, and keep him in sickness and in health; and, forsaking all others, keep thee only unto him, so long as ye both shall live?'

'I will.'

'Who giveth this Woman to be—'

'Josselyn! Are you in there? Open up, for the love of God!' Someone was pounding furiously at the back door. 'Quick, man! There's not a minute to waste! Open up!'

Daniel got to his feet. 'That's Kersey's voice,' he said. He looked down at Hannah. 'Forgive me, my love. I must see what he wants.'

She nodded and he made for the door at a lope. 'What is it?' they heard him say. 'My God, man, where have you come from?'

Kersey was winded and red-faced from the cold and his eyes were blank and wild. He had changed from his white uniform to plain jerkin and breeches, and a heavy felted cloak Daniel recognized as one of McGregor's.

'The Scotsman sent me,' he said. 'They mean to take you, sir. The militia has voted to go with the rebels, we're all in it now. Most of the men have spread out to the woods, but they still call you commander. You must clear out, if you don't want to hang or be shot.'

'I've already resigned my commission, Kersey, I have nothing to do with—'

'You haven't heard then? Some fool has shot Royallton-Smith at the inn tonight.' The sergeant's eyes looked around at the others. 'They hold you to account as commander, Major. They claim one of us did it.'

'And did you?'

Kersey's face was set and hard. 'Doesn't matter, sir. They mean to have you locked up, to keep you from leading us against the Court. Without you, we're a joke, not an army.'

'They've no proof it was one of my men. If they mean to court-martial me—'

'They don't need proof and court-martiallings! They make rules as they need them now!' Hannah gripped his arm, and behind her the boy and the women stood staring, the old parson praying softly under his breath. 'You must go!' she said. 'We are married enough!'

Julia Markham wasted no more than a moment. 'Kitty! Cut some of the veal pie in the larder, and bring a new loaf and half a cheese! And that bottle of brandy I was keeping for fruitcake! Susan, fetch Husband's old coat from the mudroom, they will not know him so easy in that!'

Josselyn drew Hannah against him and she could feel his heart slamming hard under his ribs. 'How did it happen?' he asked the sergeant. 'How was he killed?'

'Rifle shot.' Kersey was terse, as always, but his dark eyes were very bright under the beetling eyebrows and his hands gripped the stock of his gun till his nails were bright crimson. 'Through the open door as he made to leave the inn with old Siwall. Easy pickings.'

'How many shots?'

'One in the head, one in the belly.'

'Like Clinch.'

'Aye.'

'You're a rifleman, Oliver. Were you with the Twelfth?' Daniel asked him. 'The Crossed-Boners?'

Kersey's lips were set tight. 'No, sir. Haggar's Company.'

It did not strike a chord in Daniel's memory. 'Do you know any who *were* with the Twelfth?' he asked.

The big, gruff fellow thought for a moment. 'One or two from Saybrook. That fellow Fronval, the Frenchman from Fort Holland. And Simon Penny. He was with the Twelfth. Don't know what company, though.'

A pregnant girl dead. A man burnt. Many men. Hannah tried to lay together the pieces of Daniel's strange memory with what Kersey was saying. *Susannah Penny is pregnant. Simon Penny fought with the Twelfth.*

They brought the coat and Daniel put it on – a foot too short and too big in the shoulders, but sound enough as disguise. 'Hannah,' he said, 'that button of Jenny's. You must give it to Lannie McGregor.'

'There's men coming down from the Falls road!' Ethan Berge had been keeping a watch at the back door.

'You must go now, sir, out the front!' Kersey began to push Daniel towards the parlor.

'We have time enough yet.' Daniel took Hannah by the hand. 'Come, madam. If I'm to be hustled into the next world, I mean to go there a married man.' He smiled. 'Kersey, will you stand up with us? Preacher, I believe we left off at "Who giveth this Woman?" '

It was for Jennet's sake, Hannah knew that, and for the child that was not born. If Daniel died now, if they killed him, there was still property and money to come to them. Even if they called him a traitor and seized the Grange, he had sheltered enough with trustees for the children. But unless they were wed, there was no legal claim.

'Who giveth this Woman to be married to this Man?' the old parson quavered.

Daniel nudged Oliver Kersey. For a moment the thick, silent fellow only gaped, as though he did not understand what was wanted of him.

'I – I do,' he said at last. He took Hannah's right hand and put it into Daniel's. 'I give her. God help me. God help us all.'

Mr Dancer turned back to Daniel. 'Have you a ring, sir?'

'This will serve.' Josselyn bent his lips to Hannah's finger where the ring should have been. 'I Daniel take thee Hannah to my wedded Wife, to have and to hold from this day forward—'

'They have fired the boats at the ford!' cried young Ethan. 'And Cove Bridge is alight, and the ropes of old Sly's ferry! I can see them from here!'

They meant to cut off his escape. 'You must go!' whispered Hannah.

But still he would not. 'You have not said your own piece,' he told her. She murmured the words and kissed the stumps of his missing fingers. Cold, they were, so cold it frightened her.

The old man joined their hands. 'Those whom God hath joined together let no man put asunder.'

There was a crash at the front door, something slamming against it. Then came a terrible sound of wood splintering as the sheriff's men smashed through the back door, and at almost the same moment the front door gave way with a thud. A crash of glass and the jangled chime of Henry's case clock as they toppled it.

'Too late,' murmured Oliver Kersey.

Daniel stood in the center of the room as the men converged on him. There were six in all – Ketchell and Tully, with three fellows in buckskin, and the half-breed, Le Duc.

'Where is your warrant?' he asked them.

'Here.' Tully laughed and Le Duc struck out with the steel barrel of his rifle. Daniel felt the breath leave him, caving his life in upon him, and a bright pain in his ribcage took his vision away for an instant. He fell down on his knees, and somebody kicked him. In the ribs. In the side of the face. In the small of his back.

They did not stop when he was down. The kicks came again and again, and blows with them, from their fists and rifle butts. He tasted blood in his mouth and blood streamed from one ear and from a deep cut on his scalp. His broken ribs smashed against his lung and when he tried to breathe, he felt blood come into his throat and choke him.

He heard Kitty scream, and something warm fell across his own body. Julia's shrill voice cried out – words, some words, he could no longer comprehend them. Speech was beyond him, and sounds reached him through some heavy barrier. He bashed at it, forced his eyes open, staring out through a curtain of blood.

Hannah lay still, her body sprawled across him where Le Duc had struck her down. Daniel tried to move, but he could not. 'No more!' roared Kersey, and lifted her up in his arms.

Through all this the door had stood open; beyond it the dry, grainy snow still spat itself out of a roiling, wind-twisted sky. The ice was heavy and bitter cold, a gleaming, inhuman universe that seemed made of white iron.

And out of the heart of it, with a set of manacles thrown over his arm, came Sheriff Marcus Tapp. 'Secure him,' he commanded.

They put chains on Daniel's ankles and more on his wrists, and tied a rope to them to drag him by. When they pulled him to his feet, he could not stand for the pain in his leg and cried out softly, a low gasping sound. He fell again, and they dragged him, out through the mudroom and down the stoop onto the thick ice. He tried to stand again, stumbled a few steps. But the pain and the shackles would not let him.

'My – wife,' he tried to say, and they hit him again. Before he lost consciousness, Daniel heard Marcus Tapp's voice, very close, like the buzz of a wasp in his ear.

'Never fear, Major. I shall take precious care of your gypsy. I fancy a woman with child.'

For Daniel, the journey to prison was endless, a long slide to the foot of the world. They dragged him by two ropes tied onto his heavy iron manacles, the sheriff's men ranging like surefooted wolves across the ice, joking and laughing as they went, and Tapp, the master of this cold metallic world, riding horseback behind them, the ropes that held Daniel tied onto his saddle horn as he lashed and swore at the slipping, floundering horse.

It was still dark and some of the men carried smoky pine torches, others long willow poles with nails in the ends of them; every few yards, they stabbed the nails into the ice, like petards to keep them from falling.

The steep hill was the worst of it. Daniel's leg was not broken, but the ankle was so badly bruised that he had no control of it, and the shackles clamped tight around the swollen joint and cut into the flesh. When he managed to stand, Tapp would spur the horse to make him run, and he crashed down again and again, to be prodded up like a beast with the sharp-pointed poles.

At last he no longer tried to stand, prod him how they might. Gripping the rope in his chained hands, he held tight to it and let them drag him, rolling from his belly to his back now and then in the hope of some relief. Over frozen thickets of bramble they pulled him, that tore at his face and his arms and his neck. Over stone fences and tree roots and the sharp stubble of the uncleared autumn fields.

Now and then the sheriff's men would stop to rest, and the pain that so long as they moved had seemed numbed by the strangeness of that frozen, glittering, treacherous universe would crash down on him, so that he would almost have begged to go on again, to be dragged forward, dragged downward to the bottom of things, where at least he might rest.

When they put a paper soldier's hat on his head and spat in his face and saluted, he hardly felt it or saw it. When they shouted insults at him, he did not hear, and when they kicked him, he no longer felt it. The pain was too ancient, its burden too heavy, to notice any new blows that fell. Some part of Daniel Josselyn had always lived in the dark, had been bred there, and now his mind took refuge in it, diving down and down to a place where no enemy could reach it.

For his body, there was no world beyond pain, and the pain was ice, and the ice was fire.

No one moved on the roads now, not even the Night

Watch. Tapp rode on silently, taking no part in the mockery beyond the constant spurring of the horse across the ice. His aloofness as somehow far worse than their scorn.

If I live, I shall kill him, Daniel thought, and the idea pleased him, was sweeter than hope to him. *I shall root out his heart.*

I am good at killing. Did I not go mad once, and kill thousands? Hack them up with my sword till they fell thick as dead leaves? Good men and bad men, old men and young boys. And women. Have I not killed women, too?

Did I not push them all together into a great pit, I all alone, and burn them with fire?

They passed Cove Bridge, its wooden cover a charred, smoking ruin, and only the stone pilings remaining.

A man is a bridge, Daniel's grandfather had long ago told him, *between time and eternity. With his feet in the honest mud and his back bent for God and the Devil to trample on. To fight their mortal battles out.*

A bridge. Some bridge with stone pilings. Taunton Bridge? Penryn Bridge? Sherwick Bridge? London Bridge?

Two hundred British, all dead on a bridge. An old parson, his face shot away and his wig hung on a branch beside him. We tipped him into the pit and she screamed when the fire took him, one shrill scream.

My father is God's chimneysweep, she told us. See how his face is grown black.

A pregnant girl with a shaven head. A sign painted in red, like blood on her scalp: Tory Whore.

A mad girl with the soles of her feet burnt. How she screamed when we locked her away.

*

All the small boats and dories and ketches tied up by the river were burnt and smoking, and Daniel's mind was dragged back from his nightmares to the present. Surely they had burnt his own sloop, too, the *Lark*.

A sweet ship, she had been, and quick to the helm. He had bought her to take him to Boston every spring and fall; in the long years of estrangement from Hannah, he had taken a mistress there. For a moment he conjured the woman's features, trying to remember if she had been real or a dream.

But he could not envision her. She was an image in water, broken and drifting.

His smashed ribs bearing down on his lungs and a pain like an arrow stabbing into him at every breath, his hands burnt raw from the ropes he clung on to, his face bleeding and torn, and his arms and legs so battered he had to take count of them to be certain they were all still attached to him, Daniel summoned his waking memory once more.

Charlotte. A pale oval face with a fringe of fair hair. Eyes that grew sharp out of weariness, out of fear. Were they blue eyes? Or grey?

But this portrait he imposed from empirical knowledge, like facts from a history, his brain drawing an image that might have been anyone. He could no longer see his wife's face behind his closed eyes, nor the faces of his mother and brothers, nor his father's face. Even his grandfather's, that most loved of them all, would not come now to help him.

Gone, he thought. *Burnt away. Melted like ice.*

How fragile we are, and how transient, how we move in a mist and brush against one another and are suddenly gone. How we leave unknown damage behind.

As they dragged him along, drawn curtains would part

and women's faces would look out of them into the darkness, wide-eyed and terrible. Now and then he glimpsed them, their guttering candles. Their glittering eyes made of ice.

It is all down to women. They make us do mad things gladly, for a place to harbor in.

Three women, three Tory sisters hanged upside-down, one dead, one raving, and one very young, that I slept with. How gently she took me, her small, flat breasts silken under my palm, and her body so cold, like the ice. How she screamed when she rose to me, her death scream. I love you, she said. You are the world to me. When you go, I will cease to exist. Though I walk on the earth with the small feet of animals, I will cease to be here in myself.

One scream, shrill, like a woman in travail. To break the knot that held us. To cut me to pieces with love.

I have a little sister, the mad one said, the burned one. I have a little sister and she hath no breasts. She is a queen in Sheba. Solomon sings for her pleasure, and spices make sweet her marriage bed.

When they reached the jail, he was no longer conscious. There were only two cells in the place, and they dragged him inside and chained him up to the wall like a felon, his ankles still shackled.

No one tended him. No one questioned him. McGregor the constable was not to be seen.

In the other cell, old Dickie Bunche the madman, who had murdered his shrewish wife twenty-five years before and would live here till he died, snored peaceably on his pallet of straw.

But Daniel did not hear him. The faces that eluded him

waking had come back to him now, in the heavy, nerve-drugged sleep of pain and exhaustion and the relief of not moving any more.

Charlotte's face, worn by weakness and four years of anger and bitterness. The face of his mistress, vain and loveless and void. He could not even remember her name.

Three women, three Tory sisters, stripped naked and hanged upside-down from an apple tree in a churchyard.

The eldest, brown-haired. Her I buried, with the child near eight months grown in her.

The second, black-haired, that they had tortured. Her they took from me, raving and weeping and wild.

But the last and most precious, the one no one wanted, fair and pale and sweet and young, so thin I took count of her bones through the skin. So young she might have been my daughter.

I am a queen in Sheba, she said, and I came to believe her. King Solomon sings me to sleep.

THIRTY-TWO

Laying Out the Blocks

Hannah woke some time near midmorning to find herself swathed in quilts and laid on the kitchen settle, as Julia sponged her bruised face gently with comfrey-water for the thousandth time since midnight.

'Is he living?' she whispered. 'Where is he taken?'

'Daniel was alive when they left here, that is all I can tell you. But lie still, now. I feared you would never wake. Have you pain in your belly?'

Hannah tried to sit up, but as soon as she moved she felt dizzy and sick. 'How long have I slept?' she said. 'He's hurt, I must help him, I must take him medicines, I—'

'Answer me! Have you any pain?'

The import of the question suddenly reached her and stunned her and the rush of worried questions stopped. 'Only in my head,' Hannah said meekly.

Julia sighed. 'Well, that part of you is hard enough to weather, God knows. Did you think you could fight off that brute with a toast-rack?' The old woman held a cup to her lips. 'It's only pennyroyal. To fend off a miscarriage.'

'You're sure it's not valerian? Because I must not sleep again, not until I've seen Daniel. And I must speak to Siwall. Aunt—'

'Sally has run off with Jem. Yes, I know. Dick Dancer came early this morning to fetch his father to the inn, and he told us the news. When I think how she gulled me, flitting in and out all day yesterday—'

'But Aunt, Sally has taken—'

'All our savings. I know that, too. I found the empty box when I picked up the wreck of our clock.' Julia's voice was so calm that she might have been speaking of the box full of old stockings they had saved to be cut up for braiding into a hearthrug. 'If forty pounds rids my hearth of a thief and a lying deceiver,' she said, 'it is little enough to pay. Jem stole better than three hundred in silver from his father, so Dick says, and it does my heart good to hear it, after what Siwall had done by his sheriff's hand.'

'Master Siwall covets my nephew's house and land,' came a voice from the passage, 'and this Riot Act has given him grounds to seize upon it.'

A moment later, to Hannah's amazement, Lady Sibylla stumped into the room. The sheriff's men had omitted to burn an old rowboat at the Grange, and with John English in the prow to break the river ice and Jenks and Owen to carry her up the slippery hill to the farmhouse, Daniel's aunt had reached Two Mills not long after daylight.

'If Siwall makes Daniel out a traitor,' she continued, 'and all these good fellows with him, why, he may buy up the Grange for a whistle, and much of the rest of the county besides!'

Ten months ago, when their troubles first began with the death of young Anthea Emory, Uncle Henry had said much the same thing. *When a human price is paid dear in this world, it's most often for land or for money. Money buys power, and you must have enough to look like you've got plenty more.*

Look like. Siwall was not what he seemed, perhaps he had never been.

'I must go to Burnt Hill,' Hannah said suddenly, and tried to get up.

But Sibylla reached out her walking stick and pushed her gently down again. 'If you try to prowl about on this ice, my girl, you will fall and make an end to that child. Is that what you wish to give to my nephew, another dead son?'

'No, of course not. But I must *do* something.'

The old dowager lowered herself wearily onto a chair by the fire, creaking a bit as her tight stays expanded. 'Since Mr Kersey brought the news of my nephew's arrest,' she said, 'I have been half the night and all of the morning considering. That man Siwall and Daniel – they soldiered together, did they not?'

Hannah rubbed her eyes with her hand and winced when she touched her bruised cheekbone. 'For a time,' she replied. 'But not long, I think. Men were sometimes cut off from their regiments and served any they might be attached to.'

Sibylla sighed. 'No doubt it is somehow connected. In this wild outpost of yours, everything starts and ends in a war.'

Hannah sipped at the cup of pennyroyal tea. 'I do not think Siwall killed Clinch himself, and from what Mr Kersey told Daniel, he surely could not have shot Master Royallton-Smith.'

'And unless men with broken necks rise up and turn into assassins, Caesar, too, is absolved,' said Sibylla. 'Yet Siwall was eager to make the poor fellow seem guilty and hurry him to the gallows. Why was that, do you think?'

A basket of pieces for her marriage quilt lay on the floor by the settle, and Hannah took up one of the basted blocks and smoothed it out on her lap.

Triangles. What in life is not made of them? God Himself bore their shape, and more than one war has been built so, this one included.

The rich. The poor. The land they both desire.

With land, power. With power, the fear of losing that power.

She turned the block around so that the pieced triangle lay on its side, the whole design altered.

Siwall. Clinch. Caesar. What one does in the darkness, the other two know of. To be rid of Clinch would not be enough, unless he is rid of Caesar, too.

Again she turned the block, the point of the triangle downward now, the irresistible shape of a funnel.

A man. A wife. A marriage. A third thing they become, once they are joined, that is less than each and greater than both. A box with three corners, too narrow to live in?

Siwall. Siwall's wife. Siwall's mistress?

But what has Siwall's mistress – if there is one – to do with Daniel's past?

Hannah thought of the bright-colored pieces of this same new quilt that she had scattered last night on top of the other, the older pattern already in the frame. One motive strewn over the other. A triangle from one pattern laid across a square from the next to make a new shape, a random tumble of colors.

A marriage, she thought again. *The back and front of the same page. Rosepath. Tabby. Here lyeth one who lived by taking.*

There must be a sensible sequence of things, a clear

pattern. Hannah would have it no other way. But she could not discover it.

'My nephew's letter of resignation must be taken to Colonel Scribner as soon as the coach road will bear a rider,' Sibylla was saying. 'Mr English will go himself, I am certain. Then, if we can provide them the scoundrel who killed these two fellows, they may perhaps listen to reason and let Daniel go free.'

'Reason? Hah!'

Julia set the empty cup aside and fetched Henry's pipe from the mantel. She filled it from the box on the shelf, lit it with a paper spill, took a deep puff and sighed with relief.

'Such men are not creatures of reason,' she said. 'Besides, we have no sufficient grounds for deduction, especially in Smith's case. Joshua says the shots came out of nowhere.'

'Aye, Mother Markham, so they did. And a wild scream with them.'

The innkeeper shuffled into the room, Henry's felt slippers on his pigeon-toed feet and an old shawl of Julia's wrapped around him against the chill. Little Peter rode on his arm, delighted and babbling.

'One cry and no more,' Josh went on, 'as you said Dancer heard in the woods. But you must not trouble yourself over it now.' He bent to kiss her forehead soberly. 'There, how's our bride? I thought you'd sleep the clock round.'

'I am well enough,' she replied.

Joshua smiled. It was always her covert to hide behind. 'Never you fear, my dear,' he said. 'We shall sort all this out and have Daniel by your side again.'

She caught his hard, square hand and squeezed it gratefully. Dolly had chosen well for a husband; Josh Lamb was much like the old ash tree in the yard. It might lose a branch or two in a gale now and then, but its roots were deep and it did not topple easily.

'Where is Dolly?' she asked him. 'And how is Uncle?'

'He's awake, too, bless his heart!' Dolly's face peered in from the workroom, tired, but all wreathed in smiles.

A bell jangled, the tinny one they put on the old ewe so the lambs would be sure to find her. 'Hannah! Where's our Hannah, now?' Henry's voice called out.

It was still weak, and the speech a bit slurred. But it was the same voice as before, the same calm, sensible mind directing it. The world had not toppled after all. Uncle was home again – though a bit the worse for wear.

'I shall rue the hour I put that bell in his hands,' laughed Dolly. 'And I swear, he will eat us out of house and home before he's done!'

'Don't give him too much at the first,' Hannah cautioned. 'His hand, how is that? You must give him a ball of wool to squeeze on, to get back the suppleness. And his vision? His speech seems a little altered, but it's early to tell. Oh, do let me go in and see him!'

'Don't you dare move!' Dolly commanded. 'Joshua, never let her get up yet!'

Outnumbered for the moment, Hannah leaned back. But just then Jennet trailed in from the kitchen, munching one of Dolly's corn dodgers, and came to snuggle against her, to be kissed and stroked and hugged and kissed again.

'Happy birthday, my autumn flower,' her mother whispered. 'You shall have a father before Christmas yet, that I swear.'

*

It was not until Hannah had submitted to a breakfast of Indian pudding and milk and sat watching Jennet at work with her spindle that she remembered the almanac Dick Dancer had left in her keeping. It lay almost at her elbow on the seat of her aunt's old rocker, and she took it up now and began to turn over the pages.

It seemed nothing more than the usual almanac: dates for planting – root crops in the waning moon, leaf crops in the waxing, and so on; predictions for the first frost, the first robin, the likelihood of rains and snows; a few riddles and mottoes and children's rhymes and tales.

But at the center a single leaf had been carefully turned down, and when she opened the dog-eared sheets to that page, Hannah discovered that someone had made a painstaking drawing in the margin.

Six sets of parallel lines had been laid in, using a straight-edge and a fine-sharpened quill, with the shade of brownish-green ink that could be made from black walnut shells boiled down to an extract.

There were four lines in each set and the sets crossed to make perfect squares. Between the lines, some of the spaces had been carefully filled in with the pen to make patterns, small charts that might be followed when pieces were laid.

Or threads. Might it not be threads laid onto the bed of a loom, and warped through the heddles? A weaver's pattern-book, set out on the scraps that were handy? This time she had used her husband's old outworn almanac instead of the back of his copybook page.

And he, perhaps, had claimed it back again, shoved it away in that same greatcoat whose lost button lay hidden in the leaves by the body. When he crouched by the track, the rifle in his hands, the book had slipped out unnoticed, to be dusted with snow, tripped-over by Dick as he searched through the bushes. And at last brought here, to Two Mills. What she held in her hands, Hannah was almost certain, was a tracery of the life's work of that same woman whose scream Dick had heard in the woods.

'Aunt, come and look at this.' Breathless, Hannah turned the book from side to side. 'A weaving pattern, could it be?'

'Yes, it might be. Let's ask Dolly.'

'Ask me what?' Hannah's cousin looked in from the kitchen and they set the problem before her. There were patterns on the margins of several pages, and Dolly squinted hard to make them out.

'Well, this one's a quilt pattern, surely,' she said. 'See there, it's China Dish, that you and Mama have now in the frame. And this one's Cross and Crown. But not all are for quilting. There's too much blank space unpieced in the centers, it would take yards of plain fabric. No woman with sense enough to draw such a pattern would waste so much new goods cutting it up for a quilt.'

Julia nodded. 'But a weaver could fill it with plain tabby for background,' she said.

Tabby. Rosepath. Monks Belt.

Dolly turned the pages over one by one. 'Look! We are right! This one here *is* a weaver's grid, for I know the pattern myself. It's Candle in the Wilderness, Susannah Penny set me a coverlet like it, remember?'

Candle in the Wilderness. Flame in the Forest. Star of the Forest. Patterns had many names and many variations, grown and derived from each other like ears from the same stalk of corn.

Susannah Penny, whose husband was a rifleman of the Twelfth.

Sibylla had been shut out of the reasoning long enough. 'What is this little paltry scrap of paper, madam, and how did you come by it?'

'The peddler and his father found it in the woods, not far from where Daniel and I stumbled over the body,' Hannah told her.

Lady Sibylla shivered. 'The peddler's father? I wonder he did not find a door at the crack of a boulder and pipe the village children to perdition through it, little troll that he is. But these patterns, now. What do they signify?'

Hannah did not care for the way things were shaping. 'Some of them are too difficult for most women's skill. Dolly,' she said, 'could any besides Susannah Penny weave an over-shot pattern like Candle in the Wilderness?'

'Old Lady Holroyd, but she can't bear to sit so long at the treadles these days. Perhaps Leah, Mrs Kersey, she's clever – though I don't know that her loom will carry so many sheds, nor Ann Whitney's, neither. But there's little Mary Luckett. You must ask Sarah McGregor. She would know, she knows every pattern that's set hereabout and who weaves it.'

Sarah. Leah. Susannah. All three with child. All my friends and my sisters.

No, Hannah would not have it. She put the few badly sewn pages away in her pocket. 'Weaver-women trade their patterns the way small boys trade conkers in the horse-chestnut season,' she said. 'It means nothing.'

Sibylla's bird's-eyes flashed determined fire. 'Aye, madam,' she said with a sniff. 'As clouds in the morning mean nothing but rain.'

THIRTY-THREE

Piecing the Evidence:
The Fires That Forged Them

SUSANNAH JERUSHA BAGGETT PENNY

Married woman. Age 37. Wife of Simon Penny, yeoman, Blackapple Farm, Sable Brook. Born Susannah Heron, Bredmouth, Maine, 1749. Signs her name and knows her letters, but cannot read beyond simple verses. Married Nathaniel Baggett, cooper, Bredmouth, December 24, 1767. Three children, George, Margaret, and Axel. The town of Bredmouth refused to surrender its harbor to British gunships and was bombarded and burnt to a rubble, November, 1775. Husband and son George killed, house and cooper's shop burnt. Bodies never recovered. Son Axel later died of his burns. Susannah Baggett, widow, and Margaret her daughter, lived after in York State at the village of Chelm. Married Simon Penny, 1777, came to Rufford, Maine, April, 1779. four children, Frederick, Seth, Winifred, and Jerusha. Daughter Margaret married Cyrus Kent, physician and surgeon, June, 1786.

Susannah Penny bears the old scars of burns on the right side of her face and along the back of her right hand and arm, where her gown caught alight in carrying out her son Axel, then a child of two years, from the burning house of Mr Baggett, then her husband.

She is a fine spinster and weaver, well-known for her shot-over patterns, and has taught many in Rufford her skill.

My mother speaks little of that time of the burning, how my father and brothers were lost. I was but four then, and when I sleep I still dream of it sometimes, and it seems like a travelling peep show at the Midsummer Fair. I sit up all night at my loom, then, as my mother does, to work the bad memory through and make use of it.

It is always a dirty month for us, is November. It was just before dawn on November the nineteenth when they started the shelling, and that day the sun never came up on Bredmouth, Maine, nor on my mother since.

The shop roof buckled in upon Father and Georgie and there was no hope of them. But Mother threw me out of the kitchen window and went back to fetch Axel. I heard her give a scream and I saw her run out of the shop door with her gown afire and Axel in her arms. His sweet hair was burning and his hands were all black, and I knew the fire had already took him. He lived but the one night, with her rocking him and holding his mouth to her breast long after I saw he had gone.

THE BURNING BRIDE

There was nothing left in Bredmouth. It was a little place, a harbor the size of a cove that was little use but for fishing boats and coasters.

But my father died for it, and Georgie and Axel, too. And some part of my mother went with them, burned away by the fire. She has new children now and she'll soon have another, and she is fond of Mr Penny, her husband. Only when a human thing is burnt in the soul, there is a great, hollow space no one can see nor come into. Nothing fills it. But sometimes mad things dance in that clearing, and make women run wild in the dark.

—*Margaret Kent, daughter of Susannah Penny*

PHOEBE MARIA PRAISEGOD LUCKETT

Widow. Age 26. Presently keeps house for her brother, Edward Praisegod, joiner and carpenter, Nagg's Bluff. Born Pelham, Devon, 1760. Unable to read or write, signs with a double cross and circle. Apprenticed to Mrs Elizabeth Sprigget of Exeter, weaver and dressmaker, at the age of eleven. Accompanied Mrs Sprigget to Boston, where she was employed by that lady to do piece-weaving for the coastal trade. Married Zebulon Luckett, a common soldier in the 12th Massachusetts Rifles, on November 23, 1778 in Boston. One son, Saul, born 1779. Husband killed in ambush, January, 1780, at Tebbett's Wood outside Morristown, New Jersey, by marauding Tories. She has a good voice for singing and is skilled at embroidery and needlework, and excels at the weaving of fine coverlids and shawls from patterns of her own devising.

Mrs Luckett does not fancy her given name of Phoebe and is called Mary instead, and sometimes Chick.

We are Quakers and we do not believe in war and the bearing of weapons. When my sister Mary wrote us to say she was wed to a soldier, my father took to his bed and my mother could not eat nor sleep for mourning her.

My own wife was dead and I had then but little to hold me in England, so I came here to find our Chick and look after her, and bring her back home if I could. For Mary was but eighteen and my mother feared that this Luckett had betrayed her as soldiers will, and she too proud to tell us the truth.

I saw Zebulon Luckett but the once, in Boston. Nineteen, he was, a farmer lad and plain as a gatepost. But his hands were big and kind and his heart the same, and he loved the lass dearly, that was clear enough. When they sent the Twelfth away from Boston, he asked me to bring her up here to Maine, to his father, old Master Enoch. And once I was here, here I stayed, and set up my carpenter's shop.

When the news came to us that Zeb was dead, Mary had no rest but she must find him and say him farewell at his grave. And I knew she could not, for them that killed him left him for the ravens and wolves to work their revenge on him. And when he was found, there was scarce enough left to bury. I hid the letter a long time and did not tell her the truth of it, how ill they had used him. She ran away twice to seek after him and I feared she would do as much again, and be lost to me. So at last I read her the letter aloud and kept back nothing.

When she heard it, she cried out aloud like some knife had cut her. A terrible cry it was. I can hear it yet, when I'm alone.

For two days she sat at the loom I had built her and would not get up nor lie down nor eat nor drink nor sleep. So I sat up, too, watching over her, but the third night I dropped off to sleep, and at morning I woke to her singing, that old song of Bridal Bower that all the girls sing when they wed.

'Zeb came here to see me in the night,' she says. 'He looked in at the window and smiled at my weaving. That's coming up nicely, my dear,' says he. And then he walked away again, leading his pony and whistling.'

Ever since that day, waking and sleeping, Mary carries that letter about her, though she cannot read any word that is writ there. Many nights she is wakeful, staring into the fire and expecting him, and when she lies sleeping she holds the bolster against her, like as if it was Zeb.

We see what we need to in this world, to keep us from breaking. But perhaps he does come to her.

If God is anyways kind, then the dead must grieve for the living and watch over them, and their love does not end at the grave.

—*Edward Praisegod, Joiner, Brother of Mary Luckett*

LEAH ELINOR WOODARD KERSEY

Married woman. Age 23. Born Fallbrook, New Hampshire, 1764. Father Reverend Fitzwilliam

Woodard, rector of St Barnabas Church, Fallbrook.
Father and brother died May 16, 1779, killed by patriot
troops. One sister, Sarah, also deceased. Married Oliver
Kersey, yeoman, then sergeant, Haggar's Company,
Twelfth Massachusetts Rifles, August, 1780, when she
was four months with child. Lear Kersey is quiet and
dutiful, and is skilled at the loom and at many kinds of
women's work, i.e. spinning, quilting, chandlery, etc.
She reads and ciphers and writes her own name in a
middling hand. Mrs Kersey has no living children.
Sometimes called Nellie for her middle name, Elinor,
and other fond names besides.

She's a sweet loving soul, is Leah Kersey. She had once
a sister called Sarah, and she tenders me for her sake,
now she's dead, and calls me friend. Besides, we are
both weavers by nature and we took to each other at
once, for it's a strange kind of work, and some women
only do it as they scrub clothes or empty slops, because
it is there to be done. But Leah puts her soul to the
threads, as I do, and weaves a garment of pride to cover
over the hurt and the shame that living has put on her.
And so do I the same.

Before Husband found me, I was a wanderer. Men
used me and cast me away again, and sometimes I
offered my body for money or shelter, because I came
to believe I was worth little else in the world.

Now I think different, and that is McGregor's
doing, because he sees me, what I am and have been
and might be, and he treasures my heart and makes it
whole.

But Kersey is different. He's a good enough

creature, kind and solid, and I think Leah takes some comfort of him, though she is full young for a man of his age. I ask no questions and she tells me no more than she wishes.

Only there be some men that eat women alive if they love them, as a fire eats kindling. And I fear Mr Kersey is one.

—*Sarah Firth McGregor, Wife of*
Constable Lachlan McGregor

THIRTY-FOUR

Prisoners

That same bitter cold morning, at about the hour Josh Lamb and John English lowered the body of Jonathan Markham into a grave hacked out of the hillside behind his father's house, Daniel Josselyn woke in his prison to a woman's soft hands washing the blood from his face.

'Hannah,' he tried to say, but she clapped a palm over his mouth.

He had hung there all night in chains attached to great iron rings in the wall, his arms dragged up and sidewise and his legs splayed out so that he could not lie at his full length and could never relax the muscles of his neck and shoulders and back. He tried to open his eyes, but he could not; the beating had left them swollen and stuck shut with matter, and when he tried to move his eyelids they felt as though a sharp stick were inside them. His lips were cut and bruised and he had bitten his tongue so that it, too, was swollen. But when he forced it to move round the cave of his mouth, he felt only one broken tooth, and his jaw seemed to work well enough.

He was yet very weak and under his ribs there was a hollowness, something like hunger only harsher, like some animal trying to gnaw its way out.

The woman's hand lifted from his mouth and he tried again to speak. But again she prevented him. 'I'm not Hannah,' she whispered. 'They will not let her come.' The voice was somewhat distracted. He almost remembered it, but pain sends many voices and all are familiar.

'They have taken the keys from McGregor,' she went on, 'but they don't think they need fear me. Only I have not the key to the irons.'

'Who are you? Your name?' Daniel murmured – or tried to.

She laid the cold, wet rag across his eyes. 'There's blood when you cough. I'm afraid they have hurt you deep, somewhere inside.'

When she touched the place over his right lung where his ribs were broken, he felt a searing pain like a hot knife go through him, the animal inside suddenly clawing and wild.

'I – can't see,' he said. 'Is it day?'

Perhaps, he thought, *I will never see Hannah's face again.* It made his whole body shudder to think of it, and the woman put her arms round him to keep him still. 'Who are you?' he repeated. He could hear his voice fading, as if he were walking away from himself.

'I'm a poor woman, like your wife. Tapp's men take it as a fine joke that they kept you from your marriage bed.'

'My – wife?'

He thought for a moment she was speaking of Charlotte, but then he remembered. Hannah's rose-colored gown with the two undone buttons. Her weight when she fell on him. Her silence through it all, that was loud as a scream.

'They struck her down,' he mumbled. 'How is she – the child – does it live?'

'I've heard nothing, except what Tapp's men brag of. Nothing moves on the roads yet, for the ice. They will not hold the court today.'

She leaned over him, wiping the dried blood from his ear, and he could feel the tight, heavy swell of her body.

'You are with child, too,' he said softly.

'It will not live much longer. I have no birth in me since the War.' She finished her work and drew back again. 'Tomorrow the sheriff will take you to Salcombe. You must not be here when he comes for you.'

'My friend Colonel Scribner is there, he will speak for me.'

'Don't be a fool. You will never reach Salcombe.'

'Why?' he whispered. 'Why do they want my life?'

Daniel closed his eyes again. It was hard to speak, as much for the cold that made his teeth chatter as for the swelling in his mouth. The only warmth in the place was a charcoal burner in the passageway between the two cells, and the wet rag she had laid on his eyes was already stiff with cold. His hands in the icy manacles felt numb, nearly frozen. Someone had stolen his boots and he could not even move his feet to keep them from freezing, because of the shackles and chains.

The woman was chafing his fingers. 'Here, try to swallow this.' She spooned some warm gruel into his mouth, but his throat was too swollen. He coughed again, and more blood came with it.

'Ah, I am sorry,' she said, and he felt her bend over him, felt her mouth brush his forehead and move down to his cheeks. 'You were ever gentle and kind.'

'Who are you?' he said again. 'How do you know me?' She did not reply, and he felt her warmth draw away from him. 'Tell my wife I am living,' he said. 'I beg you.'

But the woman had already gone.

As for Hannah, she too was a prisoner that morning.

Her aunt would not allow her to venture out of the house to see Jonathan buried. Instead, the hired girls went with Julia and Dolly, and the midwife was left to mind her sick uncle and the two children. Even that, Aunt Julia insisted, was more than she ought to do.

The men had sanded the paths and the slope, and had laid down some precious salt along with it, for the sake of not slipping and dropping the coffin. Thus assisted, Lady Sibylla had sent to the Grange for Hobble and gone off in the direction of town with a gleam in her eye.

The house was empty, silent, the ruined clock no longer telling the quarter-hours. There was only the crackle of the fire and the occasional bubble of venison stew in the kettle, and the sound of icicles now and then falling from the eaves. In his sickbed, Uncle Henry dozed peacefully, ignorant of where the others had gone, still unaware of his youngest son's death and only half-remembering what had set off his seizure, as though it had been some strange dream.

Even the children had no need of a playmate. In the next room, Jennet busied herself at the small loom, working the treadles with an uneven rhythm; little Peter made a pig's breakfast of the forgotten Training Cake that still stood on the cooling rack, and then curled up to sleep by the hearth.

Hannah put on her spectacles and sat down to her quilting, but it would not do, her heart was not in it. Then she opened her journal and took up her pen, but that would not do either, and she could no longer concentrate on the rest of the weaving patterns in the worn little almanac. Spinning – she tangled the thread and put a great knot in it. Hetcheling the driest of the flax – her fingers grew sore from the paddles. Darning the hole in Jenny's Sunday stocking – there were more holes than stocking.

Besides, what were such foolish matters now? She paced back and forth from kitchen to workroom, from window to door to window again, bootheels gritting the sand on the floor and brows lowered.

If I were a man, she thought, *I would take up Uncle's musket and march to that jail and make them let me see Daniel! If not for this ice, I would do such things to Marcus Tapp—*

Suddenly Hannah stopped in her tracks. Why should a bit of ice prevent her, if she might be of comfort to Daniel? There had been a nor-easter four years ago, and Uncle Henry had made himself cleated pattens to get to the barn for the milking, she remembered them. Where were they now? Julia never threw anything away.

She went into the mudroom and began to rummage around on the shelves and under the hooks where the cloaks hung. Old rusty trammels and pot hooks, a trivet or two. Some tin pots with holes that were waiting for Soames, the old travelling tinker. A pair of dulled sugar cutters. Half a dozen wooden clogs in different sizes.

Ah! There now! In a box at the back of the highest shelf, Hannah found them, a pair of oversized wooden soles with leather straps and buckles to fasten over the instep. Instead of the usual iron rings on the bottom to keep one's feet from sinking into the spring mud, Uncle Henry had attached pieces of iron, flat on one side and sharp-toothed on the other, four to each foot for balance.

She sat down on the washbench and buckled them over her boots. Then she threw her cloak around her and stepped gingerly out onto the ice.

One step. Two. Three. The sharp iron teeth dug into the ice like strong claws, and Hannah found she could walk almost normally. A good thing it was, too, for she did not have to wait long for a chance to try them out.

'Mrs Trevor! Mrs Trevor, ma'am!' It was Ethan Berge, coming up from the mill helter-skelter, pulling himself along by clutching the bushes at the side of the path as he ran.

'Mrs Josselyn, Ethan,' Hannah corrected him. It was the first time she had called herself so.

'Sorry, ma'am.' The boy puffed with exertion. 'Only old Siwall's groom's down below at the mill with a sleigh, and he says will you come to Burnt Hill. Mrs Jem's took very sick with brain fever and they fear for her life. You won't go, though, will you?'

She gave a sour laugh. 'To Burnt Hill, after last night? Why, the man's barking mad! Still . . .'

Hannah's fury died quickly, overcome by her common sense. *Fool*, she thought. *Save your tantrums. What better way to get into Siwall's house and question his servants than through the front door, by invitation of the master?*

'Ethan, give me your arm,' she said. 'The hill path is too slippery even for pattens. I'll need your help getting down.'

The boy stared. 'But you can't! Mistress said you wasn't to go out on the ice. She'll have nine kinds of a fit!'

'Ethan.'

'Yes, missus?'

'Will you give me your arm to assist me? Or must I coast down the hill on my backside?'

Siwall's sleigh was a fast cutter, very light, and his horses were well shod for the ice. Besides, the freshly sanded roads and the November noonday sun had combined to make the going much easier than Hannah had feared.

But it was a two-edged sword. If horse could travel, the Regulators would not be long in striking back at the sheriff for Johnnie's death. Daniel would be helpless in the jail, a pawn for whichever side proved the strongest.

And if Sibylla was right, if Siwall feared something Daniel knew of his history, then he could not let that information be told to Colonel Scribner and to the court at Salcombe. Daniel must die with the stain of a traitor on him, so the rich acres of timberland and the house could be seized, and the truth discounted as seditious lies.

I must have him out and away before morning, she thought, *and Jenny with him, where they can none of them find us. Fort Holland until he is strong enough. Then perhaps over the border to Brunswick, or down into York State. From where we might get a ship.*

The burning of bridges and boats and guy-ropes had been little more than a gesture to put fear in the rebels. Sly's ferry was already running, ropes or no ropes, being poled through a narrow channel of open water by two or three longshoremen from the docks under the old man's surly orders.

Burnt Hill manor was silent and grim as they drove up

the lane, the curtains drawn and no horses moving but their own. Neddy Bottoms, the groom, had said little, but when they reached the last turning, he pulled up the horse out of sight of the house.

He was a clumsy fellow with spectacles that never stayed on his nose and a suit of old clothes that had once fit his father but were six inches too small for the son in every direction. He drank too much sometimes and gambled at cockfights and quoted odds and ends of mangled Scripture that would make a cat laugh. Still, Hannah had never known him raise a whip to a horse, a fist to a woman, nor his voice to a child.

'What is it, Neddy?' she asked him. 'Why have we stopped?'

He took off his spectacles and wiped them. 'You take care in that house, ma'am. There's danger in it, and shuffling sands, like the Bible do say. Principles and towers, they'm all falling down. Oh, Master may shut folk in behind locked doors now, but he's come summat late to it.'

'You mean Master Jem? But he's gone off, I'm told.'

'Aye, and our wages with him! We must all work the winter for bed-and-found or be turned off to beg.'

Hannah took a moment to absorb this. 'Neddy, what did you mean just now? Lock folk in? If Jem is away off, then who is locked in at Burnt Hill? And where is your master this morning?'

'Oh, he'm gone to shovel old Clinch in the ground, ma'am, and good riddance to bad fodder, if you pardon me saying. No, no, 'tis young missus I mean, bless her! Mercy Lewis says she was all the night banging on her chamber door and weeping for her Dada that's shot dead last night, but they would not let her out. And now she's took poorly. Maybe dying, they say.'

'Drive on, Neddy,' she told him. 'We shall see about that!'

The room into which Hannah was ushered was very dark, the long window shuttered from the inside and a single candle burning. The pictures and mirrors had all been draped with black crape in mourning for Royallton-Smith, and the china-gilt clock had been stopped at half-past eight.

From behind thick dark-green bed curtains came the sound of a rather determined sniffling that had worn itself out hours ago and was now kept alive by sheer force of will. The girl Harriet had drawn the covers up over her head so that nothing could be seen of her but a hunched, lumpy shape that heaved now and then and gave vent to a half-hearted sob.

Hannah threw open the shutters and drew the heavy draperies back from the bed with a whoosh. 'I was told you were dying, Mistress Siwall,' she said. 'Of the brain fever, was it not?'

'I want to. I mean to. I will if I can.' Harriet's voice was raw and hoarse; so then, some of the grief, at least, was genuine. But it gave every appearance of being more for herself than for her dead father. 'I would die in a minute if they'd let me,' she said. 'Only I probably wouldn't manage it, you know, for I never do anything right.'

'Well, my dear, if you mean to die of brain fever, the first thing required is a brain.' Hannah snatched away the coverlet. 'And you won't grow one lying there like a pumpkin in a cornfield. Get up and dress yourself! Let me see you, how you are.'

It was a telling inspection. Harriet Royallton-Smith in a ballgown, with a feather fan fluttering in front of her and a fine necklace at her throat might have been – well, not handsome, certainly. But acceptable. A pale, patchy face with dark eyes like raisins in a bun. Brownish, lusterless hair in two braids. A bosom – *was* there a bosom? And now, after hours of weeping—

'I'm a fright, ain't I? Mama always vowed I was, she was glad to be rid of me. And Jem said so, too.' The girl threw back the rest of the covers and sat up on the edge of the bed. 'I wasn't very good at *that*, either. At— *you* know. My wife's duty.'

'Converse, you mean. Intercourse.'

'Yes.' Harriet shuddered. 'It hurts so, I think it's too big, you know. And I had to keep my eyes closed all the time, or else when I saw it I got vaporish. So I said I was ill, and then he would leave me alone.'

Hannah could not help smiling a little. 'And you're not ill now, either. Are you?'

'No, of course not. Not really.' Harriet dabbed at her eyes with a corner of her nightdress. 'Only I'm sorry Papa's dead. I think Siwall killed him. He must have. He's an old terror for all his praying.'

'That's impossible. Mr Siwall and your father were side by side and the shot came from out on the common, through the open door.'

'Well then, somebody meant to shoot Siwall and shot Pa instead, by chance!'

Ah, thought Hannah. So there were signs of a brain after all.

'I told Pa-in-law last night I would divorce Jem for adultery and have back my dowry,' the girl went on. 'It was all they ever wanted of me, and I don't think it's fair they should have it, not now. I could have a divorce, you know, now Jem's run off with Sally. So they locked me in here and took the key away, and I screamed all night and banged on the door, and when I stopped screaming, they said I was mad and sent for Dr Kent.' She stopped for breath. 'Only he won't come, he never does since I told him I had the putrid sore throat and he found it was only the toothache. So I made Mercy get Neddy Bottoms to fetch you instead, for I had to speak to somebody, didn't I?'

'Harriet, listen to me. Would you really divorce Jem?'

'Of course! Only I shall go to Paris. Such things are nicer there. And I do *long* to see Marie Antoinette and the little Dauphin, and the balls at Versailles and— '

'Your money – it's not in Jem's hands, is it?'

'No, it's invested, that's what Papa told me. Only I think Siwall has spent it all, because Mercy says they have nothing to pay the servants and Mrs Kemp's always groaning about the bills from Boston and Portsmouth, and they would not give Jem more than a paltry allowance, and they made us come here to live though I wanted a house on Beacon Street that Jem promised me.'

The barrage suddenly stopped and the girl's shape drooped. 'Is he really dead, then?' she said. 'Is Papa dead? They would not let me see him.'

'Yes, I'm afraid so,' Hannah told her gently. 'Your father is dead.'

She expected more tears, but there were none. The girl's face was almost pretty as she sat there, her head lowered, her fingers twisting the bedclothes.

'I shall miss Pa,' Harriet murmured. 'I never saw much of him, he was busy with his wars and his politics. Nor of Mama, neither. She sent me to school for the sake of her nerves, to Mrs Blacket's Academy when I was seven.' She looked up. 'I can speak French, you know, and dance the gavotte! I'm not stupid!'

'Of course not.'

'I don't miss Mrs Blacket, but I *shall* miss Papa, I think. He meant to be kind to me and nobody else ever meant to be kind to me, or not kind, or meant me anything at all.'

Her eyes filled with tears, now, but they were not for her father. All her life Harriet Royallton-Smith had been little more than a minor piece in some elegant board game, to be used and bargained-for and ignored when her service was done.

'I don't really want to die, Mrs Trevor,' she said. 'Not really. Only I don't want any children and I don't want to be married, not ever. I want to be free. Just like you.'

THIRTY-FIVE

Husbands and Wives

'What have you done with my husband?'

Hannah marched into the constable's office, and Marcus Tapp looked up from his papers and smiled faintly. 'Husband?' he said. 'That word comes something hard to your tongue, does it not? Or have you turned meek and dutiful now?'

She did not rise to the bait. 'What right had you to take him? You know he has nothing to do with these deaths.'

'You heard the Militia Act read. Josselyn is their commander. One of his men shot Clinch and Royallton-Smith.'

'You have no proof of that! The shot came from a distance, unseen!'

Tapp shrugged. 'Just now, I don't need proof. Someone must pay, and he's elected.'

'Because it suits Mr Siwall to have him out of the way! But why suddenly now? Is it only the money, the property? Or is it more?'

'You never stop, do you? That mind of yours.' His strange, lucent eyes studied her and he paced back and forth in the narrow anteroom. 'But do tell me. Inasmuch as the word has any meaning beyond the banal, do you *love* this new husband of yours? Do the birds fall swooning from the branches when he humps you and calls you his mouse?'

'Is there nothing human you do not make mock of?' Hannah studied him, trying to get past her anger. 'Is there no one you care for in all the world?'

'No one, by God.' He stopped in his tracks and looked at her, eyes narrowed and cold. 'Besides, I'm not human. It costs too bloody much.'

'Why do you take Siwall's orders? You are stronger than he is. Smarter.'

The sheriff shrugged. 'He had money. I had none. Now I have some of his. In time, I'll have most of it.'

'So Clinch believed. It did not keep him living.'

'I'm not Clinch. I'll outlive the lot of you. Perhaps I'll buy Mapleton Grange when they've seized it. But I'll keep a bed there for you.'

'What if Siwall's money were gone? What would you do then?'

He laughed. 'Sell his balls for gunstones.'

'What else would you sell?' Hannah came a step nearer. 'You have no loyalty. But you have information.'

He shrugged. 'Perhaps.'

'I wish to see the Muster List of the militia. You have it, do you not?'

'Alas. I fear you wouldn't meet my price.'

She took another step, within arm's length of him. 'Name it.'

He took her hand and pulled her close and kissed her. A strange kiss, not harsh and invading as she had expected, not a conquest. When he had touched her before, Tapp had tried to take her cheaply. This was a different man, one she had not encountered.

He frightened her more than the other.

'Now let me see my husband,' Hannah whispered. 'And give me the book.'

Tapp drew away, annoyed. 'A single taste of your mouth is not worth so much. You may have one or the other. Which is it?'

'My husband,' she said.

He still kept her hand in his two, like a box closed tight on her. 'A wise choice,' he said. 'I had no intention of letting you look at the book.'

Marcus Tapp bent his head suddenly and kissed her again, and this time his mouth was open and hungry, his tongue coming deep into her.

'Tomorrow morning, I take him to Salcombe,' he murmured. 'It's a treacherous road, Gypsy, for prisoners. But there's a night before the morning. And if you care to pay it, freedom always has its price.'

Marcus Tapp unlocked the door of the cell. 'Five minutes,' he said, and disappeared into the anteroom.

Hannah was shaken and sick, and the stench of the place almost made her retch. It was very dark and cold, with not even a pallet laid on the straw that covered the hard dirt floor. The single window was shuttered and she nearly stumbled over the wreck of her husband before she could see him. But Daniel did not wake.

'Dear God, what have they done?' she whispered.

Her fingers found two broken ribs – no, three – and when she pulled up the shirt, almost every inch of his chest was black and swollen and bloody where they had kicked him and dragged him.

There was blood in his mouth. If it came from inside him, there was little help for him, not even from surgeons. Hannah laid her head against him, hearing his heart's steady throbbing. She detected a wheeze where the lung was pressed by the broken bone, but no bubbling sound from blood in the cave of the chest.

Bruising inside the lung, she thought. *That will heal*. It was the only explanation. And besides, it was what she needed to believe.

Still he did not move in the chains nor try to speak to her. 'Daniel, you must wake,' she said into his ears. 'You must help me.'

He moved slightly, tried to reach for her. He had heard her a dozen times during the night and he could not be sure of her now, that she was real.

'Are you living?' he whispered.

She put her mouth to his swollen eyes, very gently, barely touching him. 'Does this feel like a phantom?'

'I can't see. I can't see you.'

'Your eyes are swollen shut. They will mend.'

It was more than she knew, but she must give him something to hold to.

'I will come for you tonight,' she said, 'as soon as it is dark.'

'Hannah, you must not! Let me know you're safe at home, you and Jennet and – and this one – and then I shall manage.'

'Safe?' Her voice shook as she chafed his cold hands. 'They will bring me your body home safe, and I have seen enough of dead men's bodies! *I will have you living!*

Suddenly all her piecing and reasoning crashed down around her. Siwall, Clinch, Smith – Hannah Trevor did not care any longer for puzzles and reasons, and if there were answers to be found, then let someone else find them. The only thing that mattered was here, what was made in them, between them, that they did not drift down into death.

'Christ, Daniel,' she whispered, as she had on their first night together. 'Please. Please. Please. Please. Please.'

'Ahh – ahhh-ahhh-ahhhhyiiiiieeeeeeehhhhhh!'

Hannah heard Sarah's first broken scream as she turned up the path to McGregor's Forge, Uncle Henry's pattens digging into the sanded ice of the dooryard. As she reached the house door, it burst open and the burly Scotsman charged out to meet her.

'Thank God you've come! I sent the lad, but your aunt said you'd gone off to Siwall's.' McGregor was shaken, his wild hair matted down to his head and his eyes weary and dull. 'How did you know?'

'I didn't. How long has she labored?'

'Near twelve hours. She can't bear it much longer.'

'Yes she can, she will have to. Who is with her?'

'Leah Kersey, she's tarried the night here for the storm,' he said. 'And old Mrs O'Donnell from the end of the lane. I could find no others.'

It was not the best prospect, Hannah had to admit it. Two pregnant women and an old lady near seventy. But it would have to do.

'You must help us yourself, Lannie,' she told him. 'Go and bring in some clean ice and break it up fine, for Sarah to suck on. It will ease her, and her ease will help the child.'

He would have gone off like a shot, but he paused for a moment. 'How's Dan, then? Have you seen him?'

'For a moment, that was all they would give me. He is very ill-used. But alive.'

'Tapp's bastards took my keys from me, Hannah. They put a gun to my boy's head and I could not resist them.'

'And besides, you have taken your oath as constable.' She knew him well enough to guess at his motives.

But Lachlan spat into the fire. 'Ach, I've left all that. There was a time I'd have died before I broke my honor. But when an oath is not made between equals, it's not honor, it's tinder and straw.'

In Sarah's warm kitchen, the midwife found that Leah and the old Irishwoman had done everything right – the bed of clean quilts by the hearthfire, the half-sitting position. But the child had a mind of its own.

McGregor's wife pushed back her soaking hair and looked up at Hannah. 'It's wrong, isn't it? I shall die.'

It was always there at a borning, the spectre of dying, the other side of the treacherous coin of hope.

'Let me see,' the midwife said. Carefully, with Leah Kersey's wide, frightened eyes upon her, Hannah felt inside Sarah where the child lay. Nothing blocked. Nothing turned amiss. When she put her hand to Sarah's swollen belly, she could feel the small heart beating.

'I think you must get up and walk, Sarah.' The women stared, but the midwife was not daunted. 'It will come quicker if you move. Lannie will help you.'

McGregor had come in with the crushed ice and Sarah sucked at it gratefully, his big square paw stroking and stroking her hair. He gulped at Hannah's latest instruction. But he bent down and lifted Sarah gently up onto her feet. 'Come then,' he said softly.

Sarah leaned on him, her face against his shoulder. 'My back aches me,' she murmured. 'Your kind hands would ease it, I think. My dear love.'

Between the pains, he walked her back and forth from kitchen to bedchamber to parlor and back to the kitchen again, singing snatches of old Scots tunes as he went – 'Waly, Waly', 'The Bonnie Blue Bell', 'The Boatman of Cairn'. In an hour, the spasms were coming every three minutes by McGregor's old timepiece, and in another quarter hour the pushing began.

Able to bear it no longer, the Scotsman went into his smithy to pace up and down by himself, and when it was done, Hannah came in to tell him. 'It's a strong little girl,' she said, 'and Sarah's thriving. She'll be up and about in two days or three. Your daughter is born the same day as my Jennet, that's a fine thing.'

'But she's whole, you say, she's not—'

Hannah smiled. 'Not like Jennet, no. This one has a strong pair of lungs and she makes good use of them.'

'Forgive a fool,' he said, shamefaced.

She reached up and kissed his rough, bearded cheek. 'Sarah chose well for a husband.'

McGregor rubbed the kiss away, embarrassed. 'When she asked would I ease her back for her, I thought my fool heart would crack. My Sarah's never asked me to touch her before.' He stared down at his oversized hands. 'It's all been my doing, the marriage. This bairnie. Oh, she went along with it, for I gave her scant choice. But I never thought – to be loved.'

He went in and lifted Sarah gently into the clean bed Leah had made up for her, while the women finished scrubbing the kitchen and putting the bloodstained sheets and shifts to soak.

When it was done, Mrs O'Donnell took leave of them, but Leah lingered at Sarah's loom, laying in a few threads on the pattern of Flame in the Forest that was her own invention. Hannah stood at the back of the loom bench, watching the pattern of red triangle-shaped flames grow up a thread at a time.

'Leah, your weaver's book,' she said. 'How do you keep it?'

'Why – as most women do,' the girl replied. 'Just some old pages stitched up together.'

'Not on the margins of an almanac?'

'Almanac?'

'*Tom Tearaway's Almanac*, yes.'

Leah laughed. 'Husband puts no stock in planting dates and moon signs and such-like. Why do you ask?'

'Oh nothing. I found one, that is all, with some patterns in it. And Sarah said you had misplaced your patterns.'

'Never mind. I will find them again. Then I will come to set your warp for Jennet.'

'Do not think of it,' Hannah said. 'Not till your time has come and all is well.'

'I think it will not come,' Leah told her. 'Or if it does, I will die of it this time. I am not so strong as Sarah. I have not a heart anymore, I have put it away in the ground.'

'You must not say so! This new child is yet growing and living. I will be with you, and so will your husband, too, as Sarah's was just now.'

'Oh, yes. Mr Kersey will be there. And the child will die.'

'But – he would not harm it? He seems such a good man. You have told me more than once that you love him.'

'How could I not? But they are so heavy. The child will be smashed by the weight of them.'

'What weight? What do you mean?'

'Why, the stones,' said the weaver, as she pushed home the shuttle. 'His great stones. His silence, that weighs down his heart.'

THIRTY-SIX

How She Walked
Through the Fire

There was much to be done before nightfall, and Hannah must do it alone. In her own room at the Mills, she made a thick bundle of quilts to warm Daniel and cushion the jolting of his body, and a few clothes for herself and Jennet, as well. The child would miss Arthur the cat, but there was nothing for it; he must be left behind. Hannah's few shillings in savings and her journal must go with them, of course, and Jenny's cornhusk doll for comfort.

And the almanac, too, with its puzzle of weaving grids – for the habit of thinking was a hard one to break.

Then came the worst part – to wait till the house fell silent at sundown, and the women were out doing the milking and settling the livestock for the night. When the back door had at last slammed shut behind them and Kitty's chatter died away in the cold, clear dusk, Hannah came quietly down the back stair and into the workroom, happy to find her uncle dozing again in his bed. Working quickly and quietly, she made up a basket – food and tea, some stubs of candle, the second-best tinderbox, and some loose fibers of waste flax for kindling. A few half-finished blocks of her new piecing, the wedding quilt of Bridges Burning, and a needle and scissors and thread.

Then into her stillroom for some herbs that hung drying there, and one or two small earthenware pots of ointments and infusions. Anything else, she would trade for as they travelled, or gather in spring wherever they were.

Last of all, she took up the bottle of laudanum Dr Kent had given her for her uncle and slipped it into her pocket.

Concealing the basket under the turn of the front stairs, she led a puzzled Jennet to their chamber and dressed her for the journey. She herself put on her second-best gown, the good dark-green wool gabardine – too tight, now, of course, but more interesting with one or two laces left gaping – and her finest silk-knit stockings, a relic of old days in Boston.

Under her gown she could feel the weight of the laudanum bottle in her embroidered linen pocket, pressing its shape against her thigh.

Hannah took a last look round the little, slant-ceilinged bedchamber. Then putting a finger to her lips, she took the child by the hand and tiptoed down the front stairs to where she had left their bundles.

Out the front door they went, then waited to see if the coast was clear. It was full dark now, at near six o'clock, and Hannah could see her aunt's lantern moving about in the cowshed. There, now they were finished, going back to the house. The girls were laughing, stamping in the cold like a pair of shrill-voiced colts. Then Julia, plodding and determined, the lantern bobbing its circle of light before her up the path to the house.

I will never see her again, thought Hannah, and the

darkness clattered down on her. She paused and drew two or three deep breaths of the cold evening air.

Jennet went with her mother quietly enough while she saddled the steady little mare, Flash, and settled the baggage upon her. But when Hannah turned to help her mount, the little girl had gone.

The moon was not full up yet and it was very dark, but Hannah could not risk a lantern lest Julia should see her and stop her. She felt her way out at the stable door, leading the pony, selected one of her uncle's small splitting axes from the chopping block to take with her, then looked around the moonlit yard for Jennet. In a minute the child came running back, carrying something in her two hands.

It was an old game between them and nothing would do but Hannah must hold out her own two hands to receive the gift. Usually it was only a bird's egg or a stone or a dew worm from some puddle, but they must all be received with a grace and a smile and a hug.

She felt the hoarded treasures slip onto her palms – cold, round, hard. More blessed buttons! Well, at least it wasn't another dead mouse.

Hannah kissed Jenny's cheek for thanks and dropped the buttons into the basket with the herbs. Then she mounted Flash and, pulling Jennet up in front of her, set off for the Grange ford. In the distance, she could see the torches of Tapp's sentries patrolling the banks near the town; there was a curfew tonight, and anyone out past nine would be arrested.

The pony's hooves broke through the ice once or twice, and the cold water splashed up to Hannah's boot tops. 'Hush, my old love,' the midwife whispered, patting Flash's neck fondly. 'You'll soon be warm in a stable again, and a fine groom to brush you.'

My groom, she thought suddenly. *My stable, I am mistress here now.* It was absurd, as though she had ridden up to some castle and declared herself queen. She would never belong in such a place.

She dismounted and went – as she had always done – to the servants' door at the back, keeping tight hold of Jenny's small hand. At her knock, there was a sound of felt slippers slapping the floorboards, and in a moment a crack of light appeared under the door.

'Who are you?' said Mrs Twig's plummy voice. 'We do not open to pirates!'

'It is – your master's wife,' said Hannah. 'I must speak to Lady Sibylla.'

She found Daniel's great-aunt in the nearly empty library, bent over the small pine desk. Its top was piled high with ledgers and account books, a rack of five wax candles shedding an extravagant light on the columns of figures.

'I thought you would come.' The old lady's voice rang in the cold silence. 'Have you seen him?'

'Yes. I must take him away tonight. He will not live otherwise.'

Sibylla nodded, the ranks of carefully powdered curls on her head bobbing. 'That blackguard sheriff must keep the keys. How will you get them?'

Hannah did not meet her gaze. 'I will do as I must,' she replied.

Sibylla said nothing more, only let her shadowed eyelids fall.

'There is a small sledge in your stables,' Hannah went on. 'I will take it, if you please, and a good horse to pull it, well broke to harness. My aunt's mare is not strong enough. And some clothes for my husband.'

'Take what you will. The place is your own now.' Sibylla glanced round the room. 'What is left of it.'

It was true, the house was much changed since Charlotte's death. Had she taken the leisure, Hannah might have been shocked at the look of it.

'You see he has scoured himself for your sake,' said the old lady. The eyelids opened and the small bright eyes, clear amber in the candlelight, fixed upon Hannah. 'Would you take him with nothing? If they ruin him?'

'I did not wed spinets and cherrywood tables and lolling chairs.'

Sibylla tapped a ringed finger on one of the ledgers. Then suddenly she stood up, her cane hitting the floor with a whack. 'Where will you go? How shall I find you?'

'He has friends in the Outward.' Hannah could think no further than the shelter of the unmapped woods.

But Sibylla was well satisfied. 'That rascally Dutchman – yes, that will do, I can send him word. But the old pirate will be no help without money to bribe him.'

She reached into the drawer of Daniel's desk and took out a small kidskin bag that jingled with coin. Beside it lay an iron key, and both of these she gave to Hannah.

'In the tackroom of the stable, below where the harness hangs, there is a box,' she said. 'This key will open it; inside are my nephew's weapons. A pair of dueling pistols, a good rifle. Take them. And this.'

Sibylla took off one of the rings from her finger, a gold band set with a single small emerald. It had been there a long while and the knuckle would scarcely let it slip off. 'It is no proper wedding ring,' she said, 'but it will do for the time.'

Hannah held the ring up to the light of a candle. Inside, where the finger had lain long against it, some initials were cut in the gold: *BF to His dearest S. Armor vincit omnia.*

'Why, I cannot,' she said softly. 'Your own gift from Mr Franklin?'

'I had not the courage to use it as my dear Badger intended,' the old lady replied. 'But it suits you well enough.'

The sledge was light and strong and fast, and the horse – a steady grey called Griffin – was surefooted and quick to the rein even on the ice. They drove along the North Bank road, past Burnt Hill and the houses of most of the Selectmen, crossed on Sly's torchlit ferry, and drove toward Lamb's Inn.

In the kitchen, she found Persia taking a leg of mutton from the roasting pan. The clock was striking half-past seven, an hour and a half until curfew. 'I must go on an errand,' Hannah said. 'Will you keep my daughter here? No need to trouble my cousin or Master Lamb. I cannot be long.'

'I will keep her! I will watch at the window for you.' The voice was Jemima's. She came gingerly into the room, a thin, worn, spinsterish figure with an awkward shuffling walk, her careful cap missing tonight and her dull black hair falling in crisp little ringlets down over her shoulders. 'Tirzah is sleeping, the troublesome old baggage,' she said, 'and I've nothing to do till my sister is brought home at last.'

Hannah's eyes opened wider. 'Have you a sister hereabouts, Jemima? Do I know her?'

The peddler's daughter shrugged and began to braid up

her hair, very tight. 'No one knows her,' she murmured. 'I had a bad dream of her once, how she struggled and dug her sharp claws into living. She was someone till yesterday morning, and stronger than I am. But I fear she is dead in her soul.'

Hannah could spare no time to unravel the maze of Jemima's mind; she drove safely away from the inn without being seen by Josh or Dolly. But at the edge of the common, a horseman stopped her, a burly man waving a lantern.

'Get you home, missus! No one abroad after nine!' he shouted.

'I must see Sheriff Tapp,' Hannah said. 'Where does he lodge when he's here in the village?'

'Tapp? Oh, aye. Empty house up past Maid's Lane. Siwall owns it. Woman killt there, nobody else wants it. Gives me the creeps.'

Hannah shuddered as he rode away. Anthea Emory's old cottage, he meant, where Will Quaid had murdered his lover. She herself had found the girl's body, lying raped and strangled in the bitter cold bedchamber.

But she could not let phantoms deter her. She turned the sledge up the lane.

There was smoke from the chimney, and when Marcus Tapp opened the door to her knock, she was surprised to find the kitchen clean and reasonably warm. It seemed odd to think of him seeking comfort of any kind, even a good fire on a cold night.

'Well now,' he said. 'Here's a gypsy come calling. I wonder what she's selling this night.'

Hannah stepped past him into the small room. Anthea's things were still there – a scrubbed pine table and two or three joint-stools, a dry sink with a water bucket and pitcher, a small dresser with wooden trenchers, and a few pieces of worn pewter. On the table a candle, its flame dancing in the draft.

Tapp closed the door and slid home the bolt, like the sound of the rifles on the common when Johnnie was hanged.

'I am come to pay your price,' Hannah said.

'And what price would that be?'

'For my husband's freedom.'

'Ah. That.' He came a step nearer. 'If I let him go, I take a great risk. I suppose you are worth it?'

'You may say the Regulators came and attacked you and took him.'

'Mmmm. And you'll be happy to fetch me a clout on the head to prove it true.'

She moved nearer the fire. The empty wicker cage still hung there, in which the dead girl had kept a little finch. Hannah could not bear to see it and she took it down and set it by the hob.

'Well now,' Tapp said. She could feel him very close to her. 'I could never resist a gypsy's bargain. Besides, it's nothing to me if Josselyn freezes to death in the forest or gets his neck stretched in Salcombe. You have my word upon it. Tomorrow he shall go free.'

'You are not renowned for the keeping of bargains. First give me the keys.'

'Oh, no. When we've finished.'

He turned her to face him. She closed her eyes and his fingers began to unfasten the clasp of her cloak.

'Why hesitate?' he said. 'You're trembling.'

'That should please you.'

'I don't need your fear. But why take it so to heart? After all, I can't get you pregnant a second time.'

The cloak fell to the floor. He let her go and began to light candles. Two, three, five, seven, setting them in saucers and leaning them in pots, till the room was as bright as a ballroom.

'There, now, that's better. I want to see you, plain as day.'

He sat down on a stool and took off his boots. Forcing her fingers to obey her, Hannah began to unfasten the laces of her bodice.

'No stays,' he said, watching her. 'I thought not. That's right, now the skirt.'

'I— Please, have you any drink? Any brandy?'

'Surely, surely. I am remiss. A gentleman ought always to offer a lady refreshments beforehand.' He laughed softly. 'Old Clinch always swore you were a toper, but I didn't believe him.'

Tapp went to the dresser and fetched two mugs, then poured some brandy into each of them from a leather-sheathed flask on the table.

Hannah's hand found the laudanum bottle in her pocket. If she used too much, she would kill him. And why not? Why leave such an enemy behind to hound them and perhaps kill them one day? No, she thought, pour the whole bottle in, let him die.

Daniel had once spoken to her of a line men cross during battles that changes the soul forever, the whole self lost and never again to be found. It was the line where freedom lives, if it lives anywhere, with chaos on one side and responsibility on the other.

I must walk into this fire, she thought. *There is no other way to live.*

The cup. The bottle. Marcus Tapp, undoing his breeches and pulling his shirt over his head, his face for an instant obscured.

Hannah poured a dollop of laudanum into the mug, and a drop or two more for good measure. If there was not enough, he would do as he liked with her, and she had no intention of that. Enough to make him sleep till morning and after, to let her find the keys to Daniel's cell and the shackles, to let them drive away and be long gone before he woke.

She put the bottle quickly away and picked up the undrugged brandy.

'More?' he said.

'No. I – can't drink as a man does.' It would tickle his vanity, perhaps, and make him drink his own down. She looked modestly away from him and sipped at her cup. 'It is almost too strong for a woman,' she said.

He came to the table and downed his own drink in a single gulp, then pulled her against him and untied her skirt with one hand, the other beginning to rub her breasts very slowly, very gently, the thin cambrick shift slipping back and forth under his palm. Unwillingly, helplessly, she could feel herself rise to him, her nipples hardening and the familiar wet darkness flooding up between her legs.

'You finish it,' he said. 'I want to watch you.'

Hannah undid the ties of her petticoat and let it fall with the skirt, so that she stood in her knee-length shift and her stockings and boots. Tapp bent down and unfastened them, reaching up under the shift to roll down the fine stockings.

Last came the shift. She lifted it off and as it covered her face for a moment, she felt his mouth between her breasts and his fingertips moving across her swelling belly. He was trembling, too, she could feel him. Then his tongue on her, his fingers slipping between her legs, dipping gently inside her.

Almost tender, he was, as though he knew it would give her more pain than ill-usage. As though he almost believed he might be loved.

'Look at me,' he said, and pulled the shift off her. 'Open your eyes.'

He was naked too, now, his sex stiff and hard, huge in the bright candlelight. Her eyes flickered shut again.

'Look at me!' he commanded her, and forced her eyelids open by the skin of her forehead, his fingers still wet where he had felt of her. 'Say you want me. You know it's true, your body is proof of it! Say it, goddamn you!'

'I— I— want you.'

'Again!'

'I want you.'

'More than him. More than your husband. More than any husband.'

'More. God. Please.'

Let him fall now. Let me have given him too much, enough to kill three men. Christ, take my freedom away from me. God, let him die.

'Shhhh,' he said, suddenly gentle again. He turned her around to face the wall and bent her forward a little, leaning her against the dry sink. Over it was his shaving mirror, and when she saw her face in it, Hannah's eyes closed again.

'No. I want you to see yourself. I want you to watch yourself betray him.' Again he forced her eyes open, pulling her head up and back by her hair. 'Say you love me.'

I did not use enough, she thought. *He should be swooning. Too late. It's too late.*

'Say you love me!'

But she did not say it.

His free hand cupped her breast and she could feel his mouth kissing her shoulders very gently, moving down the valley of her spine. His sex was hard and throbbing, she could feel it against her. Then for a moment he lurched, bumping into her shoulder, and hope surged up in her. The drug was enough, after all. In a minute he would crash down on the floor.

'I won't hurt you,' he said. 'Only you must watch. See. The face in the mirror? After tonight, do you think he will find love in that?'

He put his foot between her ankles and shoved them apart, bent her a little farther over the sink. Hannah could not move and could see nothing but her own face before her. An old woman looked back at her, used-up and sour and half-wild.

Then Marcus Tapp made a soft, surprised grunting sound and lurched again, pulling her with him, almost toppling the both of them backwards.

'You bitch!' he cried. 'You – y-you tricked me! The drink!'

Hannah grabbed for his razor on the sink, but it fell to the floor out of reach. She kicked backwards with all her strength and tried to get free of him. He was stumbling, reeling. But he did not let her go, his hands were like shackles around her, like the clenched hands of the dead.

One hand still gripping her hair, he forced her down with his knee and lunged, all his strength barely able to manage it. Helpless, she felt his seed flood into her and his body arch backwards.

She made no sound. There was only the rattle of the earthenware pitcher and basin, rhythmic and regular, as his helpless thrusting rocked the washstand they leaned on. The crackle of the fire. The slight rush of the wind through the planks of the floor.

Then he fell, a terrible crushing weight on her. She pushed him away, threw him backwards onto the floor. Her legs were sticky and hot with the stuff of him and she stared down at it. Where did it come from? Something dead he had left inside her that leaked out despair?

Hannah glanced again at her face in the mirror, and thought for a moment she was seeing a ghost.

She was someone till yesterday morning, Jemima's voice echoed, *and dug her claws into living. But now she is dead in her soul.*

THIRTY-SEVEN

Piecing the Evidence:
On the Nature of Ghosts

NOTICE OF REWARD
ADVERTISEMENT
PORTSMOUTH BEACON, 15 JULY, 1779

Master Moses Dancer of Portsmouth will pay a reward of twenty pound silver for information as to the whereabouts of one Leah Elinor Woodard, his godchild, who was last seen 13 May 1779, during the Action of the Seventh Regiment, Massachusetts Regulars, to secure the Tory enclave of Fallbrook, Tennant County, State of Hampshire, following the victory at Taunton Bridge. She is of middling height, able-bodied though slender. Handsome of feature, eyes light blue or light grey, pale complexion, hair very fair and fine. She bears a small mole on her left arm, but was otherwise unmarked when last seen.

At the time of her disappearance, Leah Woodard had attained to the age of sixteen years.

Master Dancer declares his god-daughter an excellent weaver and spinster. Her voice is soft and her manners those of a gentlewoman. She is sometimes called Nell for her middle name of Elinor, and sometimes Sheba, for the sake of her twin brother, Solomon, now deceased.

The report of her disappearance from Fallbrook was filed

by one Captain Daniel Josselyn with the Office of Civilian Deployment, Continental Army, Fort Liberty (formerly Fort Reserve).

Nota Bene: Unconfirmed reports of the fair-haired ghost of a young girl have been rumored from time to time in the woods about Taunton and Fallbrook, accompanied by a single shriek, as of pain. When observed, she does not reply when any name is called out and is never seen twice in the same location.

Of Leah Woodard, no sound information is forward. She is believed to be dead.

Notice of Decease
Coroner's Court, Pelham, Commonwealth of Massachusetts, 28 August 1780, Mrs Letitia Woodard, Relict of Fitzwilliam Woodard, Tory and Traitor

According to Master Jabez Peele, Landlord, the Blue Anchor Inn, the woman known as Queenie, heretofore Letitia Woodard, late wife of Fitzwilliam Woodard, infamous Tory and executed traitor of Fallbrook, a nursery of treason in the state of Hampshire, cut her own throat with a scrap of broken looking glass during the night of 27 August 1780, in a fit of madness while she lay alone in a hired chamber. Said Queenie had been since her husband's decease the common law wife of Master Richard Eliphalet Dancer, chapman and peddler, and was said to have suffered frequent seizures of madness, in which she walked in her sleep and often proclaimed herself the ghost of Queen Charlotte, Queen Mary of Scots and other such lewd and dishonorable tyrantesses.

Jemima Woodard, her only daughter yet living, age 20 years, was lately examined by the Common Court for a madness of a more virulent sort than the mother's, having resulted in the death of a bitch dog belonging to Mr Isaiah Bright of this township. The woman was sentenced to be placed in Mt. Hope Asylum, Hope Island, Massachusetts.

At Mr Dancer's request, said Jemima Woodard his stepdaughter by common law, was sold into indenture to him for the term of fifteen years, on condition she be rendered incapable of producing any offspring, which would almost certainly run mad in their turn. This, according to Dr Tobias Boswell, County Surgeon, Pelham, may be conveniently performed by the regular ingestion of ergot, or rye smut, to abort any possible conception. Ergot will also prevent headache and regulate the monthly courses, making the patient tractable and content, as in women the organs of bearing are directly related to the size, strength, and scope of the brain.

Ergot may produce bad dreams and delusions, but these will be nothing of harm to the people at large. Though these dreams may cause alarm and despondency in the patient, this may be easily allayed by a sound bleeding every fortnight, and a regular purge.

The first winter Tom and me come here from Falmouth, Tom took a bad fever. Old Mrs Markham, she dosed him with cold water root and poulticed with onions, but it done little good at the first.

So I sent for Sam Clinch, and he comes huffing in

and begins to bleed poor Tom and clister him and I know not what-all, till at last it grew late in the night.

'You may go to your bed by the fire,' Clinch says. Well, I'd been watching four nights, and could scarce hold my head up, and I laid me down on my pallet and slept.

In the dark I woke sudden, and felt his hands on me. I cried out for my honor, but he stilled me. 'Now, now then,' he says, and claps a hand on my nipple.

I was younger then and had but two babes, and my teeth was still white and my hair not so thin as now. I had red hair in them days, like a copper halfpenny and down to my knees.

'How else shall you pay for your husband's care, may I ask?' says Clinch. 'You owe me ten shillings already and another five for my medicines. If he lasts, why confound you, 'twill be thirty or more! You're a woman of sense and you will not go back on a debt.'

I hear Tom toss in the bed, and smell the sick sweat on him, and I feel Clinch's hand slide up under my night-shift. And we had no hard money at all to pay the bill.

So I lay with him that night and two nights more, and the fourth night he comes with another man. 'This here's my friend Nathan Jenkins,' he says, as they stood in the shadow, 'and he's a fine gentleman that I know you will favor, and then your debt shall be paid.'

I did not see Jenkins, for they struck out the candle and put the firescreen before the hearth to break the light. And I thought as he came to me that I might lie so with a ghost of one that was dead, and I put out my hand to see, would it go through his body. For he did not speak and made no sound, not even when he came to his work. And when he lay in my arms, I heard he did weep and his body did shake with his sobbing. And I reached up to touch his cheek and found it dry, as the dead are clean and dry in their shrouds.

And in the night, as he slept, I did hear his voice speaking. 'What have I done?' he says. 'If any should know me, I am ruined forever.' And then, 'I am dead. I am dead.'

My third boy, Jack, is Clinch's bastard I think, for he favors him some. I did not accuse Clinch and I said nothing to Tom of this Jenkins, nor never shall. But as soon as Tom found me with child, he did not ask again to brush down my hair by the fire at night, and he went into debt to old Siwall to buy us a farm near five mile from the town, where none would come near me. And in time, being kind as he is, he forgave me.

But this summer he lay six weeks in the debtors' jail and came away with a fever that never will leave him, and does not speak, nor look me in my eye, for I think he knows now what I did to preserve him before, and is shamed in his soul.

For now I am near forty and my honor is wasted, and no man would seek out my favors. I am glad Clinch is dead, and I care not who was that dead soul Nathan Jenkins. I would rut with all the ghosts in hell to have my Thomas back again.

—*Elizabeth Whittemore, wife of Thomas Whittemore, Foreclosed Farmer, Sable Creek*

THIRTY-EIGHT

Fugitives

After Marcus Tapp crashed down unconscious at last, Hannah dared not take the time to wash herself clean of him. She dressed quickly, then went about finding the keys; they were no challenge, he had hung them on a nail driven into the mantleshelf. The muster book took longer, but she found it, too, on a high shelf of the dresser.

She barely glanced at her enemy, only enough to see he was breathing. He seemed something long dead as he lay there, an old rack of bones, the heart that had moved them rotted away and gone.

She left all his cruel candles burning and went gratefully out into the dark, closing the door carefully behind her so nothing would seem to be wrong. *Why did you not kill him?* asked a small voice inside her throbbing head. *Fool. Go back and kill him now, but a knife in his heart.*

Hannah turned and walked back a few steps, but a foot from the stoop, she was seized with a terrible nausea. She bent over, vomiting till there was no more left in her, till she could almost feel her ribs scrape her backbone. Finding an icicle fallen under the eaves, she wiped her hot face with it over and over, sucking a little of the cold, clean water to give herself courage.

But she did not go back to kill Tapp.

Instead, she got into the sledge and drove down Maid's Lane again and past the Forge, stopping a few yards short of the town jail, in the dark ell of the cooper's shop. There was a torch in a holder near the door and she could see the shadows of men inside, and hear their dark laughter.

'Stay back and wait my signal,' said McGregor's voice behind her.

'How did you know?' Hannah whispered.

'Daniel's aunt sent me word not an hour since.'

The big Scotsman did not ask how she had come by the keys in her hand, only snatched up the torch from the doorway and brandished it over his head once or twice. Another torch flared on the hilltop across the river, near the arsenal. Then there was gunfire, the sound of men shouting.

McGregor ran to the door of the jail and began to bang his fist on it. 'Away out, you fools! Regulators, they're after the cannon!' The door opened and two swarthy faces peered out at him, blinking in the torchlight. 'Away with you!' he said. 'I'm safe to be left with him, I haven't the keys to his irons. Out, now, or Tapp will have your hides!'

The firing on the hillside grew more intense, and now and then the cries of the wounded could be heard – or so it seemed. In the darkness, Hannah held her breath as the sheriff's wild mercenaries ran soft-footed in their Indian leggings, to ride bareback away to Great Meadow.

McGregor quenched the torch in the water bucket inside the door. 'The keys to his irons?' he said, his voice raw and angry.

She handed them over. He took up the cell keys from the desk and pinched out the candle on the constable's desk, and they moved through the thick, stinking darkness into the narrow corridor that led to the cells.

'Pray God you cropped him,' growled the Scotsman. There was no need to say whom he meant.

'He is living,' she said. 'But he'll sleep for some hours. Did they really come for the cannon?'

'Ach, 'tis only Kersey and one or two others, waving lights about and firing in the air, and screaming like fey-folk at daybreak.'

They opened the heavy oaken door and went to where Josselyn was lying. McGregor unfastened the shackles and his big arms lifted the battered body up.

At first Daniel did not seem conscious. But in a second more his quiet voice came. 'Let me try to walk.'

'Nay, there's no time.' McGregor's huge arm caught him and Hannah supported him from the other side, out of the cells and into the cold, sweet air of the high street. From Great Meadow ridge came more shouting, more torches moving, the rattle of occasional gunfire.

'I hope to God Kersey can turn into moonshine,' muttered McGregor as he helped settle Daniel in the sledge.

'You must find a safe place yourself.' Josselyn gripped his friend's hand. 'They'll know who to blame for this.'

McGregor pulled a quilt over him. 'I'm coming with you,' he said. 'There's many fled into the forests, gathering for a march on the court. I mean to stand with them. Kersey will see to my wife and the young ones, he's a good, sound fellow.'

*

In less than ten minutes more they were gathering a sleepy Jennet into the sledge at Lamb's Inn.

'Wait! Take this!'

Jemima Dancer came shuffling out from the kitchen with something wrapped up in heavy flannel. A warming stone, Hannah could feel the heat of it.

'God's eye, they do say, is on the sparrow,' Daniel heard the peddler's daughter say as she reached out a thin hand to touch his bruised face. 'Poor sparrow. God was sleeping, I see.'

He could yet scarcely open his eyes for the swelling, but a shadow reached him in the glow from the lantern she carried. A slender shape, paler than the night, with black hair falling downward.

Downward, he thought. *Her arms hanging downwards, how they caught at me and the fingernails clawed at my face when I set her upright. Her feet were burnt, she cried out and I lifted her, carried her.*

Tell us the truth, they said, and when she told it, they burned her again.

Three women. Three sisters. One dead. Sarah. One mad. Jemima. One I might almost have loved. Sheba. Sheba, whom Solomon treasured and called Little Sister.

'The traitor of Fallbrook,' he whispered.

The firing on the ridge had stopped and it grew preternaturally still.

'Away, now, or we're too late for it!' McGregor dug his heels into Lizzie's sides and Hannah snapped the reins over Griffin's back.

They dared not risk the high road for fear of Tapp's patrols, nor carry any lantern to light them. The safest path was the

Falls road that wound high above the South Bank, to come out over Two Mills Farm and end at Blackthorne Falls.

Before they reached the woods, eager, scudding clouds had covered the moon, making it darker than ever. The westward trail ended, forking north and south at the foot of the small spill of half-frozen water that splashed down from an outcropping of granite onto a deep, narrow, gravel bed.

'Which way?'

McGregor deferred to Josselyn's knowledge of these woods. Daniel had hunted here, trapped with the old Dutchman's Indian runners, wintered some months each year with his logging crews.

Weary, still unable to see, Daniel tried to consider. What they needed was a stronghold where they might lay up for some days and rest. An unpredictable place where there was sound shelter with a clear enough view in all directions – and more than one way out.

They would never get so far as Fort Holland tonight. Already Daniel could feel himself begin to drift again, as he had in the prison, the pain in his ribs a dull grinding and his bruised face sending a bolt through him with every rut or tree root the sledge runners struck. He had not tasted the blood in his mouth for some hours, but now it was there again, something scraped loose by the jarring. He felt weaker, and his hand gripped the seat of the sledge to keep from slumping over.

'There's an old farm,' he said, and Hannah had to lean towards him to hear the words. 'Siwall owns it, but no one has taken it. To the south, off the Salcombe road about ten miles, and then west. There's a cut through the woods and a trail.'

Very dark, it was, like driving through thick smoke once

they entered the trees. Bare branches clawed at them and the fine barbs of the cedars and junipers slapped their faces raw and would not be plucked out. Once Jennet woke and began to wail and they had to stop and quiet her, the sound more risk than the waste of time.

All along, McGregor rode silent ahead of them, hacking away what branches he could with the ax Hannah had brought from Henry's barn. Here and there in the distance, they could see the faint glow of small campfires through the trees.

'Sheriff's men?' she asked the Scotsman. 'Or Regulators?'

'Men from downriver caught at the Muster,' he told her grimly. 'They're most of them debtors and they dare not go home.'

Two miles they went, three, five. A moose loomed up in front of them and McGregor's horse almost crashed into it. Lizzie reared, screaming, and old Griffin jerked the sledge suddenly forward, almost spilling them out.

The sky was heavy with clouds now, and a light, dry snow had begun to fall. Daniel seemed to be sleeping, and Hannah put out a hand to touch his face. There was blood on his lips. She clenched the reins in her fists, pulled another quilt over Jennet to keep off the snow, and drove on.

Another mile, the snow falling thicker, the sledge runners silent but for the ice-covered tree roots they now and then struck.

Then a voice from the darkness and the soft gleam of a

lantern, veiled by the curtain of snow. 'Who is it? Bastards or poor folks?'

'Friends,' cried McGregor. 'A sick man and his woman and childie.'

'Come in with us, then, *brawd*. You won't be the first this night, nor likely the last.'

Two young boys and a short, stocky man with a heavy Welsh accent stepped out of a clump of bracken. While his father kept lookout, the eldest boy took Griffin by the bridle and helped Hannah to turn the sledge down a gentle slope between overhanging pine boughs, then into a clearing. There was a cabin of four ample rooms, a fine large barn, and a cornfield long harvested, the dry stalks rattling as the snow struck them. It was beginning to cover the ice more thickly now, and the going was easier.

'I am Ifor Jones,' the man said, 'and these great devils are Davy and Huw, my youngest boys.' He held the lantern up to peer at Daniel's face. 'Oh, now, a fair job some bastard has made of him. Come, let's have him in where it's warm.'

Other shapes began to appear from the darkness – some from the barn and some from the cabin. One or two came from under a cart pulled up in the dooryard, and some emerged from the trees and the snow, carrying torches or lanterns. Behind the men, cautiously, came one or two women, shawls over their heads and cloaks pulled round them, and a few cold, sleepy children clinging close to their skirts.

'I'll take her,' said one of the men, and lifted Jennet up in his arms, as the Welshman and McGregor carried Daniel into the house through the silent, watching strangers. He was unconscious now, his arms hanging limp and his head dangling.

'It's Josselyn,' Hannah heard someone say, and they let the torchlight fall on his features to be sure of him. 'I heard they'd took him.'

'So then. He'll be with the Cause after all. If he lives.'

'Put the little one with the babes, here in the trundle. It's warm by the chimney.' A round, pink-cheeked woman laid a hand on Daniel's bruised, swollen forehead. 'There is cold, he is! But he has fever, I think, underneath it. I will make him a bed by the fire, where we can tend him.'

She began to pull quilts and woven coverlets from a chest in the corner, and Hannah laid out a pallet a few feet from the hearth. When it was ready, the men lowered Daniel's long shape carefully down. A half-dozen of the watchers from outside had come into the house, now, one or two women among them.

'Well, you lot of puddings, what are you looking at? Huw, bring in some water for the kettle, there's a good boy, and put it on the hook to boil! Now, then, off to your beds, every one of you, and let us work!' Ifor's wife turned to Hannah and smiled as the men filed out. 'Welshmen are terrible old lads for a fight, see, and I have been wed to mine these twenty-three years. I've seen worse than your man is, believe me. Though not often.' She took the midwife's hand and squeezed it. 'Carys, that is my name.'

'I am Hannah Trev— Hannah Josselyn.'

'Oh, I knew you by those curls, and the scarlet riding hood. You tended Hitty Ballam with her third, and I was one of her women. You don't remember me.' She laughed. 'Nobody ever does, but it suits me as well.'

*

Between them, the women undressed Daniel there by the fire and Hannah washed him. As the warm water touched him, the nerves in the bruised skin began to come alive, making the muscles twitch and jump.

His feet, which had been resting on Jemima's warming stone as they drove, were fairly warm, and his toes were not frostbitten. His hands were very cold, especially the stumps of his two missing fingers, in which the blood did not move very well. She held them to her face and breathed her warm breath on them, chafing them gently. There were marks on his wrists from the shackles, thin cuts that would leave scars almost the match of her own when they healed.

Carys poked among the bundles of herbs in the basket. 'This is comfrey, that will do for his ankle,' she said. 'But what for the inside of him, where that blood comes from? I have wiped it twice from his lips and every time he coughs, it is back again.'

Hannah's fingers were searching him, feeling the spot where his ribs were broken. 'I think it is his lung that bleeds, but there is no puncture.' She bent her head to his chest. 'Come and listen.'

Carys did so, her tongue between her teeth for concentration. 'A little wheezing, but you are right. If the bone had gone through, he would not have lived so long. A small hemorrhage, then? From the beating, like a bruise on the inside that keeps rubbing open and bleeding? That will heal with proper rest.'

'God knows I hope that is all.' Hannah let her hands lie on his arm, and when she looked down she could see herself shaking. She clenched her fists hard and stood up. 'The swelling in his eyes will need ice. He will gain courage if he has back his vision.'

'Husband!' At Carys's voice Ifor Jones looked in at the door, his rifle laid across his arm. 'Bring us in a bucket of snow, my dear. Clean, mind you!'

In Hannah's pocket the rest of the bottle of laudanum made a weight like an iron. But she could not bring herself to use the poppy on Daniel. Not yet.

'I have comfrey and burdock,' she said. 'Have you shepherd's purse? And knotgrass?'

'There's a clump at the back of the barn, my dear. Davy!'

The boy was quickly dispatched with a lantern and basket, and Carys unfastened a bunch of dried shepherd's purse from a hook in one of the beams.

'I don't suppose there is mistletoe?' Hannah asked her. 'Only the leaves, not the berries.'

Ifor set down the bucket of ice and chuckled. 'Now how should a Welshman be living without mistletoe? Hah! We're all heathen Druids, you know!'

He went off to fetch it, still chuckling, and Carys piled snow in a huckaback towel and laid it gently across Daniel's eyes, packing more snow around his bruised chest and covering it with a blanket to keep it in place. It would soon melt, and they would be kept busy wringing out compresses from the icy water. Once she had all the ingredients, Hannah could brew up a tea that would help stop the bleeding in the lung.

But for the moment, there was nothing more to do.

'Take this, girl, and sit.' Carys brought a mug of steaming tea and poured in a dollop of honey. 'You'll fall down on my floor in a minute.'

'My daughter, Jennet—'

'She's sound asleep. That's a pretty name, Jennet. Not Welsh, is it? Drink your tea!'

Hannah obeyed her gratefully, sipping the hot, sweet drink. There was a small loom in the corner, a plain pattern of checkerwork set on it, blue-and-white, such as men fancied for shirts.

'You're a weaver, then?' she said.

'Oh, we Welsh are great weavers,' Carys replied. 'At home I had a fine loom. Sixteen harnesses, it had, and I'd a book of patterns as thick as a Bible! I have the book yet, but I use it seldom now.'

Another Hannah, in another world, would have asked if she knew any woman who wove such patterns as there were in the margins of the old almanac packed away in her bundle. Had they husbands? Were the husbands riflemen? Did they write tombstone verses? Had they buttons to lose, and had they lost them?

But the deaths of Clinch and Royallton-Smith, the buttons, the gravemaker's verse and the weaver's grids – all that mysterious business seemed far behind her now, all her rational questions the merest absurdities, smothered in shame as they were.

For Marcus Tapp's victory was still there, deep inside her, still smeared on her body. No matter how often she washed, it would always be there, she would never be free of him.

That was the real victory, not the seed he had left in her. He had built a wall of shame that would shut her away from Daniel, from everything she had loved and half-feared and denied and wanted in spite of herself to believe in, almost more than she wanted to breathe.

Only one thing she clung to. *I did not say I loved him*, she thought. *I did not sell him that.*

The menfolk came in with the herbs, and she brewed up the tea. Carys held Daniel's head up and Hannah soaked a corner of clean linen rag in the hot drink, let it cool slightly, and put it into his mouth. If he choked, he might hemorrhage again, worse than before, and drown in his own blood.

At the first sip he coughed, but very little blood came with it, the cold compresses already doing their work.

After an hour, he was able to sip from the cup – though he did not seem to wake when she held it to his mouth. Hannah made up a poultice of the comfrey for his ankle and put more cold cloths on his chest.

Then he slept, very deep, his mouth falling open like Jenny's. Carys dozed on the settle, but Hannah lay down on the floor beside Daniel, at arm's length, her fingertips barely touching his arm.

At last she, too, slept, for when she looked up there was a pale streak of daylight through the east-facing window. She sat up and bent over him, lifting the poultice from his leg.

'This bed is damned hard,' he mumbled. 'Where have you couched me, on my coffin?'

She laughed softly, and the sound of it surprised her. She had not thought she would laugh anymore in this world. 'There'll be no eternal rest for you yet, sir,' she told him. 'Open your eyes now, and see where you are.'

He reached up and took away the wet towel from his eyes. For a moment his swollen eyelids labored. 'I can't,' he said. 'It's no use.'

'Try again.'

He obeyed and the left lid fluttered open. The right would not, it was still stuck shut with matter. 'I see light,' he said softly. 'But I cannot see you.'

She fetched a warm wet cloth and dribbled a few drops on his lashes. 'There, try one more time.'

This time his eyes opened and he looked at her. But he did not smile.

'Ah, I see you,' he whispered. 'I know what you've done for me. What I have cost you.'

Hannah turned her face away. She had forgotten how deeply he saw her, that he must read the great shame in her eyes. 'Daniel,' she began, 'I have – had no—'

He was quick to cut her off. 'No rest. I know, my poor love. Nor McGregor neither. If he hadn't got those keys from Tapp, I should still be chained up to that wall.'

Then he did not know, after all! She almost dropped from relief.

Daniel took her hand in his own. 'Hannah? Are you ill? Are you harmed?'

'Oh now, there is a man for you!' cried Carys, waking up from her doze. 'She's worn to a whisker with tending the brute, and there he lies warm by the fire and asks what is the matter!' The Welshwoman looked at Hannah's face, a close assessing gaze. 'But he's right, love. You are not well. What can I do for you, now?'

Hannah stood in the middle of the room, her hands hanging limp at her sides, her fingers clenching into fists, then opening again.

'Is – is there never a room to myself here? I – I must wash some dirt away.'

THIRTY-NINE

Old Women's Fires

'I observe you have a reckless habit of bullying women, Master Sheriff! Remove these men at once!'

Sibylla stood at the head of the staircase looking down at the five armed men who had just burst in at the front door of Mapleton Grange.

Mrs Twig lay in a whimpering heap of starched ruffles and petticoats at the foot of the stair, and Charlotte's little maid, Abby, had locked herself into the cellar with Thankful, the kitchen maid. As for faithful Jenks and kind-hearted Owen, they were sprawled where Tapp's woodsmen-mercenaries had left them – wigs askew, livery torn, and two black eyes and a bloody nose between them.

Marcus Tapp pulled aside the splinters of the fine carved oak door and stepped through them into the hall. 'Where is Josselyn?' he said. 'I will have him.'

Sibylla peered at him down her long nose. 'Did you think he would wait for you here on his doorstep? Or have you come for something else?'

'Old hag, I'm in no mood to palter.' The sheriff was

thick-tongued and unshaven this morning, his pale eyes watery and ringed with black.

He gave a nod to his men and they began to range through the house like a pack of dogs hunting carrion. The big ox Tully and the ferret-faced Ketchell shoved Twig's bulk out of their way and went into the kitchen, and in a moment Sibylla could hear the crash of their rifle butts as they smashed crockery and glass and threw kettles and bed-warmers down from their hooks.

The half-breed Le Duc and another buckskinned marauder pushed past the old lady and began to ransack the bedchambers beyond her; she could hear the tearing of cloth and the clatter of curtain rods as they demolished Charlotte's old room, so carefully preserved until now. Le Duc emerged, grinning, a pearl ear-drop dangling from his left ear and the contents of Charlotte's jewelbox spilling out of his scrip.

From the library came the sound of books crashing out of their cases and onto the polished floor. Then the drawers of Daniel's desk being pulled out and smashed – papers tossed about, inkwells thrown at the newly painted walls, blotting sand spilled on the floorboards.

In a moment, Renard came out, sullen and angry and empty-handed.

'Where are Josselyn's papers?' Tapp turned to Sibylla. 'His account books. His military dispatches, his letters. I will have them, or I will bring this pile down around your ears.'

'I think not. Siwall covets it, and a ruin is no use to him.' The old lady's changeable eyes were very black and very bright. 'There are no papers here,' she said.

'Lying bitch.'

Not a nerve twitched in Sibylla's powdered face and not an eyelash flickered. 'I have been called hag and bitch by better than you, sir. Such words come like spring rain now, they refresh me.' She came down a step to stand eye to eye with him.

'I must have those papers, all of them!' he insisted.

'You mean Siwall must have them. But he's soon for the chop, is he not? Mr Inskip has already scampered off to the woods. Oh, you are skating very thin, my dear sheriff. You have wagered yourself on the wrong pair of dice.'

Tapp drew a breath. 'Will you give me those papers or not?'

'I have said. I have nothing to give.'

'Then find every book in this house, you dogs!' he commanded, his raised voice echoing in the cavern of the hallway. 'Every letter and paper. Take them into the yard and burn them.'

The deputies who had gathered to their leashes fanned out again. From the kitchen came Mrs Twig's cookery books, and a pile of her treasured receipts for everything from soap to brown ale written out by hand in copybooks and on the backs of Daniel's reports. From upstairs came Sibylla's own books and a bundle of letters signed 'Your Fondest Badger'. And Charlotte's letters, too, some from Daniel and many from her mother in England. And account books and receipts of old bills – every trace of this household that had once been so thriving and seemed now to have crashed to an end.

Most of all, from Daniel's library, came armload after armload of fine leatherbound books – Herodotus, Livy, Ovid, Homer, Virgil, Sophocles. Shakespeare, Chaucer, Spenser, John Donne, Milton, Dr Johnson, Swift, Pope, Montaigne, Erasmus, Cervantes. John Locke, Franklin, Thomas Paine, Jefferson.

'Oh, ma'am,' cried Twig, 'All Master's books that his grandsire left him!'

Sibylla looked down the stair and out through the open door where the woodsmen were tearing the precious pages from the bindings to make them catch quicker.

'He has read them,' she said calmly as the smoke began to rise. 'Minds do not burn with such paltry fires.'

Not an hour after the sheriff's men had gone, Lady Sibylla Josselyn was to be found perching herself with an irritated snort on a damask lolling chair in Lawyer Napier's library, her coiffure in perfect order and her gown fit for an audience at court.

'In three days more, Mr Siwall will open this Debtors' Court of his, will he not?' she demanded.

The old fellow motioned to his musty clerk to stir up the fire, and then poured his guest a small glass of sherry. 'It was put off on account of the storm and the – er – troubles. But I believe that is his present – er – plan, to be sure.'

'Are you a man, Master Lawyer?' Sibylla drank down the sherry in one gulp. 'Or are you only another creature of Siwall's?'

'Now, now, ma'am. I realize that your nephew's troubles—'

'Those same troubles are caused by his generosity and his need for peace and quiet. I am another breed of dog, sir. I thrive on contention. I find Mr Siwall is some four thousand pound in arrears in his debts to my nephew. I wish to take an action against Hamilton Siwall in this fine court of his, on Major Josselyn's behalf.'

Napier gaped at her. 'But – er – you cannot mean—'

'To attach the fellow for debt! Indeed I can,' Sibylla crowed, 'and *shall*! Let Siwall pluck out the mote from his own eye before he goes looking for dust mites in others'. He has further bills, I am told, with Mr Lamb at the inn and Mr Sanderson the joiner, and at Markham's mill for the sawing of boards. I have spoke to them and they all mean to join with me in this execution.'

'But – but— ' the old lawyer stammered, 'Master Siwall is a jurist, ma'am! He is a magistrate, a representative to General Court, a man of weight and distinction!'

'And lawyers are like physicians, eh? They close ranks to defend one another? Now I see how the wind blows you!'

'Why— No, madam! But – er – you are only—'

'A woman – and an Englishwoman, at that. Those points I shall not debate with you. But an action is already afoot by my nephew's solicitor in Boston on behalf of his interests there. Mr English has gone to the Commonwealth Court with my commission, by way of Fort Hendly at Salcombe. By the day after tomorrow, the attachment should be filed.'

'But over four thousand pound, in hard silver? No man has so much to hand!'

'Nearer five, sir, with interest at the same rates Siwall himself charges. It is no more to a man of his extravagance than twenty pounds to a poor man. Besides, the excuse has never deterred him when others have offered it. It shall not hinder me now.'

'You— You would not attach Mr Siwall's *person*, if he cannot pay?'

'Clap him into debtors' jail? The devil I wouldn't!'

Thomas Napier leaned back in his chair. 'Well, I'm fired and buttered,' he murmured, and fanned himself with the tail of his wig. 'And salted, too, 'pon my word!'

'I must have someone to speak for Daniel here,' she went on, 'in the Rufford court. To bring a man from Boston would take a week, and there is no time. Will you be that spokesman?' Sibylla stood up and walked round the desk to look down into the old barrister's face. 'I think you are no poltroon, sir. Your reputation is solid, even so far as Philadelphia. I have written long since to Mr Franklin to inquire of you.'

The old man poured himself another glass of sherry and downed it, then poured out another.

'I presume – er – there is evidence of this debt you speak of?' he asked her when he had drunk it. 'Tangible? Able to be examined?'

'Account books. Personal notes-of-hand signed over to my nephew by Siwall. Letters of intent going back some five years.'

'But – er – I was told that the sheriff had seized all—'

'They are hid where fire will not burn, sir, never fear me for that.'

'And Major Josselyn, where is he now?'

'If I knew, I would not consider it safe to tell you. You must prove me your probity first.' She began to stamp back and forth before the fire, her cane whacking the floor at every step. 'This debt is good smoke. If I can, I will use it to drive out the rats from their corners. But even the money is not enough, I think, to kill for. Siwall comes for Daniel's life, sir. It must be some threat to his own that drives him.'

The old fellow frowned. 'It is an easy thing for prosperous men to deceive themselves and one another for the sake of their pocketbooks. I have winked, madam. I fear I cannot deny it.' He looked up at Sibylla. 'But I am not the only Selectman who deplores Siwall's choice of a sheriff, and now with the Riot Act, Tapp has extraordinary and dangerous powers.'

'When Siwall falls, Tapp will fall with him,' she told him. 'Bribery, collusion. Perhaps worse. Such things may be proven, if men will but speak.'

He shook his head. 'The law is not always right, but we cannot leave quiet citizens defenseless. And with this insurrection and the Riot Act—'

'Black Caesar lay already in his grave on the night Smith was shot, yet they make no search for another assassin, they question no one and take no statements of evidence. Instead they come straight to my nephew and label him traitor. Why, sir? Why is that?'

'You mean—'

The old woman nodded. 'Daniel has a fine house and ten thousand acres of timberland. I have done what I may to put some part of it into the hands of trustees for his daughter. But Royallton-Smith, too, had a daughter. She had a dowry, and before her father could claim it back on the night of her husband's desertion, he was shot to death.

The lawyer considered. 'So, then. Siwall and Tapp may know well enough who has killed these two fellows?'

Sibylla sank down in the chair again. 'I am a rational woman and this is no rational business,' she said. 'But I fear Daniel cannot be freed till the killer is found and the whole business unravelled.'

'Then we must find and unravel, ma'am. Find and unravel!' Napier poured two more glasses of sherry. 'I can wink no longer! I will file an execution for debt against Hamilton Siwall in your nephew's name today.'

*

'Have a care, Ethan! You mustn't let the knot slip!'

'I can't see, Mistress. Kitty, bring me the lantern here.'

'No, we can't risk a light!'

The wellsweep groaned as Julia raised it, but what was tied to the rope that hung down into the well was no bucket of water – though it was almost as heavy. It was an oilskin pouch, dipped in thick tallow to make it waterproof, and tied round and round with leather thongs.

'Hah! We have it!' cried Lady Sibylla, as Owen caught the pouch and hugged it tight.

It was now well after dark, but the curfew would not take effect for two hours or more, and Sibylla felt the need of company before she went back to Daniel's empty house. Still, she shivered a little as she entered the warm, bright workroom of Two Mills; Reverend Samuel Dancer was there, sitting beside Henry Markham's bed and reading aloud to the miller from one of Fordyce's *Sermons*.

'An excellent invention of mine, if I do say so!' Julia turned the waxed script over and over. 'Not a leak or a crack anywhere. See how the water beads up? You did well to send it here to us last evening, or Tapp would surely have it by now.'

'Where is Mother?' Hearing her voice, Henry sat up, confused for a moment, interrupting the sermon. 'Has she gone to some birthing with our Hannah?'

'Here I am, Husband.' Julia went to lay a hand on him. She had told him of Jonathan's death, but he seemed scarcely to grasp it, and she had not yet had the heart to tell him about Hannah's going, too. If he had wakened to the ordinary world of dull chores and small pleasures, his mind might have healed with as much success as his body. But he had not. Nothing was as it had been; things at Two Mills would never be quite the same again, and neither would Henry.

As for Arthur the cat, he wound around everyone's legs, but none of them were Jennet's and they did not suit him. Sibylla sat down on the settle and took him up on her lap, but he gave a low growl and pushed away with his back feet, thumping down to the floor and marching off with his one good ear laid back.

'He misses the child,' said the dowager with a sigh. 'Poor brute, he's as great a fool as I am.'

The Reminder, having finished his sermon, came to sit in the rocker by the hearth; drawing the half-finished green sock on its four needles from the roll of his wig, he began to knit a row around.

'Will you give the papers to Lawyer Napier?' Julia asked the old lady.

Sibylla helped herself to a pipe of tobacco. 'Only such as he needs. The rest are no danger to Siwall.'

'If he has wronged one, a man may see danger in lambs in a meadow,' the old man murmured. His needles were still clattering, but the stitches had slipped off and the knitted piece lay on the floor.

'I will not abide any more of your riddles, sir! Speak plain, like a Christian!' Sibylla demanded. 'What lamb has Siwall wronged?'

'Ah, names often change. Faces rot, so they say, in the grave. But I know her. Jemima knows her. And yesterday, when he spoke from the platform, I saw him at last and I knew him as well. I was there when he took her from her father's hearth and delivered her unto evil. Little Leah, my godchild. I thought I should never see her alive in the world again. But all things come back again. All things are interest compounded. All things in this world are profit and all things are loss.'

'His name, Mr Dancer! We must have a name!'

He looked up at her. 'His name is Legion, ma'am, for he is many. They called him Nathan Jenkins the Tory in Taunton and Fallbrook. But here his name is Siwall.'

FORTY

Piecing the Evidence:
On the Nature of Hazard

To believe – as Hannah Trevor and Lady Sibylla had always done – in the traditional concept of mystery unravelled, of mortal puzzles neatly solved, is to believe that even sudden and violent death must somehow be rational, that it presupposes a discernible motive and the control of a rational God.

But when he fired his rifle at Samuel Clinch on the night of the hunt, Oliver Kersey did not care whom he killed. He scarcely knew the man, and Clinch had had, as it happened, nothing whatever to do with the conception of Sheba's bastard child.

When he fired his rifle into the bar-parlor of Lamb's Inn on the night of the Muster, Kersey had meant to hit Hamilton Siwall – though he had not fathered the child, either. In both cases, he aimed not at men but at circumstance – at the appearance of wealth, the arrogance of position. At the closed wall of power that had locked him out of the world all his life.

He might as well have fired at an empty suit of clothes,

or shot through the window of a coach on the post road at any well-dressed stranger who passed.

These facts – and the fact that he hit Master Royallton-Smith, who did not deserve it, instead of Siwall, who did – were a measure of the role of chance, of pure blind hazard, in human events.

On his way back from delivering the drunken Phinney Rugg to his less-than-appreciative wife, Kersey had seen Siwall's coach at the door of Lamb's Inn. Chance, hazard, had brought it there. Hazard had sent the storm that made the coachman leave early for Salcombe.

Kersey had meant to wait for Siwall and follow him home, to kill him in some lonely lane, to strike at the heart of power as it had struck at him. But hazard opened the door of Lamb's Inn and set Siwall's hard, angry, frightened shape against the light like a figure chalked out on a straw target. Hazard raised the wind that blew the door shut just as Kersey, hunched down against the sleet in the shadow of the gibbet, put his gun to his shoulder and aimed.

When the door opened again, he assumed that Siwall would still be the man who stood there, and he scarcely noticed the changed size and shape of his target. He fired once, and the shape of power – for indeed, the incarnation of it no longer mattered – crumpled and fell.

In the War they had sent him out to shoot British officers from ambush, to pick them off from a distance, as many as he could without regard to their rank. Aim at their heart, they said, strike down their leaders, their power. Use their own fear as your weapon.

He ranged alone through the winter woods, dressed in white like the landscape and slipping among the dark trees with snow-shoes on his feet and only his rifle for company.

He found he could make his thick, absurd body almost disappear in the snow, and in time he had learned to *become* snow – cold, impartial, silent, regarding no chance as greater than the next.

Breed terror, they had told him. Become the terror you breed.

Till he began to love Leah Woodard, the girl-wife he called Sheba, he had found in this coldness a perfection of power far greater than the bitter epitaphs he composed for his personless victims – like the one he had written for Clinch.

The dead and the bullets that killed them were a random collision of atoms he could feel no personal regret for. They absolved him of guilt and of failure. Hazard, chance, ruled the world, and he was its agent.

Always innocent. Always clean.

He had exchanged this seamless and beautiful control over circumstance for the love of the girl Sheba, but that love, too, had been chance.

It had been autumn, some five months after the Battle of Taunton Bridge in the foothills of the New Hampshire mountains, a small square of recalcitrant Tory country near a former British barracks called Fort Reserve. There had been many battles in those days, and they, too, were mostly chance. A Patriot patrol met with a party of Tory raiders or British from the garrison and took them or was taken, depending on the weather, the state of the roads, the shortage of rations. There was no beef nor mutton for the army, and you ate what you could. Dead horses and mules, dogs shot in some farmyard. Porcupine, weasel, even mole.

If weasel was all you chanced to find, then you ate it. It had a sweet, sickening flavor that made your gorge rise and affected your aim. Kersey had once had General Howe in his sights, but the taste of the stewed owl he had eaten for breakfast made him vomit, and when he had finished, the general was well out of range.

A joke made the rounds of the Continental Army that if Jefferson had had to eat boiled boots for breakfast as the troops did, there'd have been no Declaration of Independence and George III would be dancing the jig in Philadelphia.

'Please, have you any food, sir?'

It was September, the leaves just beginning to turn. Kersey had spent the night in a thicket of scrub oaks and dead fern, with a rock at his back like a headstone, and the girl's voice was a whisper in his ear as she bent low above him. He grabbed for her, pulled her down against him. She was very slight, very young, and her body was shaking. She did not resist him, only lay in his arms as though she had fallen there out of the sky.

They had shaved off her hair, as the patriot mobs did to camp-girls who slept with the British. It had grown in now, a soft, fine cap the color of straw on her delicate skull.

'Are you a Tory?' he said. 'Will your friends come down on me and hang me?'

'I have no friends,' she told him. 'I need answer to no one. Have you nothing to eat? Some cheese or a crust?'

Kersey sat up, keeping her trapped against him. He could

feel the small buttons of her nipples, like a man's or a child's, press against him as he dug in his scrip for the food.

He gave her a few overripe plums he had picked in some orchard and a handful of crusts he had saved. She gobbled the fruit, half-choking on the sour juice. So young, she seemed. So fine in her bones.

When she had finished, she laid her two hands on his face. 'You will stay with me now,' she said. 'And not fight anymore. Our war is over. We shall live.'

He laughed softly. 'You don't know me. You're a child. How old are you, fourteen, fifteen?'

'Near sixteen,' she said.

'I'm old enough to be your father, girl!' He let his hand stroke her. 'What's your name, then, since I've fed you?'

'Sheba,' she said.

'Ah, Bathsheba.'

'No, sir. Sheba the queen.'

He smiled at this fancy, but it suited her. There was pride in her eyes. 'Where are your people?' he asked her. 'Where's your own father? Your brothers and sisters?'

'My father is dead,' she replied, and began to kiss him, very gently.

He had never been kissed so. He had bought love, now and then even taken it by force. He felt he could scarcely bear the slight, willing pressure of her lips on his forehead.

'I have had too many sisters,' she said, 'I don't want any more. You are the world to me now. I will love you and keep you.'

Absurd as it was, Oliver Kersey could not bear the temptation of loving, of believing in this slight girl. But he tried to push her away before it was too late.

'You're a Tory whore!' he cried, forgetting to keep his

voice lowered. 'Do you think I can't see you, your hair they have shaved? No woman cuts her hair so short from choice!'

'I heard a shout! She's come this way!' cried a man's voice out of nowhere. Then there was a sound of boots crashing through the brush.

Kersey clapped a hand over the girl's mouth and pulled her down to hide under the long fronds of dead fern. In a minute the patrol came into view, three British soldiers and their sergeant, tracking carefully over the footsteps she had left in the leaves.

Sheba lay tight against him, her arms clasped round his body. He could feel her warm breath on his neck and the softness of the new-grown hair. 'Please,' she whispered. 'Help me. Don't betray me.'

'What have you done?' Kersey whispered, once the British had passed by them. 'Soldiers don't hurt women unless they've done murder or treason or worse!'

'Do you see those leaves?' she said. 'How they are taken and used?'

A slight wind had come up and the dry leaves of maples and alders blew up on the trail, their colors tangled. They fell apart and rose again with the next gust, and tangled with others, in new combinations of chance and change, none remembering nor regarding the rest. Only the feet of the soldiers that stepped them down in the mud imposed human decision on hazard.

On the post road below the woods a peddler's wagon passed, brightly painted, its tar-blackened canvas made of the sails of some ship. On the seat beside the driver sat a woman and a faded, black-haired young girl. Sheba glanced down at her mother and her sister Jemima on the seat of

Dick Dancer's wagon and knew them, though Kersey did not.

But she looked away, and let them go.

'I am no more guilty than one leaf is guilty of another. I am not theirs, nor anyone's,' she told him, and he thought she was speaking still of the soldiers. 'But I am yours, if you will have me. I love you. I will stay with you.'

So human choice born of the girl's private despair imposed itself upon the pure chance of their meeting and began to create for Oliver Kersey the love he had ached for as a boy. He asked Sheba no more questions. He had ceased to believe in the truth or to care if he knew it. That night, in a half-hidden barn on a farmstead the raiders had burned, he heard for the first time the strange, shrill cry she had made when he took her, like a rabbit in the jaws of a fox.

And hazard was still at its work on the night of the Muster. Siwall's life, Dick Dancer's life and Jemima's, Daniel Josselyn's, Hannah Trevor's – all their hopes and loves and private sins drifted together and apart like dry leaves on a pathway, and when they collided with Oliver Kersey's, there was no clockmaker-God who controlled them. All they had in common was the workings of chance, and their own stubborn wills and clouded minds.

I am clean, Kersey thought as he crouched in the sleet by the gibbet, watching the body of Royallton-Smith crumple to a bloody rubble on the floor of the inn. *Chance has no shame and I have no shame. I am clean, like the ice. Like fire.*

Out of the dark, he heard Sheba's single, wild cry, saw her run through the storm towards him. Already people were rushing out of the inn. Tapp's horse was tied up at the jail; he would be there himself in a moment.

Lorenzo Newcomb saw them there in the storm, but he did not suspect who had shot Smith. 'Go and warn Josselyn!' he cried.

'What?' Kersey mumbled. 'Why?' Sheba had reached him and she clung to him, panting, one hand holding her belly.

'You heard the Riot Act!' Newcomb shouted. 'They'll blame the militia, now the vote has gone against the courts. And Josselyn's at the head of us!'

It had never occurred to Kersey that a decent man, someone he valued, might be blamed. He could not think, could not reason. What use was reason against such a wind?

'They will call Daniel a traitor!' Sheba screamed above the storm. 'Go to Two Mills and warn them! You must go! You must!'

'No! I can't leave you!'

Her soft eyes narrowed and grew hard as they had at the cabin, when she spoke of the debt she had paid for him. 'Why, be damned, then,' she told him. 'I will go by myself, and I will not come back!'

'Nooooooooooooooooo!!!' he cried, and swooped her up in his arms. 'You will kill the child! You will kill me!'

So he did as she asked him, as he must. Stood up with Josselyn at his marriage. Saw him taken, beaten, his woman struck down.

Shame smothered Oliver Kersey. The glass walls of the prison rose around him again.

I am a traitor, he thought. *She has made me a traitor. She and the bastard child.*

*

'Are they safe away?' Kersey asked, when he came back to the Forge from the ruse at the arsenal.

McGregor was nowhere to be seen. The boy Robbie was asleep, the two women alone, Leah weaving and Sarah nursing her new daughter in the bed against the far wall. Kersey glanced away from her, abashed, and poured some hot tea from the pot on the table.

'They are gone off in a sledge,' Leah told him. 'But I fear Daniel will not live. When I tried to give him porridge this morning, he choked on it and bled. He is very weak. Very sick.'

Her voice was torn, and when he looked down at her face there were tears, like fragments of glass that had fallen there.

Her husband stared. 'Daniel, you call him? Why do you weep for him? I haven't seen you weep since the first child died in you.'

'I may be sorry for a hurt man,' she said, and went on with the weaving, the shuttle moving back and forth, back and forth between the raised sheds, as the pedals thumped their steady rhythm. 'He is gentle.'

'No! It is more!'

The two halves of Oliver Kersey shattered apart again as they had in the prison. Nothing was whole, no one to be trusted; the world fell away from him. He stared at Leah's swollen body where she sat on the loom bench, and hated her.

But he still loved the child, just as he had loved Jennet Trevor when he held her that morning, a thing of hope against the blank of the future. It was a dream now, that night Jennet had long ago spent with them at the cottage, like one of their own dead children come back from the grave.

I want a child, he thought. *I want to father life and leave it living behind me. I want to die and rise again. Free. Free.*

His hands tore at each other, the nails digging into the skin. He struck the teapot from the table and it crashed and broke on the floor. Sarah cried out from the bed, but he did not remember her, could not think who she was or where the cry came from. *A bird*, he thought. *A jay come to mock me. Thief, thief, thief.*

'Why did I not think, when you wanted to warn him?' he cried out. '*He* had you as he had Hannah Trevor! *He* paid my debts when you took him; Josselyn is rich, he could pay any debt! You love him! You have never loved me! No wonder my sons are all dead!'

Still the loom pedals thumped and the shuttle flew in and out, carrying the colors. 'Don't talk like a fool. You don't know,' she said. 'Back in Hampshire, after Taunton. Daniel was kind to me, kind to my sisters.'

'Liar! You have no sisters!'

'I was shamed, I could not bring myself to tell you. You know nothing of those days. I love you, nobody else. I'm not the same as I was then, you have helped me. Let me tell you how it was.'

'I know enough! You're carrying Josselyn's brat, that is why you mourn for him, why you forced me to help him!'

Suddenly the random fragments of circumstance made a rational pattern that absolved him. Whatever happened to Daniel Josselyn, he deserved it. The blind whirl of the universe had decreed it. The senseless made terrible sense.

And Kersey was its soldier, its impartial weapon. He must strike at the center. He must put an end to what smashed him, what tore at the rightness of things. 'I must kill him,' he whispered.

Imposing the pattern that satisfied him, he invented piece after piece, snipping them to fit and forcing them in at the corners. The ones that did not fit, that belonged to other lives, other terrors, other chances, he let fall and tramped down until they disappeared, till the answer was simple and perfect – though totally wrong.

His rifle in one hand, Kersey gripped Leah's arm with the other; he dragged her from the loom bench and across the room to the door where her cloak was.

Sheba is dead, he thought. *This other, this faithless bitch Leah, has come to deceive me, to live in Sheba's sweet body and speak with her voice.*

And I, too, am dead. He has killed my heart and eaten it. Josselyn has shamed me to death.

'You're mad! You will kill her!' cried Sarah McGregor. 'Where will you take her?'

Kersey turned at the door and looked back. 'To hell,' he said. 'Where I am bound.'

FORTY-ONE

The Stronghold

Daniel was slower to mend than Hannah had hoped. If he had been able to rest at the Welshman's snug cottage for a few days, until his bruised lung began to heal properly, things might have been different.

But on the third morning, McGregor came into the kitchen looking worried, with another man tramping behind him. He was round and barrel-chested, with corn-yellow hair that fell straight down to his shoulders from a bald spot on the top of his head. He wore buckskin leggings over his breeches and a round-brimmed hat like a preacher, and on his shoulder rode a young raccoon, bright-eyed and chattering.

Piet Soutendieck, the Dutch trader by whom Fort Holland, Daniel's lumbering camp in the woods, had been named, ruled the Outward like a king for as many miles as his Indian runners could enforce his dominion. If you craved his help or his silence, or even his patience, he would find you a way to pay for it. Daniel might own the timberland, but Uncle Piet owned the woods, and he demanded fair tribute for assistance or information.

Sometimes his tax was in money, but if you had none, he would settle for whatever caught his fancy: a book of sermons or a Bible – he had many and read them all, over and over; a fine long-stemmed clay pipe – he despised the cheap cob pipes of the farmers; or a bright piece of cloth for his Indian wives. One of them walked a few paces behind him now, dressed in bright calico and wrapped against the cold in a bearskin cloak.

'So, Dah-niel!' cried the Dutchman. 'Ha ha! I seen a man once, got run over by six oxen, looked better than you!'

He squatted down by Carys's fire and relit his pipe, and the raccoon jumped lightfoot from his shoulder. Jennet, who had been practicing sign-talk with her father, went running to pet the wild creature. It began to sniff her and climbed up her skirt, to perch wide-eyed on her shoulder.

The little girl's mouth opened in her strange, silent laugh. As a replacement for Arthur, the raccoon did not come up to measure, of course. When you put your hand to his throat, you could not feel him rumble, and his tail hung down instead of waving aloft like a flag. But his fur was soft and his eyes were bright and he was silent and wild and had secrets, just as she did. When she held him, she felt less alone.

For nearly three days now, Jennet had been robbed of her usual balance. Her self-made routines were all missing, and nobody gave her new ones. There were no chores to do, no eggs to gather, no table to set. When she went to the loom, Carys gently removed her. When she wandered outside, the refugee farmers' boys teased her and washed her face with snow. Daniel slept most of the day in the bed at the far end of the kitchen, and she was not allowed to climb on him or even to sit on his lap when they practiced.

And the worst of it was Hannah. She moved silently around the kitchen, helping Carys with the cooking, and now and then she went out to doctor one of the refugee women.

But she did not laugh as she ought to, nor tease and play games, nor write in her journal-book and let Jennet make lines with the pen. It was even worse now than it had been at home, when Jenny could not climb up and be hugged. Hannah was the thread that connected Jennet Trevor to the universe of hearing, speaking things, and now the last few fibers of that thread had somehow been broken.

At first the child had been angry, and then guilty and afraid, certain she had done some great wrong and was being punished for it. She felt alone among strangers, and she watched Daniel and Hannah with wide, cautious eyes, dodging behind the settle or into some doorway when they came near. When they gave her food, she ate greedily, stuffing part away in her pocket in case they might never feed her again.

By night, when she and her mother lay side by side on the pallet by the hearth, with Man-friend in the bed across the room, Hannah pulled her so close she grew frightened, and bad pictures came when she slept.

I must go, she thought, feeling her mother's wet face on her shoulder. *It is wrong and I am wrong. I must go away from here soon.*

In Jennet's pocket, muddled in with the bread crusts and cheese rinds and dried apple slices, lay the pewter button she had long ago pulled from Oliver Kersey's waistcoat in the small house in the woods. She had known him at once when he lifted her up and carried her high on his shoulders at the peddler's wagon. She had pulled off another button from his greatcoat, then, to go with the other, and gave up her treasure to fill the empty box in the clock at Two Mills. When she fetched the buttons from her horde in the playhouse, she offered them all to her mother, even the prize pewter button, to make Hannah love her again.

But her mother did not want the buttons, she had not even glanced at them. Hannah was not Hannah anymore, she was stranger than the pale-haired woman in the woods had been, more silent and distant.

As she sat holding the raccoon with one hand, Jennet reached with the other hand to feel in her pocket. The man's waistcoat button was still there, she had taken it back again, rummaging in her mother's basket. It was smooth and bright and cool to her fingers, and she salvaged some hope from it.

I will go and find my other friends, and live there, she thought.

'Luisa!'

Piet motioned to the Indian woman and she came to peer at Daniel. She touched his shoulders and the place where his heart was. She walked round and round his chair, and laid her two hands on his back between the shoulder blades, all the while singing in a high monotone that came and went like a wind, her eyes half-closed and her head thrown back.

Then she removed her bearskin cloak and sat down cross-legged by the hearth, a bright-bordered shawl pulled close round her shoulders. She untied a bundle from one of its corners and threw something onto the fire. It caught with a puff, and a sweet, smoky smell filled the room.

'Ground-up wolf's tooth and the claw of an owl.' The Dutchman grinned at Daniel. 'To give you wisdom, and strength against enemies. Goddamn, you got plenty of them, what I hear.'

'He says Tapp's in the woods, Dan, camped not five miles from here, to the north-east.' McGregor dashed the dregs of his tea into the fire. 'We can't bide any longer. Wherever we go to, we'd best be away.'

Carys had come in with an armful of wood and busied herself stirring a pot of wild turkey and dumplings. As she worked, she seemed unable to take her eyes from the Indian woman, Luisa. Finally she rummaged about in Hannah's basket of herbs for something and sat down on the bench of her loom, fiddling about with the beater.

Hannah came quietly down from the loft and when Jennet drew near her and showed her the new pet, she kissed the child's hair absently and turned away, to sit quietly by the fire with her hands in her lap.

As Piet and McGregor wrangled over the virtues of one stronghold or another, Daniel sat watching his wife. She had scarcely slept in almost four nights, but her distance was not only from weariness and worry. Something had gone from her, once they were out of the village her direction seemed to leave her. Hannah was lost and where she had gone, he could no longer reach her.

She helped Carys about the house in the daytime, but when she had leisure she did not take up the piecework she had brought in her basket. She studied the falling of ash in the fire as though it were the page of some book, or went up to the storage loft where she might be alone. She avoided his bed and lay on a pallet with Jenny, and when he woke in the night he could see the gleam of her eyes staring into the firelit dark.

The first night, Daniel said nothing. But the second, he could no longer bear it. 'Hannah?' he had said to her softly. 'Will you not come to me? Be with me?'

She got up from the pallet of quilts and came to sit beside him. She took his hand, but she said nothing. He tried to coax her down against him, but she would not.

'No, I'll hurt you,' she murmured. 'You're not long enough healed.'

'Come and kiss me.'

'I mustn't. Your mouth.'

'Hannah.'

Relenting, she had bent and let her lips touch his own, a mere whisper. Then she had slipped away again, back to the dark, to lie silent and sleepless. As he watched her now, she moved with a reticence he had never known in her, and her dark eyes would not meet his own.

'I got a good place for hiding. Better than the old Jowett place,' Piet was saying, 'and closer than the Fort.' He grinned, his blue eyes sparkling. 'I take you there, English. No charge.'

Daniel's eyes narrowed and he turned them on the old Dutchman. 'You're grown damn generous all of a sudden. Or have you already sold me to Tapp?'

'Nah.' Soutendieck spat into the fire. 'I got a score with him. He hires away half my crew to ride with him. He takes one of my daughters, doesn't pay for her. She's good-looking, I could sell her for three horses, maybe four. But not now. I beat her and sent her away.'

In Piet's world, every slight unavenged was a threat to

his hold over the wild men who obeyed him. If you robbed him, you paid him back double. If you didn't, they might find your bones at spring thaw.

Leaning on a stout stick to support his weak ankle, Daniel went out with the men to make ready for the journey, and Carys came to help Hannah pack up the bundles.

'Here, I am half-blind from studying on these patterns,' she said. In her hand was the almanac Mr Dancer had found, with the weaving grids drawn in the margins. 'They are fine ones, and a joy it was to think how I might weave them, if I was home again by Caer Ydris.' She sighed and packed the few loosely stitched pages away in Hannah's basket. 'Only none here is so fine as that one, I'm thinking.'

She nodded at the bright shawl Piet's Indian woman was wearing. Until now, Hannah had barely glanced at it; for the past two days such things had brought her little comfort.

Now she gazed at the pattern and her memory snatched at it: a bright double border of deep blue mingled with crimson, the red threads growing into the shape of a flame and then blending back into the blue again.

'Flame in the Forest,' said Hannah in a whisper. 'On a background of tabby.'

It was the same design as the one Leah Kersey had set on Sarah's loom at the Forge. The pattern she had lost and could not set again without counting out the threads from the finished piece.

'I thought I might find the grids in your book here,' said Carys ruefully, 'and I took it to study on. But there's no luck for the wicked.'

'Then you saw no such design there?' Hannah breathed deep with relief. So it was not Leah after all.

'Oh, no. The best patterns we keep to ourselves, in our own heads, and they come out of the fingers when least we expect them.' She put an arm around Hannah and planted a kiss on her cheek. 'And the worst patterns, too. Eh, my love?'

McGregor gave up his steady mare, Lizzie, to Daniel, the bundles and baskets stowed safely behind him, and Hannah rode bareback on Griffin, with Jennet pulled close against her. The Scotsman tied on a pair of snowshoes made of bent willow saplings and rawhide – a gift from Ifor Jones – and loped ahead of them along the snowy ground that rose slowly to the west, with old Soutendieck keeping a steady pace at the head of them all to lead the way, his own snowshoes broad as a pair of barges.

The snow lent them silence, the only sounds the whoosh of the willow hoops through the unbroken track and the muffled hooves of the two horses. A woodpecker rattled in the crown of an oak tree, and a flock of kinglets chattered as they flew from one tree to another, their scarlet crowns a flash of fire against the heavy-hung branches. Now and then a limb creaked with the weight of slowly melting ice, and a burden of wet snow fell with a plop to the ground underneath.

The weather was warming into autumn again. Soon the tracks would be a sea of mud that would slow down pursuit to a crawl. Till the ground hardened and froze deep, or until it snowed again, they would have time.

After almost two hours, they stopped to rest and give oats to the horses. But Daniel would not dismount for fear of not getting up again. He had wrapped the reins around his wrist, and his gloved hands clung to the saddlehorn. His face was very pale, but flushed bright rose across the cheekbones. Once he felt Hannah glance at him, and he was careful to wipe the back of his hand across his mouth before he smiled at her. But this time, when he looked down at his hand, there was no blood on his glove.

When they set out again, Daniel's mind began to wander. He was riding through green, quiet country, not so wild as this. Spring, it was, all the orchards blooming. In the deep of the woods, purple and white trillium flowered, and blue bunches of wood phlox like a carpet at the roadside.

Like home, he had thought. There had always been wildflowers to gather in springtime, to bring home in great greedy armloads for May-poling time, and leave in baskets on the doorsteps of sweethearts.

Was it England? No. The bridge was not stone, it was wood, built of rough-hewn pine logs.

> *Taunton Bridge is burning down,*
> *Burning down, burning down.*
> *No one lives now in Fallbrook Town,*
> *My fair lady.*

A small place, a half-dozen narrow streets. They had told him it was a harbor for Tories escaping to Canada. There were many such villages from Virginia to Maine, like coaching inns where the hunted could rest and be safe until they moved on to the north, to Upper Canada and Brunswick and Halifax. Others came, too, rich merchants from Boston with their moneybags. Turncoats. Deserters.

A peaceful, quiet place to hold so many sins.

What is your name? Daniel had asked her. The girl was young, and the bruises the women had left when they stripped her and beat her and shaved off her hair scarcely marred her. She was perfect, a single perfect thing that survived. Her skin white as a trillium blossom, her shaved head as frail as a fine china cup found whole in some ruin.

Call me Sheba, she told him. *Solomon was my brother, but he and my father are killed.*

When he tried to remember, her face was a patchwork of many women's faces. Charlotte's prim mouth, Hannah's eyes, the long nose of his mistress in Boston.

How old are you? Fourteen, fifteen? he had asked her.

Twenty, she told him. A lie, and he knew it. *I will stay with you now. You will not betray me. I require your kindness*, she said.

Daniel knew he should push her away, that she was too young and they had used her very ill. But he could not. He was tired, he had spent the last days wading through a desert of dead men, dead women. He wrapped her in his army cloak and they found shelter in a small ruined cottage. One of its walls was half-gone and the spring night flooded in, full of the voices of the dead he had been sent there to count over and bury.

Secure Fallbrook, they had told him.

It meant, bury the bodies. A few were left living – women, old men, children. He had found this girl and her sister alive in an orchard next to a small, whitewashed stone church.

Three women hanged in a blossoming apple tree. One dead, the child dead inside her. The second was mad, raving. When he cut her down, she began to claw at him and sink her teeth in his hands. He had gentled her, stroked her dark hair like a wild cat, trying to soothe her. In the end, they had locked her away.

But this third one, this fair, delicate shell of a child. No one claimed her. *Sheba!* the mad girl had screamed as they took her away. *Little sister! Where is she gone?*

And so she was. The past drained away from her, childhood a dream she had suffered from. All gone.

You're too young, he had said when she lay down beside him, her mouth already searching him. She was practiced. British soldiers had taken her, used her, returned her, taken her again, like her sister before her. Daniel had begun to take depositions, to piece out their story.

All that week he had moved like a dead man. There had been too many to bury one at a time, their bodies too long in the open to wait for a preacher. He ordered a pit dug at the edge of the town near the bridge, and the bodies slid into it from planks, her father and brother and sister among them, as though they were buried at sea, her shrill cry like the keening of a gull.

They had burned them all, then filled in the trench with more bodies. More burning. The smoke so heavy the men could not breathe. Many ran away and did not come back, and Daniel had not the heart to punish the ones who were caught by the sergeants.

You are the first, she lied, her soft hands slipping over him. *A gift I have saved you. I have waited so long for you. Where have you been?*

Daniel required the giving of kindness as much as she needed to have it. A single perfect thing, unruined. *Christ, I want to live*, he thought, and clung on to her as they took one another. *I want to belong to the living. I want my Hannah back again.*

Twice that night he made love to the girl, gently, as though he might break her in pieces like the women in his dreams. When he glimpsed her face in the moonlight through the broken wall, it was older, the eyes darker and larger. When he touched her shaved head, it was Hannah's cropped brown hair he touched, her ghost he had summoned, speaking her name in the darkness.

In the morning, he had found the girl gone.

When Daniel woke from the daze of memory, it was cold again and he was back in the Maine woods. He opened his eyes and found he could not unlock his hands from their grip on the saddlehorn. Hannah rode very close to him, now and then reaching a hand out to steady him. McGregor led his horse, and they had braced his body into the saddle with rolled quilts and bundles to keep him from falling.

Ahead of them, two or three hundred yards to the left down an overgrown path, the Dutchman loped forward, his snowshoes kicking up miniature blizzards as the others moved on in his wake.

It was dusk when they reached their stronghold, an old two-room cottage on a high rocky slope looking down through a small meadow where a stream ran across lichen-covered rocks. As a farm it was hopeless, the buyers deluded and cheated. Nothing would grow here, there were no cleared fields, no orchards planted. Someone had begun to lay walls for a stable, but most of them had long since toppled.

'Poor bastards,' mumbled McGregor. 'Sold out and gone.'

This was one of Siwall's holdings, it could be nothing else. Below the cabin in every direction were acres of deadenings, the girdled oaks and pines and maples grey and broken, their branches long fallen and their rotting trunks stark and bare in the gathering dark. A flock of ravens flapped overhead, their strange baritone voices calling directions. From the west came the bark of a coyote, just beginning his evening hunt.

Daniel drew a deep, painful breath and looked around him. They had come no more than eight or nine miles as the crow flies, but their path had wound up and up, moving always westward, deeper into the woods.

The old Dutchman was right. It was a stronghold. The dead trees made poor cover for anyone riding in, and spark would fire twenty or thirty acres in the space of a few minutes, and flush out any enemy who got as near as the foot of the slope.

'Good place, yah, English?' Uncle Piet came to help him dismount. 'The roof got no holes yet.'

'It will do well enough,' Daniel told him.

McGregor brought wood for a fire and carried in their things from the horses. Carys had sent enough food to last them a week, more if they were careful, and whoever had built the cabin had set his chimney in the wall that divided the two rooms, with hearths in both bedchamber and kitchen so both could be heated from one load of wood.

There was an old rope bedframe and they tightened the sagging lengths of crisscrossed hemp as best they could. A small cove of white pines grew by the corner of the house, and McGregor cut branches for a mattress. Once Hannah had spread her quilts on them, they made a fine, fragrant bed, and Daniel was too weary to resist lying down when they bid him.

He slept quickly and deeply, and Hannah went about the business of cleaning out a family of mice from the old beehive oven, sweeping the floor with a branch of the pine, and unpacking and sorting the food and medicines they had brought with them. Carys had sent an old stewpot to cook in; Hannah raked some coals onto the hearthstone and began to think of Jennet's supper.

Work was the best thing. You could smother almost anything in work.

As for the Dutchman, he sat cross-legged by the kitchen fire, his wet boots steaming and his eyes on the little girl; Jenny moved cautiously around the small room, Piet's raccoon trailing behind her as she took stock of the landmarks.

'His Lordship's bastard, I bet. I heard about her, the one that don't talk.' Soutendieck grinned as Hannah glanced at him – a sharp look, but not angry. 'I got four wives here, and two more back in Holland. One son with my church-wife in Amsterdam – the son-of-a-whore, he would kill me and eat me! Bastards are better. If they like you, they stick.'

'Is Luisa your church-wife?' she asked him.

'Nah.' He laughed. 'Her I bought from her father, the old

heathen. Got six horses with her. Good ones, too, brought good price up in Salcombe.'

'But you must value her greater than horses. You give her very fine clothes.' Hannah cut some of Ifor's venison into the pot. 'That was a handsome shawl she was wearing. Did she weave it herself?'

'I trade for it,' Piet told her. 'The fool's got no money, he wants rum and molasses – Kersey, that's his name. His woman, she's smart, she weaves good.' He shrugged. 'Once I thought I would trade him for one of them tombstones he makes. Fine granite, with a verse on, I seen them one time in his stable. But, the devil! I took the shawl instead.'

FORTY-TWO

Piecing the Evidence

MUSTER LIST

TWELFTH MASSACHUSETTS RIFLES, THIRD DIVISION
BATTLES OF TAUNTON BRIDGE AND FALLBROOK
COMPANIES: HAGGAR'S, SHERWELL'S, WICKHAM'S,
CHURCHEL'S, GRIME'S.
13 MAY 1779

\# Anstey, Jacob, lieutenant, Haggar's Company.
   Arrowsmith, Henry, private soldier, Haggar's.
   Brightman, Thomas, private soldier, Haggar's.
\# Byard, Elimelech, sergeant, Sherwell's Company.
X Carne, Timothy, private soldier, Sherwell's.
X Callwood, Geoffrey, private soldier, Wickham's.
   Clinch, Samuel, General Surgeon, Grimes's Company.
X Dammerell, John, private soldier, Sherwell's.
X Dommett, John, private soldier, Haggar's.
\# Earle, Abraham, sergeant, Wickham's.
X Eggins, Noah, private soldier, Sherwell's.
X Fifield, Amos, private soldier, Wickham's.
   Fewings, Joshua, private soldier, Haggar's.
   Fronval, George, Corporal Sherwell's.
\# Furneaux, Peter, private soldier, Sherwell's.
   Gillard, Titus, sergeant, Sherwell's.
   Gleave, Ezra, private soldier, Haggar's.

\# Haggar, Edward, captain, Haggar's Company.
\# Hickson, Luke, private soldier, Sherwell's.
  Jepson, Matthew, corporal, Haggar's Company.
  Kennerley, Jude, private soldier, Wickham's.
  Kersey, Oliver, sergeant, Haggar's Company.
X Lawry, Hosea, private soldier, Sherwell's.
X Littlechild, Jonathan, private soldier, Haggar's.
  Maunder, Patrick, private soldier, Sherwell's.
\# Pavey, Samuel, private soldier, Haggar's.
  Pinckney, Rufus, private soldier, Wickham's.
  Petrie, Joseph, sergeant, Haggar's Company.
\# Rideout, Hezekiah, corporal, Wickham's Company.
  Sherwell, Jonas, captain, Sherwell's Company.
\# Trewin, Jacob, private soldier, Haggar's.
\# Tween, Charles, private soldier, Churchel's.
  Venning, William, sergeant, Grimes's.
  Witheridge, James, private soldier, Haggar's.
\# Wrayford, Benjamin, private soldier, Grimes's.
  Yarrow, Stephen, private soldier, Sherwell's.
X Zenas, Jotham, private soldier, Grimes's.

A mark of # indicates the decease of that soldier in the course of the action aforenamed. A mark of X indicates the disappearance of that soldier; such men are to be held missing-in-action. If discovered unwounded and in hiding after no longer a period than forty-eight hours, they will be forced to run the gauntlet of their fellows, and to receive one hundred stripes of the lash laid on in sequences of twenty strokes for eight days in succession, two days' time to elapse between each, so that those incorrigible and dishonorable fellows accustomed to such desertions may feel their punishments more for being lashed upon wounds not yet healed.

If discovered unwounded and in hiding after more than seven days, any such villains will be court-martialled for desertion and shot for treason.

DEPOSITION OF WILLIAM VENNING, SERGEANT, GRIMES'S COMPANY, TWELFTH MASSACHUSETTS RIFLES FT. RESERVE 16 MAY 1779 APPENDED IN EVIDENCE TO THE MUSTER LIST OF THIRTEEN MAY

I, William Venning, do hereby depose that the body of one Nathan Jenkins, Tory Civilian attached to His Majesty's Third Grenadiers, Ft. Reserve and listed as deceased following the glorious victory of the Patriot forces at Taunton Bridge, Hampshire, is in fact the body of one Private Jotham Zenas, Twelfth Massachusetts, listed as missing or deserted. The body was dressed in civilian clothing like many private soldiers, more especially riflemen, and that circumstance gave no alarm, but that no shot nor powder was discovered upon it. The corpse was recovered with some others in the fourth quadrant, south bank, Taunton Woods and delivered to the Company Surgeon, Dr Samuel Clinch, at the hospital tent, second quadrant, south bank, for verification of decease. The military papers of Jotham Zenas were not discovered, and it is not known by what manner be came to be in possession of the papers of said Nathan Jenkins, as enemy sympathizer. Jotham Zenas was shot in the back of the head at close range.

FORTY-THREE

Piecing the Evidence:

REGARDING THE RAIDS UPON FALLBROOK
PROCEEDINGS OF THE OFFICE OF CIVILIAN
DEPLOYMENT
SEVENTH MASSACHUSETTS REGIMENT,
PINE TREE COMPANY
CAPTAIN DANIEL JOSSELYN, COMMANDANT
FT. LIBERTY, NEW HAMPSHIRE
WITNESS, LEAH ELINOR WOODARD
CORPORAL PHILIP SWEET, CLERK
15 MAY 1779

CAPTAIN JOSSELYN: Will you kindly state your name and your father's name?

WITNESS: Leah Woodard. But I am never called Leah. My sisters call me Biddy and my Ma calls me Nellie, but my brother Sol calls me Sheba. We are twins. Oh, yes! Twins run in families, so they say, perhaps one day I shall have some. Only my father, he is dead, and Sol is dead, and so is Sarah, and I know where Ma and Jemima are gone. Gone. Gone. Gone, my true love is gone, and the violets grow on his grave.

JOSSELYN: Don't be afraid, my dear. You aren't afraid of me?

WITNESS: No. You are kind. My father used to say that

God was merciful, only I don't think He's known to
be kind.

JOSSELYN: Not in the catechism I have studied of late.
But will you help us by talking a bit more slowly,
Sheba? The clerk can't set it down so fast.

WITNESS: I require your gentleness. Please don't send me
away.

JOSSELYN: No. Of course not. But what's your father's
name? Will you say it?

WITNESS: He is dead. They hanged him and shot him. I
saw them take him and Sol to the belfry, and then
I heard the bells ring, only it wasn't time for
service. I heard the bells ring and ring, and then I
heard the gun. They dragged him out and put him in
the leaves under the butternut tree, and hung up his
wig on a branch. The butternut tree lost its leaves in
the springtime and died soon after. Is not that strange?

JOSSELYN: Mr Sweet, set down in the record that the
young lady's father was parson of St Barnabas Church,
Fallbrook. Reverend Master Fitzwilliam Woodard.
Church of England. Hanged up by the hands and shot
twice in the face, after torture. And his son with him.

CLERK: But who will identify—

JOSSELYN: I will. I found them. Under the butternut tree,
as she says.

CLERK: Disposition of bodies?

JOSSELYN: Burnt, in the pit with the rest.

WITNESS: I saw him. I saw Papa burning, like Jemima. I
am burning, too. Can you not see?

JOSSELYN: And you cried out, did you not, when your
father was burnt?

WITNESS: Fitzbilly, that's what they called Pa. His friends.

He had lots of friends and he wasn't a Tory, though he could not swear against the king for the sake of his cloth. I don't think he was anything, only a parson. I don't know where he has gone now. People go away when they die, but I don't think it's to heaven. They hanged him and shot him and shot Solomon, my brother, and I don't think they have them that's hanged into heaven, do they? If you know where they are gone, come and tell me. Say you will tell me! I require to know!

JOSSELYN: Mr Sweet, fetch the lady some grog from that bottle. And some bread and cheese, too. How long since you have eaten properly, Sheba? You are very thin.

WITNESS: Oh, I don't eat. I live on air, now they've made me a whore.

JOSSELYN: Who made you so?

WITNESS: Soldiers.

JOSSELYN: British Soldiers? Americans?

WITNESS: They had red coats. But some of them didn't. Some had fine silk coats, blue and rose-color and brown, with brocade.

JOSSELYN: Civilians? Not soldiers?

WITNESS: Oh, all men are soldiers. But some wear other clothes, that's all, to fool you. He did, Nathan Jenkins did. First he came and took Sarah away here to the Fort for their dances. A great Michaelmas Ball. My father wept.

JOSSELYN: Did your father resist them?

WITNESS: He was old. He could not fight, only argue. And weep.

JOSSELYN: What became of Sarah, your sister?

WITNESS: She was gone two days the first time. Then they began to come oftener. I thought soldiers must do nothing but dance. At last a soldier took Sarah and did not bring her back for near a month. After that, Mr Jenkins came and took me instead.

JOSSELYN: What was your age at that time?

WITNESS: Fourteen. No, fifteen. I'm sixteen now. Well, almost.

JOSSELYN: Who was he, this Jenkins?

WITNESS: A gentleman. I liked him and Pa liked him at first, for he wasn't a soldier. He said he was a Tory, a lawyer, he meant to be rich and meet all the rich Tories from Boston that stopped at the Fort, he said they would make him his fortune. We had him to dine once, he said grace at table and Jemima thought him unctuous. That's a funny word, unctuous! Jemima knows all such words, she is mad over books.

JOSSELYN: What was his age, this man Jenkins? What did he look like?

WITNESS: He was not so old as Pa and not so young as you, and he had a red face and no proper wig, just his own hair, only powdered. Going thin at the back.

JOSSELYN: So you knew him as a friend? You went with him willingly?

WITNESS: Only the first time. I was never let go to a party before, not without Mama. So I did not mind, though Papa didn't like it. But the soldiers were with him, all laughing and their red cloaks flashing. Like handsome red birds. I wore my best gown, my blue with the cream-colored ribbons.

JOSSELYN: Did they come for your sister Jemima?

WITNESS: No, sir. He didn't want Jemima. I don't know

why, for she's cleverer than I am, and kinder than
Sarah. But they say she is plain, and plain girls never
marry. I shall marry one day, and have a handsome
husband and all sorts of children. And a fine coach.
Where – where is my Jemima?

JOSSELYN: She's safe. Do not fear for her.

WITNESS: Oh, I don't. She's very good with her needle,
and though women of talent are not meant to be
happy in general, they may always survive if they will.
If they will. If they—

JOSSELYN: Sheba? Leah! Don't leave me!

WITNESS: What? Where is this place? I want to go home
now.

JOSSELYN: Sip some of the rum, my dear.

WITNESS: I was gone just then. I heard you speak, but I
was not here to answer.

JOSSELYN: I know that. Where had you gone?

WITNESS: A quiet place, where the dead are. The dead
have no wars. Nothing burns them, and when they
suffer, their tears are not wet. You have seen them.
You have been in that place.

JOSSELYN: It's name is despair, my dear. Only fools have
not been there.

WITNESS: Am— Am I mad, sir?

JOSSELYN: I don't think so.

WITNESS: Will Jemima always be mad now?

JOSSELYN: I don't know, Sheba. Many in war are mad in
bits and pieces. With some, it comes and goes.

WITNESS: They put coals to her feet, to make her tell
where I was hiding.

JOSSELYN: I saw the burns. I know.

WITNESS: I heard her cry out that she didn't know where

I was, and indeed she didn't, for I had been gone from our house near a fortnight. But when she told them the truth, they said she lied and burnt her more. I don't know where the coals came from. Maybe from the neighbors. My Mama don't keep many fires in May, she says it's wasteful.

JOSSELYN: Who put the coals to Jemima's feet? Who came to seek you?

WITNESS: Men. Some men. There were women with them, wild, angry women. I hid in the grain bin. There were rats. There always are.

JOSSELYN: These men, were they raiders? Did they rob your father's house? Is that why they killed him?

WITNESS: They said I betrayed the British troops, and we all must be punished, and I must be shown to the town for a traitor and a whore.

JOSSELYN: And did you betray the troops at the fort? Did you give information to our side? The Patriot side?

WITNESS: I told Nathan Jenkins that Major Braddock had told me his first column would move out on the Tuesday and cross Taunton Bridge. That was all! I knew nothing else! How should I ride to Portsmouth and tell the rebel garrison?

JOSSELYN: Let us return to this Nate Jenkins, Sheba. What happened when he brought you here to the Fort?

WITNESS: He said I was bidden to dinner at the officers' table. Only there was no dinner at all, only a poky little room with a bed and a candle, and a bowl of oranges on the table, beginning to spoil. I heard singing and laughing outside, very loud, and I tried to get out of the room, only I could not and I screamed

and screamed, but no one heard me. I wept and my
eyes grew very sore, and I sat on the floor and pounded
my fists on it. I was very tired, and at last I fell asleep.
I think he must have been listening at the door, for
he never came in till I was quiet.

JOSSELYN: Who came in? Jenkins?

WITNESS: No. A man in silk coat and breeches. Very
grand. There were rich men in Fallbrook, on their
way north from Boston.

JOSSELYN: Tories?

WITNESS: Yes. They came to Pa's church sometimes, to
Evensong. The officers always gave parties and balls
for them.

JOSSELYN: What was the name of this man, did he tell
you?

WITNESS: He had no name. 'You must be generous to
me,' he said. 'You must be a good girl and do all as I
tell you, and I will be kind.' Only it was not kind,
was it?

JOSSELYN: You did not resist him? This rich man?

WITNESS: At first I didn't know what he wanted. He
began to unhook me and I cried out and he put the
bolster in my mouth and made me bite on it. Nobody
told me. It hurt, first a lot and then not so much. He
petted me and kissed my face. I didn't know.

JOSSELYN: Did he take you home? This Jenkins? As he
had done your sister?

WITNESS: Yes. Only the next night they came again to
fetch me. But the man was not the same.

JOSSELYN: A civilian?

WITNESS: No. A soldier. He knocked Pa down and made
his nose bleed. After that, Jenkins did not come again

until April. They kept me a fortnight. They took me home, and then the first raiders came, on the night before the fight at Taunton Bridge.

JOSSELYN: There was more than a party of raiders?

WITNESS: Yes.

JOSSELYN: Patriots? Tories?

WITNESS: I do not know, sir. To me, they were the same. Only the first ones said I was a Tory whore. They dragged me out into the yard and tore off my clothes and burned them. Then they beat me and shaved off my hair with a straight-edge. My father was watching. I did not like him to see me. But they made him watch me and look at my body. I heard him howl.

JOSSELYN: And your sisters? Sarah? Jemima?

WITNESS: Sarah was with child by the men at the fort. The first night, my mother hid her in the root cellar, for fear she'd miscarry. She had tried to get rid of it, but Pa said that was a crime and she must bear it and love it and God would forgive her her sins. Only I didn't know what sins they were, you see. She did nothing but put on her new cream-colored gown and the lace Pa had brought her from Portsmouth. She was sweet on Davy Griffin of the Lancers, she thought if she went he might ask her to marry. It went wrong, though. If God had been kinder, it would not have gone wrong.

JOSSELYN: Tell me about the second raiders.

WITNESS: They came after Taunton Bridge, just before you came and found us. They were Tories, they called me a Patriot spy. I ran away after the first ones came – the Patriot women who shaved off my hair. I stole clothes from some bushes, that someone had set out

416

to dry. I meant to stay away, but I could not, I got hungry. I came home again, only I hid in the barn. I was shamed to come in, for my father's sake, because he had seen me so shamed. And I saw when they hanged him and Solomon, my dear brother, and when they still could not find me, they took Sarah and Jemima and would hang them too. But because they were women, they feared to shoot them, and Sarah with child.

JOSSELYN: Only you could not bear to see it.

WITNESS: I screamed, like I did when you put Pa and Solomon into the burning pit. I came out from the grain bin and stood in the orchard and screamed. And they took me and dragged me all through the town, and then they hung me up with my sisters, upside-down. They said traitors must be hung so, for it took longer to die upside-down. But then you came and found us. Jemima thought you were only a man, like the others. But I knew you were better. When you lifted me down, your hands were kind. Are you God, do you think? I should like to think so, for Pa's sake.

JOSSELYN: Sheba. Did Major Braddock tell any other than you when the British column would ride out of Ft. Reserve? When it would cross Taunton Bridge? How many soldiers would be with them?

WITNESS: It was spoke in his sleep, as he lay with me. I don't know who else he told. But he gave me a shilling and a hank of blue ribbon, after. They always gave something, and them that was not kind gave most.

JOSSELYN: Did Nathan Jenkins ask you to tell him what you learned from the officers who lay with you?

WITNESS: Oh yes, sir. He said if I was a good girl and told him the truth, he would take me home. He promised. He—

JOSSELYN: Did he never lie with you himself?

WITNESS: Once, sir. Only once. And he wept all night long, just like you.

FORTY-FOUR

How He Kept Her
from Waste

Leaving Daniel and Hannah in the house by the deadening, McGregor rode back that same night to Ifor Jones's cabin where the others were gathered, and the Dutchman, too, left them.

Hannah barred the plank door and made up a pallet for Jenny. Piet had left her the raccoon and the little girl had been delighted to find it would eat from her hand, just as Arthur sometimes deigned to. She fished in her pocket for a rind of cheese, and the animal gobbled it down. Jennet gave a soft sound, almost a laugh, and suddenly Hannah went to her daughter and lifted her up in her arms.

The child in my body must bear it, she thought, *for the sake of the child that is already here.* But Jennet wriggled and squirmed and would not be held. She snatched up the raccoon and went to sit with it in the farthest, darkest corner, as if she were invisible. She was sullen and angry and unreachable, all her affection centered on the little wild creature.

All gone, Hannah thought. *Even Jenny. Gone.*

Hannah Trevor had lived for nearly twenty years on the strength of her pride, but she had surrendered the last inch of it to Marcus Tapp in that small, death-ridden cottage. Betrayed something, someone, besides Daniel.

There was a girl she remembered – an oval face and long ash-brown hair and dark eyes that always carried a laugh somewhere in them. A girl who fussed over new gowns and giggled with her friends when a handsome young officer rode past in the street. She had trusted the world then, that it would take her as she was – not so handsome as many but brighter than most, a woman of energy and skill and pride the equal of most men, of kindness and sympathy greater than most.

But that girl had lived long ago, before James, before Daniel. Nothing was left of her now, that girl-Hannah. Only a ghost, like the faded grey trees in the deadening. Whenever she closed her eyes, Hannah could see her own face in Tapp's shaving mirror – an old woman, wasted and used-up and lost, too tired to live and too frightened to die.

She began to undress, folding her clothes carefully in a pile on the bench in the corner, until she stood naked in the unsteady half-circle of firelight. Her hands traced the swell of her breasts, then moved down to her belly, holding the barely perceptible weight of the child as though she could already pick it up, lift it, see the color of its eyes and the soft helpless down of its hair.

But it did not seem real, did not reach her. An aberration was all that could ever be born from her now. A dreamless thing without hope. Hannah's hands slipped away from her body. There was no healing in them for her as there had been for others. She had used it all up.

If I could lie down now and sleep and not wake up, she thought. *But God is not so kind.*

One last flicker of her passion for freedom was left in her, and she clutched at it. It was very cold in the room now, and she put on her nightdress, then quenched the stub of candle and put another stick of pine onto the fire; it flared up very bright and the clean scent of pitch filled the room.

She held out her hand again to Jennet, who sat silent and wide-eyed in the far corner. But the child did not come to her, would not even look at her.

Hannah could hear Daniel's breathing from the next room, the crackle of the pine boughs whenever he moved. When she thought of her passion for him, how she had let him enter every part of her and become her, she felt it must have been some other woman, that he was a stranger who sheltered under the same roof, now, and could not have known the woman she was now.

Then she reached into her pocket and took out the bottle of laudanum. On her knees by the fire, Hannah poured the milky liquid into a tin cup. It would be bitter, but that was as it should be. For a moment she let her eyelids close, thinking of poppies, a huge crimson field of them, like fire and blood that danced on the high floor of the world.

All of it. Drain the last drop and finish it. You are strong enough yet to be free.

She lifted the cup to her mouth, felt her lips touch the cold metal rim, tasted the bitter kiss of the opiate.

'God damn you! What do you think you're doing?'

Daniel dashed the cup away and the laudanum spat on the fire. He took up the bottle, his hand shaking. In his other hand was the Muster Book she had taken from Marcus Tapp's kitchen.

He smashed the glass vial against the stone of the hearth and the sharp slivers flew out in a dozen directions. She could hear the breath come like cold wind through his clenched teeth and feel the strange heat that came from his anger. For awhile Hannah said nothing, her shadow hunched, gnomelike, in front of the fire.

'How long were you watching me?' she asked him at last.

Daniel stood above her, very tall, very still in the firelight, his words slow and quiet now, deliberate. 'I – was looking for a clean shirt in your bundle, and I – found the book. The Muster Book. You got it from Tapp?'

'Yes.'

'How?'

'You know how.'

'And the keys? To the irons?'

'Yes. The keys, too.'

'Christ.'

She saw his shadow bend double, his arms locked around him. Then she saw him move, heard his fist strike something – the planks of the wall, the windowsill.

'Strike at me, if you like to,' she murmured. 'I am your property now. What more have they left us?'

Once or twice more, she heard Daniel's fist strike the wall, heard the slight groan as he used his sore muscles. Then the blows ended. For a long while he could not speak, but she could still feel his body's straining, locked tight with rage, striving to gain back its balance again.

More minutes passed. To Hannah, they seemed like an hour.

At last she felt him, the stillness of him very near to her. His long fingers touched her hair, knotted themselves in her curls. She drew away an inch, her head bent.

'You shun me,' Daniel whispered.

He stood isolate in the middle of the bare little room, his hands hanging down at his sides and his face turned away from her. 'I don't blame you,' he said. 'If I hadn't made you marry, if I hadn't been so set on it— It was pride. My pride.'

His voice declined to a whisper, till she had to strain to hear him. He was leaving her, disappearing from the circle of flickering light they both lived in.

'If I hadn't delayed for the muttering of a few words, I might have spared you this. I am to blame,' he said softly. 'I am. Nobody else.'

Had he cursed her and called her a whore, had he struck her or spat in her face, Hannah might have borne it and remained cold and unshaken.

But not this.

Her shoulders hunched and her breath came in shivers, great shuddering tearless sobs like the broken fragments of the poison vial. They made her body bend double and her hands reach out in the darkness. There was only the floor to cling on to and she braced herself, palms flat down on the bare, rough boards.

Daniel bent over her, a steady, quiet shape like a tree that had grown there. She felt his hands under her armpits, lifting her up till he smashed her against him, her feet off the floor and her face in his shoulder. She felt him gasp when she touched his bruised chest where the rib was broken. But he was strong in himself. He did not let her go.

The sobs stopped, then began again, deeper and deeper, like a drowning thing gasping for air. His hand braced her head like a child's and he rocked her back and forth, back and forth, murmuring softly, some wordless, animal language. Something truer and older, more human than words.

Jennet drew out of the shadows to watch them and the little raccoon climbed onto the mantelshelf and curled up to sleep. Still they stood there, arms locked around each other.

'Will you tell me how it was?' he said at last.

'I wash and wash and I'll never be clean again.' Hannah tried to move away from him. 'I'm – so cold,' she said.

He would not let her go. 'Let me warm you. Tell me, give me something to carry. Otherwise we will break.'

So, in the end, she could not keep it back from him, could not leave him to imagine it worse than it had been. 'I – ga-gave him laudanum,' she said. 'In brandy.'

Daniel had gathered her down with him into a corner, his back braced on the wall and her body drawn across him like a rope on an anchor, not able to think anymore of his bruises and his weakness. She took his hands and gripped them, her fingers locked tight onto him.

'I thought it would drug him,' she went on, 'that he would sleep before – before— But he is very strong, and I don't know much of opium. It wasn't – enough – and— '

'Did he strike you? Hurt you?'

Stupid question, he thought. *Stupid fool*. She was all hurt. If you cut open her flesh, hurt would lie like a hard white bone in her. If you opened the bone, all the marrow was hurt.

'Forgive me,' he whispered. 'Forgive me, forgive me.' It was all he could say. He held her tighter, his face in her hair.

She could not tell him all of it, how her ghost had looked back from the mirror, how it still watched her and haunted her. But she had to go on.

'I could have – borne with his harshness. But until the last moment when he knew I had tricked him, he was gentle. I think he knew it was worse so. For me. He— Wanted more than my body.' Hannah was silent for a moment, her mouth buried against Daniel's neck. 'I should have killed him,' she whispered. 'Once he slept from the drug, I should have gone back and slit his throat.'

'You? Kill a helpless man? Never.'

'Tapp is no man. He's a jackal.'

'I have known you take pity on worse.'

But I will take none, Daniel thought. *If I find him, he is dead.*

He said no more, only stroked back her curls from her forehead, locked his fingers in her own and held them, breathed his warm breath on the cool skin of her neck. For a long while they sat silent, the child watching them, puzzled. Then at last Jennet lay down and they could hear her soft breathing grow deeper, steadier.

Daniel went to lay a quilt over her, then turned back to Hannah.

'Come,' he said, and held out a hand. 'The bed will hold two of us.'

She shuddered. 'My dear, I cannot. You must give me time.'

He nodded. 'Come to bed anyway. It is warmer with two.'

Too spent to resist any longer, she followed him into the bedchamber, the flames from the double hearth making the darkness liquid, as though they swam in a black sea. He sat on the edge of the pine-scented bed, watching her, never taking his eyes from her.

Hannah lay down beside him. Very still. Very pale in the dark, like a long bridge of light in the white nightdress she wore. Even before he touched her, Daniel could feel her wild shaking begin again, soundless and tearless, as it had been before she wept.

'You are not afraid of me?' he asked her.

'God forbid. Only – I am so tired of living,' she said dully. 'The war is too long, I can't fight anymore. I think I – have lost – myself.'

'Come, then. Let us look for Hannah Trevor, where she has gone.'

Daniel sat beside her, touching her slowly, his fingertips moving over her as he had so often seen her own hands do, sensing out damage, finding the knots of fear to unlock them, pushing the shame away like dust from a glass. What she could not do for herself, he must do in her stead, be her midwife.

His body's passion for her was no less, but it was mixed with something else now, a concern so vivid and intense he seemed almost to feel the touch of Tapp's hands on his own body, feel himself entered and used as she had been. With the shame and filth and scorn of the prison still heavy upon him, Daniel understood Hannah Trevor as he had never done before.

He cared for her more than freedom or vengeance. Far more than he cared for himself.

He did not kiss her, made no effort to rouse her. Only now and then he laid his palms flat against her thigh or her arm or her shoulder, like a piece of herself that was missing and must be fitted just where it belonged. A piece of himself that would otherwise drift away like flotsam. Inside her, he imagined the child being conceived a second time.

From time to time Daniel bent his face to hers, listening.

Hannah said no words he could fathom, the soft sounds she made almost like Jennet's.

At last she slept, and he lay down beside her and held her against him, pulling the quilts over them both.

It was still deep dark when they woke and he told her his own memories – the fragments of fact he had gleaned from the Muster Book, the bad dreams his day and night in the prison had brought back to him.

They lay side by side, not touching, as if separation might make thought clearer, answers easier to come by. The window was shuttered and the fire had burned very low. Outside there was a sound of water dripping from the eaves. The ice was melting, the burden of snow sliding down the slant roof to land with a soft squelch on the ground below.

Hannah told him, then, about the weaving grids and what Piet had said of Kersey's tombstones. 'It squares with what Leah told me. "His great stones," she said, and I did not comprehend her. But the weaving grids, the feet burned as Jemima's were burnt, and her father's . . .'

'Oh yes, it makes sense,' Daniel said. 'But if Oliver Kersey killed Clinch and Smith, it must somehow be connected to all of this I have told you, and so to Leah and to me. Only I cannot see how.'

He pushed back the quilts and sat up on the edge of the bed.

'I was shot not long after she left me,' he went on. 'Sniper fire, from ambush, as we made our way back to Portsmouth barracks. I took fever, and except for these few teasing images, it burned Taunton out of my mind. I wanted to live. I wanted you.'

'*Was* there a traitor of Fallbrook?'

'Our scouts told us the British had sent out a small advance troop, we thought that's all we'd be facing. When we saw it was the main column, it was too late to retreat. We had only light guns, we weren't prepared for it. Their men just kept coming, as if the dead rose up again as soon as we killed them.'

She could feel the bed shake from the grip of his hands.

'No one could have known the whole truth in advance,' he said, 'or they would have sent us more troops, better artillery. If this Nathan Jenkins betrayed the British column to us, his information was muddled, it was wrong.'

'Or it was lies.'

Daniel shook his head. 'Who knows? A brag. A taunt, such as a soldier in his rutting may mumble to a captive girl who only half understands.'

'And repeats to the man who seems her only friend.' Hannah took up the thread of it. 'Nathan Jenkins, who had sat at her father's table in the parsonage. Who had promised to take her back home.'

Daniel nodded. 'And this Jenkins, who sells anything for money, has someone in the Patriot camp to pass the knowledge to.'

'You think it was Clinch?'

'It's bizarre, Hannah, but makes a mad kind of sense,' he said. 'Clinch was always half drunk. When Jenkins passed him the information, he'd have been too addle-brained to get it straight – how many troops, when they would travel, who would be in command. And wrong information is worse than none.' Daniel's fist struck the bedframe. 'Our men charged onto that bridge, too, we couldn't hold them. They were trapped there and caught in our own guns. Some jumped off into the water and were killed. Some ran for the woods. Once the British abandoned Fort Reserve and went packing, we called it a great shining victory. But we lost near as many as they.'

'And the village?' Hannah thought of the women – still spinning and churning, still sweeping their hearthstones clear of last night's ash, as though the world had not ended on a bridge a half-mile down the road.

'The Patriots said the Fallbrook folk were Tories and scourged them,' Daniel said. 'Next night the Tories came and said they were Patriot spies who'd betrayed the British column, and scourged them again.'

Hannah felt his hand reach out and find her own, needing some balance against his memories.

'Jemima tried to scratch my eyes out when I took her down,' he went on. 'I had to tie her hands while I tended her feet where they'd burnt her. That day in the woods when I saw Clinch's feet, I began to remember. First she struck and then she began to weep. To put out the fires, she said. I must put out the fires. There was a madhouse nearby, and somebody told me her mother had been taken there. I sent Jemima to be with her, and Dancer and his father must have found the both of them there.'

Daniel reached over to stir up the fire; Hannah got out of the bed and came round it to sit by his side.

'Twig deals with all the peddlers who come to the Grange,' he said, 'so I never met Dancer, never saw his father till that night you and I were wed. In these years she has passed as the peddler's daughter, Jemima may have been ten times at my door and come near her own sister's cottage a half-dozen times, there in the woods. I wouldn't have known her, any more than I knew poor Leah. Always with her head bent, always sheltered behind Kersey.'

A wild creature frightened with fire will carry the scent of it in him forever, like a madness, thought Hannah. *Like a coal of despair in the heart. Every child Leah conceived, the fires of Taunton took from her. And from Kersey, too. Her losses are his.*

'And this man Jenkins?' she said. 'Who was he? Why did he put his papers onto a dead man?'

Daniel frowned. 'A civilian Tory – there were many who served with the British Regulars, volunteer troops that came and went as they chose. An ambitious man, surely, who meant to be rich himself and didn't mind who he ruined.'

'A man like Ham Siwall?'

Daniel shook his head. 'I remember all the rest, but I can't place Siwall in the midst of it. I wish I could, but I can't.'

'Did you not say Fallbrook village was known for sheltering turncoats and deserters as well as Tories?'

He turned round to look at her. 'You think Siwall turned coat when he left us after Saratoga?'

Hannah sighed. 'I suppose it doesn't make sense. The British were losing then.'

Daniel considered. 'Yes, but it's possible! We *looked* like losing for want of provision, at Valley Forge and after. If Jenkins— If *Siwall* saw that, thought he spied a way to use it to his advantage— There was a thriving black market in shoe leather and horsemeat and blankets just then, too. Quick profit. A quicker disappearance.'

'And once he'd got Clinch to put his papers onto a dead man and fiddle the Muster Book, Nathan Jenkins, the traitor of Fallbrook, would be listed as dead. He could go anywhere. Become anyone.'

'Hannah.' Josselyn paused. 'I think there was no Nathan Jenkins. I think he *was* Hamilton Siwall. What better hold could Clinch have had on him? Why else would he turn on me so, but that he feared I might soon remember?'

'Until Sarah Firth wed McGregor, Leah almost never came into the town,' Hannah said. 'If Siwall glimpsed her these last few months— He had been with her a long while at Fallbrook, he knew her far better than you did.'

'How Siwall must have feared me all these years,' Daniel said softly. 'He knew I was in command at Fallbrook, that I might have found some trace of who he was. But I have no sign of it. So long as we were yet partners, he thought he was sure of me. He braved it out, put a bold face on it. But such a long fear – it eats into the soul.'

'When you quarreled,' said Hannah, 'he grew more and more fearful. And Clinch was always there to remind him, to bait him, always bleeding his pocketbook. No matter how much money Siwall made, it all slipped away. He was a sham. A fine house. A fine carriage. Fine clothes.'

'Whenever he could, he tried to use law against me,' Daniel continued. 'The business of Mrs Emory's death, then of James's murder. On the morning of Muster, he even offered to bribe me, to buy me.'

'As he had bought Clinch.' Hannah sighed. 'But you still have no proof, my love. Nothing to say Hamilton Siwall and Jenkins are one and the same. Nothing a court will accept.'

'No.' His voice was determined now. 'I can't place him at Taunton or Fallbrook. But he thinks I can. I mean to let him be sure of it. Fear will rattle the truth from him, whatever it is.'

'You will bring Tapp's army down on you!'

Daniel got up and felt his way to the window. The shutter latched on the inside and he opened it. The moon was out and the air had a softer edge, the snow on the ground sunk a good two or three inches since morning.

'I want an end to it, Hannah,' he said softly. 'I want him to answer. Otherwise this will claim us forever. Look around you, what we are left with.'

A kit fox trotted out of the pine grove, tail dragging, and bounded away. In the distance, at the foot of the hill, the pale, jagged trunks of Siwall's deadening stood like an army of ghosts.

Hannah's voice was a knife in the darkness. 'How shall I fight for you, my own good heart?'

'Find me paper and ink, and a pen,' he said.

FORTY-FIVE

Piecing the Evidence:

LETTER OF DANIEL JOSSELYN, ESQUIRE
TO HAMILTON SIWALL, MAGISTRATE,
BURNT HILL MANOR, RUFFORD
9 NOVEMBER 1786

My dear Sir,

You will perhaps be surprised to discover that I am not the
ghost you did your best to make of me. But I have lately
conversed with many lost souls, in your prison and after. I have
met there with the spectre of one Nathan Jenkins, the Traitor
of Fallbrook, and known him at last, and sorted his misdeeds by
the light of a fire that has burned in my mind since the Battle of
Taunton.

His face is your face, Master Siwall. I know you now, what
you are.

I was a friend to your brother Artemas, as good-hearted a
gentleman as I have met with, and when I saw you grieve for
his dying, even mad as he was, I thought the better of you in
spite of our quarrel. Though you owed me a large sum, I could
not reckon a man's life as you do, at how many shillings and
pence he may bring by his fall. I could not pursue your good
name as you have pursued mine and many others, to ruin you
and make nothing of you.

I will not scruple so carefully now in your behalf.

Once I had come to learn of your raw dealings, even though we were no longer partners, my peace of mind left me. I suffered from war-dreams and began, these last months, to walk in my sleep and to wander, knowing something long hid at the back of my mind must be come by, pulled out to the light and confronted.

Now I have waked from those dreams. I know you, and I know Nathan Jenkins, and I know they are one, made one flesh by your greed. Your poor brother perhaps knew it too, and the knowledge prolonged and worsened his madness, till the blow that struck him down at last was a mercy of God.

Your son has turned thief and deserted you. Master Royallton-Smith, whom you thought to use as a stairway to power, is dead, and his daughter will not, I think, hesitate to sue for her dowry that was meant to pay your debts. As for Tapp, he is a jackal. He will leave you as soon as you no longer have money to buy him. For all I know, he has already gone. Your creditors in Boston and Philadelphia will close in on you soon, as you have closed in on others. Your lady I know but little. That she is proud is a byword, however, and once your credit is broken, I hazard she will turn from you too.

I do not judge you and I do not seek vengeance. I want only my good name restored and the taint of a traitor-father removed from my children. I have achieved written proofs of your guilt in the betrayal of Taunton, that you were then on the Tory side, having deserted our forces after the Battle of Saratoga. The name of Tory — even the whisper of it — will destroy your position, your fortune, and your safety among us. You yourself have been loud in the clamor against those who remained genuinely loyal to the King's side, and soon you will be hounded and driven to exile as you have hounded others. And for what cause? For position, to think yourself better than poor men? Soon you will learn once again to be poor, and shame will ride on your shoulder of a greater weight than any debtors' jail can stamp upon an honest farmer.

As our column rode out of Fallbrook, I was shot in the back from ambush, from a clump of trees near a millpond. I slumped over my horse with the wound and looked down at the water, and I saw reflected there for an instant the figure of a man, a gun in his hand, a face flushed with fear that I have all these years taken for anger and choler. Your face, Mr Siwall, that might otherwise have been the face of my friend.

I saw you and knew you, but fever and wounds drove the memory from me. I see clearly now.

I will not bear the name of traitor in your stead, but if you present me written proof of the dropping of all charges against me and all claims upon my life and my property under the Riot Act laws, with the Seal of the Court and the signatures of the Justices plain upon it, I will give you what proofs I have of your guilt as a turncoat and will guarantee to keep your secret to my grave. My wife and I, you may be certain, shall not stay longer in this country, once we are free to leave it in peace. You may have what you can claim of it, and welcome.

There is a spring in a great rock below a deadening, ten mile beyond Blackthorne Falls and five mile south-east of Ft. Holland. Come there alone, and bring the proof of my exoneration with you, before dusk on the Twelfth of November, in two days from now.

If you do not come, I shall send my own proofs to my lawyers in Boston, there to be presented to the General Court and the Magistrates General, and to General West, commander of the Continental Army from which you deserted. Court-martial, disgrace, exile or execution can be the only results.

One last word. You are alone, Master Siwall. Every human bond, every urge towards tenderness, every moment an ordinary

man treasures and craves, you have forfeited for the phantoms
of power and position and the money that secures them. It was
your holy cause. It was your only faith, and all your hope and
love. It seemed an endless dance, but now it is ended.

You have paid a high price. It has all slipped away from you,
like the smoke of Taunton's dead.

But you still have a soul. The girl Sheba told me once that
you wept in her arms as you used her. Weep again, and
remember better times and better men.

Yours faithfully, as you know me,
Daniel Josselyn, Esquire

FORTY-SIX

The Runaway

The eleventh of November dawned sunny and bright and cold upon Rufford, the snow gone and the ice on the Manitac broken up to choppy, dangerous islands that kept the few skiffs and fishing dories still intact from risking the treacherous current.

But in and out among the jagged, half-melted ice floes a canoe hollowed out from a birch trunk travelled fearlessly in and out of the swirling rapids that formed around each obstruction. It was paddled by a brown-skinned, strong-shouldered young man of not more than twenty, his black hair drawn into a topknot of hawks' feathers, a gold ring glistening in each ear.

They knew him well enough in the village; he was Jean-le-Petit, old Piet Soutendieck's messenger. Reaching the dock at Lamb's Inn, he moored the canoe to a ring in the pilings and jumped lightly ashore, his white teeth gleaming in a grin of delight as Lady Sibylla's black-lacquered chair passed him, the two liveried bearers grunting hard, their breath steaming in the cold.

The door of the whitewashed Meeting House was propped open, the oaken benches inside packed with silent men and women, so many they filled the narrow aisle and spilled out into the yard. None was armed, and there was no sign of the militia which not quite three days before had voted to resist this meeting of the Debtors' Court.

The door of Lamb's Inn swung open and the three justices emerged, an armed deputy on either side of them and Sheriff Marcus Tapp walking before them, his own gun carried casually over his arm. He was formally attired, wearing his chain of office on the breast of an elegant black velvet coat and a waistcoat of deep blue brocade, his sword – less efficient than the guns he usually fancied, but more impressive – worn in a looped and tasseled belt at his side.

The judges were wigged and robed for their sitting, but their faces were tense and every leaf the chilly November wind blew across their path made them start and glance around the common for enemies.

Behind them, skirting the buildings like a shadow, his moccasined feet making scarcely a sound on the cobbles, Jean-le-Petit followed, waiting his moment with all the aplomb of an actor about to step onto the stage.

'Oyez, oyez, the Court of Common Pleas of the County of Sussex is now in session, Honorable Justices Hamilton Siwall, Patrick Tyler and Simeon Madderly presiding. God save the Commonwealth.'

The clerk, stout little Timothy Bottrill, took his place at a high desk just under the pulpit, while the justices sat in state by the altar in three canebacked chairs with a plain pine table before them.

'Master Clerk, read the list of those summoned.' Patrick Tyler was the justice from Wybrow, a quiet man of middle age who kept his sympathies to himself.

There was a stir at the back of the room and the spectators parted to admit Sibylla's chair. With Julia Markham and her daughter, Dolly Lamb, walking beside it, it continued along the crowded aisle till it reached the table where the white-wigged lawyers stood mumbling to one another.

The crowd's muttering grew louder and the clerk struck his desk with the gavel. 'Order in the well of the court!' he cried.

The chair stopped its progress and Lady Sibylla emerged. She was dressed in crimson silk and a cloak of black velvet, her white hair piled high and topped with a veil of fine black lace held by a silver comb.

The effect was as calculated as Tapp's finery and the justices' wigs; unless summoned or charged, a woman was not allowed to speak in the court. But if she could not speak, Sibylla Josselyn would certainly be seen.

Siwall's face was purplish-red. 'Proceed, Master Clerk,' he demanded.

Timothy Bottrill slid his short legs down with a dangerous lurch from the high desk and took up his sheaf of papers. 'For debt,' he read out, 'in the matter of thirty-six pound, owed to one Hamilton Siwall. Lorenzo Newcomb, yeoman. Appear before the Bench.'

No one came up the aisle to stand before the assembled justices. Little Renzo Newcomb was out in the woods with the others, and everyone knew it.

'For debt, in the matter of twenty-one pound, eight shillings, owed to one Isaiah Hobart. Geoffrey Hemmings, master joiner. Appear before the Bench.'

Again, no one came to the summons. More names were called: Thomas Whittemore, Amos Drewel, Thomas Flynn. All were missing. The justices muttered like bees in a hive.

'Master Sheriff!' cried Siwall. 'To the bench, sir!'

'Your Honor.' Tapp strode to the well of the court, the chain guard jingling on the pommel of his sword.

'What knowledge have you of the whereabouts of these fellows?' Tyler asked him.

The sheriff shrugged. 'They are fled to the woods with the escaped Traitor Josselyn.'

'Hah!' Old Madderly drew a long breath through his nose. He was near seventy, gouty and impatient – but with a mind of his own. 'I'd sooner think you an archbishop, sir,' he told Marcus Tapp, 'than Dan Josselyn a villain.'

'If— If Your Honors please. There is yet one debtor's name to be read.' The little clerk was jittering, his forehead beaded with sweat though the room was not heated. He took out his handkerchief and mopped his face.

'Well then,' huffed Siwall, 'get on with it!'

'For— For debt,' Master Bottrill read out, 'in the matter of four thousand three hundred pound, thirty shillings and three pence, with interest compounded at twelve percent over five years outstanding, four thousand eight hundred and sixteen pound, less the grace of the shillings and pence, to Daniel Josselyn, Esquire, one— One Hamilton Siwall. Appear before— Appear before the Bench.'

For a moment, Siwall could only stare at the other justices. Tyler's sober features were blank and old Madderly could not repress a chuckle.

'This – this is an outrage! A slander!' Siwall fell back in his chair.

'No, sir, it is not.' Lawyer Napier rose, his thin form

unshaken. 'I have before me bills-of-hand, gentlemen. Receipts and ledger pages to account for every last farthing of the amount we have quoted. Copies have been filed with the clerk.'

Patrick Tyler spoke quietly. 'Can you pay the sum, Siwall, or not?'

'Near five thousand pound in hard coin?' Hamilton Siwall stood up from his chair for a moment, then sat down again. 'I – know no man who could pay such sum all at once.'

His eyes were stunned, as though someone had struck him. If he had expected a counterattack from Daniel, it had not been this. He looked over at Marcus Tapp, but the sheriff's handsome face was unreadable, only the pale eyes faintly lighted. Beyond him the crowd of spectators sat murmuring now and then to each other, the half-wild deputies stationed at every door.

'Mr Napier,' Justice Tyler began, 'is your principal prepared to wait for the payment of this sum? Will he accept an amount in earnest?'

The old lawyer glanced at Sybilla and she shook her head, the silver comb dancing. 'No sir,' he told the bench. 'He will not.'

'But surely you – you would not attach the gentleman's own person for surety?' Patrick Tyler could not quite bring himself to accept it. 'To dishonor such a prominent man by sending him to prison as a common debtor—'

'Oh aye, poor men have no honor,' growled someone.

'And he's no commonplace debtor, is Siwall,' came another voice from the gallery. 'When *he* pisses in the straw, his muck turns to gold, I warrant.'

Siwall got up again and began to pace back and forth in the small, bare little church.

'This debt is a fraud and a humbug,' he declared. 'Whose word will you credit, sirs, that of a gentleman, a magistrate, a representative to the General Court, a moderator of Rufford congregation? Or an accused traitor, a known debaucher of women, who espouses the cause of these ruffians here, that spew out their foul scorn upon me? I will bear it, God will help me to bear it. Only let me alone with these bills and receipts and in less than a day I will show them as counterfeits, trumped up by a desperate brigand to shift his blame to me!'

'We must take great care in this matter,' said Patrick Tyler quietly. 'As a member of government, Mr Siwall's disgrace brings the whole of our great nation into disrepute and makes us the scorn of our enemies. Besides, if Josselyn is court-martialled, his property is forfeit and all his debtors are relieved of the obligation to pay. We must not act rashly. All may be resolved if the traitor is convicted.'

'Ha!' Old Madderly was not impressed. 'But Josselyn *ain't* been convicted, has he? Ain't even been heard on the charge! Held without counsel, sir! Suspension of *habeus* whazzit! Dragged about like a dog!'

'He did not wait to be tried, sir.' Siwall was gaining some confidence now. 'Daniel Josselyn fled to those same rebels who struck down Dr Clinch and Master Royallton-Smith and—'

'Hey-up! Thought you said 'twas the black feller killed old Clinch? What's become of that tale, eh? Now it's rebels and draggle-tail farmers that done 'em both in, is it?'

The cagey old justice laid out a pinch of snuff on his hand and drew it in with two quick, deliberate snorts. He sneezed mightily, wiped his nose on the sleeve of his gown, and fixed his baleful eye on Siwall, who was still pacing up and down, up and down, the narrow nave of the church.

'There's aught amiss here, Master Siwall,' Simeon Madderly said. 'I can't see it, but damme, I can smell it! And I shall badger it out, sir! Mind that. I shall badger it out in the end!'

'If I may, Your Honors.' Napier stood very still, his bony knuckles braced on the table before him. 'The question is simple. Do all men now stand equal before the law in this nation? Or may that law be bought by appearance, by a fine coat and a fancy carriage, whether substance supports them or not?'

Tyler and old Madderly put their heads together for a moment. While they deliberated, the silent figure of Jean-le-Petit made its way through the crowd and down the aisle to where Siwall stood. The half-breed said nothing, only laid a light hand on the magistrate's sleeve. Siwall turned, staring down at the handwriting on a sheet of cheap copybook paper, folded in quarters and sealed with the wax of a tallow candle.

'Order in court!' cried Mr Bottrill, as Jean disappeared again into the crowd. Siwall shoved the letter quickly into the pocket of his waistcoat.

'In view of the magnitude of the debt that is claimed against Master Hamilton Siwall,' Tyler began, 'and in view of the fact that its principal, Major Josselyn, is not present himself in the court and has left prosecution of the amount so long as to come suddenly and without warning upon the accused—'

'Pah!' growled old Madderly. 'In view of the fact that *you'd* let him off quacking and *I'd* have him hauled and carted, you mean, and there's none but the bugger himself to break the vote between us.'

A few in the gallery sniggered, but Patrick Tyler ignored them. 'The Court allows Master Siwall the space of a fortnight to settle his debt,' he concluded, 'or he shall find his person attached for surety of payment and confined in Salcombe Jail.'

'Nobody gave my Harry a bloody fortnight!' cried one of the women. 'They whisked him to prison in the wink of an eye, and he owed but ten pound!'

'And paid it twice over, if any had troubled the marking it down!' shouted another.

'Aye, that's right, What of the reckoning? We've all been two-timed, if not *three*!'

'Where's Squeezer Inskip, his bailiff, run off to, eh? Where's the record books gone to? Let Siwall answer to that!'

As the shouting grew louder, Hamilton Siwall approached the justices. His breath was very quick and shallow and the veins in his neck were distended, the blood swelling under his skin till it seemed almost transparent.

'I must have more than a mere fortnight, gentlemen,' he said to the bench in a voice too low to be heard by the gallery. 'My funds are invested in Boston, and the state of the weather and the roads—'

'A fortnight, sir.' Tyler's sober face tilted a little away from him. 'You hear the shouts of these fellows. Besides, we can tempt the law no further.'

Defeated, Hamilton Siwall turned too quickly away from the bench and stumbled, his balance deserting him. He fell against the lawyers' consulting table and leaned there, a hand over his mouth as though he would retch.

When he looked up, his eyes met Sibylla's. 'Ah,' she said. 'Master Nathan Jenkins, if I do not mistake.'

'You – you are mad!' he whispered. 'God will strike you for this.'

'Strike me He will, for my sins have been great.' The old lady stood up, her bright eyes fixed upon him. 'Why not go to hell, sir, and wait for me there?'

Only just able to sit his horse without reeling, Daniel had ridden out with his letter in search of the Dutchman and found Jean-le-Petit instead, in a small encampment of trappers preparing a cache for their winter furs no more than three miles from the stronghold. A word of instruction, an exchange of some of the silver Sibylla had sent with them, and the bargain was struck that sent Jean to the village.

But the woods were full of rumors just now, and along every trail a dozen eyes watched each lone traveller who passed by. Before noon, word had spread to the farmers and debtors camped near Ifor Jones's cottage – and half a dozen others in a ragged circle from Sable Brook to the Falls – that Daniel Josselyn was recovered, that he had been seen on horseback, riding north toward Fort Holland, and that surely he would join them after all.

Through that day and the next, men came straggling out of the deadening and up the small rise to make camp by the brook and gather wood for their fires, to smoke one another's last dregs of tobacco and talk through the rights and wrongs of things. Some rode, but most came on foot, their boots heavy with mud from the snow that had melted. It had left all but a few trails sodden and too treacherous to travel with oxcarts. Many of the women and children had gone to their own homes, but a few picked their way through the mud to the stronghold at their husbands' sides, skirts kilted up to their knees, the children running and playing tag, making a holiday of it.

But most of the men were alone. As Hannah moved among the fires tending their small hurts, putting ointments on chilblains and poulticing bruises, they seemed to her somehow insubstantial, like grave, watchful souls who had lost all the force of their living.

'How long do you think this will last?' she heard them murmuring. 'I left my woman with scarce enough wood for a month's fires.'

Or: 'If it lasts till the spring, Annie'll need a man for the plowing. Where the money will come from to pay one, God knows.'

Or: 'We've a child on the way again. Susan bore the first one alone when I was at war. If this business lasts past a month I must go home, for I won't leave her alone so long again.'

'We are all traitors now,' said another. 'We can never go back till it's done.'

Josh Lamb arrived just before noon on the eleventh, and McGregor came trotting in on old Lizzie by sundown. John English had stayed behind to look after Sibylla and the other women as best he might, but Simon Penny was there, and Drewel and Whittemore.

Stephen Anson came too, moving like a wild thing from campfire to campfire, crying of freedom and tyranny and the rights of man. When he spoke of the Cause, they all knew he spoke of his dead father and his mad, broken mother, and they pitied him.

But the rest of his talk was all noble words, and they no longer cared for them. It was living they needed, not causes.

'There, now.' Evening had almost fallen when Hannah straightened up from binding a Saybrook man's ankle. 'You may walk on it, but spare the weight with a stick.'

'You're a good lass,' the man said with a grin. 'And not bad to look at, neither. I'd wed you myself, but my Bess might not like it.'

'Why, this lady's taken, George!' cried a big man in a red-checkered shirt. 'She's just lately wed to the Major!'

'Let us sing home the bride, then!' cried a man with a penny-whistle, and he struck up 'Step We Gaily'.

Susannah Penny brought a branch of bittersweet and twined it in Hannah's dark hair, and some of the others held pine boughs above her. Arms linked together, the men seemed almost to carry her with their deep voices as they walked on either side of her, the song lifting them.

> Red her cheeks as rowans are,
> Bright her eye as any star,
> Fairest bride of all by far,
> Come to grace thy wedding.

But Jennet Trevor heard no music. Only a fragmented dream of the speaking world entered her silence and sang her to sleep that night.

The small cabin was crowded with women and children now, and none of them knew her. Yesterday, two of the boys had pulled her down and smeared her braids with mud; strange women had washed her and fed her. Strange faces looked down at her when they put her to bed. Hannah came to kiss her goodnight, but by daylight she scarcely had time from her work to draw a breath, and when Man-friend wandered out among the campfires, he did not pick Jenny up to ride on his shoulders. He led her by the hand, but there was no laughter in him and she could not ask him why.

Josh Lamb was there, but he had no sweet cider to give Jennet, and none of Dolly's gingerbread and apple tarts. She missed Arthur and Silly-boots and her playhouse and her own bed to sleep in. Everything was gone, and the world had caved in on her. Even the racoon Piet had left her was banished to the lean-to stable, kept in an old withy basket they had found for a cage, where she must feed him on morsels through the bars.

It was all strange, a changed, rifled world she could not fathom.

Jennet's mind closed in upon itself; her universe had shrunk to the size of her own body and her skin seemed an armor that no one could penetrate. She was a freak. A mooncalf, who did not deserve to be loved.

Anger flooded over her, through her. *I am not like them,* she thought. *I am something else, something better.*

Her mouth opened wide and she tried to make a sound come out. But there were no sounds left. The half-formed cries that made her mother's name would not come to her. Her anger enveloped her, muffled the sounds she could now only think of. Jennet was silent again, as she had been when she ran away to the woods and found the Man-Who-Has-Buttons.

I will go to him now, she decided. *I will take him the shiny button and he will lift me up and carry me to the woman with pale hair. I will live with them now, and make Annnhhh-Ahhh sorry.*

Thus determined, no logic could stop Jennet Trevor.

When no one was looking, she put on her blue cloak and slipped out of the cabin. In the lean-to, she took the raccoon from his basket and set him on her shoulder; she could feel his warm fur against her temple and the thump of his tail against her back, and how he trembled with happiness when her small hand lay upon him. The women had made biscuits that morning with what flour was left, and she fed him a crumb of one.

Then she ran down the hillside to where the dead trees were. Nobody noticed her, the men were marching and drilling to keep themselves warm. In less than the time it took to walk from one end of the little yard to the other, Jennet had disappeared.

She went on through the deadening, clambering over fallen logs. Now and then she had to stop and untangle her cloak from the brambles, and when a family of rats scuttled out of a tree stump, she followed them for a while to see if she could catch one, if its fur would be soft and she could make a pet of it, too.

She could no longer see the cabin at the head of the rise, could not even see the smoke that came from its chimney. All around her were the dead trees, grey and ragged. Wild milkweed vines climbed all over them, leafless and bare now, but very tough, very stubborn. They caught at her boots and made her fall and when she got up, she went another way.

Not many birds lived here, only now and then a great black-winged raven flew over like a shadow, and an owl peered sleepily down from a branch. The sky was pale blue-grey and clouds had begun to drift in from the north-west. Hours passed, but time meant nothing to Jennet. She was hungry, but the raccoon had eaten all the biscuit crumbs. She took some crusts of bread and a bit of jerked venison from her pocket – the food she had been hoarding – and ate them.

The precious pewter button had come with them and it lay in her hand, gleaming in the golden-grey afternoon. The man would be glad to see her, glad to have back his button. It was a treasure, he must have been sad to be without it.

She polished it on the wool of her old blue cloak, put it back in her pocket again, and looked around for the little raccoon. He was gone, wandered off to shuffle in a clump of dry, waist-high swale grass where Jenny could not see him.

For a long time she looked for him, in and out of the tangled fallen limbs and the leafless creepers and the burrs that caught in her petticoat and scratched her small legs till they bled. There was no horizon now, the sky overhead pale gold with a shading of blue, the thin clouds overspreading it. A cold wind had come up, blowing dry, dead leaves in swirling clouds that seemed, when they settled, to make things look different, to turn directions upside down.

I will go home now, the child thought. *Some other day I will find Man-Who-Has-Buttons. Now I will go back to woman-friend.*

'Annhhh-Ahhhh,' she tried to make her throat say. But it would not, fear tightened it. Even the distant humming she knew was wind and the dim crackle of running water from the small stream did not reach her, for her fear smothered them. The invisible tympanum of her senses was lost here, the world grey and tangled and all the same, the acres of dead trees without color, the stench of waste and decay like a heavy weight upon them.

'Annhh-Ahhhh!' the child cried out again, a strangled squawk like the cry of a bird brought down by a hawk.

Suddenly terrified, Jennet broke out of the dead trees

and saw him there, Man-Who-Has-Buttons, waiting on the path as though she had willed him to her. Oliver Kersey held open his arms for her, and the deaf child ran to be closed into them, held tight and lifted.

'I am your father,' he whispered into the soft tendrils that curled round her face. 'I have waited so long.'

By the fire in the stronghold kitchen, Hannah Trevor felt a sharp pain in her belly, as if a wire were being pulled tight from her breast to her groin. She sat down on the rickety bench, forcing herself to breathe deeply, willing the child in her to live.

In a moment the pain eased and she looked around for her daughter. But she knew without looking that it was too late.

Daniel came in from the yard and when he saw how she sat there, hunched over her belly, the flush of cold left his cheeks and he knelt down beside her. 'What is it? What can I do?' he said.

The wire inside Hannah tightened again, cruel and relentless. 'My Jennet,' she whispered. 'She is gone.'

FORTY-SEVEN

The Refiner's Fire

It was midafternoon on the twelfth of November when the men spread out among the dead trees to look for the deaf child. Though they knew she could not hear them, they cried out her name at first, more for their own sakes than hers. But after a time they grew silent, their hopes of her drained by the death in the place. Still they walked on through the maze of the ruined trees, crashing through undergrowth and breaking away the dead limbs, calling to one another now and then as they did at the hunt.

From the narrow, muddy trail down which her husband led the heavy-chested old workhorse she rode on, Leah Kersey heard the crackling of branches at a distance, and thought they were fire.

Since the night he had dragged her away from Sarah McGregor's bedside, Oliver Kersey's fury had waned. He was not by nature a cruel man; even his losses had not drained away all his love for her. With her, even if she had been used by other men and discarded, his own humanity still existed. Cuckold he might be, but if he lost Sheba, he would die like a smothered spark.

Of her more distant past, of Taunton and Fallbrook and the man Nathan Jenkins, she had still told him nothing. But if he had known, it would scarcely have mattered. He could see only her distended body, all his tenderness spent on the child he could not call his own so long as the stranger whose seed had conceived it still breathed on the earth.

It was more than a physical jealousy. It was equivalence he coveted, to be used as an equal and valued accordingly. England or America, colonial or free citizen – all his life every rich man had sneered at him, scorned him, used him as a fool for his class and his bluntness. Every controller, every taker, every grinder of men and user of women – they all stood in their numbers before him, and they all had Dan Josselyn's face.

Kersey's conviction of the rightness of his journey – of his cause – never wavered. Far more than the doubtful, worried men who camped in the yard of the stronghold, he was in his own mind a soldier of universal justice, and he had only one enemy – the wrong one.

'Have you seen Josselyn?' he had asked at the cottage of Carys and Ifor. 'Where is he hidden?'

The Welshman sized him up: another desperate farmer, this one with a wife in her eighth month at least. 'What do you want with him?'

'He has cheated me,' Kersey said. 'He owes me a great debt and I mean to make him pay.'

Ifor consulted his sensible wife. 'I don't like the look of that fellow,' he murmured. 'Shall I tell which way they went when they left here? Or shall I send this pair by another way?'

Carys frowned. 'Ah, now,' she said, 'look at the poor girl, she's no more than a few days from labor, and dragged all this way through the snow and the mud! Whatever her man wants with Daniel, it's Hannah *she* is wanting, I'm certain of that.' She squeezed her husband's thick hand. 'You are kind to be worried, my love. But you must tell where the midwife is gone.'

Not two hours after Kersey and Sheba had left the Jones farm, Redoubtable creaked and rattled her way down the muddy slope from the main trail and into the yard. The brightly painted wagon drew up at the door where Ifor was chopping wood for his wife's baking fire, but before Dick Dancer could open his mouth in greeting, Jemima flew out at the back like a thin, pale bird.

'Where is little sister?' she shrilled. 'Have you seen her? Has she not been here?'

She spun like a top in the yard, her lusterless black hair escaping from under her cap, its strings untied and flapping like a broken rigging.

Dick came down from the wagon. 'Have you seen a young, fair woman and a dark man with her, grizzled and near old enough to be her pa? We found their cart by the side of the road some three or four mile back, but there was no sign of them nor their animal. If he's done the poor child any harm—'

'Mrs Kersey is well enough, sir – though far gone in her time, to be sure. They were here early this morning, but now they have gone.' Carys spoke from the doorway, wiping her hands on her wrapper. 'On the south track, to the deadening.'

'But you can never take your wagon,' Ifor told them. 'You'll lose an axle the first mile.'

It was then near dusk on the eleventh of November, the day Daniel's letter reached Hamilton Siwall. But Jemima Dancer cared nothing for letters, nothing for traitors, and nothing for any debts but those that may never be paid.

'Lost and found and lost again,' she said, and sank down on the cold, muddy ground of the dooryard, the strange silent tears streaming down her face. 'I have lost my sweet soul. I run and I run, a-trying to catch it. But I shall never clasp it more in this world.'

'And I saw a new heaven and a new earth,' came a thin, cobweb-voice from the back of the wagon. Inside a candle glowed and Reverend Moses Dancer's small shadow swayed back and forth beneath the canvas, his knitting needles clicking. 'And I saw the holy city, new Jerusalem, coming down from God out of heaven, prepared as a bride adorned for her husband.'

Ifor Jones was kind to a fault, but he took no one for granted. Besides, the young woman was mad, or the next thing to it. 'What do you want with Kersey's woman?' he said.

The old man climbed down from the wagonbox; his knitting still in his hands, he crouched down near Jemima. She leaned against him, sobbing softly.

'I saw Leah and knew her,' he said, 'and so did Jemima. I failed their poor father, who was ever a friend to me. I was but a scholar, a travelling schoolmaster, but I took his cloth upon me for his goodness' sake, and I wished myself a parson and learned all the words of it. But God has not found me worthy. I have spent my life in a miscalculation. Interest compounded. Seven and sixpence. Bankrupt. Beggared. Overdrawn.'

Dick picked up the old man and led him gently away from Jemima. 'You see us as we are, sir,' he said to Ifor. 'A Flying Dutchman, and I her captain. But our port is in sight now. We've looked for the lass these seven years. This lady, my daughter as I call her, is her only living sister. All the rest of her family were lost.'

'Ah. The War.' The Welshman looked down at Jemima.

'My horses are nigh spent,' Dick went on. 'If you have any beast you might lend us to go on with, I will pay for its hire. The old chap's game, but his shins don't travel easy afoot. And Jemima grows faint from her medicine.'

The Reminder went to where Carys stood in the doorway and took her hands. 'Do not fear us for harm ma'am,' he said softly. 'The world is a rock and when it spins out of time, some things human break off and fall into darkness. He looked down at Jemima. 'But my godchild, my Leah – such sweetness comes only once in the world.'

He held Carys's hands to his cheeks; they were dry and cold, and she thought of old books she had sometimes turned over, though she could not read any of the words.

'I dare not die till I see her again,' the old man said, 'that God has not spoilt her with using. Otherwise, I should rather be damned.'

Ifor Jones looked from one of the strange little group to the other. 'I will lend you two horses,' he said, and kissed his wife's warm cheek.

*

When dusk neared, the men searching for Jennet returned to the cabin for torches, branches of the same white pine they had worn with such jaunty defiance in their hat brims a few days before.

But Daniel did not return with the others. 'Husband says he meant to ride to the fort,' Susannah Penny told Hannah, 'in case Uncle Piet's men have found the child.'

'He has not gone to the Dutchman. He is gone to meet Siwall, to have it out with him.'

Hannah threw her red riding hood around her and opened the door to the gathering dark. The colder air had drawn up a soft ground fog, the sky above the acres of deadening a strange salmon color heaped with clouds of deep blue and crimson.

The strange pain in her belly had not returned and no blood had followed it. The child was autonomous, the pain its strike after freedom, to clutch at its own life without her protection. Hannah felt strangely light, as if some bond that restrained her had at last given way.

'You cannot go!' Susannah Penny gripped her arm. 'Wait for Josh Lamb to go with you, or send someone to find the Scotchman. The sheriff may be there!'

Hannah took up Daniel's pistol from the corner. 'If God is just,' she said, 'so he will.'

An outcropping of granite overhung the fork of the trail where the two great sections of Siwall's deadenings parted, and from it an underground spring bubbled up through the rock. Wary of ambush, Daniel did not approach it directly; he came on foot through the pale sentinels of the broken tree trunks, to pause among a clump of mountain cranberry bushes and wait.

The colors of the sky blended and darkened to a blue-black still lit from behind by the westering sun, and ground fog began to fill the ruined woods to nearly the height of a man. At last there was a sound of horse's hooves on the track, the leaves stirring. An owl called from somewhere nearby, and in a minute a lone rider came into sight.

It was too dark to see the spring in the rock now, but easy to hear it as it fell onto the gravel bed below and trickled away to the south-west. The hoofbeats stopped and the rider pulled up: a thickset body slightly hunched, the head in its tricorne bent low as the rider dismounted and filled his cupped hands with water, then held them to his lips.

'It is strange, it is not? Pure water in such a place.' Daniel's voice rang in the half-dark.

At the sound of it, Siwall's body convulsed as though he had been hit by a bullet. But he calmed himself, forced his hands steady while he finished drinking. 'Have you come here to kill me?' he said. 'Or will your rascally friends do it for you from ambush, as they killed Royallton-Smith?'

I know who killed Smith,' Josselyn replied. 'And Sam Clinch. So far as I know, it had nothing to do with the rebellion. But a good deal, perhaps, to do with you.'

'I killed no one!'

'No. But their deaths were convenient, they relieved you of burdens. Blackmail. Fear of discovery. You let Caesar die to be rid of him. But then, Caesar was no one. As all poor men are.'

Siwall laughed. 'You were born rich, you had always the luxury of making poverty a virtue. When I was a tradesman's son in Bristol, I reaped the contempt of your kind.'

'It didn't make your brother Artemas bitter and harsh. It didn't fill him with greed.'

'Artie was a dreamer. I'm not. He thought he could be like you, read the books you read, mimic your fine gentleman's manners. But only one thing makes a gentleman of a tradesman's son. Money. I've fought hard, I've earnt what I have! From a boy, I wanted nothing but the power to trample the lot of you!'

'And have more with me,' said Daniel. 'Leah Woodard. Her sisters. Near three hundred men at Taunton Bridge, English and American. But by then it no longer mattered, did it? So long as the price was high enough?' His foot snapped a stick and Siwall dodged behind his horse for cover. 'Don't cringe,' Daniel told him. 'What have I to gain by killing you?'

'Vengeance.'

'For Taunton?'

Siwall scoffed. 'If you think to make me admit to treason in the hearing of whoever lies hidden in those woods yonder, you may think again. Vengeance for – for the loss of your reputation, I meant.'

'Though of course you had nothing to do with that either?'

'You chose the side you would be on, when I came to you on the morning of Muster! All the Selectmen heard you!'

Daniel drew a step closer. In the woods, there were lights to be seen through the fog now, the torches of the men come out again to look for Jenny. By the custom of hunters, they called to each other with the voices of owls.

'It is something late to play this farce with me, Siwall,' Josselyn said. 'Have you brought a dismissal of the charges your tame sheriff has trumped up against me, or have you not?'

'I've brought nothing, sir.' Siwall drew away from his horse, a black bulk in darkness. 'But if you come peacefully back to the village and withdraw the execution for debt you have lodged against me—'

'Ah.' Daniel smiled in the dark. So, then, Sibylla had not been idle. 'I think not.'

One of the torches moved steadily closer, down the path that divided the deadenings. 'Wh – what are those lights?' Hamilton Siwall's voice shook. 'You betray your word! You said you meant to come alone!'

'But *you* are not alone. Are you?' There was a sound of Daniel's rifle being primed and cocked. 'Mister Tapp, sir!' he called into the darkness. 'Why not join us? I like to see a tame dog dance.'

From the other side of the track, beyond Siwall, another gun was primed and cocked, the kiss of metal on metal. 'I am many things, Major,' came Marcus Tapp's voice. 'But tame I am not.'

He stepped out onto the path, his rifle shouldered and aimed in the direction of Josselyn's voice. He was dressed as he had been in the courtroom, the chain of his office gleaming around his neck and the dress sword clanking in his sword belt.

Daniel stood opposite, a shadow aiming at a shadow. *Absurd*, he thought. *In this darkness, we are all three the same.*

'Where are your buckskinned thugs?' he said. 'Or have they tired of soldiering for you already?'

'I don't need them. I could kill you right now,' Tapp told him. 'It would give me great pleasure, and the law would applaud me.'

'But it wouldn't fill your pockets.'

The sheriff laughed softly. 'Neither will Siwall. He couldn't pay for a two-shilling whore, now, let alone an army. My men are all gone.'

Daniel could no longer feel his finger where it lay on the trigger. It was no part of him now, it had a will and a life of its own. He could see nothing in the darkness but the picture of Hannah with Marcus Tapp's naked body upon her, his hard pale arms around her, hands cupping her swollen breasts.

He was gentle, she said. He kissed me gently, and wanted my love.

'You could sell him.' Daniel felt the blood pound in his ears, all the half-healed bruises throbbing, so that his body had the strength of a primed weapon. 'Master Siwall himself is a great believer in merchandise.'

'Sell him to whom?' Tapp said. 'To you?'

'To Colonel Scribner at Salcombe. He deserted the Continental Army after the Battle of Saratoga and joined the British forces at Fort Reserve as a civilian volunteer. A Tory called Nathan Jenkins. I have the proofs. From your own Muster Book.'

'He's lying!' Siwall cried. 'Kill him! I shall get money again! I have friends in Boston will lend me twice over the debt!'

Tapp ignored him, his attention on Daniel. 'So your Gypsy gave you the book, did she?' He spat into the darkness. 'She lay with me willingly, did she tell you that? How she cried out with pleasure?'

A sound came from Daniel, so sudden he thought for a moment some one of the others had made it, that one of the men in the woods had found Jennet. His will was all concentrated in the finger that lay on the trigger. He pulled it back and fired.

Where she ran down the narrow path between the dead, jagged trees, Hannah heard his sharp cry and the shot. Inside her, the child pulled tight the wire of connection. She doubled over for a moment, soundless, and then ran on.

Tapp's head jerked sideways, but he did not move from where he stood, a tall shadow. His laugh was a short, harsh bark.

'I have yet two ears,' he said. 'Next time aim for the other. As to this Nathan Jenkins you speak of, Siwall uses many names when the heat's on him, half the whores at Edes's talk of it. Try another story, Major. That one's stale.'

The random shot had been foolish. Now he must prime again, ram another ball down the barrel. Daniel wished for his pistols, but he had come out without them. In this darkness, a sword was no use at all.

'I was in charge of the securing of Fallbrook, in Hampshire,' he said. 'I took testimony concerning this Jenkins. Before the Battle of Taunton Bridge, he gave false information to the patriot spies. Then, with the help of Samuel Clinch, who was company surgeon, he put his papers—'

'I am no traitor! The information was not false! I didn't know, the fool girl didn't tell me, she— ' Siwall's thick shadow crumpled. He was down on his knees. 'She was only a child, then,' he said. His face turned up, but the sky was a blanket of darkness and fog. 'I am lost now. God help me. God forgive me. I am lost these many years.'

*

At the edge of the woods where he had camped with his wife and the deaf child, Oliver Kersey heard Daniel's cry and the shot. A few yards more through the dark and he saw them.

Chance had brought him here. Chance put his enemies once again in his power. Like a stray leaf, it had blown him from place to place in the world, till its purpose was complete. The dead trees watched over him like a regiment of shame-ravaged spirits in the huge tomb of the darkness, the torches flaring like candles as they had on the night of Clinch's death, the owl-men calling and calling.

Sheba ran clumsily up to him, holding a child by the hand, his child. A girl-child with red hair in two plaits, one of the dead children come back to life, risen up and found wandering, as he had found her before. She had come to him out of the dead trees at dusk, one of his own pewter buttons in her small hand, to jump up in his arms.

His heart swelled with joy as he held her. Where had she been hiding all these years? Under the stones he had carved for her brothers and sisters?

Regret, he would call her. Regret, born of shame.

Now he stroked Jennet Trevor's hair and kissed her tenderly, and Sheba lifted up her own face to him gently. 'Leave this,' she whispered. 'You are the world to me, I want no one but you. Let us live and be satisfied. Let us go home, my dear heart, and leave all these dead.'

Still Kersey would not. *Josselyn*, he thought. *I must have Josselyn down.* The glass walls of shame had closed round him again; his prison self was not yet clean. He stared down the barrel of his gun at the three indistinguishable shapes in the dark of the clearing.

One is kneeling, a thick man. A fool. A shape like a monkey. Shoot him last, when the others have fallen. The weakest of enemies last.

One is quiet, scarcely moving. Josselyn is quiet. When his orders come, they are quiet and cool, like forged iron dropped into cold water.

One is wearing a sword. Josselyn wears a sword, like a gentleman. Power carries a sword made of scorn.

But which was he? Which was Josselyn's shape? Kersey's gun swivelled, the aim shifting from Daniel's tall shadow to Marcus Tapp's and back again, then lowering a little to compass Siwall.

'Which – which one is the guilty?' he asked Sheba.

'None! All! If you shoot,' she told him, 'I will leave you!'

The words were an ache in her. All these years she had witnessed his steady, silent labor, how his passion was not only for her body. He loved her and treasured her. But treasures are things to be owned. To be pressed under stones.

'My sister is in the town,' she said. 'Her friends will take me away from you. You will never see me again. I swear it!'

'Liar!' cried Oliver Kersey. 'You will go to him, if I don't kill him! To Josselyn!'

The gun barrel swivelled again. *The sword*, he thought. *The sword is power. Kill the sword.*

He need not get close to them, his skill let him keep at a distance. Kersey fitted a square of oiled cloth over the end of the barrel, laid on a lead ball, and rammed it home. In the clearing, Marcus Tapp heard the dim sound and spun on his heel. He fired into the barren woods, but his bullet buried itself in the soft, dead trunk of a girdled maple.

Now we are equal again, thought Daniel. In a single smooth motion, he primed his own rifle, rammed the ball home, took aim at Tapp's shadow. *I could kill him now*, he thought, and his finger shook on the trigger, squeezed it a hair's breadth.

But war had made killing harder for him instead of easier. Daniel Josselyn hated guns, their cold, precise weight an obscenity to him.

He let the trigger creep back to its full-cocked position. Took his finger a little away.

The sound of Tapp's shot echoed, coming from everywhere, nowhere. Hannah ran the last few steps down the path, her torch flaring. Its light fell suddenly on the three shadowed figures in the clearing.

'You,' she said, and aimed the pistol at Tapp.

The uncertain light of the torch turned the darkness to liquid. Kersey grew confused, rubbed his eyes with his coat sleeve. Faces danced madly, shapes came and went. In the deadenings, more lights moved now, coming closer. The owls' voices turned to the voices of men.

'Have you seen her?' one of the searchers cried. 'Where is she?'

'Gone,' called another voice. 'Gone away.'

Sheba, he thought. *Sheba is gone. I can never have her back again. Perhaps I have dreamed her. Dreamed all the dead, how they lie under stones.*

His aim drifted from one of the men to the other. Which was guilty? It had ceased, now, to matter. *All*, he thought. *Kill them all.*

'I wanted to live!' Siwall was saying to Daniel. 'I had nothing! Your kind made me nothing.'

Hannah lighted another torch from the first, the dead

branch of a tree, and propped it up on a stump at the edge of the deadening. 'Pick up your ruin and carry it.' She spoke to Siwall, but her eyes were still fixed on the sheriff. 'The woman you used is still cleaner than you.'

'No one was unkind to her, they were gentlemen!' Siwall's voice was a squeak. 'All gentlemen, of good families! When she told me the column was leaving, I knew it would bring me enough to put an end to it. Do you think I liked posing and posturing? Toadying to such arrogant bastards?'

They were gentlemen one minute and bastards the next, and between them he failed and floundered, even now needing to think well of himself. If Hamilton Siwall stole, if he whored, if he bled the poor, it was God's will, who had put them on earth to be fodder.

'I had to clear some kind of profit!' he cried in the darkness. 'Nothing is built out of nothing!'

'You knew what would be waiting for us at Taunton, you must have.' Daniel's voice was quiet. 'You were there, you saw the column forming! You let it go on.'

'It couldn't be helped! I had to protect myself! I paid Clinch. I'd have paid you, too.'

'But Clinch wanted it all, did he not?' Hannah drew a step nearer. 'All Harriet's dowry?'

'I gave him fifty pound on the night of the hunt,' Siwall told her, 'but he would not be satisfied. I prayed God would help me. Release me. And He did. I didn't kill Clinch! It was the hand of God!'

'Does He dance like a clown to your piping?' Hannah held the torch close to Siwall's features, to see him.

'All these years, you said nothing, you did not remember.' His broad shoulders heaving, Siwall looked up again at Josselyn. 'I did not think you had seen me that day in Taunton Woods.'

'You were right. I saw nothing.'

'But the letter you wrote me—'

'It brought you here.'

Tapp began to laugh softly, as Daniel continued. 'You used Leah Kersey and threw her away,' he said to Siwall. 'As you have tried to use me.'

In the woods, Oliver Kersey heard the words. *Used her.*

He could see in his mind the monkey-shape of Hamilton Siwall hunched over Sheba's fragile body, his sex ramming into her over and over, the heat of him clouding the glass of the small, single window. The debt that could never be paid.

'*You* used her!' he cried, and fired.

Siwall's body lurched forward. The bullet had struck in his back, between the shoulder blades. He fell on his face in the mud that was beginning to freeze now, as the night-cold grew deeper.

Not dead.

The gun stock was braced on Kersey's shoulder and the backfire had knocked him off balance. But true to his custom he began to reload.

Always two shots. Never leave a wounded thing living. Pain makes hurt creatures fierce. Gives them nothing to lose.

Jennet Trevor was caught close against Leah's swollen body, crouched down in the leaves. She had heard the shots from a great distance, but they were no more to her than the sound of someone clapping hands in a room beyond a wall.

'Hannah, get down!' Daniel shouted. He dived towards her, and Tapp made for the cover of a fallen tree.

Hannah.

The child heard the familiar word as others heard the

sound of a clock that strikes every hour – it was habit, the comfort of custom. It was home.

'Hannah, for Christ's sake, get down! It's Kersey! Do you not hear me!'

Whatever force made Hannah cleave to the dying, made her care with an impartial kindness for whatever was broken or damaged, that same force now kept her motionless there in the clearing, torch in one hand and pistol in the other. It was beyond voice, beyond moral imperative. It was the force of her own mortality, the gravitational pull of almost forty years of living, free or not free.

She was what she was.

Without her will, almost without her conscious knowledge, her feet carried her towards the body of the dying man. In the woods Kersey rammed his bullet home.

Daniel was up in a moment. The pain in his ribs had returned, hot and white and furious, but he could not give in to it. Dodging in the shadows, he quenched the second torch and ran towards his wife.

He snatched the torch from her hand and threw it into the deadening, pulling her down in the dark, smashing her against him so hard that he wanted to scream. She seemed numbed, unable to think or to function.

'Hannah!' he cried again, trying to rouse her. 'Don't leave me!'

The familiar sound reached Jennet once more. The world returned to her and her throat remembered the feeling of sound. 'Annnhhh-Ahhhhhhh!' she cried, and broke free of Leah's arms.

Kersey fired, and a second bullet made Siwall's body jump where it lay. This time in the head, the back of the skull shattered. Dead.

With a sizzle, the half-rotten wood of a tree trunk had caught from the dying flame of Hannah's discarded torch. More of the dead trees caught alight from the first. The hunters were shouting, now, crashing out of the fire-trap. Bushes began to blaze, and dead vines draped themselves, burning, in the jagged arms of dead branches, dropping fire like snow to the fallen trees below where weasels and rats and skunks scuttled, scolding, to escape their own refuge.

Kersey primed his gun again. *Two left*, he thought. *Only two bastards left in the world.*

But only one shape could be seen in the clearing – Jennet Trevor's.

He could no longer distinguish between it and the others – Tapp's body, Daniel's, the midwife's, the little girl's. He no longer considered their guilt or their innocence. He was killing the scorn of God.

Kersey aimed at the child's head, as he had been taught in the army. The head first. Then the belly. The back, if you must. Take no compass of honor. Kill for pride, kill for justice. Define it as you care to, and then kill again.

'Ayieeeeeeeeeee!'

With a great, shrill cry, Leah crashed past her husband and into the clearing, her body between the child and the path of his bullet. The burning trees were yet too far off to threaten them, for most of the fire was spreading downhill to the northward, away from them. The other section to the south, nearer the stronghold, had not yet caught.

But the burning trees were like huge candles, they lighted everything brightly now – the dead man on the ground, the child, the pregnant woman.

Daniel dived after Jennet, pulled her away, fell with her and rolled sideways into the shadows, a great pain like a wound in his chest though he knew he had not been shot. He lay fighting for breath, Jennet's small arms around him gripping hard. Hannah was a few yards away, alone in the fringe of the burning trees. Sparks floated down at them, the air luminous and strange and transparent.

'Sheba!' Kersey's cry was torn from him. 'Do not leave me, my soul!'

His shape loomed up from the burning woods – a thick, peasant body, meant for years of hopeless labor. A body that had always betrayed him, always belied his mind, his talent, his dreams. Long ago, he had written a verse for his gravestone, and it came to him now.

> *Here lyeth one who carved in stone,*
> *The flesh grown cold that warmed his bones.*
> *He ruined none, though many scorned him,*
> *Six feet of dirt now all that warms him.*
> *Through all his life, few learned to prize him.*
> *But worms are kind. They won't despise him.*

He came out of the woods towards Sheba. The child in her had begun to move, she could feel her belly change shape with its struggling. A great pain struck her, different from the agony of the five miscarriages.

This is birth, she thought, and her breath quickened, her mouth open like Jennet's. 'Life,' she said aloud.

She was all Kersey could see now, all he could think of, that he could no longer possess her. The alien child owned her now.

He held the gun to her belly. 'I love you,' he said. 'I forgive you all your sins.'

Sheba did not move when he pulled back the trigger. The gun joined them, married them.

Then from a distance a woman's cry reached them, and the sound of a horse's hooves on the track. 'Little sister! She is gone!' called Jemima's high, furious voice.

Marcus Tapp had hidden himself in the deadening, but the fire drove him out now, his pale eyes lit by the burning. His sword was drawn and pointed at Kersey's chest as the rifleman turned.

'You damned fool,' Tapp said. 'She's worth ten of you. I know.'

'You!' the marksman gasped. 'It was you that had her? But – Josselyn, I—'

'I wiped out your debts for her sake,' said the sheriff. 'I never struck a better bargain. I – could have – loved her.' He looked at Hannah, then at Leah. 'Almost. Almost.'

Kersey groaned, and the sheriff could no longer bear it. 'You want vengeance for her bastard? Here it is.'

Tapp lunged at Oliver Kersey and the blade went home, a soft sound like the falling of ripe fruit from a tree. In almost the same instant, Kersey fired. As Marcus Tapp had known he would.

For a split of a second the two clung together like lovers, like brothers, as ancient as statues carved from the same fine stone, the gun and the sword, joining them in the tunnel of the woods that burned away on either side.

Kersey's body crumpled, but Tapp stood for an instant, his eyes fixed on Leah. 'Say – say you loved me,' he whispered. And then he fell.

Leah's labor had begun, she lay doubled over on the ground. From the path to the eastward a thin, frantic figure came running, dark hair flying. Jemima bent over her sister, and in a moment the old man and the peddler came up on horseback.

Hannah knelt beside Kersey's wife, her ear against the struggling belly to listen for the heartbeat of the child. It was strong, and she could almost be certain it was double. Twins, as she had predicted.

She laid a hand on Jemima's arm. 'It was you who burnt the dead man's feet, with your candle?'

Dancer's daughter – how else should she be thought of? – looked up at Hannah. 'I burn as I am burnt,' she said.

In a moment McGregor rode into the clearing, and Josh Lamb behind him, grim-faced at the sight that confronted them.

There was no time to take thought for the dead; they must think of the living, or the fire would take them all. Josh lifted Jennet up behind him, but Leah was too deep in labor to ride now. They began to make a travois, finding branches and tying them with one of the strong, leafless vines.

Only the old man remained with the dead, moving from one to the other, murmuring prayers and snatches of scripture.

Though he could not live, Marcus Tapp was not yet dead. He lay on his back, the strange eyes staring up at the fire that drew nearer and nearer, eating the deadening. His breath came in great dragging gasps that could scarcely be told from the groans of the woman in labor. Hannah's pistol was still in her hand and he looked up at it, his white teeth flashing for an instant, a flicker of smile.

'Finish it, Gypsy,' he whispered. 'The honor is yours.'

Hannah raised the gun and aimed it. Daniel was near,

but he could not touch her now, could not even speak to her. It was the last battle of her war, and he could only watch her.

But he moved in her, lived in her. In her mind, his quiet voice spoke.

It is the last kiss he demands of you, my heart. If you shoot, he will enter you and never leave. He will drive out my ghost from your bones.

The long barrel of the dueling pistol shook as Hannah pulled back the trigger. She wanted to kill Marcus Tapp. She understood Kersey, how his hand had struck at anything, everything, struggling to be clean again, to be whole and himself.

The sheriff was braced for the bullet, his eyes closed. In the bright, burning air, Hannah Trevor saw her own face as it had been in Tapp's mirror: ruined, used, captive. An old face, like Jemima's. A face without a life.

She looked past the reflection at Daniel.

I want you to watch yourself betray him, Tapp's voice echoed in her memory. It was what he wanted, even now.

'Do your own work,' she said, and laid the pistol on the ground within reach of Marcus Tapp's fingers. 'I am not your instrument. I never was.'

They heard the single shot as they walked up the hill, the little stream flowing cold and clear beside them. The fire had caught a few trees in the south section of deadening now, and the limbs and vines blazed in mad, tangled patterns against the dark sky that hung above the dead. By morning, the land Siwall had coveted would lie open and charred and clean from the foot of the hill to the Manitac, their own cold river that probed its way inland, branching north and south.

To the westward the great living trees still stretched away, half a continent deep in temptation and hope.

'I saw the dead, small and great, stand before God.'

The Mortal Reminder trudged behind them, his voice all but drowned by the cries of the woman in labor.

'And a book was opened. Which is the book of life.'

FORTY-EIGHT

The Journal
of Hannah Trevor

24 December, the year 1786

I write this upon the Eve of Christmas, a bitter cold day with snow from the north-east. I cannot applaud it for travel, but it sweetens my heart.

It is long since I have found ink to write with. Made some from the husks of a butternut tree Husband found near the Dutchman's fort. It is watery and skippish. But it serves.

We bide still at the Stronghold. There is a force of Militia at Rufford and pardons are proffered by the Governor at Boston to all who will return and sign an oath of loyalty, renouncing their Cause. The men are cold and hungry and have no heart left for fighting, and may have gone. Lachlan McGregor has gone with them, and Josh Lamb. He will keep my lost cousin's son, Peter, and raise him, and Dolly will have a child to make her glad at last.

But the debts of the poor remain, and the prisons are hungry. Power keeps to its kingdom, no matter who rules.

There is no pardon offered my husband. He is not blamed for the deaths of Siwall and Tapp, but he will not denounce his men and forswear them. The law will not pursue him, but the charge of treason will not be dropped and his property is already seized. Mapleton Grange is bought at sheriff's auction by Master Cain, the rope-spinner, who is raised to the Magistrate's bench.

When the head of the Monster of Greed is cut off, two new ones spring up in its place. I wish him well of his power, that he may use it far better than Siwall. But I do not like the man.

As soon as we may, we shall go into exile from Massachusetts and Maine. We shall go to Daniel's aunt in Halifax until my son is born, where no charge hangs over us.

Thanks to Lady Sibylla's exertions, we are not bankrupts. My Uncle Markham's debts are paid and my Aunt sends me now and then some small comfort.

Husband mends slowly and spends much time teaching my daughter. We are poor, but not broken.

I should not much have cared to be rich.

Still I think of the words of Jem Siwall, that human things have no choice but to Pound or be Pounded. The war goes on without end, and somewhere between Hammer and Anvil, we snatch life as we may.

And mourn the wasted dead. I have had time now to weep for my Johnnie. God give him quiet rest.

Leah Kersey has gone with Master Dancer's wagon to Gull's Isle, where she and Jemima will stay awhile with Mrs Annable's women, to regain themselves. Delivered twin children on the night of the burning, a son, William, who lived but till daylight, and a fine daughter, Sarah, who thrives.

I have broke the vial of ergot that poisoned the life of Jemima, and Mr Dancer will never give her more. Her mind begins to clear, I think. But all poisons are not of human giving. Pray God her sister and the new child will heal her as no tincture can.

I have all my life longed for a sister, and had none but my women who need me. Wherever we go, I shall keep to my work.

Aunt sent me my marriage gown to keep for daughter, but I have traded it for two pair of hens from Welsh Farm, and Husband gave one of our horses for a small cow, very fresh. I churn in a shaking-jar. A tedious task, but my daughter takes her turn.

Daniel has brought me flour and sugar and ginger from the Fort and I make this day a crowd of ginger men for my daughter, from the receipt of Carys Jones.

> Welsh Ginger Men
> Take three pound of flour and grate into it a nutmeg, two ounces candied ginger cut very fine, with cinnamon, mace and coriander. Mix with one pound sugar mashed with the pestle, and three teaspoons pearl ash for leaven, melted in cream. In summer, rub all this same very fine with a pound of good butter. In winter, when the butter be too cold for the rubbing, warm it with some of the sugar and pour as syrup into the spiced flour. Take four good eggs, or eight in the season of brooding, and add to the mixture. Knead in currants or dried cherries or citron. Work on a floured cloth till the men be stiff enough to roll, and cut them in their shapes to your fancy. Bake them very brisk on a bread stone, not long enough to scorch.

My Aunt Markham has sent me enough scraps to finish the

piecing of my marriage quilt, Bridges Burning, which pattern I set down here for the keeping of Jennet, my daughter, and for my son, who may have some day a wife with woman's skills.

Bridges Burning

The pieced top I shall carry with us to the westward, where my husband's dreams are set. I shall quilt it wherever I may, for sure, there are women and needles in the Ohio country and along the Missouri, and a sound enough stitch will hold in a wilderness.

Mistress Jones tells me she has heard Reverend Dancer say he is never a parson but only a schoolmaster. I think I shall not tell Husband. If Daniel and I be not man and wife, we are one.

I woke this morning in the dark to find my love had carried in branches of pine and bittersweet as I slept and twined them about my bedplace. He lit candles and sat by me and sang old songs, God Rest Ye Merry and Lully, Lullay and the Cumberland Wassail.

He came to me then as of old, with great sweetness.

I am clean, and my son in my body forgives me, and sings. Writ by Hannah Trevor in her own poor hand. 1786.

Author's Note

Many of the confrontations represented in *The Burning Bride* are telescoped from actual events in Massachusetts during the winter of 1786–87. Daniel Shays, the reluctant leader of the rebel farmers, was not pardoned when the Riot Act was repealed. He fled to a refuge in the Vermont mountains, defended by his neighbors and dodging arrest by persistent sheriffs until his eventual pardon. His beloved first wife, Abigail, disappeared or died – from what cause, historians have never discovered – and Shays ended his days as a quiet, ceremonious old man whose second wife ran a tavern in central New York and provided all the liquor he needed to drown out the past. He died at eighty-four, poor and obscure. No marker was put upon his grave.

The nor-easter that came down upon New England in early December of 1786 put an end to the organized resistance of the Regulators, as they called themselves, and most were forced to sign the loyalty oath and give up their cause for the sake of survival. Debtors' prisons continued to exist for almost another thirty years, but concessions were made to allow men whose persons were attached for debt to work actively at day labor in order to earn their release. The old, the sick, and the unskilled still died in prison, and those put to day labor were often used little better than slaves.

In 1787, the new Constitution replaced the unstable Articles of Confederation, and George Washington took office as president. The granting of the vote to all white males regardless of property made the county conventions seem unnecessary and centered power in the federal system. Within Maine, the anger of the poor was quelled by land grants and by the separation of Maine from Massachusetts.

But the gap between rich and poor was never adequately bridged; by the early 1800s another generation of Regulators had begun to resist sheriff's auctions and raid the shops of overpriced merchants, as the so-called Malta War began.

Acknowledgments

Historical fiction owes a great debt to the many scholars upon whose careful research we novelists rely. The list of works consulted in preparing the Hannah Trevor trilogy contains almost four hundred books and documents, many journals on microfilm, cookbooks, songbooks, books on quilt patterns and weaving grids, diagrams of the workings of eighteenth-century mills, looms, toast racks – everything that went to build the New England world of 1786. In particular, I wish to express my gratitude to the work of Mary Beth Norton, Laurel Thatcher Ulrich, Linda Kerber, Mary Ann Mason, Wallace Brown, Barbara Clark Smith, Edith Hary, Charles Elventon Nash, Reuben Thwaites, Jane Nylander, Alice Morse Earle, Judith Walzer-Leavitt, Walter Blumenthal, Lee Agger, Elizabeth Anthony Dexter, Linda Grant DePauw, Samuel E. Morison, Marion L. Starkey, and David Szatmary.